When Magics Meet

By

Jeffrey C. Dillow

Art: J.C. Dillow

ISBN: 978-0-9966154-0-2

High Fantasy Publications

FIRST EDITION

www.HighFantasyBooks.com

Other Publications by this author include:

High Fantasy

Adventures in High Fantasy

Goldchester

Wizards and Warriors

Murder in Irliss

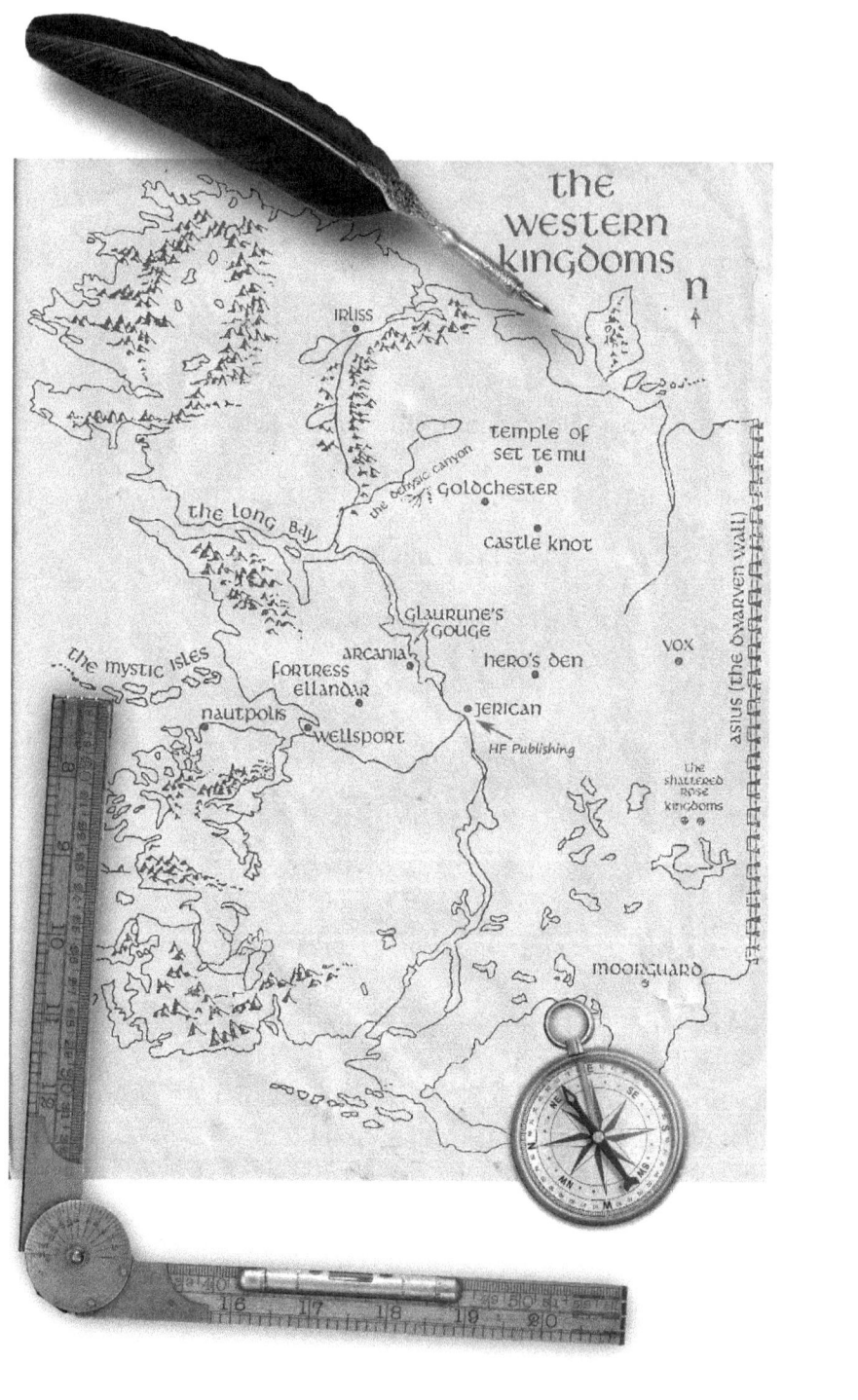

The tiny bubble plays briefly around the flask's bottom. Reluctantly the bubble rises through the thick yellowish liquid calling on its brothers to follow it on a trek to fresh air. Its quest is interrupted, only briefly when it bounces into a parrot's feather, spins around, and trickles on past in a quickening rise to the top. Bobbing on the surface the bubble explodes giving up its shape for the freedom above.

-the alchemists' journey

CONTENTS

CHAPTER ONE

The Abduction

He likes to dabble in the mysterious and is often found pondering over boiling test tubes and books with recordings of various experiments.

- of Alchemists, from the treatise of High Fantasy

Affensash feeds the sparks tiny twigs of oak and ash until his distillery flickers to life. The new light settles into a warm glow and begins to play along the walls of the cold stone chamber, discovering in its dance the crucibles, flasks, and bowls of precious metal shavings butted up against the black night shadows.

He grumbles half out loud, "Alchemy is a difficult science." Then he thinks, "My wife will simply have to understand that."

Turning a small hand crank causes a wooden door to open in the ceiling. The moonlight is reluctant at first. Then it enters the room and joins the dance of lights, white-washing a table of powders, jars, and twisting tubes.

Too much!

With a slight adjustment of the crank the moon is refocused on a small empty jar, the ultimate receptacle of all this twisting science.

Certain experiments must be performed when the forces of the sun and moon are just right. It is simply a hazard of the job that some of these experiments must be performed at such ungodly hours. It also doesn't hurt to perform them when she is asleep.

Two puffs of green cloud float to a thin canopy. Affensash stretches his slight frame, barely reaching the tube at the canopy's top. Adjusting it a little the gas travels on toward the small jar.

Affensash was an apprentice long before he met his wife. You would think Laurallin would be more reasonable about her demands on his time. Things can't always move along a schedule. They don't always go as planned.

He had a grueling apprenticeship at an ill-equipped shop in Wellsport. The finer schools at Jerican or the premier laboratories of the Pentacles were financially out of the question. A farmer and his wife could only afford to indulge their son's passion for so long. The rhythmic cycle of the planting and harvesting always pulled him away from his studies for long periods of time.

As he learned his craft at Wellsport he often wondered what true marvels were being taught at the finer schools. Why are even the simple formulas more potent when brewed in those high mountain peaks? Is it that boiling temperatures change in high places or is it because they are so much closer to the gods? If Affensash were a betting man, which he is not, he would bet on the gods.

He brushes a dirty hand across his sandy-brown hair and removes the small jar from its premier location. Then he fills it with a green-blue powder. Cupping the jar in his hand he whirls the powder around until the inside of the jar is coated with a translucent haze. He dumps the excess out and carefully inspects the jar for any spotty areas. Satisfied, he replaces the jar and turns to examine the liquid's progress through the distillery.

Affensash loves his alchemy lab. To him it represents a microcosm that he can control. The world outside his shop is jumbled and vast with too many unanswered questions. Here in his lab he can impose his will.

Suddenly, there is a crash followed by a choking cloud of powder. Well, sometimes he can impose his will. Affensash stumbles back into a chair covering his nose and mouth with his sleeve. A fit of sneezing erupts from the shadows. A red face covered in yellowish powder peeks ashamedly from between two straw baskets.

"Ruefin," chokes Affensash, "What have you done this time?"

Ruefin, a miniature red fox, whines plaintively and ducks back into the shadows. The glint of a darting tongue is all that can be seen of Affensash's tiny pet.

"Ruefin, don't lick that off!" coughs Affensash.

He snatches Ruefin by the nape of the neck and pulls him from his hiding place.

"You will end up hairless, or a toad, or both, if you aren't more careful around my chemicals."

A rag from the table saves poor Ruefin's tongue the bitter ordeal of cleaning his face.

Ruefin is unceremoniously dropped out of harm's way deep into the pocket of Affensash's brown robe. Still choking, Affensash dampens a cloth to clean the mess. With half a laugh he restores his precious powder to a new container.

Normally, Laurallin would be helping with this mess. She is busy with the baby now and no longer has the time to help in the alchemy business as she once did. Her absence means he must spend even more time in the lab.

"You know, Ruefin," Affensash begins, still cleaning at the mess on the floor. "When I first joined the Alchemy Guild she was actually proud of me. When I took my vows of secrecies to the brotherhood she stood close to me. I remember that night very well. It was a celebration then. It was our celebration."

Placing a rag over the top of the jar, Affensash walks over to the wall and gazes up at the gun hanging there: An arquebus, the first firepowder weapon the Guild allows you to carry. How to use the gun is one of the Guild's most carefully guarded secrets.

"I believe, Ruefin, old boy that she expected I would have earned my pistols by now. It's not as easy to advance on your talent alone. Back then Ruefin..."

"Aff'fff'ensash," comes a voice from outside the little chamber.

"She knows better than to interrupt me now," snaps Affensash. "She probably needs help with the baby. That little girl is truly an alchemist's child. I mean, Ruefin, she is always bubbling... from both ends."

The first drops of a long trail of thick syrupy liquid drips into the jar. The moonlight is temporarily blocked by a shadow. A light mist begins to creep through an open window.

"What?" Affensash asks. "The almanac calls for a clear night. This will ruin the potion."

A quick turn of the crank and more moonlight washes into the lab. A gust of wind blows a window shutter open and more unwanted mist fills the room.

"What's going on?" Affensash blurts in half-panicked tones. "If the night is misty my light potion will be murky. It will be worth only half as much in the market tomorrow!"

"Affensash," the voice comes more clearly this time.

"Please dear, I am at a crucial point," answers Affensash in a practiced voice. It's loud enough she will hopefully hear, but not too loud to wake the baby.

Affensash grabs a clear liquid vile from a shelf, dips a syringe in, and fills it with the liquid. Walking to the beam of moonlight, he sprays the clear liquid into the air creating a sparkling cloud. Kneeling, he watches the cloud float downward and gather on the lip of the jar. From outside his chamber the mist suddenly pours through the window and nearly fills the room.

"Affensash, do you not hear me?" comes the voice again.

Exasperated, Affensash falls back into his chair. "Ruined," he mumbles.

"I'm sorry, allow me to help."

Shocked by the nearness of the voice, Affensash spins out of his chair and ducks behind a large sack. From a dark corner a light bursts. Three figures stand clearly visible in the radiant light. The light is actually glowing from one of them, filling the room as if it were daylight.

"Is that better?" asks the splendid female who is radiating so brightly.

"Wha?" stutters Affensash.

"Is the light better for your chemicals?" she replies.

Glancing at the all but forgotten jar, Affensash stammers, "Uhh, no not actually. It's quite ruined now but, uhh, I can make another."

The woman folds her arms and the light goes out. The two men on either side turn to the walls and quickly light the lanterns hanging there. The woman is breathtaking even though she is dressed in every day traveling clothes like her male companions. Her hair is yellow gold and shoulder length. It frames her face like a shining aura beneath her raised hood. Her face is clean and unmarked, very unusual for the women Affensash knows. Her figure is full and her waist is small, giving shape even to her traveling apparel. Affensash may not recognize *who* they are, but he knows all too well *what* they are. They are members of the True One's Guild. Unlike his newly formed Alchemy Guild, the Wizard's Guild is old and their members powerful.

"I am Diane. Forgive our intrusion, good sir, but we called to you several times and you would not reply. I hope we haven't ruined anything of major importance."

"Am I dead?" Affensash asks in flat even tones.

"Why no, of course you're not dead," Diane answers confused.

Still crouching behind the sack, Affensash considers his next actions carefully. Where he had been laboring to make a potion of light that any commoner could use, these people produced light seemingly by just thinking about it. He knows what they are capable of doing.

Cautiously he asks, "Why am I honored with such esteemed visitors at so late an hour?" Affensash glances towards his arquebus hanging on the wall. Just then Ruefin pops his head out the top of his pocket, startling everyone. Ruefin sniffs the air, looks around, and starts panting.

"Step from behind there, Affensash," says the mystic figure on the right. "We are but flesh and blood like you. I am Glenwall. Good lord man! We have traveled a long way and could use some common hospitality."

Glenwall is about the same size as Diane, but very stout. His face sports a well-trimmed beard streaked with gray. Despite his bulk, his features are sharply defined, giving him an almost wolfish appearance. His body is scented with ointments, something that Ruefin seems to notice. Scented oils mean two different things to a wizard and an alchemist.

Hesitantly, Affensash steps forward, brushing his robe. "Of course, of course. Let me get you something."

He walks over to a table by the door. Reaching down for a pitcher of water, his hand suddenly swings for the lever on the door. It partially opens. Glenwall slams his shoulder into it, knocking it closed again. From someplace behind Affensash a light blue trail of light streaks across the room and wraps around him. Securely bound by the magical threads, Affensash falls to the floor like a bag of flour.

"Let him go," commands Diane.

"I think we had better explain in a little more depth why we are here," says the wizard who cast the binding spell. "It seems our host isn't in a very hospitable mood." The third wizard is Terrell, a tall young man with brown gentle hair and eyes.

Glenwall bends down by Affensash to inspect the bindings. The hem of a fine cloth robe with delicate gold trimmings slips from underneath his traveling garment. He touches the bindings with the palm of his hand and the power of the spell is absorbed. The bindings loosen and fall away. The wizard's hand glows blue and the spell disappears. Affensash is helped briskly to his feet.

"We haven't started off quite as well as we had planned," chuckles the wizard. Turning to Diane he says, "Perhaps it would be better to get on with our mission and return immediately."

"I think you are right," she replies." Affensash we are here to take you back with us to the Isles."

"You mean the Mystic Isles?" Affensash stammers.

"If you prefer to call it that you may," she replies. "There, Enchantraen, an Elder of our Guild and members of your own Alchemy Guild wish to speak with you."

"What do you want from me? What's the purpose?"

"We are to take you to the Isles and that is all we know," says Terrell trying to sound reassuring.

"How can I trust you?"

"You are to go. You have no other choice. Take a few minutes and prepare yourself," says Diane in a low calm voice.

Affensash's steel gray eyes become cold and calculating. Fleeting thoughts pass through his mind about fighting his way out. However, the safety of his family could be at stake.

"I wish only to say good-bye to my family."

The door is opened by Terrell and they file out of the little laboratory and down the hall in a gloomy procession. The wizards seem to know exactly where to go in his house. They quietly open the door to the bedchambers. Immediately, Affensash senses something is not right.

Before the question is asked, Diane answers, "They are alright. They will sleep until the morning. At that time one of your own guild members will come to let them know that you are gone."

The alchemist crosses the room to his wife's side. Slowly he bends down and kisses her. His knees purposefully touch the side of the bed jarring it slightly.

"Laurallin will not wake, Alchemist. Please do not try anything foolish," Diane whispers.

Quietly, without noticing her words, he crosses to Dannia's crib. In the moonlight the baby looks so helpless. When awake she is such a firm strong child. It is hard to realize how vulnerable she actually is when sleeping this way. She seems so small, not at all a large bundle of work and responsibility. She is so quiet. Stooping over, Affensash slowly lifts the blankets to guard the child as best he can from the cooling night.

With a kiss, Affensash and the others are gone. Vanished!

The mist clears and the night air blows through the creaking shutters. In the eerie hours before dawn no one notices the small object left hidden under the child's coverlet.

CHAPTER TWO

The Huntress Awakens

His knowledge is sacred and a carefully guarded secret of his guild.

- of Alchemists, from the treatise of High Fantasy

Laurallin eases out from beneath the covers in the morning to find Affensash, as usual, gone. Her slim long legs extend and tentatively touch the cold stone floor. This must be the first time in six months that she slept through the night and wakes up feeling rested. One last long lean stretch and she topples out of bed. A quick check in the crib and she can tell that Dannia, their baby girl, is fine. Going to a small table, she picks up a heavy bone comb and runs it through her long, silky chestnut hair. Looking at her reflection in a large bowl of water, she carefully ties her hair back with a simple off-white string. Walking to the hearth, she swings the tea kettle on a large wrought iron hook over the fire.

Throwing logs she gathered the night before into the hearth, she stirs the coals and the embers blaze. And thus starts another normal day. The same as every day for the past eight months since Dannia was born. The tea will be ready soon. After being up all night in the laboratory, Affensash will need it.

Opening the door, she walks down the hallway with the usual grace in her steps. She expects to find him slumped over his table snoring. Of course she will have to scold him. But by midday, with a warm meal and rest, Affensash will be just fine. Some days, after a successful night, she might have to run one of his concoctions to the market before noon. The door to the lab swings back and Laurallin finds the room empty. Empty? Surprised, she opens another door and calls outside.

"Affensash, where are you?"

No reply. The baby begins to cry. Realizing for the first time that something is wrong, she goes to pick up the baby and then searches once more.

"Hush little one. Let's go find where daddy is hiding." Bending over to lift the child, she notices a small talisman hidden beneath the covers. Something is wrong.

"You won't find him here," a deep voice comes from behind her and a strong hand grabs her shoulder!

Stunned, she bolts upright. Instantly she reacts. Her leg swings back and catches the man in the stomach.

"Whommphhh…," the man doubles over caught off-guard by the attack.

Grabbing her heavy iron from the table, a lightning-quick bang on the back of the neck sends the man into unconsciousness.

Forty minutes later, the man's senses start to blur back into focus. He finds himself tied to a sturdy chair with Laurallin pacing in front of him bouncing the baby in her arms.

"Good morning," Laurallin says in a calm serious voice. "Are you ready to talk now? I'm sorry I can't offer you tea, but I just don't appreciate visitors who come in unannounced."

Shaking his groggy head, he tries to focus on the pacing woman, "I am a friend. I'm a messenger from your husband's Guild."

"Good, good," she replies, "then it shouldn't be necessary to use that on you to find out what's going on around here." Laurallin motions to the fire where the iron glows red hot. "Did I mention that I don't appreciate unannounced visitors?"

Stunned, the man sits quietly, afraid to speak. Laurallin slides Dannia into her seat and picks up a bowl of warm cheese grits. Spoon feeding the baby, she begins her questions without looking at the man.

"What is your name?"

"I am Lucius. Really, this isn't necessary. I'm a friend."

"Friends are people I know. I don't know you and I don't appreciate you breaking into my house. Dannia you little piglet stop spitting that out!" She wipes up the spill of the giggling baby and turns a deadly expression towards Lucius.

Dannia somehow feels the calm comfort of her mother's demeanor. To her, it is happy time. Lucius, on the other hand, cannot escape the deadly gaze of Laurallin when she asks, "Where is my husband?"

"He has been called away on confidential Guild business. He is safe and will probably return in a few months. I have some silver tams in my pack that will see you through until he returns," Lucius says and gestures with his head towards his pack lying in the corner.

"Yes, I know about the tams. I counted them while you were resting. I also noticed the two pistols that were hidden under your shirt. My husband tells me that it is a symbol that you are doing well in the Alchemy Guild." Blowing on the spoon, she shovels a bite into an eager little mouth.

"Well, yes I suppose I'm doing all right. But listen, I'm here to offer you a safe place to stay with members of the Guild while your husband is away."

She can't resist a chuckle when she glances over at the bound-up man. "No, for some reason I feel safer here." After a few more bites, she returns to a more serious mood. "You haven't answered my question. Where is my husband?"

"I am only supposed to tell you that he is away on Guild business. It is better for the Guild that you don't know anything else."

"Listen to me and listen carefully." She stands up and walks over to Lucius.

"I don't care for the Guild very much right now. I don't care for you very much right now either. What I do care about is the safety of my husband. I know he wouldn't have left me for any reason without telling me first. He was taken from here without a choice. I also know that you are no simple messenger. Your pistols say that much. You are going to tell me where my husband is now, or you will tell me where he is when I'm through with my ironing. Either way, Lucius, I'm going to know."

Her brown eyes stare straight through Lucius and he believes her! She turns around, sits back down, and continues feeding Dannia.

Sweat breaks out on Lucius's forehead. "I really don't know that much. It has something to do with being on assignment someplace north of here. Really, that's all I know. The reason they sent me instead of a common messenger was to insure your safety when you are traveling to a new location."

Laurallin puts the bowl down and walks over to the wall. There she removes a knife from her hunting belt, turns, and walks back towards Lucius.

"This is ludicrous! I just came here at the request of the Guild to assist you!" Lucius strains at the leather straps, but they won't break. Kicking out with his legs, he manages to rise briefly. He and the chair tumble sideways. With a loud bang, Lucius ends up on his side in the middle of the floor. The loud noise startles the baby and she cries. In one easy motion, Laurallin dips down and slashes with the knife. The bindings fall away, but Lucius stays on the floor stunned and breathing heavily.

"Well, get up, Alchemist. You've done what you have come for."

Lucius rises, rubbing at the swelling in his wrists caused by the leather straps. He stands at least a full head taller than Laurallin.

"You will find your things hanging in the tree outside. Go back to your Guild and tell them I am fine, but I want my husband back."

Lucius manages to calm himself. "I can still take you back if you like. You may find waiting with others more comfortable than alone here by yourself."

"I have no intention of going with you *or* of being by myself. Please leave now." She walks away, turning her back to the man, and picks up the baby.

Quickly, Lucius walks over and swings the outside door open.

"You will have to reload your pistols," Laurallin explains. "My husband would never tell me the secrets of his craft, but I know enough to wet down the powder of an Alchemist's gun."

With a huff, Lucius is out and slams the door behind him.

Cracking the shutter, Laurallin watches Lucius walk down the lane away from the house. The baby quiets down as Laurallin bounces her briskly in her arms. Suddenly remembering the talisman she found under the baby's cover, she bends over the crib and examines it. It is her own talisman, a symbol of the power of Dorre, her tribe's shaman. Studying it for a moment, she is uncertain what it means. Memories of her childhood race through her mind at the touch of the talisman. She sees the great herds of horses roaming through the grasslands while the Hebelcaan tribesmen race after the strays. She vividly remembers her father, their chief, leading the tribe to fresh fields as the seasons change. Laurallin is surprised at her reaction. She hadn't consciously realized how much she missed them all.

The Shaman of her tribe has great powers, many of which are beyond her understanding. The Shaman is not a true wizard. He works his powers with his mind. Some call him a Sensitive or Mystic of the mind. Whatever it means, it is as good a place as any to start.

"Why this Aff?" she mumbles out loud. "What are you trying to tell me?" What the symbol means is unclear, but where it is telling her to go is certain.

Gathering a few things, mostly for the baby, she prepares to leave. Her family should not be far from here. They probably are moving west so that the herd can take advantage of the spring grass in the large plains just south of the Pentacle mountain range. She should be able to reach them in three days, or even sooner, if she can pick up the tribe's trail quickly.

With only the barest necessities, she walks out to the rickety corral fence. She is always embarrassed to saddle up Affensash's old nag. The beast is a far cry from the horseflesh she rode while growing up.

Sensie was her horse and her friend. They grew up together in the wild fields. Laurallin can almost smell the fresh grass and feel the hot sun of the steamy spring days they spent together. She remembers lying on her back watching the clouds race overhead and listening to Sensie's steady nibbling of the grass.

Her adolescence was a worrisome, wonderful time and Sensie shared it all with her. Her father took away Sensie when she dared to marry Affensash against his wishes. It crushed her. It pains her still. She hasn't faced her father since.

A short whistle and the old nag comes over and obediently lowers her head. She nuzzles Laurallin's shoulder for affection. Laurallin laughs. At least the old girl has a tender heart. By the time the horse is saddled, Dannia is crying again inside the house.

Hurrying back inside, Laurallin soothes the baby with kind words. The words must do as a substitute for her tender touch. She has too much to do right now and no time to cuddle the child as is their usual routine for this time of the morning.

Her house clothes drop around her slim ankles. She must leave behind the soft cotton array of the country wife. Going to a drawer, she pulls out the tougher buckskin clothing traditional for the women of her tribe. Sliding the briefs up her naturally smooth legs, she finds the buckskin tough and stiff from long neglect in her drawer. The short dress slips easily overhead, but stops and pulls tight at her waist. A little adjusting on the drawstrings that bind the sides and the dress tumbles down the rest of the way stopping just short of mid-thigh.

"Well, pumpkin, it looks like you have had a slight effect on my figure after all," she says to Dannia, who has found a stray leaf carried in by the wind. Absently, Laurallin remembers the scandal it caused when she first showed up in town wearing her tribe's clothes. It was quite a contrast to the long dresses of the town women. From behind a shelf of dishes in a dusty corner, she pulls out her bow. She tests the wood by bending and examining it for stress or damage. Satisfied, she wraps it around her leg and forces it down, looping the end of the string over the top notch. Holding it up, she pulls the string taut to her cheek. It's been a long time since she has used the hunting bow. Of course Hebelcaan don't practice shooting a bow standing. They always practice from a full gallop.

The thought of the journey starts to excite her despite the disappearance of her Affensash. She hadn't realized how much she missed the outdoors. It was a part of her. The fields, the forests and the mountains are a part of her lineage. It was a heritage she had ignored too long.

Taking the blanket, she wraps Dannia up into a neat little papoose and slings her over her back. Then, Laurallin gathers her quiver and the last of her things, and bolts the door behind her. Lashing her traveling gear across the rump of the horse, she walks the old nag down the long lane towards the road. At the end of the lane Laurallin sees the egg woman making her way from house to house selling her produce. The old woman is shocked when she sees Laurallin's Hebelcaan riding clothes.

"Watch over the house for me old woman," Laurallin shouts. "You may live in it if you like until I return." Mounting up, Laurallin rides past the woman who is in too much shock to say anything.

With a whistle and a click, Laurallin tries to goad the old nag into a canter. The old horse can only manage a sort of shuffle-walk. "Oh, Affensash," she mumbles somewhat disappointed. "How will I ever find you this way?"

Away she rides with the rising sun in search of her family tribe. Perhaps there she can discover the secret to the sudden appearance of the talisman. Onward they clop, Laurallin straddling the badly swaying nag; Dannia already asleep behind her.

CHAPTER THREE

Treachery on the Isles

He can use potions and gunpowder weapons, create and cure poisons.
The Alchemy Guild often views its work as the most important function in
their crude society.

- of Alchemists, from the treatise of High Fantasy

The dizzy black spinning lasts a short while. Affensash's feet land suddenly on wet stone. His equilibrium returns, but his vision does not. His hands immediately flail about and find a handhold in a thin wool cloak.

"You are safe, Affensash. There is no reason to be alarmed," says a comforting female voice.

"I'm blind."

Light suddenly rushes in and Affensash can now see he is in a small room. One of the wizards is standing by an open door.

"Is that better?" Terrell asks with a smile. "You are on what you call the Mystic Isles, near the labyrinth of Elder Edla, our founder. There are reasons why it would not be appropriate for you to be seen in the main palace at this time. We must go and announce our return. Please remain here and you will be instructed further."

The three wizards begin to file out of the cell into the well-lit hallway.

"Wait! Am I a prisoner?" shouts Affensash.

The door is closed and Affensash feels very much alone. His tiny world has been violated. The order of his life has been altered, leaving him confused. Extending his hands, he searches the cell for a seat or cot to sit down on. Something squeals and bites down on his finger.

Rats!

Suddenly his pocket wiggles and Ruefin pops his head up with a growl. The little fox jumps to the rescue. In the darkness all Affensash can hear are the growls and snaps and dozens of scratching paws making an exodus from the room.

The room goes quiet. A cold nose nuzzles his hand and he withdraws it in alarm. Then comes the familiar tug on the pants and Affensash knows that it is Ruefin wanting to be picked up.

With Ruefin wrapped in his arms, and the little fox's warm fur against his face, Affensash sinks down along the side of a wall and sits with his knees bent under him.

Affensash just cannot believe what is happening. The Alchemy Guild and the True One's Guild have had, at best, an uneasy truce through the years. Why would his Alchemy Guild be cooperating with these "poof and spoof" wizards of the True Ones Guild? One of the primary goals of the Alchemy Guild is to discredit unfounded superstitions and to impose the art of science over all the other lesser practices.

Affensash never liked wizards. "It is my misfortune to be alive during the time when wizards wield such great power," he would say to Laurallin. When he was at Wellsport, the most powerful wizards once swaggered through the streets putting on shows, unashamed and boastful. Some of them just took what they wanted and moved on. And when two of them disagreed with each other, it was just better to clear the streets and let them have at it. Better to clean up the mess than to be part of the mess.

They probably brought me here, Affensash surmises, to torture the secrets of my Guild from me. Why me? I haven't even earned my pistols yet. The three that brought me here certainly had enough power to bring in a bigger fish than me. Whatever the reason, it must be deviant. Affensash reasons away, lost in the endless possibilities that present themselves now that he is away from his lab.

In the cold dark corner of his cell, Affensash tries to remember as much as he can about this type of magic. As if by reasoning alone he could somehow free himself from this situation. No, he remembers, the

True Ones Guild believes in the untainted study of magic void of demonic intervention. He knows at least that much about wizards, having talked to a few lesser ones during his apprenticeship.

Light bursts into the cell. Affensash involuntarily jumps to his feet. His eyes try to focus, but they are too slow.

A small voice pleads, "Come, come quickly!"

A delicate hand wraps around a finger and tugs for Affensash to follow. Out in the hallway his eyes adjust and he can see the back of a tiny blonde-haired girl urgently pulling him along.

"Where are we going?" Affensash asks, dropping Ruefin back into his familiar pocket.

"You are in danger here," she replies! "I've asked for help, but there isn't time to wait!"

Down a myriad of corridors they both rush, the little girl breathing heavily under the stress. They stop and she peers around a corner down a long corridor.

"Come quickly and say nothing," she continues glancing over her shoulder at the alchemist.

Affensash gasps and jerks his hand out of hers. He thought she was a little girl. She's not; at least not a human girl.

"Who; what are you?" His voice is too loud and the girl follows his outburst with a series of hisses.

"I'm a 'Tuatha'," she replies briskly, and green eyes, with slits for pupils, blaze angrily. She grabs him and starts down the corridor.

Affensash pulls his arm back again and asks "What's a Tooth-tha?"

A gray smoke suddenly bellows from around a corner. She pushes him back into an alcove.

"It looks as though you will never find out," she despondently answers.

Looking around the corner Affensash sees the gas filling the corridor and bellowing down toward them. It doesn't take a trained alchemist to know the gas is deadly. Across the hallway is an open door and a stairway leading up.

"This way quickly! The gas looks too dense to float up the stairs," Affensash takes the girl's hand and runs for the door.

The gas actually seems to quicken as if in pursuit.

"Oh, I think this one will manage to make it all the way to the top," she answers in panicked tones.

He has only just arrived, but his training tells him anywhere is better than here with that gas. Up and around the spiral staircase Affensash and the girl run. They fly at dizzying speed until Affensash stumbles and falls, sliding part way back down the stairs. Gasping and rubbing his bruised skin, Affensash starts to get up when he hears it. The gas rises up the staircase.

It comes!

Instead of hissing like rising steam, it comes making sounds like large thick claws scraping against the stones. Steadily it rises breathless, mindless, scraping.

"What is it?" Affensash asks, bewildered with panic.

"I don't know," she replies simply and helps him to his feet. Up they go again, the scraping sound much closer now.

It is gaining.

Out of breath, they see two thin doors at the top of the stairs. The girl is the first to reach them, but the doors won't open. At a dead run, Affensash smashes his shoulder into them, nearly knocking the doors off their hinges. The momentum of Affensash's charge sends the girl through the door, out onto a small balcony tumbling up and over the railing.

A cry curdles the air and Affensash lunges after her. He clutches her by the wrist while his other hand flails for the railing. Fingers grab, but the weight and momentum are too much. They both drop another two feet where he finally finds a hold on an ornamental flag. The girl swings below him, smashing against the side of the high stone tower.

Wide-eyed, Affensash looks around. They have stumbled over a mirador or watch tower's balcony. The ground is at least six hundred feet below.

Ruefin pops his head out of the pocket, shakes his ears, and looks quizzically at his master.

After a brief pause, the girl shouts up, "I think, Affensash .....I would rather....take...my...chances with that gas than down here with you. Get me back up there!"

Not being a muscular man, Affensash already feels his fingers slipping.

"Grab my robe! I need both hands."

The girl uses her free hand and wraps the tail of his robe around it. Testing it, she finally lets go and Affensash grabs the flagpole. Throwing his legs up, he wraps them tightly around the pole. The sudden shift in his robe knocks poor Ruefin out of the pocket. Quick reflexes allow the little pet to snap a firm hold onto the robe. Six hundred feet above the ground, his legs and feet wrapped around a flagpole, a girl and tiny fox dangling beneath his tearing robe, Affensash comes to an immediate realization.

"Well?" shouts the girl.

"This is it," pants Affensash, "I can't move any further!"

"Tremendous, Alchemist," she replies exasperated.

Reaching up, she grabs Ruefin by the scruff of the neck and balances him on her shoulder. Hand over hand she climbs up the cloak, reaches around Affensash, and latches onto the flagpole. Placing her foot in the middle of his stomach, she boosts herself on top of the flagpole where she can climb over the railing. With her feet firmly on the balcony, she puts Ruefin down and races over to the doors and closes them.

"Hey, what about me?" shouts Affensash, barely holding on below.

She pops her head over the balcony, looks down and says, "I think we're both safer if you stay down there." She disappears back over the rail and starts to slide a stone chair in front of the doors.

"I'm slipping!" Affensash screams.

"All right, all right," she says and takes out a small knife and cuts the extra rope from the flag. Tying one end to the railing, she lowers the other end to Affensash. With the girl tugging on the rope, Affensash is able to climb back, where exhausted, he collapses on the balcony.

Before he can enjoy the solid stone beneath his feet, she shouts for him to stand up and help her with a heavy stone bench. Their danger is far from over.

"Wait! That won't work. It is gas remember." Affensash takes off his cloak and stuffs it in the crack under the door. "Now let's get the bench." They barely get the bench in place when something thuds against the door.

The girl walks over to the balcony's edge and stares blindly at the buildings below. Her breathing is controlled, but her face is white and sweaty-pale. Confused, Affensash touches her on the arm and tells her not to be afraid. She is deathly cold and is already deep into a trance.

A second thud resounds against the doors.

Affensash glances at the door and then back at the girl. He realizes that he has been left, at least temporarily, to his own resources to survive this ordeal. The third thud causes the hinges to scream and the bench to rumble. A claw gouges solidly into the weakening doors.

Affensash spots two large porcelain urns on either side of the doors. They each have a tight golden lid with flowers sitting on top of them. Dumping the flowers of one of the urns, Affensash formulates a plan. The lid pops off and rolls in circles around the balcony. Reaching to his side, he grabs his powder-horn and sprinkles the dark firepowder around the bottom of the urn. He reaches into his pocket and carefully places his flint at his feet. His plan is to capture the gas in the urn and then burn it or at least create an explosion large enough to harm it.

The next thud sounds much more concentrated and with greater force than the previous ones.

Pulling his knife, he goes to examine the doors. Running his hands over the wood, he discovers the area most damaged and cracking. He chops at the area with his knife and it weakens further.

The next thud sounds and the area starts to splinter.

Back to the urn, Affensash wraps his arm around the top and lifts. The urn doesn't budge. Sweat breaks out on the alchemist's brow. The door is splintering. It looks as though it will break apart exactly where he expected.

Again, Affensash lifts, and this time the urn rises! Straining with a new strength born from fear, Affensash manages to lift the heavy urn to the top of the stone bench and rolls it to the area where the door is breaking. Taking his dagger, he stabs again at the door. The creature smashes against it on the other side. The wood splits open!

Through the crack the gas rushes, going straight into the urn. Grabbing the lid, Affensash tries to force it over the opening of the urn. A small amount of the gas hovers outside the lip. The lid bumps against it as if it were a solid object! Amazed at the density of the gas, Affensash pushes harder. It feels as though he is pushing the tail of a mammal into a cage.

Affensash's wrist brushes against the gas and he yells as it burns and blisters. Still, he manages to secure the lid. Affensash starts to reach for his flint when the urn suddenly rocks and rolls towards the end of the bench. Bending low Affensash catches the urn just as it topples off the end.

"It mustn't smash!"

Much heavier than before, Affensash strains to stop the fall and sets the urn down carefully. The creature shifts its weight, bashing against the side of the container. The sudden shift causes Affensash to lose his balance. He staggers back until his foot catches on the leg of a stone chair. His back smashes against the railing. The weight of the urn carries him up and over once more.

Down they plummet over the balcony together!

The sudden movement wakes the girl from her trance. She runs to the rail and looks over. Relieved, she sees Affensash hanging on the flag pole once more; the urn falling below him. Midway down the urn breaks apart. Luckily, the gas is too far away and the wind harmlessly carries it out to the open sea.

"You know, Alchemist. I think you like it down there," she says amazed at Affensash's uncanny ability to survive.

Lowering the rope again, she helps the ashen-faced alchemist back onto the balcony. Sinking to the floor, Affensash pulls a hanky from his pocket and wipes his clammy brow. Ruefin runs to comfort him with a barrage of enthusiastic licks.

"You're going to be really good at this I think," she muses, looking down at the panting, quivering bundle of man.

"Thanks," he says, looking quizzically at the girl. "You know though, I haven't earned my pistols yet."

"I know, you have mentioned that," she laughs, sliding down beside him.

"Well tell me. What's a 'Tooth-tha"?" Affensash pants.

"I'm a Tuatha, you goose," she laughs again. "A 'too-a-tha', not a 'tooth-tha'. Haven't you heard of the green-eyed elves from across the sea? I am an elf! My parents sent me here to both teach and learn from the Elders in the True Ones Guild."

"No, I'm afraid I really don't know much about magic. I've been studying most of ..."

A faint sound comes from the railing. Affensash rolls forward pulling his knife. "It's come back," whispers Affensash.

Tink. Tink, tink.

Light glints off of silver hooks that look like tiny wisps of string.

Tink. Another catches on the side of the balcony. Affensash steps forward just as the first leg hooks over the rail.

Instead of seeing a hideous beast, a child appears. First one and then another. Each appears as quietly as the first. Collectively they make no more noise than a wind chime on a warm summer night.

Surprised by the sudden number appearing, the alchemist lets the blade drop from his hand.

"Tooth-tha," Affensash mutters.

The girl gives Affensash an annoyed look. "I summoned them here. They are the only ones I could trust who could make it to us in time. "

"The creature in the smoke I spoke of is floating along the waves of the sea waiting for the tide to bring it back to shore. You must gather some others and drive it away. I am to take Affensash to meet with Elder Enchantraen. He expects to meet Affensash as soon as possible. Mark well though! Few are to know of his presence. His life here is in danger. We barely escaped this time by the good alchemist's wits and cannot risk another encounter." The girl gives Affensash a sideways glance and smiles.

One of the Tuatha hands the girl a bundle of the thin silver string. Affensash bends over to grab Ruefin and drops him back into his pocket.

Faint silver light flickers around his waist. With a tug, Affensash is caught off balance and once more finds himself falling over the railing.

His hands flailing around grab and hold onto the girl's tunic, although it is not necessary. The silver rope around his waist is securely fastened.

"We are late," the girl says letting the silver string glide through her fingers. Affensash gasps and gulps for air. "Besides, I thought you would be used to this by now."

"You could have told me," is all that Affensash manages to get out.

"We cannot be seen walking the halls. I have another way to Edla's throne."

Downward they glide. Affensash cannot look below at the rocky shore. Instead, he focuses on the silver thread. His alchemist mind tries to understand what is happening. There must be a winch or some device slowly letting out the string, but Affensash cannot find any.

Baffled, but beginning to relax, Affensash looks away and sees a small village. Dotted along the side of several tall mountains, he can now see the palace proper. It is massive. It is a seamless flow of man-inspired beauty with an architecture that blends perfectly with the top of the coarse rocky terrain.

The descent ends with a little drop. The string falls from his waist. The elven girl motions for Affensash to follow.

"We can't take the path back up. We will be seen. We will take the boat across and we will use my rope to climb back up."

The shore line is dotted with little rowboats used to cross back and forth between the islands. At this point Affensash is weary enough to just follow.

In the boat, Affensash sits down and pulls out his book of notes. As he often does when he sees something new, he sketches it out with as much detail as he understands. He begins drawing the cliffs with a thin string dangling from it.

"What were you trying to do back there?" the girl asks quietly as she rows towards the shore.

"What?" Affensash asks looking up from his drawing.

"How did you defeat that creature?"

"Oh, you mean the gas. Well you see there are three states of matter. Water or gas will always seek to travel along the path of least resistance," Affensash begins to explain.

She looks at him with a blank stare on her face. Affensash rethinks his answer.

"Well I sort of put it in a jar and tossed it over the side."

"I saw that, but how did you get it in the urn?" she asks again.

"The path of least resistance…" and he stops. "Why don't you tell me about your rope instead? How does it work?"

"That's easy," she replies. "All I have to do is weave the *aether* around me into the rope. That way I can control the length."

Now it is Affensash who stares blankly. Looking down at his paper, he makes several big Xs through his ideas.

"You must be a mighty alchemist," she says as the boat brushes the shore line. "Come with me and I will show you." Together they leave the boat and walk over to a sheer mountain wall extending hundreds of feet tall.

"We are going up there?" Affensash asks incredulously.

She smiles and tosses the end of the string and it wraps around his waist. With the other hand, she tosses the string up into the air.

Somehow it seems to grow and catches much further up the rock wall than he expected. Up they go together gliding as effortlessly upward as they did coming down.

"You see. All I have to do is unweave the aether and up we go."

This time Affensash looks at her free hand. Her fingers are deftly making tiny motions. Swiftly and precisely the thread-like rope shortens. She pulls them up on the edge of jutting rock and repeats the motion. Up and up they go one section at a time.

"Do you see it now?" she asks. "Can you see the aether unwinding and flowing around us?"

Affensash looks around. Her words are so compelling that he wants to see something. He sees nothing, nothing except the gentle gliding motion that is produced by the skill of her fingers repeating the same pattern over and over.

On the tenth throw they reach the top. Climbing over a rock railing, they both sit down on a pathway.

Pointing up the path she says, "That way is the throne of Edla." A large white marble throne sits directly in the path and open to the sky. "Enchantraen will come up from the other way to talk with you," she states pointing in the opposite direction down the path.

Affensash is exhausted. The girl turns and drops back over the cliff.

"Wait," Affensash calls after her, but she is soon lost to the dark shadows of the cliffs.

His arms are too tired to lift. Why isn't she tired? Scribbling a few more notes, he sits down taking steady even breaths to try and calm himself.

Ruefin sniffs up and down the pathway to make sure they are safe. After he is satisfied, Ruefin returns to Affensash and curls up next to him.

"This is too much Ruefin. I don't understand any of this."
Scratching his friend's ears, they wait until their eyelids grow heavy.

"He won't do," says Enchantraen the second he sees Affensash.
With that, Elder Enchantraen turns and starts the long walk back down
the mountain.

"Wait, listen! He's perfect," shouts a bewildered man at
Enchantraen's side.

"Get him on his feet," commands the man and motions two
guards in the entourage towards Affensash.

Affensash sits up blinking his eyes, hearing the sudden
commotion. The two men briskly lift him to his feet. Affensash is not too
tired to recognize the man chasing after the Elder. It is Jabir Hayyan, the
head of the Alchemy Guild.

Affensash gives a quick little whistle and Ruefin jumps into his
arms. With a plop, his pet ends up in the safe familiar pocket. Affensash
brushes the dust off his robe and attempts to smooth back his rough
unruly hair. Laurallin always told him to carry a comb for times like these,
but as usual he is unprepared.

Jabir must have been successful in convincing Enchantraen to take
a second look. They both appear again over the edge of the path talking in
deep muffled tones. As soon as they get within ear-shot Jabir breaks off
the conversation and approaches Affensash. Elder Enchantraen in thick
white robes walks up and sits down on the throne.

Smiling, Jabir says, "Well, well, well, Affensash we meet at last.
Rest assured that your family is being well looked after. We have made
arrangements for a safe place for them to stay. We have some exciting
news to discuss with you today. I am certain you will find it most
intriguing."

Carefully looking Affensash over, Jabir says, "Oh, you still haven't progressed past your arquebus. You are still interested in earning your wheel-lock pistols aren't you?"

"Well, ah, of course I am sir. You see I would have had them by now but..."

"Never mind that now Affensash," Jabir interrupts. "I am giving you an excellent opportunity to earn them and much more. Just listen and follow my lead. We will get together and work out the specifics later. You're a good man Affensash. It's time we utilized your talents." Jabir slaps him on the back and spins to face Enchantraen.

"As I was saying Elder Enchantraen, Affensash is an excellent choice. You can see that he has a very non-distinctive appearance. His mannerisms are non-threatening and he has kept a low profile all his life despite his rugged up-bringing. He is unwanted and unheard of by the Eastern Empire. Underneath this scruffy facade, however, is the steel-hard interior of an outdoorsman."

Affensash shuffles nervously on his feet at Jabir's words.

"Yes, he was born and raised in the hard northern lands. He is a member of a tribe of fierce nomadic horsemen and has the inborn instincts of how to survive in the cold harsh weather of the high mountain ranges."

Affensash nearly chokes! Jabir walks over and rests his hand on Affensash's shoulder while smiling at Enchantraen.

"Ah sir," Affensash whispers.

"Yes Affensash, what is it?" Jabir returns impatiently.

"Ah, sir it was my wife who was born a nomadic horseman. I was born in a little town outside Jerican," continues Affensash in words barely audible to his Guild leader.

Jabir's jaw starts to drop, but he quickly collects himself. Jabir spins back around without any noticeable break in the momentum of his speech.

"When you look at him it's hard to believe the account of the smoke demon he defeated with just the aid of one small she-elf." Jabir ends his speech with a flamboyant gesture towards Affensash. "On behalf of the Alchemy Guild, let me introduce Affensash. He's our man for this assignment."

Enchantraen stands up and starts to walk towards the stairs. "You needn't work so hard to convince me of the merits of this man. My Guild is paying yours to perform a mission. If you feel this comfortable with Affensash so be it. Just remember! If the mission fails you don't get the last half of your payment."

"Oh, he will work or I wouldn't have gone to all the trouble to bring him here," Jabir concludes.

Enchantraen turns shaking his head and starts back down the path.

Affensash stands disbelieving what is happening around him.

"Wait a moment!" Affensash yells. "No one's asked me anything. You drag me out of my home and away from my family! For what?"

"Calm down Affensash. I told you we would discuss it later!" Jabir commands.

"I am truly sorry for any inconvenience this may cause you," Enchantraen says solemnly. The wizard's calm grey eyes seem to echo the truth in his statement. "I cannot meddle in the affairs of your Guild. Jabir here will explain the reasons and, I hope, the dangers of this mission. I have only enlisted the services of your Guild. It is your Guild that has chosen you to perform them. Good day Alchemist. I honestly hope we will see you again." With that Enchantraen turns and disappears down the pathway.

Jabir whirls and walks sternly up to Affensash. He towers at least two heads above the alchemist and his thick muscular frame makes quite a contrast to Affensash. Jabir's blue eyes nearly flame beneath his black hair and dark complexion.

"Never, ever correct me in front of my peers again. Do you understand me?" Jabir pauses just long enough to add the proper emphasis to his threat.

"I am sorry, Jabir, but someone has caused me a great deal of grief in these past few days. You were just talking about me as if I were an unthinking slave to be sent off somewhere without my consent. The Guild is made of free men you know."

"Don't you dare presume to tell me about the Guild. You are really starting off rather badly with me you realize. It would be a shame for you to lose your arquebus when you are so close to earning your pistols."

Jabir's stance suddenly changes and his expression softens. "Really, Affensash, I think you will like what I'm about to tell you. It is very important and worth a lot of gold tams for our Guild. You do know that the Guild will take only a portion of the gold paid for your services? The bulk of the tams will go to you and your family."

"The gold is not the problem, sir. I need to feel a little more secure about this whole assignment. That creature! Who or what wants me dead? I haven't done anything."

"Don't worry about the creature, Affensash. It was very unfortunate and believe me these people are looking into it. They will probably find some wizard's misplaced his 'hocus-pocus' or something else totally unconnected with this mission. This whole thing is really quite un-dramatic and I think I can put you at ease about the whole thing. But tell me, is your wife really the Hebelcaan tribesman?" Jabir asks motioning Affensash to walk with him to the stairs.

The two other alchemists follow behind.

"Well ah, yes sir, I aa..." Affensash begins.

Jabir looks back at one of the guards and says, "Get me the name of the alchemist who wrote me the letter recommending Affensash for this job. I want his fee returned immediately."

Looking back at Affensash, Jabir's eyes soften and he continues. "Sorry to interrupt, Affensash. Well, any how I'm sure you and your wife have spent a lot of time out in the wilds, perhaps following the tribe around. "

"No, not actually. Her father really doesn't care for me."

The first guard suppresses a laugh and whispers to the other, "I'll give you two-to-one he doesn't make it to the boat without hurting himself."

Jabir overhears the remark and spins around glaring. A tense moment passes. Then he turns back to Affensash, "Well, I'm sure you enjoy the open sky. With a wife that has had an upbringing like hers I'll bet you really enjoy hunting and fishing together. You'll need that kind of experience for this mission."

There's another long pause. Affensash closes his eyes and swallows hard. "Uh, sir, I can't cook."

The first guard can't contain himself any longer and laughs hardily.

Red faced, Jabir screams, "Dismissed!" Still bellowing commands, he asks the second guard to get him the name of the alchemist that wrote that letter!

After several moments of deep breathing, Jabir is calm again. The two of them continue down the stairs in silence while Jabir reflects on the situation.

"Listen, Affensash, you handled that creature like a hardened professional. The idea of throwing it over the balcony was brilliant. Just let me worry about the food situation. I'm sure you will come through this just fine."

"Come through what?"

"Elder Enchantraen has commissioned our Guild to do a little reconnaissance mission for him. It seems there is something disturbing this mystical stuff in the air called aether. You have heard about aether haven't you?"

Affensash cannot bear to disappoint him again, so he answers truthfully, "Yes", even if it was only a few moments ago.

"There have also been reports about things happening in the high mountain region near the Pentacle Peaks. That's where I want to send you. Your mission is to simply gather information. You are to be Enchantraen's eyes and ears. Don't worry. I've made it clear that you are not to be put into any danger. You are to look around, pay attention, and report all you see."

"If that's it why couldn't I talk to my wife and why wasn't I given time to prepare myself?"

"We don't want anyone to know where or why you are going. Enchantraen doesn't know who the enemy is, therefore, the less who know about you the better. Why do you think he asked us for help? A wizard showing up in such a place would be suspect, and any dealings the wizard had in magic would be carefully watched. There will be less reason to hide magical tricks, or whatever, from an alchemist. Believe me, Affensash, you will be just fine."

At the bottom of the stairs Affensash is huffing. They enter a small garden area where tiny buds are stretching to the rays of an early spring.

"I will make preparations and give you further instructions. Tonight there will be another meeting with Elder Enchantraen. I will be there and I would like you to come. Let him tell you in his own words what he expects from you. But for now, how do you feel about it?"

Jabir's hawk-like features smooth into a broad reassuring smile.

"I'm not sure I want to go," Affensash states flatly. "If it's not dangerous why worry about sending an alchemist? Are you sure there have been no wizards already sent to investigate this disturbance? What if there really is something wrong up there? I've seen wizard's duels. In clashes over power there is no safe place."

"Believe me, Affensash; I know this for a fact." Jabir stops and looks squarely into Affensash's eyes. "I wouldn't send you up there if I thought there was any real danger. Trust me. There have been no wizards sent into those high mountain ranges for years."

CHAPTER FOUR

Relearning Old Skills

Moving while shooting a missile weapon decreases the chances of hitting the target. See missile table.

- from Missiles, in the treatise of High Fantasy

The next day Laurallin is up at the first glint of the sun. They made good time the previous day despite Affensash's good-hearted horse she is forced to ride. Dannia is still asleep bundled away in warm furs. Although it isn't necessary, Laurallin thought she would start sharpening her hunting skills before beginning the day. Quietly, cat-like, she stalks through the woods for game with her composite bow. She hopes to find a small bird or rabbit to cook for today's lunch.

It has been awhile since she was able to use the skills her father taught her. Life with Affensash just doesn't leave much time for such practices. Sitting still, she scans the woods for the slightest sound or movement. Always being careful to hunt downwind, she moves on when nothing is found. The hunt goes on that way for what may seem like hours to a city-bred hunter. To Laurallin, patience is a part of the hunt. Her tracking is deliberately slow and only hampered by the fact that she must remain close to her camp. She follows a trail through the woods where some animal has been eating the vegetation and bending branches and leaves to the side as it pushes past. The trail is clear to her but she dare not stray too far from her sleeping child.

Finally, she hears a bold rustling in the leaves as the creatures of the woods begin to stir with the early morning light. Step after carefully planted step, she closes in on her prey. Over a small hill and just through a thicket she finally spots it. A wild boar!

The creature would provide more meat than they need, but her heart begins to race with the excitement of the hunt. Imagine, her first time out and to find so handsome a prize. Even from this distance she is certain she can hit the creature. Lifting her bow, she looks for an unhindered path to loose the arrow through the trees. She aims just to the left of the boar and waits, inhaling slowly to steady her aim.

The boar grubs around for a short time and then starts to meander off to the right. Just when Laurallin thinks she is going to lose him, he changes direction and heads back left. The strain on her muscles from holding the bow taut begins to tell. The boar steps into the path and the arrow flies. It strikes with a solid thud, but the quivering in her arm keeps it from becoming the kill shot. The boar squeals and runs painfully in circles.

Laurallin quickly readies the next arrow, but the boar charges off through the thicket and is lost from sight. A wise hunter would track the boar and kill it. A wounded animal like that can be one of the most dangerous creatures in the woods, not to mention the unnecessary suffering it must go through. Disgusted, Laurallin lowers the tip of her arrow. She was a good hunter, but not the best.

She has already been away from Dannia too long and she dare not continue on an extensive hunt that could take them far from her destination.

Laurallin turns and stretches to relieve the cramping. She starts back toward Dannia at a good run. A rabbit leaps from hiding in a bush. In one blurred motion Laurallin raises the bow, aims and fells the rabbit as she runs.

Stopping for a moment, she realizes what she has just done. Running or riding while you shoot should make the shot much more difficult. Her training comes back to her naturally. She really is a Hebelcaan, and a daughter of the chief.

Drawing her dagger, she goes over to clean the rabbit before returning to camp. Halfway through cleaning her game she hears the frantic snorts of the old plow horse. Standing upright, the color drains from her face. The boar must have circled around and stumbled into her camp!

Dropping the rabbit, Laurallin sprints through the woods with visions of Dannia flashing through her mind. She is not far from the camp. She sees the horse rearing and pawing the air, but the foliage blocks all sight of the boar or Dannia. She begins screaming at the top of her lungs, not from fear, but with the hope of scaring the boar away.

Faster still she runs directly to the camp. Ten feet away she sees the boar stamping its hoof making ready for a charge against the horse. With the speed and instincts of a natural huntress, she springs from a rock straight at the boar. Leg muscles taught and back arched, she flies full length, and with one strike her dagger takes what her bow could not.

Rolling on her side, she avoids the horse's descending hooves. Up, and back on her feet, she allows herself a deep breath of relief. She sees Dannia proudly sitting on her furs having squirmed free of the covers. Catching her mother's eyes, Dannia smiles, sticks her tongue out, and gives a long playful "plehhhhh", then topples over and starts crawling towards her.

Laurallin drops heavily next to Dannia and laughs in relief. "Maybe we should just concentrate on finding your father!"

CHAPTER FIVE

Secret Meetings

A potion is a liquid that affects the bodily functions whether taken externally or internally. It is not magical in that it does not use aether even though its effects may be similar or identical to magic.

- of Alchemists, from the treatise of High Fantasy

Jabir has provided Affensash with a room. It is complete with all the necessities of an alchemist, and that helps him pass the nervous hours while waiting for the coming meeting with Elder Enchantraen.

Holding a dull red flask up to a candle, Affensash watches, as the liquid thins out and bubbles. Affensash knows so many of his formulas by heart that he can work on them mechanically, freeing his mind for more serious matters. He always seems to do his best thinking while tinkering around a lab.

When the liquid seems thin enough, Affensash walks over to a second flask that has a tube running out the bottom. The tube goes down to a third flask, but halfway down the tube is an odd little contraption. A pinwheel is attached to the tube that rotates. It adds precisely the right amount of air to the passing liquid, while at the same time mixing it with a second liquid. Carefully measuring the dull red fluid, Affensash pours it in, drop by drop, while slowly blowing on the pinwheel.

Jabir's story about sending an alchemist to investigate seems plausible enough, but there are still a lot of things that trouble Affensash. Why all this secrecy at the Mystic Isles? Maybe the True Ones Guild is not really behind this mission and Affensash is being made a pawn of an over-ambitious wizard? Elder Enchantraen could be using him for his own personal gain. What about the attack? Three wizard's bring him to an island where he has to be rescued by a young elf? It's too coincidental that such a fearsome beast strayed loose of its master and just happened to attack him out of all the other inhabitants of the island.

Picking up the bottom flask, Affensash begins stirring it with a glass rod. Placing the flask on a wire stand, he moves a stocky candle beneath it. Then he mixes in a coarse white powder.

Although he has never met Jabir before, the chief alchemist's reputation is well-known. Jabir has been criticized as being more of a merchant than an alchemist. He is always willing to hire out Guild members and to commit the Guild to nearly anything for the right price. When gold is part of the formula, Affensash wonders if Jabir can be trusted about anything.

The liquid begins to smoke. Affensash accidently inhales a whiff making him dizzy. Grabbing a cork, he stuffs it in the flask before the whole concoction evaporates.

Shaking his head, Affensash mumbles to Ruefin yawning in the corner, "The sleep potion is a little more potent than usual."

Walking over to his case, he places the flask with his others, including the light potion he made just before being taken to the isles. Like a good alchemist, he goes back to the table and methodically begins the whole process again.

The biggest threat to Affensash is having been taken from his lab. He always equated his small cramped room of twisting tubes with security. The experience has left him more shaken than he cares to admit. Being forced into the world he fought so long to avoid is frightening for him. It is only natural that he now distrusts everything and everybody in it, well maybe not everyone.

The edges of his mind touch on thoughts of Laurallin. To directly think about her now would be too much. He just can't mix his fright with feelings of longing and loneliness. They are safe. He blocks out the fleeting images of his wife and Dannia, and manages the only way he knows how. He engrosses himself in his work. Affensash passes the time, all the while trying to create order and make sense out of the senselessness around him.

When a Tuatha finally brings a late meal, Ruefin is ready and anxious to eat. Gobbling down the food, Affensash gathers a few things and is quickly led away through a maze of old stone passages. The maze is so long and complex that Affensash prays he never gets lost. Finally they come to a passage that dead-ends at a set of double doors.

The guide stops and Affensash mistakes his meaning as a sign to go on alone. He starts to take a step forward when the Tuatha says, "Stop! Can't you see it?"

Affensash stares and through the torchlight, begins to make out a light blue shimmer in the air.

"The area is warded!" explains the Tuatha. "Wait a moment. They know we are here."

Affensash takes out his book and writes *warded*, and dashes off a few notes.

After a brief pause, the oak doors at the end of the hall creak open. Like a wave from an ocean, darkness rushes out of the doors and the torches on the walls dim and fade to black. Affensash stands dead still, uncertain what to do. Three little spheres of light race from the darkness and they whisk once around the two of them. They stop to hover before Affensash.

"These are the were-lights of Elder Enchantraen," the Tuatha explains. "They will take you safely from here. I guess I am not supposed to go any further."

The small spheres of light hover tentatively as if waiting for Affensash to follow.

"What do you mean, you 'guess' you are not to go any further!"

The Tuatha steps away and disappears into the darkness.

"Hey, come back here." The corridor is still and Affensash stands alone in the eerie were-light. "Hello! Enchantraen? I could use a little help."

Silence.

Affensash waits a few moments, still uncertain what to do. "Listen, I refuse to go any further unless I get a real live escort."

Echo: Silence.

"That's it! Sometimes you must stand your ground; I'm not budging until I get an escort." To show them that he means business, Affensash sits down and crosses his arms.

All is quiet and Affensash begins to feel confident that they know he is serious. Then he notices that the were-lights are beginning to move toward the oak doors.

"Hey wait. You can't do that to me."

Just as the lights pass through the doors and begin to disappear down the hallway, Affensash jumps up and runs after them.

"All right, all right, I understand now. Just slow down," he yells after the floating spheres, but they continue their quickening pace not heeding his pleas.

The spheres fly around a corner and Affensash temporarily loses sight of them. At a dead run, he starts to puff and only just manages to catch a glimpse of them.

"Hey! Hold on!" he shouts wheezing loudly now.

The ominous sound of footsteps causes him to look back jerkily over his shoulder. He catches only impressions of darkness.

"Just my echo, just my echo," he hisses between pants, but manages to quicken his pace anyway.

With three sizzles, the lights pass through a crack between two closed doors and Affensash is left in total darkness. Relying on his memory of the corridor, he runs blindly along stretching his arms out in front of him. Misjudging where the end of the corridor is, Affensash collides with a thud against the doors. They burst open, knocking him off balance and he stumbles into the room.   A low chair catches him at the knees and he falls forward sliding part way down a table. He twists over and stops flat on his back looking up at the ceiling in a well-lit room.

Ruefin squeals, pops out of his pocket and runs for cover. As his eyes refocus, faces appear looking down at him.

"Is he dead?" someone asks. "I told you he wouldn't make it to the dock without seriously hurting himself," says the familiar voice of a guard Affensash met earlier.

Jabir's face appears and rough hands jerk him from the table. "Get up," Jabir screeches.

Once he is righted, Affensash sees that he has finally made it to the meeting room. Enchantraen, Jabir, and several others are gathered around the table.

"SS .. Something's out there," Affensash stutters pointing to the door.

"Silence you fool. This is embarrassing enough without you looking so scared and incompetent," Jabir hisses. "He is just a little over-anxious, Elder Enchantraen," Jabir continues loudly now looking towards the great wizard.

Turning back to Affensash, he shoves him down in a chair and whispers, "Do you think you can manage to sit here quietly without hurting yourself until this is over?"

Punctuating his comment with a purposeful narrowing of his eyes, Jabir returns to his own seat at the table. Red-faced, Affensash isn't willing to argue. Even Ruefin seems too embarrassed to join him and sits quietly in a dark corner, cleaning his paws and sniffing something unusual in the air.

"Welcome, friend Affensash. Jabir was just assuring us that your natural born hunting skills will see you through this little adventure unharmed," Enchantraen says skeptically.

A low chuckle arises from around the table. Looking the room over, Affensash discovers that Jabir has attended the meeting with two alchemist guards. Naturally, Enchantraen is there, but there are also three other wizards that Affensash has never seen before. There is also a fourth man that looks distinctly different than the rest. He is a rough-looking man wearing hunting clothes, looking like he has just stepped off the trail. Unconsciously, Affensash stares at the man.

A low base growl from a dark corner sends Ruefin scurrying across the room. Jumping onto Affensash's shoulder in one leap, he dives with a yap into his pocket. The sudden charge of his friend causes Affensash, whose nerves are already frayed, to jump from his chair.

A jet-black jaguar looms out of the dark corner, strokes its sleek deadly head against the leg of the enigmatic man, and disappears back into the corner again.

"Sorry, friend Affensash," the man says genuinely concerned. Standing, he extends a hand and says, "I am Benolic, squire and animal master for Enchantraen. I hope Teela didn't scare you. Every now and then she becomes very protective."

"Benolic is a friend who came to the isles about the same time I arrived. He insists that, in my elevated position as an Elder, I should have a bodyguard," interrupts Enchantraen. "But please sit now. We have important business to conclude."

The three little were-lights dance around Enchantraen's head adding a certain kind of majesty to this already stately wizard.

"The discovery of the disturbances at the Pentacles came to my attention when an alarming number of True Ones reported failures in their spells. Several have even trekked to these isles to seek training and comfort, believing that their powers were leaving them, and that soon they would be wizards no more. Using the powers available to me as an Elder, I attempted to search the area with the telepathic powers of Edla's Throne."

A scowl passes over the Elder's face. "I have found that the Pentacles are closed to my vision. I do not wish to concern the council of the Elders, or as you know them, the Circle of Truth, without investigating the matter on my own first. I do, however, believe that the problem is growing, as more and more reports of spells failing come to me. I do not wish to send True Ones to investigate because they may be powerless to defend themselves under the circumstances."

"Some of my trusted colleagues were so insistent on investigating for themselves that I had to send a few away to keep them busy elsewhere. I trust the rest of you have learned from friend Johona's mistakes and don't wish to join him on his recruiting adventures in the south." Enchantraen looks challengingly around the table at the other three wizards.

One of the wizards seems unable to contain himself despite Enchantraen's meaningful glare. "Johona may not have been very diplomatic, but his reasoning was sound. Suppose the Eastern Empire has devised a way to neutralize the aether-drawing powers of the True Ones. Our whole Guild could be in serious danger. We should investigate such dangers ourselves and act upon them immediately. We shouldn't trust our fate to outsiders." The wizard looks almost apologetically towards Affensash.

"My personal feud with the Eastern Empire is no secret to anybody. But the True Ones Guild is supposed to be neutral to worldly politics. I am trying to be objective about the matter," Enchantraen replies bluntly.

The statement of the first wizard gives a second wizard enough courage to speak his mind. "What of Elder Chinit? That beautiful she-devil has openly rebuked you at council meetings. Besides, the attack on Affensash has not been satisfactorily answered in my opinion."

"That is Guild business!" Enchantraen objects. "We do not speak of family problems in front of outsiders!"

"But that is precisely the point," blurts out the third wizard. "This is Guild business, our Guild's business. How do we know that they can be trusted with so serious a matter?" pointing directly at Jabir.

Enchantraen stands and slams a fist on the table.

"No one is to be trusted. Remember, we are not the only magic users in this world. We always distrust the Planear and Namonic magic users. But even among the aether-using wizards only sixty or seventy percent belong to the True Ones Guild and we should carefully consider them as well. This is just the first prudent step in the investigation. It is my first step and my wish is to proceed with caution. We will not name our enemy until we have proof."

Suddenly, a loud scraping sound like a giant claw descends from the top to the bottom of the doors that lead to the room. Before anyone can react the doors explode!

"I told you, Jabir that something was out there!" Affensash shouts.

A chance piece from the large oak doors flies across the room and strikes Enchantraen on the head, sending the great wizard reeling.

"There's your proof!" shouts one of the wizards, mistaking Affensash's statement as an accusation against Jabir. "Jabir is the traitor!" With that he leaps across the table grabbing the chief alchemist by the throat.

Enchantraen succumbs to the blow and fades the rest of the way into unconsciousness. When a wizard stops concentrating on a spell, the spell stops. Enchantraen's were-lights go out, throwing the room into chaotic darkness.

Shots from the alchemist guards' guns ring out and the great panther springs, attacking an unknown assailant. Men shout and in the scuffle Affensash is knocked from his chair into the corner. The room is in total chaos and Affensash can't see a thing.

Suddenly, the roar of an attacking creature drowns out even the panther's frantic growling. The death gurgle of a man sends a foreboding shock-wave through Affensash's bones.

Reacting quickly, Affensash pulls two vials from his belt. Shaking the first vial, a dim light appears and then fills the room. Affensash sees Jabir wrestling with the wizard who jumped across the table at him. By the doorway rests the mangled body of one of the alchemist guards, apparently dead. At the other end of the room, standing over the unconscious body of Enchantraen is Benolic and one of the wizards. But in the door is the frightening form that Affensash sensed in the corridor. A large, nearly transparent creature stands over the mangled body of the alchemist.

The creature is immense, with a large mouth and several vicious rows of teeth. The only other distinguishable part of the creature is a light-green liquid that seems to emit from its pores and flows down, outlining its otherwise invisible body. The liquid gathers in hissing puddles on the floor. The creature is so large that it is having trouble fitting through the doorway. The stones on the archway begin to crack and crumble as the creature strains to enter the room.

The panther is riding on the creature's back, tearing viciously at the invisible flesh. The light potion in his hand makes Affensash the prime target of the creature's next attack. It swings its massive jaws towards him. Affensash winds-up to throw the second vial, his sleep potion, at the hideous beast.

Just then Jabir heaves the wizard off of him and stands drawing his pistols from his belt. The vial crashes on the back of the chief alchemist's head causing his shot to go wild. Turning groggily towards Affensash Jabir manages a look of total disbelief before he succumbs to the effect of the potion and crumbles to the floor.

The swinging jaws of the creature slam into Affensash sending the light vile smashing against the back wall. For Affensash the closing darkness doesn't matter. The force of the creature's blow, and a whiff of his own potion, also sends him spinning into unconsciousness.

CHAPTER SIX

Friends Again

This subclass deals with the non-magical abilities of the mind.

- of Sensitives, from the treatise of High Fantasy

Laurallin quickly finds the trail. The Hebelcaan are making no attempt to cover their movements. A sign the tribe is doing well. The trip has been easy. Spring has supplied the two with plenty of small game and Laurallin finds the hunting a refreshing change. Dannia has been introduced to a few of the delicacies of the wild and has adapted her appetite accordingly. In fact, she has actually gained weight.

Laurallin knows she is closing in on the tribe. The trail is fresh. If she had a fast horse she would probably reach them by nightfall. One thing she has learned as the daughter of a nomad chief is that you don't get any place in a hurry in this country. Up and over a hill she walks, leading the horse behind her. Dannia is strapped to the poor animal's back, tugging incessantly at the blanket wrapped around her.

Laurallin stops. Something is coming! She can neither hear nor see it, but horses are approaching. The terrain is bad cover at this point if there is any trouble. Tugging on the reins, she pulls Dannia and the horse into a clump of bushes. There she strings her bow and waits.

Only a few moments pass when she sees them. Outriders! They are the scouts for her father's tribe. They haven't spotted her yet. Reaching into a saddle bag, she takes out a red ribbon and feather and ties it to the top of her bow. Coaxing the horse out of the bushes, she mounts up holding the bow high over her head. The two outriders pull up. Noticing her for the first time, they visually search the countryside for any others. Satisfied that she is alone, they lower their short spears and charge. Laurallin stops the horse and with lightning speed nocks an arrow. They must have seen her symbol. The markings on her bow should distinguish her as a tribe member and not an enemy. Perhaps the symbol has been changed? Confused, she watches the two men approach. Maybe an enemy discovered the sign and it now stands for treachery?

She pulls the arrow back to her ear, but holds it there. The two outriders suddenly split, fan around her, and stop about thirty feet from her on either side. She aims the arrow first at the one on the right, and then quickly turns to the left and back again. The outriders wear a light headdress and their faces are covered in a death mask, the traditional garb of her tribe when killing has to be done.

No one speaks. The outriders' horses shift their weight and stamp uneasily. Suddenly, one of the riders laughs.

"Do you not recognize the daughter of your chief?" Laurallin shouts.

"Don't you recognize an old friend when you see one?" laughs the outrider. Pulling the mask away from his face, Laurallin sees that it is Kenlin, her childhood friend. Both riders lift their spears and laugh.

Lowering her arrow, Laurallin says," You know I could have killed you both right now playing that silly game."

"I suppose you could have, that is, if you still remember how to use that thing after all these years," Kenlin laughs again mockingly.

The two outriders spur their mounts to either side of Laurallin. "It's been a long time since we have seen you. Are you going to visit your father or are you here on business?" asks Kenlin, as Laurallin goads her mount into motion.

"Both, but I prefer to speak with my father about it," Laurallin snaps, still perturbed about Kenlin's little joke.

"I'll ride ahead and tell them you are coming." Kenlin clicks his tongue and his horse breaks into a full gallop.

"You really shouldn't treat him badly. You were the one who left him if you remember," says the second remaining rider as they watch Kenlin gallop away.

"It was a childhood infatuation. Everyone is allowed to grow up aren't they? Besides, who are you to speak to me like this?"

"Excuse me, I'm Hannel. Don't you recognize me?"

Laurallin coughs, "The short fat kid with the greasy face?"

Taken aback by her abrupt reference, Hannel retorts, "Some of our childhood things are easily discarded. Others are worth keeping even when we are adults. If you are looking for your father, follow the line of hills up that way," he says, pointing to a ridge. "I will see you when you make it to camp. I must return to my duties." With a whistle and a touch on the shoulder, his great horse wheels and canters off.

Dismounting, Laurallin walks her tired horse the rest of the way up the hills. Well that could have gone better, Laurallin thinks. In a few brief sentences she managed to offend two of her old friends. Dannia is in a deep sleep swaying back and forth as Laurallin tries to get the old horse to go just a little faster.

Laurallin is disappointed with her hot temper and regrets being so short with Kenlin. But that's the way it has always been. Somehow or another she always manages to hurt him. Either he is too sensitive or she is too brash. She smiles to herself now that the scare of Kenlin's joke is over and pats the plow horse's old muzzle. Then, she is finally struck with a realization. Kenlin has grown up! He was... well... handsome. Unwittingly, she flushes and suppresses any further thoughts about him.

It is just about dusk when Laurallin finally sees her father. He is sitting still, mounted on Tsester, his magnificent black stallion, looking down over a large valley. She is certain he has seen her and is purposely posing that way to make things difficult for her. Still, he makes an impressive silhouette etched against the reddening sky. It has been too long she thinks, as she maneuvers the old horse past the boulders and tree stumps. This is going to be a difficult reunion. She walks all the way to his side before she can speak.

"Hello father, you look well," she says looking up at him.

"Nice horse," he replies not even looking down.

"Don't do this father! Don't make it any tougher than it has to be. I've missed you. It feels good just to be around you," she says placing a hand on his knee.

Looking down and patting her hand he says, "I don't suppose you have come home to stay. Your mother is getting older and misses you very much. She could, I mean, we could use an extra pair of hands right now."

With a sigh, Laurallin turns away. The same old story all over again. For the first time she looks out over the valley and it takes her breath away. The herd is grazing below. There are hundreds of beautiful horses surrounded in the thick green grasses with the red and orange dusk sky cresting the mountains. They are like a living wave in a great pond. A ripple appears when a herdsman chases in a stray. Like one, the herd moves. Frisky males rise and paw the air. Young colts scamper after their mother. Just off in the distance campfires flicker. The evening meal is being prepared for the men's return.

"The herd is much larger than I remember. The tribe seems to be doing very well," Laurallin says absently, as the peaceful memories of her childhood dance before her.

"Yes we are. We sell the half-blood horses to the Eastern Empire now and save the full-blood for the Western Kingdoms. Our stock has good blood in them. They are very much in demand from both armies."

"Oh father, how could you? They killed your brother!" Laurallin groans.

"That was in a war fifteen years ago. It was my brothers' choice to fight, not the Hebelcaan's," he says rigidly.

"I remember the stories he told me. He could name all five of the Dark Lords. He saw them butcher... "Laurallin can't finish the sentence. "I will never forgive them."

"We," he starts, then changes his thought, "The tribe needs this. By selling we can go on," the old chief says, beginning to raise his voice.

Dannia coughs and comes to wake crying.

Noticing his granddaughter for the first time, the old chief slides down off his horse. Untying the straps, Dannia drops into his arms and immediately quiets.

"She is beautiful, Laurallin." He holds her up, stretching out her arms and legs, inspecting her like a colt. "She looks just like your mother."

"I always thought she looked like you," Laurallin returns with a smile.

Looking the horse over for any other surprise bundles, he turns to her in mock disbelief. "What? Only one child?"

"Please father! City men don't breed their women like you do your mares. Affensash is kind and gentle to me. Don't start criticizing him already."

"Where is this kind and gentle man who sends his wife and child out alone in this harsh country?" he blurts sarcastically.

"He is gone, father. That is why I am here." A tear wells up in her eye.

He sees that she is serious. His sarcasm melts away as she collapses into his arms with a sob. The three of them walk down the hills arm in arm toward the camp. On the way, Laurallin explains Affensash's disappearance.

The stars are shining brightly by the time the evening meal is completed. In honor of Laurallin's return, a ceremonial ring of flame is built. The ring consists of many smaller fires built in a circle so that the whole tribe can gather around them.

With the meal finished, contentment settles over the camp, even among the younger children. All the tribe lay around the fires, women wrapped in their husband's arms; children tucked away or nestled in soft blankets asleep for the night. In the middle of the circle, walking around the inner edges of the fire is the Shaman. In a half walk and half dance he tells a story with his voice and hands. It is a story that all have heard many times and for Laurallin it brings back the fondest memories.

"In the days before, the sea was calm and smooth as glass. Across this sea the one great stallion, Hebelcaan, roamed. So great was Hebelcaan that when each of his hoofs touched the water waves flew up and raced towards the land. Each wave bore with it his son or daughter and washed them newly born upon the beach. These are the grandsires of our herd, the beginning of the four-footed people.

Hebelcaan came but once to the shore. There he spoke to only one man. That man was the tribes ' first chief. The man asked to sit upon the back of Hebelcaan so that he could ride and see the world. Hebelcaan thought on the matter for a moment and decided they were both in need. If the man would care and look after Hebelcaan's children for all the years to come, Hebelcaan would consent to the man's wishes. The man agreed because he could not think of a greater splendor. The ride on Hebelcaan's back took two years. The man saw the world like no other man has ever seen it. From this experience the man grew wise, wiser than all other men.

At the shore Hebelcaan knelt and let the man slide from his broad strong back. There all of Hebelcaan's children waited to be cared for. Hebelcaan bid the man to make good his promise. First the man arranged the children into a herd. Those who were the strongest and bravest would be the leaders. But even organized this way the herd was too large for one man to care for. So the man called on all of his children to come and make good his promise. The children came and he arranged them into the tribe. Man and horse were brothers.

Hebelcaan saw this and was satisfied. For keeping his promise Hebelcaan named the man Chief among the tribe. With his children cared for Hebelcaan now spends his days playing and running freely upon the seas.

As long as the waves wash upon the shore we know that Hebelcaan lives. As long as Hebelcaan lives, we the tribe will keep our promise and care for the four-footed people who are his children."

The Shaman continues his song, gesturing with his hands to indicate the steady crashing of the waves. By the end of his story, the mood of the tribe is relaxed. Laurallin glances around the fire and catches Kenlin staring at her. Both are embarrassed and avert their eyes at the same time. The Shaman is making ready for his last duties of the evening.

In the center of the fires he lays out small blankets and various tools of his craft. It is the time when the tribesmen may bring up their sick for healing or ask the Shaman to perform other tasks. Seeing the future for profit or love is a very popular request, especially among the young. Usually, the answers to such questions are so vague that it is hard to take any real action on the advice. None-the-less, the young people usually spend hours giggling and contemplating the results. One by one, the people disappear into the ring and then return. Laurallin waits impatiently. Several times she stands and moves towards the Shaman, but another reaches him first. Kenlin is also trying to reach the Shaman with the same results. Eventually, they end up standing closer together. Kenlin is closest to the fire. The reflection of the blaze gives the illusion that his firm muscular body is actually cast of bronze. His eyes raise and lower unable to ignore the slim figure beside him.

"Please don't stare Kenlin. You are making me nervous," Laurallin whispers.

"I'm sorry," he says, lowering his eyes. "It has been a long time since I have seen you."

They both gaze nervously at the fire. Laurallin starts to move, but sees that another will beat her to the Shaman.

"Are you happy now Laurallin? I remember how uneasy you were before you left."

"Yes I'm happy now," Laurallin replies and for the first time she softens her tone, "but it is different than I expected."

"We miss you around here you know," and he coughs nervously into his hand, "but I am truly glad things have worked out well for you."

"What about you Kenlin? You're getting a little old to be running loose. Tribal law says that you must marry soon. Who is the wife to be?"

"Well there is ..."

Just then a tribesman leaves the Shaman and Laurallin sees her chance. Two quick steps put her ahead of all others. Once inside the circle, she seats herself on the blanket across from the Shaman.

"Greetings, Daughter of our Chief. I'm glad to see you return even if it is only for a short while."

"I have made this trip Shaman especially to see you. My husband, Affensash, was taken from me in the middle of the night. I think he left this as a message." Laurallin pulls out the talisman and lays it before the Shaman. The Shaman stares at it blankly and then looks up at Laurallin.

"It is my symbol, but I don't know what it means. I know nothing of your husband or of his whereabouts."

"Please, I have come a long way," pleads Laurallin and picks up the talisman and places it in the Shaman's hand. "There must be something you can do."

He turns the talisman over and over in his palm. "Really child, I have never met your husband. My powers only reach to those... "

The Shaman stops in mid-sentence. "What's this?" he asks with a chuckle. From around the talisman, he unwinds strands of hair. "This certainly isn't Dannia's hair." Holding the strands to the side of Laurallin's head, he clearly sees that they are not hers either.

"Very clever! Very clever indeed. It seems that this is what your husband wanted me to find. This is Affensash's hair?"

"Yes, yes I think so. What does it mean?"

"Come child, it hasn't been that long. Don't you remember how I used to call to your father when he was away from the tribe?"

"I thought that was because he was the Chief. Do you mean that my husband wishes you to communicate with him?"

"Exactly! With this hair and his willingness to cooperate, I should be able to call to him just as I called to your father. Is this your wish for tonight?"

"Of course! Find him for me. Make certain he is safe. Ask him where he is so that I may go to him."

"Very well child. All this I can do for you, but you realize we must have the permission of your father, and the tribe must bear witness to the contact."

"My father will approve." Laurallin stands and turns until she sees her father. She motions for him to enter the circle. While the Chief approaches, the Shaman takes out a sharp knife and begins cutting the hair into tiny sections.

Laurallin explains to her father and as expected he consents. She turns excitedly back to the Shaman.

"Laurallin," her father calls after her. "If you really want to go after this husband of yours, your mother and I have something for you."

Taking her by the hand, he leads her outside the circle of flame and gives a short whistle while the Shaman prepares. Out of the blackness she hears a nicker and a fast set of hoof beats. A sable mare trots forward, rears in front of Laurallin, and immediately bows and dips Its head up and down as if in recognition of her.

"Father, it's Sensie! You kept her for me!" Laurallin leaps to the horse and strokes its nose and slaps its flank. The tribe does not train their horses as the rest of the Western Kingdoms do. They train them with voice and hand gestures instead of rope and whip. This emphasizes the special bonding between rider and horse. It also makes them a solid team.

"To tell you the truth daughter, the horse hasn't been much good to anyone. I haven't seen her this frisky since you left. You may have her, but I would like, in trade, to send along a few of our men to accompany you until you find your husband."

"No father, I really don't think that will be necessary. The Alchemy Guild assures me he is not in danger. However, you and mother could help by looking after Dannia until I return."

"Listen girl, the road could be dangerous even if the destination is not."

"Thank you father, but you worry too much."

The voice of the Shaman rises in a sing-song manner.

"He has already begun. I must return!"

Leaving Sensie with her father, she smiles and runs back to the circle of flame. There she finds the Shaman singing a chant and walking from fire to fire. Sitting on the blanket, Laurallin watches as the Shaman drops a tiny strand of hair into each of the fires. There is no visible result until the last strand is dropped into the final flame. Sparks and ash drift above the camp and collect around the stars.

"Affensash, we search the earth for your form as you wish of us."

The fires begin to smoke more heavily.

"Hear me, Affensash. We search the world and all the seas for your life. Your wife is here. We listen for our words in the winds. Do not be afraid. It is I, the Shaman of the Hebelcaan, and your wife, Laurallin. Talk to us. There are things we must know."

Going to the center of the circle, the Shaman lifts his arms and slowly spins around. Suddenly, the Shaman grabs his head and grimaces in pain. A faint and distant voice is heard.

"Shaman I hear you. Where are you?" The sound of waves crashing on the shore drifts in with the voice.

Still grimacing, the Shaman replies, "We are here, Affensash, at our spring camp. Where are you? Speak to us, let us know."

A long silence follows. Laurallin rises and walks to the Shaman's side.

"What is wrong? You look in pain."

"I don't know. There should be an image. Instead we hear only a faint voice. There is some resistance going on."

Looking up to the heavens, Laurallin shouts, "Where are you Affensash? Open your eyes and look around. We can't see anything!"

A voice replies clearly now. "I am on a beach at the base of the Pentacles."

"What beach?"

"I don't know."

With concern in her voice, Laurallin shouts in strong commanding tones, "Open your eyes Affensash. I might recognize the area."

Again a long pause follows. "Affensash! Let me see!" Laurallin commands.

The flames suddenly leap around her. The smoke continues to thicken and hangs over the circle. High above her an image begins to form so that the whole camp may see it. It is smoky at first, dancing in and out of their vision.

"I think I know that territory," says Hannel to Kenlin standing in the crowd.

"But why is the image forming sideways?" Others in the tribe make their guesses as to what image is forming and what location it is near the Pentacles.

The image becomes a little clearer.

"I don't think you recognize that particular mountain range," Kenlin laughs being the first to recognize the image.

Suddenly it stops shifting and snaps into focus. The naked breasts of a beautiful woman come into full view, wet hair dripping down her bare shoulders.

"He must be lying in her lap," someone shouts from the tribe!

Stunned, the Shaman loses his concentration and the communication is broken. When he looks down all he sees is the back of Laurallin leaving the circle.

"Father! Get me my horse."

CHAPTER SEVEN

Easy Sailing

Magic is the reshaping of reality. Wizards control this reshaping through the use of spells. They perform these spells by drawing power from a natural resource known as aether.

- of Wizards, from the treatise of High Fantasy

When Affensash comes to he finds himself back in his room bound to his bed. The remaining alchemist guard stands over him with his musket lying across his shoulder. Squinting to focus his eyes, Affensash tries to sit up and discovers that he can't.

"What happened?" he mutters painfully, remembering the creature.

Walking over to the side of the bed, the guard adjusts the bandages on Affensash's head.

"You're lucky Alchemist," the guard says quietly.

"I know! I was sure that thing was going to get me," Affensash replies with a moan.

"I don't mean the creature you idiot. I mean you're lucky Jabir doesn't kill you himself. In one short meeting you managed to make the Alchemy Guild a major suspect in this magic business and you nearly killed the head of our Guild as an encore."

"Ohhhhhh," Affensash groans as his memory fully returns. "What happened to that... to that creature?"

"Lucky for everyone, you went out at about the same time Enchantraen came to and cast a spell. It seemed we would all die until the Elder's hands suddenly burst to flame. In a way I simply do not understand, the wizard simply walked up and incinerated the creature! There was nothing left but a charred place on the floor."

"Who is hurt?" Affensash asks, feeling responsible.

"Almost everyone is hurt but only my friend, the other alchemist guard, was seriously injured. After the fight, Enchantraen laid hands upon him and stopped his bleeding. It was miraculous. He was nearly dead and now he is better off than you. I think there is more to these wizards than we care to admit."

"Please release me now," Affensash grunts struggling in his bindings.

"Oh, no! Not for all the gold in the Western Kingdoms. Jabir wants you bound and guarded until he can get you off this island. He says you are too dangerous to allow you to roam freely. Honestly, I think he would have killed you if he hadn't already signed the contract with Enchantraen. Because of that contract you are alive and Jabir asked me to give you this letter to complete your mission."

The guard loosens Affensash's ropes around his hands and squeezes a letter into his fingers. Affensash notices that the letter is sealed by an alchemy symbol. To be safe, Affensash licks his fingers before breaking the seal in case the letter is meant for his eyes only.

Affensash,

In light of recent events your mission now takes on new meaning. Not only will you have to ferret out the information Enchantraen has requested, you will also have to somewhat vindicate our Guild. You are to complete the first part of this mission as quickly as possible. As for the second, and I want to make this abundantly clear, you are to do as little as possible. Remember, your wife and child are tucked away in our safe keeping.

You are to complete this simple mission and to observe and report without any further trouble for all our sakes. Tomorrow morning you are going to leave this island by boat very, very quietly. You were to be escorted by those three wizards at the meeting, but they have refused. I guess they value their lives. Instead, the three wizards that originally brought you to the Isles will escort you as far as the mainland.

Once on the mainland you can make your way along the Pentacles mountain range toward High Tower.

At the bottom of the letter is the Seal of Jabir, head of the Alchemy Guild.

Affensash knows to break that seal causing the letter to flare and burn away.

Affensash remains bound-up for the remainder of the night while the guard apologizes but explains he is to remain bound on orders from Jabir.

In the morning he is thrown into a potato sack and quietly put aboard a ship. Affensash thinks the potato sack must be the guard's idea and there he remains until mid-morning. That is when Terrell feels brave enough to cut him loose.

Affensash thinks everyone took Jabir's instructions too literally. He did not do anything that warranted being bound. At least not for that long. After several hours, Affensash finally joins his three companions at the bow of the ship and quietly stares across the sea. Worrying about Laurallin's safety, he mentally reviews the written and verbal orders from Jabir and prays that he doesn't make things worse.

The orders seem simple enough. Go to the mountain ranges, observe and report everything you see. Stay out of trouble and do not get involved. Afterwards, he gets to return to his wife with a bag full of gold.

Affensash particularly likes the part about not getting involved. Exactly what he is supposed to look for was never fully explained to him. Jabir always seemed too angry to go into details. Anyway, Elder Enchantraen said too much information would tend to bias his reporting. Other than the fact that he was going to be separated from his family, and that everyone on the Mystic Isles and his Guild either hated him or was afraid of him, the whole thing sounded like a nice vacation.

Diane, the female wizard, is cordial enough, but her two companions, Glenwall and Terrell, are rather grim and silent. Glenwall in particular bothers Affensash. Glenwall is an Easterner and proud of it. The East is conqueror of the Western Kingdoms and the tales of its harsh treatment of Affensash's countrymen is widely told. Besides, one of the wizards at last night's meeting named the Eastern Empire as a possible suspect.

Glenwall's rich garments and hefty coin purse are a dead give-away that he is an Easterner. If someone from the Western Kingdoms were that rich they wouldn't dare walk around showing it off so openly. A Westerner would be robbed and beaten shortly after leaving home.

Jabir said that the three of them were supposed to take him as far as the first mainland port. From there on, Affensash was to make his way as quickly as he could to the Pentacles. He knows to avoid extensive contact with any wizards in the region. He was; however, supposed to pay careful attention to any of their peculiar activities. Affensash tried to explain that everything a wizard did was peculiar to him, but Jabir would hear nothing about it. From time to time, Jabir said he would be contacted and his reports would be passed on to Elder Enchantraen.

Simple, simple, simple!

Somehow, Affensash just can't believe Laurallin will see it that way. Where is his wife, he wonders. Maybe she missed his clue. She's safe though. He firmly believes she is all right. If he didn't, he would be off this ship and swimming for the mainland.

The ship rocks sharply and Affensash staggers away from the railing. He has always hated the sea. Dropping to his knees, he crawls over to the mast and wraps his arms around it. Not knowing much about ships, he feels that something is unusual about this one. It looks like it has a spare mast strapped horizontally across the back.

He misses Laurallin. An old ache wells-up in the bottom of his stomach. Somehow things would not feel so bad if she were here. He hasn't felt an ache like this for some time, yet he recognizes the longing clearly. Where is she? It was going to be a long separation; he only hoped she would understand when it was all over.

"We are away from the Isles' protective spells. There is nothing but clear seas ahead of us," shouts one of the shipmates.

See, there they go again talking about things he knows absolutely nothing about - *protective spells*. How could he report to the Elder what was going on at the Pentacles? They should send a wizard instead, or someone more knowledgeable in the True Ones' craft. Affensash opens his book and writes, protective spell, but then quickly scribbles it out.

The ship dips in an unusually large wave and Affensash's ache turns to a very real physical pain in the stomach.

"They're right you know," says Glenwall to Terrell, looking over the bow of the ship. Glenwall's rich gold embroidered robes whip around in the brisk wind very unlike Terrell's plain woolen brown colors.

"What's that?" asks Terrell absently.

"He's not going to make it. They've got the wrong man. Look at him," Glenwall says pointing over his shoulder. "If you sat a full bowl of soup in front of him and hid the spoon he would starve to death. He just won't make it through the rugged country of the Pentacles."

"He's not going to be alone," breaks in Diane, overhearing the conversation. Walking to Terrell's side, she gazes out over the sea.

"What do you mean? Jabir said we are to place him in a rowboat at the first sight of land. His orders are for Affensash to go alone."

"Forget it Terrell. Those were the orders from the Alchemy Guild. As a True One, I can't sit back and watch him go to his death. I am going with him," Diane retorts in determined tones.

"No Diane! We can't interfere with his Guild's wishes. Besides, we are under contract to his Guild to perform a task."

"You will be breaking the Elder's wishes," interrupts Glenwall in disbelief of Diane's words.

Diane turns and faces Glenwall, her lithe but full form contrasting to Glenwall's thick stocky frame." We are to set him adrift in the sea. After that, our work is completed and my time is my own. Listen Glenwall, we are talking about a man's life, not a technicality. I am going. Period!"

"You are going to traipse across the country risking the anger of Elder Enchantraen, not to mention your life, for that man?" Terrell asks doubtfully, pointing toward Affensash who is making his way with haste towards the side of the ship. "Why throw away a perfectly good career for that?" A sickening sound erupts behind them. "Besides, what would your fiancé say if he knew you were alone for months with another man?"

"I hardly think Johona would feel threatened by him," she says looking a little queasy herself. "Besides, he's been gone a long time and hasn't bothered to send the first message. Maybe if Johona is separated from me a short while he might learn to appreciate me a little more. He is the one that took off with those other wizards and headed south without me."

"How much further," Affensash yells from behind them. They all turn around, but no one answers.

"Here they come." Diane puts her hand above her eyes and searches the sky. A deep buzzing sound slowly becomes audible to the rest.

"Goodness Diane, you have fantastic hearing," says Terrell suddenly spotting two descending forms.

Two black spots quickly turn to glints of gold. The buzzing sound changes to a rumble and the ship's sails begin to bellow.

"Get those sails down," barks the Captain, "or they will be ripped to shreds!"

Affensash crawls back to the bow of the ship. Searching the sky in the same direction as the others, he finally sees two large creatures descending.

"Dragons," he gasps.

"No Affensash, those aren't dragons. They are the wind steeds of the Elders. Enchantraen has sent them to hurry us along on our journey. They are called Wind Drakes. Look, can't you see they have four wings instead of two, and they are slimmer than dragons?" Diane tries to explain.

The Wind Drakes descend until the water splashes and stirs from their beating wings. Affensash pulls out his book once more. They are mostly gold in color, but each scale is highlighted with blues and greens. Their eyes are coal black. On the back of each rides a Tuatha from the Mystic Isles. The crew quickly battens down all the loose items on deck. The great beasts land on the large horizontal pole that extends on either side of the back of the ship.

"I thought that was a spare mast in case the one in the middle broke," exclaims Affensash.

"No, no alchemist," Diane laughs. "The Wind Drakes are a symbol of the Elders. They could not accompany us from the port because that would mark our trip as very important. Elder Enchantraen wishes us to stay unnoticed as long as possible. They will push our ship with great speed and we should make it to the mainland by nightfall. They will leave us again when we first sight land. That way we can sail in under our own power and no one will be the wiser."

Temporarily forgetting about his stomach, Affensash stares in wide-eyed amazement as the clawed feet of the Wind Drakes wrap around the pole and the ship begins to lurch forward.

"You know I've never even seen a dragon, well, except in paintings of course. Wind Drakes will do for now."

"I have been meaning to talk to you about that Affensash," Diane says very concerned. "You wouldn't mind if I accompanied you for a while on this mission would you? Just until you catch on to what you are supposed to do."

"Well I guess not. If that's the wish of Enchantraen, but I'm married you know."

"Yes, yes I know Affensash. I promise to behave myself," Diane can't help but giggle a little.

Embarrassed, Affensash turns away. "I didn't mean that. I, ah, I just thought I was supposed to do this on my own."

"Well you will do it on your own. It's just that I don't have anything to do and I think it would be an interesting diversion."

The Wind Drakes begin to pick-up speed. The wind rushes by the ship and Affensash's ailments turn to feelings of exhilaration.

"The rumor is," Diane continues, "that there is strange magical phenomenon occurring routinely in those mountains. My fiancé wanted to go investigate it himself. He likes that sort of thing, but he was sent on a recruiting mission with another group of wizards. He will be quite interested in what I might discover."

"I know," says Affensash." I heard his name mentioned at the meeting. Johona, I believe he is called. But what sort of strange things has been occurring in the mountains?"

"It's all rather complicated Affensash. Have you ever heard of aether? It's the magical energy that the True Ones draw on to form and work our spells. We believe that threads of aether weave about us and envelope our world in mystical patterns of power. The more powerful a True One you become the more sensitive you are to these patterns of power. Elder Enchantraen has detected a disturbance in the pattern. The disturbance is somewhere around the Pentacles. Wizards have brought back tales of strange behavior from the villagers in that area. It is Enchantraen, as you know, who is concerned about this disturbance."

"For some reason the great wizard does not wish to get others in my Guild directly involved. That is why he is contracting with your Alchemy Guild. I don't think that the other Elders are aware of what Elder Enchantraen is doing. That is why the Wind Drakes were sent out later to aid us. It is all very interesting you see if you are as nosey about the True

Ones' politics as I am. Something significant is going on and I want to be a part of it."

The hours pass and Diane seems to be the only one willing to talk with Affensash. The other wizards, especially Glenwall, keep their distance. The day is unusually cloudy, but it isn't until the afternoon that the Captain becomes particularly concerned. Joining Affensash and Diane at the bow of the ship, the Captain takes part in their casual conversation. Diane notices the Captain continually looking back towards the Isles.

"Tell me, Captain," she finally says. "Looking back that way I half expect to see a giant whale come rising out of the sea and swallow us whole."

"Oh there are monsters enough in the sea, lass," the Captain replies, "but it isn't sea monsters that I'm particularly worried about at this time. These are tricky waters even for the best navigators. When you're not twisting through a maze of sharp-teethed reefs you look over your shoulder for the changing moods of the wind. You see the black line of the Isles back there?" he asks, pointing along the horizon. "The Isles act as a natural barrier to the storms that blow in from the sea. You can't see the storms until they pass over the islands and by then they are practically on top of you."

"Well, how do they look today?" Affensash breaks in, clearing his throat.

"A storm's approaching all right. I just don't know how bad or how fast. See, the Isles are really only half that long. Most of that black horizon you see is the front of the storm."

Affensash suddenly turns pale. At the very least, they are in for a rough ride before they reach the mainland. Affensash is sure his stomach won't make it to shore even if he does.

"Think I will go check on Ruefin now," Affensash excuses himself and goes below deck to rest, feeling sick and scared.

The heavy rocking of the ship and a wave breaking against the upper deck awakens Affensash early from his much needed nap. Rising out of his hammock, he goes over and opens the door of Ruefin's cage and tries to calm his rapidly pacing friend. Then he hears the unusually high pitched humming of the Wind Drakes wings and overcomes his fears enough to go up and investigate. Dropping Ruefin in his pocket, he grabs his alchemy case and climbs above. The wind is howling loudly and nearly knocks Affensash over before he can adjust to it. He sees Diane and the other two wizards huddled near the center mast of the ship.

"We've been trying to outrun the storm," shouts Diane over the crashing waves. "It came up too quickly." As she explains, Affensash watches the Wind Drakes release their grasp on the ship and streak upward like paper kites. "The Captain has ordered the Wind Drakes off. They can't manage to drive the ship in a storm like this."

A wave strikes the side of the ship and washes across the deck drenching Affensash to the bone. The helmsman tries to regain control of the ship, temporarily taken off guard by the suddenly departing Wind Drakes.

"The Captain says we will weather it all right, but my friends and I are going to make sure. When the brunt of the storm is near enough we will combine our powers and calm the waters with a spell. Together we should be powerful enough to make this pleasant sailing for the rest of the journey. Why don't you go back to your cabin? There is nothing for you to do here but get wet."

Taking heart from Diane's words, Affensash decides to stay.

"I will wait up here with you. I am not powerless myself you know," he says as he pats his alchemy case on the side. Diane gives him an appreciative smile and he edges away to give the wizards room.

In the partial shelter of a stack of barrels, Affensash watches as the wizards prepare their spell. Joining hands, the two men wait for Diane to give the signal. She gazes out to sea, apparently trying to judge the best time to start the spell.

Affensash studies her face. Suddenly, her eyes widen and she begins the chant. Curious, Affensash leaves his concealment and stares across the sea in the same direction as Diane. At first he sees nothing. Then it becomes obvious what caused Diane to start. It is so big that Affensash subconsciously overlooked it at first. A giant wave races across the sea towards them.

Running back to his shelter, Affensash watches the wizards. They each begin tracing small light blue patterns in the air. Their chant is barely audible, but it is none-the-less uniform and unbroken. As the wave approaches, Affensash's stomach begins to twist into knots. What are they waiting for? It has to be now or never!

A light-blue ring of light appears above them, fizzles and then fades. From his shelter, Affensash knows something is wrong. The wail of the storm is too loud to make out any intelligible speech, but Affensash can read the words forming on Diane's lips. She turns toward Glenwall with a look of utter bewilderment and asks, "Why?"

The wave hits with such force that the three wizards are knocked to the side of the ship. The helmsman is washed overboard and the wheel starts spinning wildly. Flipping quickly to its side, the ship threatens to capsize. Diane and Terrell are thrown up and over the railing.

"No," screams Affensash and runs to the railing to find Diane barely clinging by one hand.

Terrell is already lost to the sea. Grasping her wrist, he pulls up. Just then a second wave slams into the hull before the Captain has time to straighten her up. The ship leans-to and Affensash and Diane are thrown into the mercy of the sea. Down and under they go, helpless against the strong currents. Men scream and more are lost to the vicious waters before the ship rights itself again.

Down below the waters the world seems surrealistically quiet. Affensash struggles aimlessly, uncertain of his direction, or even where the surface of the water might be. Suddenly, there is a tug on his collar and his head breaks the top of the water. With her arm under his chin Diane starts stroking towards a floating crate.

"I can swim! I can swim," screams Affensash, and Diane lets go.

"To the crate," she yells.

Affensash can barely make her words out over the turmoil. A few yards away Affensash sees the crate and poor Ruefin paddling madly beside it. They both make it about the same time. Just as they touch it, another wave smashes into them and they are both pulled away into the swirling sea.

Affensash surfaces first and scans the water for Diane. Her head bobs up and she gasps, taking in equal amounts of sea and air. The weight of her thick traveling robes acts as an anchor and pulls her back down. Just below the surface she struggles to untangle herself. Somehow she manages to disrobe and kick her shoes off. A strong pull on her arm and Affensash helps her break to the surface once more. Gasping with burning lungs, they reach the crate and hold on for dear life. Affensash's shouts for help are swallowed by the storm and the ship quickly drifts too far away for any plausible rescue.

"Ruefin, Ruefin!" Affensash shouts, noticing for the first time that his little friend is gone.

A short way from Diane the fox surfaces looking half his normal size and pawing frantically at the water. Reaching out for the little fox, Diane is forced to let go with one hand. A wave smashes her head back against the crate and she is torn away and taken under once more.

Dazed and exhausted, her body won't respond to her minds' frantic pleas to swim. She knows she is slowly sinking down.

Wasting no time, Affensash dives in the same spot he last saw her. Reaching and kicking around in the roiling water, his foot brushes against her limp hand. He grabs and pulls, but Diane does not respond and her body barely moves. Swimming deeper, he dives underneath her. Grabbing her by the back of her thighs, he pushes and kicks. The motion raises her, but causes him to sink a little further. He feels her legs slowly kick and as she rises past him, he grabs the bottom of her feet and pushes again. She rises, but whether she breaks the surface is unknown to Affensash. The last push sends him ever deeper into the sea.

Lungs on fire, Affensash struggles for the surface. The force of the storm and the ice cold waters have taken their toll and his strokes are weak and more frantic. On he fights, the fear of an icy grave urging him to stroke one more time, and yet again.

His lungs are ready to explode and the icy water surges in. At the same time, he breaks the surface exhaling the burning death from his lungs and gasps in choking spurts for life-giving air. Limply flailing in the water, his hand grazes the wooden crate and holds on. Pulling himself up, he sees Diane dazedly completing the end of a spell. The tip of her finger glows blue like a beacon in the storm. She reaches over and touches the forehead of Affensash and whispers, "Strength, my friend."

Affensash actually feels renewed, stronger, like a second wind has surged through his body. Desperately, Affensash, Diane, and little Ruefin cling to the bobbing crate as the uncaring sea tosses them in its wild abandoned fury.

How they wash onto the shore, neither one remembers. Diane is the first to realize they are on land. She comes to her senses when she hears Affensash mumbling near her. She drags her naked and battered body across the sand to Affensash's side. The alchemist is mumbling deliriously about a Shaman and his wife. Affensash's eyes try to open, but flutter closed again.

Alone on the beach on a wind-torn night, Diane cradles her companion's head, who seems to be going in and out of consciousness. Tears of fatigue stream down her face. Sobbing, she cries out to the flickering moon, "Johona why did you leave me? Johona where are you?"

CHAPTER EIGHT

Diane's Answer

No more than ten wizards may bind together to cast a spell.

- of Wizards, from the treatise of High Fantasy

It was early spring, one month before Affensash was summoned. Winter had refused to relinquish its rule on the high mountain peaks. The sun lay frozen on the horizon and the wind bore great chunks of ice, battering away at the mountains with no respect for their ancient majesty.

The men who were gathered together on the high mountain ledge knew the full danger of the situation. The real fear lay not in the storm itself, but with the malign force driving it. Gathered in a circle, they moved in mechanical steps, their leader shouting out the rhythm of their spell. Joining their powers together and casting it as one was their best hope of survival, and at least temporary relief from the onslaught that has been haunting them throughout their expedition. In the circle, six wizards chanted. Three already had fallen outside the protective sphere of flickering lanterns and lay resting in a pool of their combined blood.

This was their fourth attempt at casting the spell. Twice before, members in the circle stumbled on the words freezing on their lips before they could complete it. One time the spell was interrupted when huge sections of the mountain broke through the warding sphere hurtling two of the wizards outside its protection. The third wizard sacrificed himself early when he established the magical lights in the lanterns that comprise the fragile warding sphere.

The paramount concern of Johona, the expedition's leader, was that many of the members would become magically exhausted. Their manna, as the Guild called it, would be used up and they would be forced to stop and rest for at least a day. Johona knew there would not be another day.

The wizards stop their march and raise their hands in unison. As one, they trace identical patterns in the air. Midway through their motions a light-blue light begins to glow from their finger tips and leaves a trail suspended in mid-air.

All around the semi-circle the same pattern is traced. The light-blue designs burn as the patterns feed off the magical energy of aether. The decorative designs seem to somehow soften the violent tempest around them. The patterns start to take on life. The tracings grow and expand. They travel along the inside of the warding sphere like creeping vines on the side of a building.

The force of the wind suddenly increases and howls. The wizards' magic is answered by yet more magic. The strain on several of the wizards is showing openly now. Relying on the innermost reserves of their manna, they feed more aether into their incantation, power on power, as more and more they strain to stay focused and complete the spell. The patterns grow until they become a canopy arching over them. Yet the spell cannot break free of the forces that contain it.

Johona calls verbally to a staff at his feet. The staff rises, wavering in the force of the gale. Obediently, it continues to the top most center of the sphere. The wizards are too entranced with their own spells to notice when the staff begins to glow blue. Like a magnet, the staff draws on the remaining aether in the area funneling it into the patterns.

The staff flares, burning and sparking like a giant fuse. The energy fed into the patterns becomes so fierce that it too begins to hiss with power in an effort to break free. The patterns expand edging their way outward.

Explosion!

A tremendous blast follows and the patterns scatter like shards of ice. For miles, the white-hot aura of the blast can be seen even in the valleys below. The mountain's ledge breaks apart, sending tons of rock and hard ice down the slope.

For half a mile, the avalanche continues fleeing from the threatening heights, taking trees, countryside, and wizards with it. Finally, it stops on another large ledge. A blanket of soft white snow cascades behind it covering its tracks, leaving the impression that nothing at all has happened.

Silence.

There is only the sound of gently falling snow. Darkness has settled around.

A cough suddenly breaks the serenity. Blood spurts across snow, red on white. A blackened hand lifts. Johona has unfortunately survived. All the others are either dead or dying below the snow. His body is broken and each breath is tainted with the red mist of his own life. Still, he manages to lift himself to the surface.

Painfully, slowly, he inches forward on his elbows dragging his useless legs behind him. Gasping, he stops and vomits across the snow. His senses fade in and out. In anguish, Johona starts to put the pieces together. Examining his body he realizes, quite matter-of-factly, that he is dead. Why his heart keeps beating is beyond his comprehension. Blood pounds in his ears.

Wait, it's not his heart that pounds, it is ... it is the sound of drums. From someplace a deep drumming echoes across the snow.

Unbelieving, Johona listens again. They are coming! The storm begins to pick-up in force. Even through the howling wind, the approaching drums are distinct. Johona struggles to a sitting position. A strange smile cracks through the freezing blood on his face. Dead men have little to fear.

With a soft spoken word, a charred staff rises from the deep snow, circles, and flies to his open hand. He sees that his staff has survived the affair as badly as he has. The once sturdy oak flakes and peels under his examination. Extending the staff, he clears a semi-circle of snow away from his body.

The drums grow louder. The approaching drums bring the storm back towards him limiting his vision to less than a few feet. A cold shudder suddenly ripples through his body that goes far deeper than the chill of the wind. Laughter uncontrollably erupts from his soul. The mad sound is whisked away with the snow and wind.

The drums stop.

Johona spits his mouth clean of the blood and makes ready for his last spell.

Three feet away the first shadow appears, black against the hard white storm.

CHAPTER NINE

Chilling Alliance

Invisibility: *This spell allows a wizard to bend light to make himself invisible to the normal eye. The total of objects or people affected per spell is determined by the wizard's skill level.*

- The Spell Book, from the treatise of High Fantasy

Traveling alone in the dark is a foolish thing to do and Laurallin has no intention of going far. She just had to leave the tribe after being humiliated. She might not know what is going on, but she knows Affensash and she doesn't have the time to explain it to her father. Sensie canters steadily along through the cloud covered night. Laurallin is more confused than hurt. The great horse seems happy and frisky despite Laurallin's solemn mood and the dismal misty night.

In the low areas, fog has settled. The two dip down into it and emerge again wet and cold. The moon darts out from behind a cloud revealing Laurallin and Sensie. The moonlight traces long lines on Laurallin's bare tanned legs and continues down the sleek strong flanks of Sensie. In the silvery light, Laurallin's buckskins and swinging hair blend perfectly with Sensie's mane and flipping tail. They ride in perfect concert as though they had never been parted. The clouds reclaim the moon and they are lost again into the night.

Laurallin never really cared for magic. The little episode around the fire makes her hate magic all the more. For her, it always seems to create more questions than it answers. If Affensash was on a beach at the base of the Pentacles then she must be very close to him. There is a little village called Mince that sits on the edge of the beaches. That will be as good a place as any to start. Mince is about a day or two away. It also has a small port. Perhaps the sailors may have news.

Let's see, Laurallin reasons, if Affensash is on Guild business maybe he is headed to the Alchemy school in the Pentacles. He always wanted to go there. I believe Affensash called it the 'Apothecary.'

Sensie stumbles on an unseen rut and Laurallin reins her to a halt. They can't travel all night like this. She needs the rest and there is no need to endanger Sensie with a broken leg. Finding a suitable place for a campsite, she releases the horse and sends Sensie off to eat and care for herself. Laurallin knows she will return in the morning when she whistles.

The air is a bit chilly, but not cold enough to build a fire. A short sleep and they will be off again in the morning. The country is rolling, with large open grasslands, where she might easily be spotted if the clouds cleared. Laurallin instead chooses a grouping of trees to bed beneath. Along with the protection there is the bonus of a thick layer of needles that she can pile for her bedding. Laurallin glances up when the moon pierces through the clouds. Standing proudly along the hillsides are groups of giant pines gathered like families.

As she unrolls a lightweight blanket, a disturbing feeling creeps through her like she is being watched. She is too wise to try and dismiss the feeling and decides to investigate instead.

Taking an extra blanket, she stuffs it down beside her and finds the darkest night shade to lie down in. After about an hour of pretending she is asleep, she slips out of the covers and crawls on her stomach until she is a safe distance from the blanket. Dagger in hand, she sits on her haunches listening intently for any sounds. The only sound she can make out is the noise of a distant horse. It is probably Sensie, but her instincts tell her that it is too early to relax. She heads towards the noise.

Quietly through the bushes, being careful to take advantage of the shadows, she circles around. Then, once again heads towards the noise. A moonbeam breaks through the clouds and races across the hills. Laurallin follows it with her eyes. She finds a horse grazing atop a small knoll. It is not Sensie.

She continues to look, but can't see any other life. The horse could be wild, but taking no chances, she begins hunting in large circles around her camp. She stops at the crest of a hill. Patiently, she watches what the moonbeams permit.

Nothing. Nothing but swaying grass, and the contours of spring foliage forming over the foothills.

In time she becomes weary and returns. Tired, but still uneasy, she slips into the covers and drops into light slumber.

In the morning she fixes herself a quick meal and whistles for Sensie. Mounting up, she starts off towards Mince. With luck she could make it by evening.

All morning long she can't lose the feeling of being watched. It takes till noon before her uneasy tensions personify. A single man on horseback is pacing her from behind. She catches a glimpse of him by accident when looking over her shoulder from the top of a large hill. She must be an easy prey to track. The lush grass leaves a perfect trail in the bright sunlight wherever Sensie goes.

Sometimes city dwellers get unusual ideas about a woman who travels alone. The thought sends a red hot flush coursing through her body. Laurallin decides to put an end to that possibility right away. Turning Sensie around she draws her bow and charges back the way she came. Quickly sizing up the rolling terrain, she determines that she can get quite close before the rider knows he has been discovered.

She is right.

Up and over a knoll she charges within several hundred feet before the rider can react. It is a big man sitting atop a great black stallion. A massive bow is slung across his back. He starts to swing his horse around, but realizes it is too late. His horse prances in a full circle and comes to a dead halt facing Lauralllin's charge. The man raises no arms against her, but watches passively. She gets almost on top of the hill before she recognizes who it is. Angrily, she pulls the arrow back and circles around the rider pointing it directly at his head.

"I should pay you back for the greeting you gave me and for one sleepless night," she shouts, bringing Sensie to a halt ten feet from the rider. His thick curly hair blows across his broad shoulders. It's Kenlin. He must have followed her from the tribe's camp.

"Stop being ridiculous Laurallin. I have only come to offer my help."

"I don't need it," she retorts lowering her arrow. "This is a family matter Kenlin and it doesn't involve you." With that, she kicks her horse and heads off towards Mince.

"Hey! Wait a moment," Kenlin shouts and follows after her. "I have something to tell you," he says, irritated, and pulls up next to her. "The Shaman said that Affensash is headed for the Pentacles."

"I've guessed that much Kenlin," Laurallin retorts.

"Then maybe you will need these!" Kenlin throws a bag of clothes at Laurallin with such force that it nearly knocks her off of Sensie. "Your mother thought you might want some extra clothes for the cold mountain air."

Righting herself as the horses continue to gallop, she looks over at Kenlin and says, "Is that all, or is there something else?"

"You should probably head to Mince first. From there, depending on what we discover, we should head directly to High Tower," Kenlin finishes in a matter-of-fact manner.

"We? Did you say we? You're not going Kenlin. Now turn that black piece of horseflesh around and get both your tails back to the tribe. I'm ..."

Before she can finish her sentence Kenlin leaps from his horse, grabs her and they both tumble to the ground. Sensie scampers ahead, turns and comes back to help her mistress, but Kenlin's stallion steps in the way. Flat on her back, Kenlin pins her arms and stares her down.

"You forget Laurallin. I was the only child in the tribe that could beat you and I always won." Kenlin's clear blue eyes spark with the dynamics of youth. Laurallin struggles, but the steel hard body of a man in his prime holds her down. His legs clamp tighter around her waist. "Don't use that tone of voice on me. I am going with you to find your husband. I can help. Once you find him you can take all your frustrations out on *him*. Now if you pretend you're a lady I will pretend I'm a gentleman and we can get the job done."

"You only won because I let you," Laurallin curses struggling to get up. She heaves with her stomach muscles but Kenlin, who weighs forty pounds more, doesn't budge. After a small struggle, Laurallin realizes the helplessness of the situation.

"All right Kenlin, but we will take it one day at a time."

Laughing, Kenlin releases her and jumps up. He barely misses her swinging foot as she kicks out.

"That's better. Now at least we can talk like two mature adults," he says. Walking back to his horse, he passes Sensie who gives him a big shove with her muzzle.

Laurallin gets up and dusts herself off. She pulls her brief buckskins back down to a respectable length and swings her chestnut hair free of the clinging leaves.

"You always have been a pain Kenlin. I guess some things never change."

Kenlin is unruffled, or maybe it is because he can never be ruffled. His hair hangs naturally and neat and his tanned body is too dark to show the scratches of the prickly grass.

"What do you think the Guild wants with your husband?" Kenlin asks as they ride towards Mince.

Laurallin, who is not all together happy with the situation, never-the-less explains it to him and gives her best set of guesses, but admits she doesn't know. The ride honestly becomes pleasant after a while and the presence of her old friend brings back memories she thought she had forgotten long ago. Despite his forward and brutish nature, Kenlin can really be quite charming.

It is hard at first for Laurallin to adjust. Kenlin is so much bigger than Affensash that he needs the big black stallion to carry him. Even mounted on Sensie this means that she always has to look up to him. Laurallin, being a Hebelcaan, admires a good horse and soon finds herself watching his stallion's muscles ripple with each easy stride. Then she notices the ripple that begins in the stallion then passes through Kenlin's taut muscular legs in perfect harmony.

Unknowingly, she stares at Kenlin's legs and turns away with a flush when he notices.

By late evening the two still haven't reached Mince, but decide to continue on. The air is warming and the clouds are clearing, leaving the night fresh and sweet smelling. It is spring in the low country even though the mountain peaks still swirl with snowy caps. Small spring flowers known as 'Pixie Flames', dot the grass fields. They shine like little pastel lanterns actually giving off iridescent glows that shimmer and bob along the hillsides. As a child, Laurallin always imagined fairies playing beneath the light, dancing in little circles.

"There is so much I miss not traveling with the tribe," Laurallin says whimsically. "It seems that time stands still out here. Nothing ages. Everything here is free and everyone in it has their freedom."

"It does Laurallin. For me nothing has changed." The gentle light silhouettes Kenlin's face and Laurallin is glad hers is hidden in the shadows of her hair.

Laurallin looks nervously at Kenlin, catching the deeper meaning of his words. Time has changed Kenlin. Sensie splashes into a small stream and it sprays up around them. They both dismount to let the horses drink. They are both tired and dirty. Laurallin walks into the stream waist deep and then sinks down into the icy water splashing away the dust. She arches her back and eases her head backward rinsing her hair.

"I think a lot about you Laurallin. When you came to the tribe I couldn't just let you depart without hearing me."

Laurallin is shivering in the water. Kenlin is standing in the stream several feet from her. The slow water ripples at his knees. Standing-up, Laurallin turns to mount Sensie, nervous about Kenlin's intentions. When she turns, Kenlin catches her in his arms and she falls forward into his long tender kiss.

The chill of the stream passes and is replaced by a passionate flush that sears unexpectedly through Laurallin. She pushes away half-heartedly, but Kenlin forces her back against him and they both sink gently into the stream. The cold stroking of the current and Kenlin's firm warm body sends a second heated ripple through her. Laurallin throws her head back and tiny droplets spray from her hair. The moon catches each one and sends them cascading back like tiny diamonds around them. Unthinking, Laurallin gives up the fight and presses her body back against Kenlin's. Her stiffening breasts find comfort and warmth. She returns Kenlin's kiss with the full force of pent-up passions.

A night bird sings and for a simple moment the world is careless and the two are centered in its seductive sigh. Pushing him gently away she says, "I have heard you now Kenlin. I am sorry that things aren't different-- but they just aren't. Let me go please."

At first Kenlin refuses. Then his arms shudder and he obeys.

Pressing her eyes against the palms of her hand, Laurallin rises from the stream shivering again. Kenlin watches her wade back to Sensie. Her clothes cling tightly around her emphasizing the slim physique this journey has restored. Water runs down her hair and back dripping in little clean splashes that are whisked away by the current.

"I think I see the lights of Mince ahead," Laurallin mumbles somewhat dazed.

Quietly they mount up and ride off, Kenlin content to leave it like that for the moment. The rest of the night they travel in cooling silence. The mountains rise up and take the moon, but the clouds clear, revealing a sky deep with stars.

They reach the small Western port of Mince. Ships only stop at Mince to deliver supplies for the small villages, or the alchemy school that is nestled in the Pentacles. When Laurallin and Kenlin arrive it is nearly midnight. The only activity is in the local pub. It seems a ship or two has docked earlier in the evening.

The pair unties their supplies from their horses and walk on together into town. If they take horses into a town like this they realize they are likely to be stolen.

"We might as well ask around at the pub before we turn in," Kenlin says breaking a long silence. "If we get some word about Affensash tonight we could get started all the earlier in the morning."

Laurallin agrees, but not before she slips on a pair of leggings to cover herself. City dwellers get a lot of wrong ideas about women out this late at night and she has learned her lesson about riding into cities in her Hebelcaan clothing.

The tavern is full of smoking pipes and loud voices. The activity is pretty robust for so late an evening. The majority of the crowd is Eastern sailors and soldiers. A few of the local villagers are still here trying to cheat the last few coins from the drunken sailors. Kenlin walks to a table in the back and places his pack under a chair. Laurallin cautiously follows.

"Would you like something?" Kenlin asks.

"No, not really. But why don't you ask that man at the bar to join us." Laurallin points to a Westerner sitting by himself.

Kenlin returns with the small warty man and three frothing mugs of ale.

"This is Pennel, a local farmer from these parts. Pennel, this is my, ah ...friend," Kenlin stutters in the introduction.

"Welcome to our little town," Pennel bows, gesturing with his free mug of ale. "I'm always glad to see visitors. What brings so fine a pair to these humble parts?"

Before Kenlin can answer, Laurallin breaks in, "We are here to meet a young alchemist on his way into the mountains. We were wondering if he has been here. His name is Affensash and he might be traveling with a woman."

"Who is this popular Affensash fellow? You are the second person this evening who has asked," Pennel says slurring his words.

"Really? We didn't know he was meeting with others," jumps in Kenlin cautiously. "Who else is asking?"

"That wizard over there," Pennel says, pointing over to a man sitting at a table full of Eastern soldiers. The man is dressed in a rich, gold-embroidered robe. He is laughing and presumably having a good time with his companions.

"I don't like the looks of that," Laurallin blurts out loud before she can catch herself.

"I know what you mean. I didn't figure grassland Westerners like you would be seen with the likes of them. Is this Affensash fellow in trouble with the authorities?" asks Pennel slyly.

"I really don't know," answers Laurallin. "Did that wizard say what he wanted with Affensash?"

"No, he just said he would pay me gold if I found him. Hey, maybe he might give me a little silver if I told him you were looking for him also?" Pennel drunkenly gets up and starts toward the Easterner's table.

Kenlin grabs the little man and spins him back into his seat. "What do you think Laurallin? Should we find out what this wizard knows?" Kenlin whispers holding Pennel down.

"We need to know, but not here in this place. Sorry Kenlin, but it looks as though we won't get much sleep tonight."

Laurallin stands and bends over nose to nose with Pennel. "Tell the wizard we will meet him alone in the hotel across the street. Alone, Pennel, or we won't be around to talk. We aren't looking for trouble. We are just being cautious." She reaches in her belt and lays a piece of copper on the table. Laurallin and Kenlin pick-up their packs and leave.

Laurallin sprints across the street and motions for Kenlin to hide down the side alley while she goes inside. Wanting to be noticed, she bursts through the front doors and bangs on the desk top waking the clerk sleeping in a back room. Slapping a gold piece on the desk's top she asks for a room.

"For that price I can't say no," the clerk yawns, squinting to see if the gold is real.

"Good! Give me the key," Laurallin says imploring with her hand. "I saw a set of stairs in the alley on the side of the building. Does that lead to this room's hallway?" Laurallin asks quickly looking over her shoulder.

"Well, yes it does."

"Good! Now listen. If anyone asks I'm in my room. Send them up immediately. Got it! Send them up immediately," she says clearly again, staring into the eyes of the clerk.

"Right, I understand," the clerk says scratching his head.

Laurallin then turns and runs back out into the street.

"Wait a moment," the clerk mumbles bewildered, "I guess I don't understand."

In the dark street, Laurallin circles around and ducks down the alley where Kenlin first disappeared. No sooner than she makes it to the shadows of the building, light fills the street as the tavern door opens and soldiers file out.

"He's coming," whispers Kenlin, "but he's not alone. We had better leave while we can."

"No," demands Laurallin. "Not yet! He may be the only one who knows about Affensash! Wait here. I will shout if I need you."

Laurallin looks down the alleyway and finds the staircase to the second floor where her room is located. Dashing up the stairs, she slams against the door breaking the lock. She grabs the door and opens it just a crack so she can see down the hallway. Then she nocks her arrow and waits.

Soon she hears the Eastern wizard coming up the stairs.

"Don't move wizard," Laurallin hisses through the door when he reaches the hallway. "We said to come alone."

Below her Kenlin covers the bottom of his face as is the tradition in the Hebelcaan tribe when killing is to be done. With his tribal death mask lowered, Kenlin sticks five arrows in the ground at his feet. His muscles tighten like granite in his arms as he pulls back the big bow. Two arrows hiss into the street stopping just short of the soldiers. In his deep bass voice Kenlin shouts, "Back to the tavern or the next round won't be in the dirt."

Searching the shadows, an Eastern soldier discovers Kenlin's large silhouette.

"It's a Hebelcaan bowman," shouts the soldier.

The Hebelcaan have a ferocious reputation even to the seasoned Eastern warriors. They instantly realize that at least several of them will die if they try to rush him openly.

"Walk this way wizard," Laurallin shouts at the top of the stairs. "Don't mutter a word."

The richly clothed wizard walks toward her stroking his thick well-trimmed beard.

Laurallin hears footsteps on the stairs below. Turning to look is all the opportunity the wizard needs to charge. Slamming his shoulder against the door, he breaks the arrow point off. He throws the door open and swings a fist at Laurallin's head. Her cat-like reflexes allow her to step back and grab the wizard's passing elbow, spinning him around. Pulling her dagger, she holds it to the wizard's throat.

"What do you know about my husband?" she demands.

Kenlin is standing halfway up the stairs waiting for the Eastern soldiers to find heart enough to charge.

"Who?" the wizard replies honestly bewildered.

"Affensash. My husband. You have been asking about him."

"He's your husband? Look, there is no need for this. I can explain. There has been a misunderstanding," he croaks choking.

"This 'misunderstanding' is about to get us killed," Kenlin observes. "The soldiers are moving."

Grabbing the wizard by the robe, Kenlin half throws him down the stairs. Laurallin follows until they reach the alley below.

"Run!" shouts Kenlin. "I can slow them down."

"There is no need for this," the wizard repeats. With a dozen Eastern soldiers moving towards them, Kenlin prepares his bow anyway.

"You haven't killed anyone yet," the wizard yells, "just hold your arrows a little more. Trust me."

Laurallin reaches for an arrow.

Before Laurallin can stop him, the wizard chants and traces brief patterns in the air. The spell is complete.

To Kenlin, it appears as though the charging soldiers blur momentarily, then continue their charge as normal. For some reason he holds his fire, listening to the wizard's plea. He has no reason to spill Eastern blood and become a fugitive at this point.

The soldiers stop!

"They're gone," shouts the lead soldier, looking down the alley directly at Kenlin.

"Hell fire," objects another. "It looked like it was going to be a good fight."

"They can't see us," whispers the Eastern wizard. "Back out of here in case one of them happens to bump into us."

The three slip away down the alley. Laurallin stays close to the wizard with dagger in hand still not trusting him. Once out of harm's way, the three walk away from town to a small clump of trees where they feel free to talk.

"I was told your husband was going to pass this way," starts the wizard. "I was to meet him and give him a message. I've been here several days and he hasn't arrived. There is a good chance he has already come and gone unnoticed."

"Why was he here, and what is he supposed to do?" asks Laurallin.

"I assure you, dear lady, that I don't know anything more about this than you do. If you like, I am preparing to leave in the morning to search for him in High Tower. You and your companion are welcome to travel with me. I have many men with me and together we will have a better chance of finding him. I do know that he will have to go to High Tower eventually. If I may be so bold as to ask, why don't you know where your own husband is?"

"It's a long story. Let's just say that it is important that I reach him and talk with him to make sure he is safe," Laurallin flatly replies.

"Well I assure you that I have his safety in mind also. That is why I must talk to him. I somehow feel that between the two of us, we will be able to find him," says the wizard. His sharp bold features turn into a smile.

"Then it's agreed! We will depart together in the morning and search for Affensash," Kenlin interrupts.

Laurallin gives him a side-glance for his impetuous answer.

"What is this message you have to give Affensash?" Kenlin continues a little more cautiously.

"Well, that is between me and Affensash. I am on my honor to discuss it with no one else. But since I'm speaking to his good friend and his wife, I can tell you that I am going to try and dissuade him from going to the Pentacles."

"There may be nothing wrong with that, ah ... what is your name anyway?" asks Laurallin.

"Together then we will find Affensash and see if we can't convince him to return home with you. Tomorrow we leave for High Tower and we will spread the word in Mince that his wife is waiting for him there, just in case we miss him. You don't know how much better I feel about this whole thing now that I have someone with me who knows him so well. Before, I wasn't even sure I'd recognize him if he walked right up and talked to me."

Turning to walk towards town, the wizard looks back from the corner of his eye and with a wry, wolfish smile that Laurallin cannot understand says, "I am a wizard of the Eastern Empire and Guild member of the 'True Ones.' My name is Glenwall and I am so glad we met."

CHAPTER TEN

Message Received

In fact, the book is a living entity that draws its life force from the wizard and is therefore only attuned to its owner.

> *- The Spell Book, from the treatise of High Fantasy*

The sun is high and burning his face when Affensash wakes the next day. Diane is clothed in pants and a shirt from a less fortunate sailor who washed up on shore. She is standing with her back to him staring out into an endless gray-blue sea. The waves are high and threateningly white. They seem to mock Diane each time they crash against the shore. Her arms are raised and Affensash hears her mumbling in the sing-song speech of spell casting. The wind whips her tattered clothes tightly around her displaying her femininity. She stands defiantly with her feet buried in the churning sand.

Shortly, bouncing along the tops of the waves comes, of all things, a book. It skips along until it reaches her feet. She bends down and cradles the book in her arms like a newborn child. Walking over to her, Affensash places his hand on her shoulder pushing back her wet tangled hair. Even drenched and ragged, Affensash is struck by the natural beauty Diane possesses. Her eyes are crystal light blue and her cheeks still glow red with the natural fire of her spirit.

"Why the summoning and so much concern over a book?" he asks, suddenly realizing how dry and parched his mouth has become.

She stands and smiles walking away from the water's edge.

"It is not a book Affensash. It is *my* book. It is a part of me. In it is the sum total of my knowledge about magic. It was given to me as a child and each page has been carefully added as each day of my life has passed."

"I have a book. I always coat each page with a wax to protect it from water," he says.

"My book is wet and soaked to the bone just like me," she manages to smile, "but just like me it will dry and recover. It is a book of spells. All True Ones have such a book. You don't always see us using our books when we cast our spells because many of the pages are memorized and we cast them by heart. The really difficult spells and the ones most recently learned are always read. I can't tell you how much trouble I would be in if I lost it. That's a good thing to remember, Affensash. If you wonder if someone is a True One look for his book. We are really good at hiding them, but if you look hard enough you can find it."

"I'm as hungry and thirsty as a ...a Wind Drake," Affensash says, making a silly buzzing noise. Ruefin runs little circles around Affensash yelping. They both resemble drowned rats.

"We are close to Mince," she says laughing at the two of them and looking around. "If I remember correctly, my fiancé has good credit there. All I want is some new clothes and a bath! I feel awful." She shakes her hair sending a salty spray through the air.

Ruefin refuses to be carried in Affensash's wet pocket and scurries off hunting ravenously for breakfast. He disappears into the thick prickly grass lining the beach.

Affensash finds himself in reasonably good spirits by the time Diane discovers a hidden spring to quench their thirst. With so many spells flying about he really isn't sure if she actually found it, or just conjured it up. But the water is wet and refreshing enough that he decides it doesn't matter. He splashes it over his salty head. Sitting down on a fallen tree the two of them rest, tired from yesterday's ordeal.

After some small talk, when Affensash is sure Diane is recovered enough, he asks her what really happened out there.

"I don't know. The spell we were casting was not that difficult. Glenwall should have had no trouble casting it. If I thought there was a reasonable chance that a combined enchantment would fail I would have cast the spell myself. The effect wouldn't have been as dramatic, but I probably could have saved the ship. It just doesn't make sense. Glenwall is an accomplished wizard. He is higher in the order than I am. He is almost as well-versed as Johona."

Her mood changes and her eyes become downcast. Her shoulders slump as though a great weight is suddenly pressing against them.

"I wonder how many died. I never did find Terrell."

"You know that's odd. Only three of us were washed up on the beach, the two of us, and the sailor. I didn't see any large chunks of wood or pieces of the ship's hull that you would expect. It's just possible that the ship survived."

"Maybe it will be waiting for us at Mince," Affensash says hopefully.

"Even if the ship survived it wouldn't continue to Mince. There would be too big a chance that a drunken sailor might say too much. No, the ship would return to the Isles. They would; however, send someone to check for us. If they discover you survived they would tell you to go on. If you were lost at sea they would have to tell Elder Enchantraen and someone else would be found to carry on," Diane concludes, scratching her salty hair for any other possibilities.

"Well, we shall soon find out. Mince can't be more than an hour away."

Just then Ruefin returns, popping suddenly between them. Affensash startles and grabs the little fox by the scruff of the neck. Ruefin hits him with a barrage of licks until Affensash is forced to stuff him down in his pocket.

The knowledge that the small port is so close gives the two the extra strength to start walking until they find a well-traveled road. It isn't long before an old farmer carrying hay, allows them to ride in the back of his wagon for the rest of the trip. Comfortable and drowsy, the two fall asleep lying next to each other, jostling back and forth along the deep, rutted road. They don't awaken until the rhythmic clopping of the horse's hooves stop.

There is still plenty of daylight left when Affensash and Diane tumble out the back of the wagon shaking the straw off. They look like a couple of vagabond peasants, hardly a pair to cause any suspicion among the locals. Stretching and limply walking to the town's only hotel, Diane calls for the clerk across the desk. He immediately comes running.

"I am Johona's fiancé," she says to the smaller man. "His credit is as good as any man's in these parts."

Eventually, when the clerk sees past the stiff and crusty clothes to the natural beauty with the sparkling eyes, he calls for the servants to draw a bath.

Affensash makes arrangements for his own room.

Diane pulls herself regally up the stairs until she reaches her room. There, she immediately sends the servants away to fetch fresh clothing and a hastily prepared list of supplies. After hours of soaking and relaxing in a feather bed, she raps on Affensash's door to be escorted to a late evening meal.

Sitting across the table from her is about all Affensash can handle. With her honey-blonde hair neatly wrapped and combed, she dines in a light pink gown with soft rose flowers gently woven into the pattern. Clumsily, Affensash tries to make polite conversation. He decides, after finding himself staring several times, that it would be better not to look at her at all.

"I think I would like to learn about this magic of yours," he says staring at the wall. "It seems that you people have limitless power and can do just about anything you want."

Diane looks up from her plate and then over to the wall that Affensash seems to be talking to.

Confused she says, "That's hardly the case! We are really quite limited in what we can do. You must understand Affensash that the True Ones magic is not like the science of alchemy. To perform real magic you must be born with certain skills. Your Guild guards and protects its secrets about potions and explosive powders. But you see ..." she reaches in a fold of her gown and brings out her book, "you can't acquire the skills of magic unless you first have the natural gift." She opens the book in front of Affensash.

He drops a helping of potatoes in his lap when he sees that the pages are blank.

"I can't read that! There is nothing there."

"Oh yes there is," she assures him handing him her napkin.

Ignoring his spill, he sets the napkin down and lifts his wine glass.

"The words are written in my blood, the pages are like my flesh, and the power is drawn through my soul."

Affensash lightly chokes on his first drink. Grabbing more napkins, Diane hands them to Affensash.

"Of course that is just a figure of speech, but as you can see we have no need to hide our secrets from those who are not adept."

"Oh yes. I see now," Affensash says observantly, still looking at the wall.

Once again Diane's eyes trail over to the wall confused.

"The founder of our Guild, Elder Edla, built a rigid learning structure for those who are adept. The purpose of his teachings is to take one's natural abilities and channel the power into a self-taught lifestyle that will allow you to progress and understand at the fastest possible rate."

Affensash makes a little grunt of understanding still looking at the wall.

"Am I boring you?" Diane finally asks.

"No! No, go right ahead. Could you pass the bottle please? I guess I'm still thirsty," Affensash replies in his most casual tone of voice.

"He, Edla that is, divided the training into five planes. At each plane level there are ten spells to learn. I am a third plane wizard. I know thirty spells that the Guild taught me, plus a few that I picked up on my own. My fiancé is a fourth plane wizard and Enchantraen is a fifth plane wizard. Enchantraen knows all the spells the Guild can teach and as an Elder the great wizard is expected to pioneer new spells and enchantments."

"Wait," Affensash blurts, an understanding suddenly popping into his head. "You said Glenwall was almost as powerful as Johona. That means he was a fourth plane wizard too."

"Exactly," Diane says, delighted that Affensash momentarily took his eyes off the wall. "Actually, the spell we tried to cast was a third plane spell, which is relatively easy for a fourth plane wizard. That is why it caught me so off-guard when Glenwall failed."

Just then the clerk comes into the dining room looking over the guests. Finding Diane's and Affensash's table, he approaches with a letter in his hand.

"Excuse me for interrupting fine lady, but I found a message your fiancé left nearly a month ago. He told me he expected you in a few days. When you didn't arrive I meant to throw it out. But here it is."

"Are you certain Johona gave you this? He has been away in the south. He shouldn't have been in this area at all," Diane says doubtfully.

"Look, it is his very own seal," the clerk replies handing her the letter and then walking away.

Anxiously she examines it, and once she is sure the seal is authentic, she breaks it and opens the letter.

My Dearest Diane,

I was certain you would follow me when you found out that Elder Enchantraen reversed his decision and decided to allow me to investigate the Pentacles' problem myself. I hope my first letter reached you in time so that when you read this one you have forgiven me for not having taken you from the start. I am excited and expect to discover a powerful new insight into magic on this expedition.

I will wait for you in High Tower for several days. If I am gone before you arrive don't concern yourself. I will return shortly. Wait and be patient. I promise it won't be long. The ways of the Elders have always been a mystery to me. What caused the sudden reversal in his decision I will never guess.

Love you forever,

Johona

"Affensash! This says Johona has been here all along," Diane says bewildered.

"That doesn't make any sense," Affensash replies even more confused. "Why would Enchantraen lie about it to me and then be so adamant about keeping other wizards away?"

"Better yet, why would an Elder withhold the first letter to me written by my own fiancé?" Diane retorts.

"I don't like this at all. Perhaps you shouldn't go any further with me. If Elder Enchantraen is lying it must be for a good reason. I could go to High Tower, find Johona, and send him back to you in a few days," Affensash says trying to sound as convincing as possible.

"Not on your life, Alchemist. If my fiancé is really in these mountains and I find that an Elder has lied, there will be hell to pay," she challenges, throwing her napkin on her plate.

Affensash hurriedly gets up and follows her to the front desk where she confronts the clerk once more.

"You know Johona," she says waving the letter at the poor man. "You are certain that it was he who gave you this letter?"

"It was Johona, for the last time. I'm sorry that the letter upsets you, but I know who gave it to me," he tells her in defense.

"Well that's it Affensash. Tomorrow we go looking for Johona despite what my Elders say," she says determined.

"Did you say your name was Affensash?" the little man questions somewhat surprised.

"Yes it is."

"It seems I have a message from your wife also."

"From my wife?" Affensash asks wide-eyed in amazement.

"Look. If you are going to give me trouble too it's not worth passing these messages along," the little man concludes, turning to walk away.

Affensash is not usually a physical man, but under the circumstances he grabs the clerk by the shoulder and spins him around. Pulling the man half over the desk, Affensash shouts, "What's the message?"

"She was here yesterday!" the clerk stutters. "She left this morning for High Tower with a caravan headed by a wizard named Glenwall. They said to tell you they will meet you there."

Affensash drops the man and looks at Diane.

"What does this mean? Is she in danger or is she under his protection?"

"I don't know any more Affensash," Diane says shaking her head. "We are being lied to by someone. Until we find out we had better stick together, trusting no one except ourselves, Laurallin, and Johona, if we can find them before they come to any harm."

"Forget about leaving tomorrow. Let's go tonight!" he says, slamming his fist down on the desktop.

Affensash bounds up the stairs to get their belongings while Diane barks out orders and a new list of supplies for the clerk to purchase.

CHAPTER ELEVEN

The Lure

The general trend of alchemy took a sudden change when several alchemists developed a powder that produced an explosive charge. This explosive powder is the newest and most carefully guarded secret of the alchemist.

- of Alchemists, from the treatise of High Fantasy

Glenwall's caravan consists of three wagons and fifteen men. Ten of the men are Eastern soldiers-of-fortune, meaning they either deserted or presently don't belong to any of the High Lord Generals' army. The other five are hired hands who are also of Eastern origin. Laurallin and Kenlin are obviously the only Westerners. Now that Laurallin is wearing her new cold weather clothes it is clearly visible they are specifically from the Hebelcaan tribe.

There is only one road leading to High Tower from Mince. It is a long winding muddy road that meanders upward through the mountains. It would take approximately three days for this leg of the journey if the weather were perfect. No one expects the weather to be perfect. Icy winds are already starting to blow and the clouds begin bellowing overhead.

Kenlin and his stallion seem to enjoy the trip. At times the stallion becomes so frisky that it is difficult for Kenlin to control him. The sleek black horse prances and sways, trying to tempt Sensie into joining its game. Sensie, like Laurallin, is much too sensible and refuses to be a part of the misbehavior. Occasionally, Kenlin allows the stallion to run ahead of the caravan to release a little of his pent-up energy.

Kenlin bends low over the neck of his stallion and they race ahead as swift and true as one of Kenlin's arrows. Together they manifest the spirit of the one great horse. To Laurallin they make the story of Hebelcaan very believable.

Laurallin might be too sensible in her head, but she yearns to throw loose the reins and charge after them. The freedom and excitement of the race churns unceasingly in her stomach. She can't. She cannot break away.

Kenlin always manages to rein back the stallion before he gets too far ahead of the others. He knows too well the dangers of being caught alone in this country. Bandits often come down from their high mountain retreats, bandits who were once Western soldiers, driven into exile by the Eastern conqueror. Now they prey like vultures on the passing merchant caravans.

Each time Kenlin returns Laurallin feels more resentful. She really doesn't understand why.

The gently sloping hills turn into a steep climb. The lush grassy plains have given way to rocks and bramble bushes. Still, here and there a spring flower sneaks through a crack and threatens to break-up the harsh terrain. Laurallin is a little relieved to be traveling in a group, although she would never admit it openly to Kenlin. She is still acting upset at him for so rashly accepting to travel along with the caravan without consulting her first.

Kenlin prances up next to Laurallin, "Come Laurallin. Let's ride together. Let's show these Easterners and their cows they sit on what Hebelcaan can do!"

Kenlin's handsome face glows with playful excitement. To Laurallin, when his face lightens he looks just like the Kenlin she remembers. Time has left him untouched.

Resentment.

"Really Kenlin, will you never grow up?" Laurallin says in harsh belittling tones. Laurallin already regrets saying it before she is even through.

The glow fades and Kenlin gallops ahead knowing better than to confront Laurallin when she is like this. He canters up next to Glenwall's wagon.

As he rides away Laurallin feels very ashamed. This time she really would have liked to talk.

Glenwall is willing to ride with Kenlin; however, Kenlin doesn't feel comfortable around him. His conversations are too polite and always patronizing.

"High Tower is an interesting town, Kenlin," Glenwall muses. "I have been there many times and it still remains a mystery to me. You wouldn't think a town could survive through these harsh winters, but every spring to my surprise, she is still sitting there nestled against the steep mountainside."

"What I don't understand," Kenlin interrupts, forgetting about Laurallin, "is why anyone would want to live there. There is plenty of land at the foot of the Pentacles that would be good for farming. The lowlands obviously have more hospitable weather."

"It's the mining that keeps them there, Kenlin. I wouldn't expect you to understand that, being a free roaming Hebelcaan, but the richness of those mines cause men to do many foolish things. They say there are ores up there that can't be found anywhere else on earth. Some of those ores are very valuable to the Alchemy Guild. That's why you find such a highly respected school as the Apothecary in this god-forbidden mountain range."

"Foolish, stupid city-dwellers," Kenlin bitterly philosophizes. "They unknowingly trade away years of their lives to line their pockets with gold. What good is money in an early grave?"

"Well-spoken Kenlin," Glenwall again blurts patronizingly. "I don't think the citizens of High Tower see it that way. When we get there I'd be careful about preaching that in front of them. Mountain people can be pretty resistant to outsider's opinions at times."

Kenlin hears a howling sound way off in the distance. "I wouldn't think wolves would be this close to the grasslands. They must be feeling brave this year," Kenlin remarks casually.

"What did you say?" Glenwall asks. His easy-going patronizing way suddenly drains from his face. Kenlin is too bewildered to answer. "I asked you a question!" Glenwall again demands.

"I said the wolves have come down from the mountains," Kenlin replies, still confused.

"That's an odd thing to say," Glenwall says fingering the folds of his robes, forcing a smile to his face.

"I heard a wolf. That's all. What's so odd about it," Kenlin questions?

As if relieved, Glenwall laughs too loudly. "Oh, I see. They have been having trouble with missing livestock. The locals have been complaining some."

Disturbed by Glenwall's odd accusations, Kenlin leaves. He has had enough of Lauralllin's abuse and Glenwall's erratic behavior. He chooses his own place in the caravan and rides alone.

The rest of the day continues in a peaceful mood. The storms manage to pass overhead and the weather stays reasonably good. When camp is set up Laurallin and Kenlin try to stay out of the Easterners' way. Being so distinctly different from the Easterners, the two Hebelcaan have little to say to the rest of the group. Laurallin is curious enough about Glenwall's message for Affensash that she manages to strike up light conversations with the wizard. But Glenwall guards his words carefully, and as the sun slips away the wizard's mood becomes more irritable. Laurallin finally gives up.

By evening Kenlin is also in bad spirits from being rejected all day by Laurallin. Laurallin realizes what she is doing to him, but she is not quite sure why. Often she deliberately strikes out to hurt him. That really isn't her way, especially towards someone she cares for. The thought 'cares for' echoes in her mind. She tries feebly to convince herself it is better this way and in the long run he will be hurt less. She can't help wondering why. When he kissed her at the stream she liked it. She liked it more than she wanted to admit. He made her feel young and desirable, and no matter how she tries, she can't suppress that feeling. He evokes feelings she likes and more importantly had forgotten existed.

By late evening the camp is quieting down. The stars come out one by one, but the wind remains cold. Kenlin sits quietly by the fire. Laurallin watches him from behind. She tries to come to grips with her feelings while absently tracing the outline of his body with her eyes. The firelight twirls in his hair, but his jaw is fixed in rigid rejection. At last her heart thaws. She walks up quietly behind him and places a blanket over his exposed shoulders and sits down beside him.

"Thank you, Kenlin, for traveling with me. I realize you are risking a lot for me. I don't think I can ever repay your kindness." They sit quietly together for hours never speaking a word. Kenlin just holds her hand as they stare into the fire.

Sensie was released to roam as she will, but tonight she and the stallion stay unusually close to camp.

"Do you hear them?" Kenlin asks.

Laurallin stirs from deep thoughts feeling lazy and warm. "What? The horses playing?"

"No, the wolves. They have been getting louder through the day," Kenlin tells her.

"Yes I've heard them, but they are so far away," she sighs. "It seems like a good night for a pack to be hunting. I wouldn't mind a little hunting myself."

"Please not tonight. I fought all day with an over-anxious horse and now I'm confronted with an overzealous female. I think you are enjoying your new freedom more than you have told me."

"There are parts of this trip I have cherished. But believe me, Kenlin, I am worried about Aff."

"We will find him. I feel certain about that, but after we find him it will be every man for himself. I still have a score to settle with him for taking you away from me." Kenlin's voice is joking and playful, but his eyes say differently.

"Please don't talk that way, Kenlin, even in jest. I love to be flattered as much as any woman, but with Affensash gone it only makes me feel guilty."

Smiling and acting as though he didn't hear her, Kenlin looks around at the quiet camp. Most of the men are already asleep, snoring loudly under thick blankets. He decides to lead the conversation away from Laurallin's husband.

"You know, Glenwall is a peculiar man. He talks to you like you are a king that he must guard every word against. Today though, he did such a turn around that it makes me wonder if he has a double personality. Of course who am I to judge personalities? You, for example! You ignore me all day, and then stay awake past a reasonable hour to make up conversation."

Laurallin smiles, her brown eyes dancing in the firelight. "I don't know about Glenwall, but I'm making up to an old friend." She leans over and gives Kenlin a hug. "Thank you again, Kenlin."

Caught off-guard he blushes. Even through his darkly tanned face Laurallin notices and smiles broadly.

"We better get some rest before daylight," Kenlin says a little embarrassed. With a deep breath, they stand and shake their blankets out. Kenlin lies down only a few feet from Laurallin. Sliding under the blankets, Kenlin takes one last look around the camp to insure that everything is in order.

Suddenly, he bolts upright. "He's gone," he hisses.

"What," Laurallin asks quietly, trying to follow Kenlin's eyes to see what he is talking about.

"Glenwall! He is gone."

Laurallin glances around and discovers the same thing.

"Maybe he is just taking care of his bodily necessities," Laurallin jokes, missing any significance to his disappearance.

"Maybe. Maybe not. Before I sleep tonight I must be sure." Grabbing his bow, Kenlin slips out of camp. Laurallin is right behind him.

The moon is nearly full and the wind is chilling. Laurallin and Kenlin make their way across rocks barely covered with enough soil to support the thin grass. The countryside is littered with occasional clumps of trees and patches of stiff, tangled bush that make walking difficult. Still, the Hebelcaan are born to this and it doesn't take long until they find Glenwall's trail. He has wandered far from the camp, farther than what would be considered safe. They come to a rocky ledge that leads to a large sink hole thirty or forty feet in diameter. Growing on the sides and middle of the sink hole are more of the sickly trees.

Laurallin looks for a stealthful way to descend when they are stopped by a low deep growl. Trying to pierce the shadows with their eyes, the hunter and his huntress crouch breathless until they hear another noise.

"I will do it! I told you I would do it."

Laurallin points into a clump of trees at the bottom of the sink hole. She shows Kenlin where Glenwall is sitting, just at the edge of a giant shadow.

"Something is not right," Kenlin whispers. "What is that in front of him?"

Laurallin looks, but sees nothing. Then they hear another growl and the tearing of flesh.

"He's in danger," Kenlin shouts suddenly rising from his hiding place. "There is something evil down there."

Jumping forward, Kenlin tumbles down the embankment charging to Glenwall's rescue. Laurallin stands and readies an arrow to cover her presumptuous companion.

Glenwall stands and turns around. He suddenly becomes visible to Laurallin as if a great shadow has left him. In the moonlight she can see that his beard is streaked with blood. Kenlin sees it too and stops.

"Glenwall, are you all right?" Kenlin shouts.

Startled, Glenwall wipes his mouth with his sleeve and clearing his throat he says, "Yes, of course."

"I thought you were being attacked. What's that blood?"

"Just found a rabbit while I was walking. I'm skinning it now," Glenwall replies holding the carcass of the animal in the moonlight. "Thank you for your concern, but it really isn't necessary. I'm fine. Please return to camp. We have a long way to travel in the morning."

Kenlin starts to walk toward him and stops when Glenwall raises his hand.

"Please Kenlin, I'm fine. Leave me. You know how we moody, old wizards like to be left alone at times."

Kenlin again starts forward until Laurallin shouts, "Come on back, Kenlin. We found him and he's fine. It's late and I'm tired."

Kenlin turns reluctantly and goes back to her.

"Thank you again," Glenwall says very meaningfully. "I will see you early in the morning."

Turning to walk back to camp, Kenlin is quiet.

"Why did you want to bother him when he asked to be left alone?" Laurallin wonders staring at Kenlin.

He looks up at her with a very puzzled expression. "Couldn't you smell it? Something was wrong."

"Smell what? He probably just wanted privacy for some unnatural wizardly reason," Laurallin says. "Wizards always do grueling unnatural things."

"Not 'True Ones'," Kenlin answers and then shudders. "It was an unnatural smell like the thick repugnant odor of a beast. He stank... of more than one death."

The two almost double back to get an answer to their questions, but decide not to. They both agree to watch Glenwall more closely through the following days. They need the protection of the caravan, but they make a pact to leave anyway if his odd behavior becomes threatening to them..

When the caravan wakes in the morning they find the ground frosty white and frozen. Laurallin hardly noticed the road's climb over the previous day, but the chilling weather is evidence that they are indeed going up. During the next two days, Laurallin speculates, the road will have a much steeper climb.

Sliding out of her covers, she shakes her stiff legs. At times like these Laurallin appreciates some of the luxuries of her routine but civilized life. She misses her soft bed and Dannia.

Glenwall's men are very efficient in breaking camp after breakfast. Soon the caravan is making good progress once again.

The whole trip Laurallin has been watching for any tracks that may leave the major road. If Affensash has gone this way she doesn't want to chance missing any side ventures he may have embarked on. At one point Laurallin finds a set of hoof prints that cross the major road. Laurallin signals to Kenlin, and unnoticed, they lag behind the rest of the caravan to inspect the tracks.

"It looks like about fifteen or twenty riders," Laurallin says examining the hoof prints.

"If I'm not mistaken they are Hebelcaan riders," Kenlin says to Laurallin's surprise. "Your father has probably sent a party to hunt down strays from the herd."

"And maybe to keep an eye on his daughter," Laurallin laughs. "The old fox hasn't found me yet by the looks of these tracks. They are headed in the wrong direction. We had better catch up to the caravan before they see we're missing."

As the day wears on she finds no other trail worth investigating. Now that Laurallin is less worried about Kenlin she begins to relax around him. Laughing and joking with him has helped her to get in touch with her emotions. She hasn't quite confronted them, but she is becoming aware of what they are. He is everything her parents ever wanted for her husband, tall, strong, and savvy of the wilds, a born leader worthy to take her father's place. Laurallin can't really understand why it didn't work out. Maybe it was because it was a rebellious period in her life. Back then, she recalls, she didn't want to do anything her parents wanted. She would like to believe it was because she fell in love with a better man, but there is a doubting voice that keeps suggesting otherwise.

A low whistle of warning suddenly gives her more to worry about than her moody contemplations. While Laurallin has been studying the sides of the road, Kenlin was scouring the hillsides for any signs of trouble. He was the first to spot a unit of Eastern cavalry riding towards them away from the direction of High Tower.

"There is no need to panic," Kenlin assures her. "For once we are riding among people of their own kind."

Glenwall spreads word through the caravan to remain calm but prepared. No one is to speak to the soldiers except him. Laurallin is surprised to see the caravan soldiers loosening swords from their scabbards and placing weapons within easy reach.

The Eastern soldiers advance in good order, but it is obvious that the troops are exhausted. Many of the soldier's blue and white uniforms are blood-stained and dirty. Some of the men are heavily bandaged. All of the soldiers, however, are able to fight, making Laurallin wonder what happened to those who were too wounded to ride. Kenlin guesses that the battle they left could not be more than a day or two behind them.

"Hail conquerors of the world. We welcome the protection of the High Lords' soldiers," Glenwall shouts when the patrol is within listening distance.

The horsemen halt in the middle of the road, quickly reforming their ranks. The procedure looks routine rather than an actual preparation for combat and no one is alarmed by it. The Captain of the patrol advances and Glenwall climbs down from his wagon to greet him.

"What purpose have you for traveling on Lord Gaoler's highways," shouts the Captain in a tone of voice that leads you to believe this is the hundredth time he has said it today.

"We are merchants carrying goods from Mince to High Tower for the profit of the Blessed Empire. Are the roads clear behind you?" Glenwall questions.

The Captain suddenly notices Laurallin and Kenlin in the back of the caravan. He moves his horse forward to get a better look.

"Let's leave the questions to me for now," he insists suddenly more interested in his duties. "Why do Hebelcaan travel with Eastern merchants if they are truly on Eastern business?"

"These two are paying for our protection through these difficult mountain passages," Glenwall lies. "We thought it no harm since the Hebelcaan openly trade horses with the Empire. It seemed to us as easy money."

Kenlin leans toward Laurallin and whispers, "We must remember how convincingly our friend lies even to his own people."

Wheeling his horse around, the Captain nearly knocks Glenwall off his feet. "What is your merchandise ... merchant?" the Captain sneers making his words sound more like a curse.

"Just odds and ends that were ordered by High Tower store-keeps to replenish their shelves," he lies again.

"Then you won't mind if we have a look beneath those canvases will you?" the Captain asks, still eyeing Laurallin and Kenlin.

With a wave of his hand, two riders break ranks and ride around him to the first wagon. Drawing swords, they cut the ropes and pull back the canvas.

"Just books," they report back to their Captain.

"Not a very profitable cargo for the Empire, merchant," he says sarcastically to Glenwall.

With a motion of his hand, he signals his riders to do the same to the second wagon. The riders do exactly as before. But this time the first rider hesitates before reporting his find.

"Alchemy guns!" he finally shouts in a quivering voice. "There is enough here to equip an army!"

"What did you say?" the Captain shouts in disbelief.

That was all the tension the caravan soldiers could stand. One of them draws a sword, leaps from the wagon, and knocks the Eastern soldier from his saddle. A chain reaction follows.

Shouts and threats turn to clashing swords. The Eastern patrol outnumbers the caravan three to one. The patrol lowers their lances and prepares to charge. The Captain whirls his mount and returns to his troops to lead the attack.

Glenwall remains where the Captain left him, at the front of the caravan, alone and exposed.

"They will cut him down like ripe wheat," Kenlin shouts and starts to race to the rescue.

It's too late Kenlin realizes. Before his horse can gain speed, the soldiers charge. Glenwall stands his ground facing the soldiers. Laurallin and Kenlin can only see the back of his stocky build. He waves his hands high in the air. Kenlin thinks he is trying to wave his attackers off until he sees a light-blue light trailing from his fingertips leaving patterns in the air. Smoke rises from sibilating rocks in a line across the road between Glenwall and the charging soldiers.

When the soldiers get within five feet of the molten line, Glenwall lowers his arms and a white hot fire leaps from the ground. Too late to stop, the soldiers charge headlong into a river of torrid fire and blazing death.

Tortured cries of men and horses burst over Laurallin and Kenlin as the first wave of heat surrounds them. They are forced to cover their faces with their arms as the smell of burning horse and human flesh mingle together.

For Glenwall this isn't enough! Reaching into his robe he pulls out a wooden coin. Laurallin can barely make out a strange symbol carved on it just before Glenwall tosses it into the inferno.

Many of the soldiers were incinerated immediately by the flames. They are the lucky ones. Screaming horses plunge through the flames, many riderless, with blazing manes and tails. Other soldiers, including the Captain, miraculously survive and manage to make it through to continue their charge. It's then that the flames take on an inhuman form. Ghastly creatures with fire for hair and diamond-like claws reach out after the surviving soldiers and pull them back to the flames. The soldiers live just long enough to watch their own bodies torn apart and their souls drunk greedily by the flaming beasts.

Laurallin turns away.

"There is nothing good about a magic that butchers and tortures men so." The screams of men and horse are deafening and her words are barely audible to Kenlin. "This goes beyond defending oneself. This should not be possible in the lives of men."

Glenwall stands unaffected before the flames. "I have fulfilled my bargain with you. Now take your booty and return to your world," he commands.

The flames and the Eastern soldiers are instantly gone.

The odor of burning flesh hangs heavily in the air. Glenwall turns and goes back to the caravan. He walks directly to the caravan soldier.

The soldier slumps to his knees, grabbing for the helpless life snaking from his body.

The effect of Glenwall's actions on the rest of the caravan is immediate and unexpected. A wagoneer jumps from the wagon to the horses, cutting them loose. Shouting and frantically beating the horses, he rides off the road back towards Mince. The rest of the men grab what they can and join the desertion.

"Come back cowards!" Glenwall shouts enraged. "How dare you run from me?"

Raising his hand, Glenwall mutters a fatal enchantment and a man bursts to flames, dying as he runs.

"I've seen enough, Kenlin. I want out of here," Laurallin whispers.

The words fall out of her mouth pitiously. The smell of burning flesh lingers in the air.

While Glenwall is shouting at his men, the two ride off in the other direction unnoticed.

By the time Glenwall spots them they are out of his spell range.

"Come back here," he yells. "When you needed help I offered my protection and my caravan. How can you desert me when I need *your* help?"

"How well our friend lies," Laurallin reminds Kenlin to ease any feelings of guilt.

Glenwall continues to shout until the two can no longer distinguish his words. Glenwall's frustration mounts and his words turn to screams. Then to the horror of Kenlin and Laurallin, his screams turn to howls, long unnatural howls that echo around the mountains and return hauntingly to their ears.

CHAPTER TWELVE

Crossing Paths

Negate: *Allows the caster to negate or dispel the effects of anything previously created by a spell or magical device.*

- The Spell Book, from the treatise of High Fantasy

It takes longer for the poor desk clerk to purchase Diane's supplies than the two had anticipated. After an hour of beating on the doors of closed shops, Affensash and Diane decide they must wait until morning. At sunrise they buy the two best horses they can find for themselves and load Ruefin with their supplies on a third.

The day is chilly and storms threaten several times, but blow over. Diane and Affensash ride their horses hard, trying to make the best time possible. The road is clear and the conversation is sparse. Both feel an urgent need to make it to High Tower in time. Affensash always thought Laurallin wouldn't wait long for him to return, but he never expected that she would get in front of him. If Glenwall can be trusted he would keep them at High Tower for at least a few days. Diane could question him all she wanted about his failure on the ship. All Affensash wanted was to make certain Laurallin was safe and to hold her in his arms.

At noon they must stop for lunch to rest the horses. Affensash dismounts, rubbing his already blistering bottom.

"I'm afraid it is going to get worse for us and the horses before we reach High Tower. I have every intention of riding these horses into exhaustion. They can rest at High Tower. If we need to travel further we can purchase fresh mounts there," Diane explains as Affensash continues rubbing.

"Do you have friends in High Tower?" Affensash asks, tossing nibbles of bread to a hungry, indignant Ruefin. The little fox has always hated cages. "Glenwall is not likely to spread our names around and we might have trouble finding where they are staying. It's going to be hard to search for them and maintain the low profile Elder Enchantraen requested."

"The people of High Tower keep to themselves," Diane states flatly. "We will have to plan our search carefully once we get there. Glenwall will find a way to contact us quietly. Remember, Elder Enchantraen didn't want any wizards in High Tower. Glenwall will have to disguise himself or stay in hiding. If he openly announces to the inhabitants that he is there then we know he can't be trusted because he is openly rebuking his Elders. The Glenwall I knew would never risk that. He has every intention of becoming an Elder himself one day."

After a quick bite, the two mount up and charge off once more. It is during this part of the day that Diane's keen ears first pick up the howling of the distant wolves.

"Isn't it unusual for wolves to be calling to each other at this time of the day?" Affensash asks Diane nervously.

"It is a little strange. We had better build a big fire tonight to keep them away from camp and the horses. We don't have time to be fooling with that sort of nonsense," Diane says stiffly.

Her confidence lets Affensash relax a little even though the wolves' howling grows closer as the day goes on. As evening settles around them, the sky finally blows in the beginning of a real storm that looks as though it means to stay. The wind blows in gusts threatening at times to lift Affensash from his saddle. Before the sun totally sets, Diane stops at a good place for camp where a small clump of trees can offer some shelter from the wind.

Affensash gathers the wood while Diane makes a shelter from blankets tied to trees. Luckily, the fire becomes good and hot before the first snow starts falling. The two settle in close to the fire huddled under one blanket. The wind whips the snow around with great force several times nearly blowing the fire out. Affensash curses each time he has to go out to gather more wood.

Huddled together shivering, they listen as the sound of the wolves baying continues around them. One long mournful howl comes from the south and is answered by several to the north.

"The wolves could become a dangerous threat in weather like this," Diane quietly informs Affensash. "They will probably hunt in large packs and settle for whatever prey they find first. The fire should hold them off for the night."

The next time Affensash goes for wood he does so with vigor. Once the fire is big enough to burn for the rest of the night, Diane and Affensash relent and fall asleep. Snuggling together, they drift off in each other's arms trying to stay warm.

The weather breaks early in the morning. The sky remains threatening and the wind blows drifts of stinging icy snow. There is about two inches accumulation, which isn't enough to hinder the horses except in some unusually high drifts. They waste no time in setting off once they are awake. The wolves are still howling around them, but it sounds like most of the wolves have moved to the west.

"I think they are tracking something," Diane concludes, listening to their yapping and barking. "They are probably chasing after a herd of wild horses or deer. Anyhow, it is clear they aren't after us."

The road is steeper now and the clouds occasionally blow fresh snow down to replace the snow that melts. The horses are holding up well, but they have to make several short stops to rest them. Working them up into a sweat in this kind of weather could kill them, and Diane has no intention of walking this far to High Tower.

The day drags on and the sky becomes worse. The short gusts of wind turn long and bitter, threatening to bring even more snow. Affensash covers his face and stares down at his saddle content to let his horse follow Diane's. They continue for hours, the wind slowing their progress and snapping bitterly around them.

Diane suddenly stops, causing Affensash to bump into her. Looking up, he sees her pointing to the road. A long black line of burnt grass crosses the road in front of them. The falling snow seems to pass around avoiding the black line, leaving it very much in contrast to the white snowy countryside. Off to the side are an overturned wagon and several bloating corpses.

"It's the caravan!" Affensash utters with a sick feeling in his stomach. He jumps from his horse and runs to check the bodies. His greatest fear is that Laurallin is among them. He starts to cross the charred line to look for more when Diane stops him.

"Don't go near that!" she commands and Affensash stops. "This is not the whole caravan. None of the bodies are Laurallin's. There are no women. There is a good chance she is all right."

"What is it?" Affensash asks as Diane dismounts and starts walking to the burnt area.

"I don't know. This is not the magic of 'True Ones'," Diane replies and stops about ten feet in front of it. "Stay here," she says handing Affensash the reins to her horse.

Taking out her magic book, she opens it to precisely the right page and starts reading aloud. As she reads, one hand forms light-blue ringlets in the air that hover momentarily and then settle over the black charred area.

With a pale face, Diane returns to Affensash's side. "We will have to camp here for the night. The snow has covered any trail the caravan might have left. It is reasonable to assume that the survivors continued on to High Tower. I have much work to do here tonight."

With Diane so visibly shaken, Affensash isn't about to protest further. He starts to make camp at a place near the charred ground, but Diane waves him away.

"Something terrible has happened here. I will have to work through most of the night to undo it. It would be best if you stayed back where it will be safer."

"Can't you tell me what it is?" Affensash asks, not sure he really wants to know.

"A great wrong has been done. There are bodies around here that you can't see. None of them are Laurallin's," she quickly interjects. "Tonight I will lay their souls to rest. If anything happens to me, ride toward High Tower in the morning. If the weather breaks you may be able to make it by tomorrow night. We should be traveling at a better pace than the caravan. You may even overtake them. Tell Johona what happens."

"Don't talk like that, Diane. Nothing is going to happen to you. We will both leave this place and find them tomorrow."

Diane smiles weakly, "Maybe so. Maybe so," and starts to help Affensash set up camp. "It seems like they met some Eastern soldiers and a skirmish followed. The Easterners must have had some magician with them because there was a magic used that I don't fully understand."

"Could it have been Glenwall who did that ghastly magic?" Affensash asks, wishing he didn't have to.

"It is possible, but let us hope not. If he did, then Laurallin is in greater danger than you can imagine," Diane says too bluntly.

Naturally, that type of remark makes Affensash imagine the most horrible things, but he manages to calm himself and attend to more productive matters.

To Affensash's surprise, Diane eats a full meal before going about her business. She explains to Affensash that she has never done anything like this before, but she has witnessed it once.

Solemnly, she builds a second shelter adjacent to the charred strip. From where Affensash sits he can just make out the fine features of her face. Diane takes out a small talisman and sets it in front of her. Affensash can only guess this to be some sort of wizardly charm. She opens her book to precisely the right page just as she had done before. And just as before, she raises her arms and begins a sing-song chant, tracing blue patterns in the air with her fingertips.

Affensash sits watching. He has no idea what to expect. To him, Diane's spell seems longer in the casting than any other he has witnessed.

The winds begin to slow. The temperature drops. Affensash grabs an extra blanket and wraps it around his feet. The wind stops all together and he realizes this all must be caused by Diane's spell.

Diane's chant becomes light and airy. She seems to be drifting off into a trance. Affensash finds it impossible to continue watching her and stay awake himself. To remain alert he shifts his eyes up and down the charred black strip, but he is too concerned to take his eyes far from Diane. He involuntarily takes a gulp of cold air.

A phantom flame ignites along the entire length of the strip. It is a cool, heatless flame, barely visible. Diane never pauses in her sing-song spell, so Affensash assumes that this too must be because of her enchantment. The phantasmal red and yellow flames seem to draw together and concentrate inches from Diane. When she ends her song she reaches down to pick-up the talisman.

A creature forms in the flames in front of Diane. It leaps forward hissing like a fire consuming a dry pine tree. Affensash jumps from his shelter with an involuntary cry. Diane barely lifts the talisman in front of her in time to ward the demon away. A sudden burst of power echoes through the hills. The demon hisses as if injured from the talisman, and retreats back to the phantom blaze.

"Do not threaten me evil one," Diane calls across the flames. Her voice seems to travel a long way off and becomes lost in another world.

With a hissing sound that cannot be called a voice, the demon asks still cringing, "Who calls me away from my comfort?"

"Diane, True Wizard and master of your fire, calls you here, demon. You have taken something from my world that does not belong to you. I have summoned you here to take it back," Diane cries boldly.

The demon hisses in pain from Diane's words. It rises again, building power to attack, but Diane lifts the talisman and the demon retreats.

"First, demon, I want an answer from you," Diane says forcefully, never looking away and never showing signs of fear or doubt.

The demon slithers forward, and if a thing of smoke and flame can smile, Affensash swears he sees the demon smirking.

"So that is what you want. You wizards always want something. Let us make a pact..."

"No!" Diane nearly throws the talisman at the demon causing it to shrink away from her. "I demand the name of the wizard who called you here before me."

The flame burns cold and steady. "There will be no pact," Diane challenges.

The hissing sound comes again, low and calm this time, "There must be a pact. There is always a pact. I cannot tell you without one."

Diane reaches down and lifts the talisman, "I have death waiting for you, demon, and it will not be an easy one. For the last time, tell me who brought you to this place."

"We have no pact!" the demon hisses.

Diane moves forward as the demon speaks and waves the talisman. The demon's body erupts, sending steam and smoke billowing, like a pail of water thrown on a smithy's forge. Diane's body becomes completely blocked from Affensash's view. When the steam clears, he sees her standing next to a resplendent image. Light beams from the image, spearing into the mist and driving it away. It is the figure of a naked man shimmering blue, the same blue as her spell patterns. Saying nothing, she walks back to her little shelter escorted by the ghostly blue shade who takes its place beside her. There she starts her spell all over again.

Diane continues to call the flame demons one by one. Affensash becomes afraid several times as Diane is barely able to ward off their attacks. Each time she tries a new line of questioning to find out who called them here, and each time they refuse to answer without a pact.

It is nearly daybreak when she summons the last demon. It too prefers to die rather than talk without a pact. Surrounded by thirty or forty shimmering shades, Diane releases them from her control. The naked spirits walk across the land like bright blue beacons, silently headed toward the east. Diane collapses on the ground from exhaustion. Affensash runs to her side, picking her up in his arms.

"They can find their own way home from here," she coughs. "We must leave this place. I fear the worst for Laurallin," she says barely able to breathe enough to say the words.

"We will rest here until you are able to travel," Affensash insists.

"We cannot stay here. We will be dead before nightfall. Take me to High Tower, Affensash. Please!" Diane says coughing, looking up through eyes she can barely keep open.

Affensash believes his first assessment of her was correct. When she came to take him away from his laboratory he thought she was an angel. Only the angels would give so much to men who did not know her and were unable to even say thank you.

With tears in his eyes, he wraps her warmly. She lays quietly, a small fragile bundle, as he packs everything away. Ruefin comes out of his hiding place and quietly curls up in a ball next to her. When he is done he lifts her to her horse, but she is too weak to ride. Still tearful, he is forced to strap her, like a sack of flour, across the horse's back. The snow blows and falls freely on the charred black line. Affensash feels it is safe to ride across it.

The weather is better than it was yesterday, but Affensash stops several times to try and force Diane to eat. Her strength is slowly coming back despite the cold wind, but she still is unable to ride. Ruefin, it seems, has taken a special liking to her and whimpers to be placed next to her each time they stop. Affensash finally has to strap his cage to her horse just to shut him up.

By mid-day Diane's breathing is steady. The wolf pack is howling to the west of them apparently hot in pursuit of some unknown prey. Affensash doesn't care as long as they leave him alone. On each new section of road he looks but cannot find any tracks from the caravan. He is hoping for Diane's sake that he can overtake any who may have survived so that she may receive help.

By late afternoon he is certain that the caravan could never have come this way. He can find no wagon tracks and there is too little snow left to drift over any that might have been made.

The wolves howl.

Affensash becomes concerned about the wolves again when he hears the howling of a new pack growling louder on the road ahead of him. Half asleep and drowsy from the night before, his mind conjures nightmares around him. At times he feels like the pack is pacing him, but at others it becomes so quiet that he starts to doze off, nearly falling from the saddle.

By late evening he catches glimpses of High Tower each time he rounds a new bend in the twisting, turning road. Ruefin becomes nervous, bringing on a second wave of nightmares. The little fox paces in his cage sniffing the air. Affensash stops and puts his little friend in his pocket as a precaution. That's when the howling closes in. He hears them now in front, as well as in back of him.

Frantically, he searches the sides of the road. Nothing.

High Tower looms so close he is deceived several times into thinking he is there. He is not.

Instinctively looking back, he sees the first beast scurry across the road behind him disappearing in the bushes. Affensash turns for his alchemy case. His fingers are numb as he fumbles for his potions.

The wolves trail him. Affensash can barely make out their shapes as they dart between the shrubs and the shadows of the setting sun. The world darkens. The wolves become more courageous, loping along beside him, but always just out of sight.

He cannot stop to rest although fatigue sets heavily on his shoulders. The pack is trying to run ahead to completely encircle them. If they can surround him they will eventually attack from all sides and he will not stand a chance.

He is at war with his nerves. Each bend gets him closer to the city and each bend seems to have a new wolf waiting to join the pack. Finally the wolves become bold and careless and Affensash spots one. It is a man! It howls and rushes off behind a boulder. The hair on Affensash's neck prickles. It must be the night shadows playing tricks on him. It must be. He desperately tries to wake Diane, but she lies limply over the saddle. Affensash knows they cannot stop.

Around the next bend he sees them, the gates to High Tower. They are two huge oak doors. Lining the road on both sides are quivering torches. Grabbing the reins of Diane's horse, he digs his heels deeply into his horse's flanks and bolts into a dead run.

The wolves attack. Two leap out in front of him, but scamper away when the horses nearly run them over. The night becomes a howling madhouse of snarling growls and leaping beasts.

He makes it to the gates. Leaping off his horse, he runs to open them.

They're locked!

He turns around expecting to find the pack at his throat, but the torches hold them at bay.

Everything is suddenly quiet.

He looks wide-eyed around in the bushes and sees glowing eyes with a glint of white fangs.

"Oh!" he quavers. "They're part human."

Turning around, he screams and bangs his fists raw against the gates. "Help us! Help us please!"

The wolves howl, circling and sizing up their prey, always edging forward.

"Stand back," comes a voice from within.

Affensash is pressed so hard against the doors he can feel the grain of the wood on his cheek. He can't move.

The doors burst open and the town militiamen charge out brandishing swords in one hand and torches in the other. The horses turn to run, but the men grab the reins and force them inside.

Affensash is picked from the ground and hurried inside. The men come back, retreating slowly, always facing the wolves, ready for an attack. Through the closing doors Affensash sees the wolves finally regain their courage and charge, but they are too late to reach the doors before they are bolted shut.

A small crowd cheers.

"Hah," says a young man coming towards Affensash. "They always wait for us to open the gate and then try to rush in. That scared the dogs," the young man laughs again. Turning a serious face towards Affensash he asks, "What is your business here at High Tower?"

Caught off-guard, Affensash pauses while he tries to recover. "We were with a caravan," he pants, "that was attacked en route to your city. All is lost except me and my wounded friend." Affensash's voice shakes. He doesn't know if his story sounds convincing enough. "She is badly hurt. Can someone help?"

Affensash unties Diane and slides her from the horse. She is barely breathing and is still unconscious.

"Wolves get her?" one militia man questions Affensash as another goes for help.

"No, not wolves, but we heard them all the way here," Affensash says in a tired voice. "What are those creatures?"

"They are beasts, plain and simple. Some of them are miners from High Tower. Others come from who knows where. They are beasts that live on the flesh of those who won't join them," the man says grimly, walking away.

A litter breaks through the crowd of militiamen. Affensash hurries to place Diane on it. A woman shoves her way through the men. Apparently she is a nurse or healer of some kind. She stoops down and examines Diane.

"Strip her and let's see," says the woman, turning Diane over and unbuttoning her shirt.

"What?" Affensash yells, but two strong arms grab him and hold him back.

The woman calls for a blanket and covers Diane from the eyes of the men. Deftly, she takes her clothes off and throws them in a pile at Affensash's feet.

"She has no marks," the woman announces. "This one can stay."

Affensash is released and runs to Diane's side looking wildly around at the crowd of faces not knowing what to expect.

"There is no room in the healing quarters," the woman says morosely to Affensash. She turns to the crowd of men saying, "Ask around and see if someone can take them in."

"I can take care of her," Affensash objects.

The woman looks at him questioningly, "She has a fever and her body has no strength to fight it. You aren't a healer and you don't look so well yourself. It will be days before she can travel again."

Seeing Affensash's wild and frightened eyes, she feels a little pity. Turning back to the men, she tells them to go ahead and take her to the inn.

Two of them pick her up and start toward the inn when Affensash objects again. "I have no money. We lost it all on our travel here," Affensash says embarrassed.

The woman looks at him with disgust. "Take her to the inn and tell the keeper that I will take care of the bill," she says blandly. Thinking a moment, she stops them again and says, "Better yet, send for Steven and tell him to enlist this one," pointing to Affensash. "You are willing to work for your keep until she is better aren't you?"

"I will do everything I can to help her," Affensash says tired and confused, not knowing who to trust, but willing to agree to anything for a moments rest.

"Good. There will be plenty for you to do," she says laughing, and walks away.

"Excuse me," Affensash yells after her. "Has anyone else from the caravan arrived?" he asks, worried about Laurallin.

"I'm sorry, but no," she says never looking back over her shoulder. "No one has walked through those gates for weeks."

Affensash feels his heart sink as he watches them carry Diane away to the nearby inn.

CHAPTER THIRTEEN

Hunters or Prey

Binding: *A magical wrap created by wizards to bind and hold victims helpless. It begins as a faint light-blue concentration of light that forms about the wizard's hands.*

- The Spell Book, from the treatise of High Fantasy

Laurallin and Kenlin ride west on the road away from Glenwall and the caravan. They continue that way until they are out of sight. Finding a second path, they turn north hoping to parallel the road for as long as possible. The riding is slow. Through the rest of the sunlit hours, the two of them ride silently, letting their horses work their own way along the path. They come to a large plateau and the ground starts to level. Looking ahead, Kenlin knows that it is a luxury that won't last for long. Soon they will be climbing again. He only hopes that the terrain does not become so rough that it forces them back onto the road where Glenwall would have an easier chance of catching them.

The wind blows in a storm and with it a stinging snow. The temperature drops making it cold enough for the snow to drift. Laurallin leans over to tell Kenlin a sudden thought. "We have to beat Glenwall to High Tower. God help us if he gets there first."

Kenlin hadn't thought of that. They could run all they wanted to, but unless they find Affensash, they will have to eventually end up at High Tower looking for him. Glenwall could wait for them there knowing they would eventually show up.

The wolves yap and call to each other from all around. They are moving closer. Both Laurallin and Kenlin know that, but neither one mentions it to the other. In all their experience neither has heard anything like it before. Wolves howling in broad daylight and continuing on through the night! Always howling and moving; getting closer.

Day finally surrenders to the night and the two are no longer on clear ground. They are forced to dismount and walk their horses up sharp rock cliffs, often having to double-back when the path becomes inaccessible. The snow will not quit, making the passage all the more difficult. Kenlin leads the way, having the most experience in these situations. They go on blindly listening to the wolves and saying nothing. Several times the horses slip, until they are finally forced to make a decision.

"We cannot take the horses through these mountains, especially in this weather," Kenlin finds himself shouting to Laurallin over the noise of the wind. "We either have to let the horses go and cross the mountains on foot, or we have to go back to the main road."

"We can't beat Glenwall to High Tower this way," Laurallin yells back, still trying to come up with another solution.

"You are assuming he is still going to High Tower. With no cargo or men to help him he may just head back to Mince," Kenlin says unconvincingly.

"Let's go back to the road, Kenlin. We are trying too hard to avoid Glenwall. You are right. He may have already forgotten about us."

Laurallin stops and turns finding it hard to locate the trail leading back down. Sensie suddenly whinnies and tries to rear. Laurallin falls out of the way. She hears a wolf growl and jumps to her feet pulling her dagger. Sensie cannot gain her footing and stumbles into Laurallin, knocking her down. Leaping from the night shadows, the wolf attacks.

Kenlin is the first to realize that it is not a normal wolf. The wolf lands on its back paws. It actually stands on its back legs growling at Laurallin, staring for just a second with coal black, intelligent eyes. Laurallin freezes, unable to grasp what is attacking her. Kenlin struggles, trying to calm his horse and reach his bow. The wolf springs for Laurallin's throat.

To Laurallin, it is like the whole scene is moving in slow motion. The wolf leaps, extending its body, snarling with rows of sharp dirty teeth. She tries to move, but her muscles won't let her. She can almost feel the wolf's teeth on her throat. From the corner of her eye, she sees Sensie attack. Raising just enough to kick with her hooves, the horse knocks the wolf aside, ruining its attack. The wolf lands on a rock beside Laurallin and tumbles down away from her.

That is all the time Laurallin needs to adjust. She is up on her feet before the beast is and turns to face it, dagger in hand. Slapping Sensie on the rump the horse moves away. Laurallin doesn't want the horse trapped so close to her where neither can do any good.

Sensie stumbles down the path just as the beast leaps again for Laurallin. She slashes her dagger in the air and the wolf twists in mid-flight just missing her flashing blade. The beast lands and springs again. This time Laurallin's blade strikes home with deadly accuracy.

In pain, the beast twists off the blade and rolls to the side with an eight inch gash in its chest, and is unable to complete its attack. Howling and thrashing in agony, it finally comes to rest and lies silent. Horrified by the looks of the man-beast, she slips around it and faces Kenlin.

"What is that thing?" she pants, still winded from the fighting.

Kenlin stands with his bow in his hand. He slips the tribal death mask over his face. Even through the swirling snow and dark night, Laurallin can see the horror in his eyes. Suddenly, they become steely gray and he raises his bow aiming it toward her.

"Kenlin," is the only word she can mutter before the tribesman shoots.

The arrow flies past her ear and strikes with a solid thud behind her. She turns just as the creature lets out a snarling growl of anguish and lopes off into the darkness. Hidden from view, it begins a tirade of haunting howls.

"It's signaling to its brothers," Laurallin shouts, "I will go kill it!" She starts off into the darkness when Kenlin stops her.

"Don't go," he commands. "You cannot kill that beast with that dagger. It will not die so easily."

Laurallin turns and casts a knowing expression his way. "You don't think it's a werebeast?"

"I think it is akin to the werewolf, but I have never heard a legend that said werewolves track by day. Laurallin didn't you see its eyes? That was a man carrying the mark of the beast."

The night air is suddenly full with replying howls to the wolf's calling. "Kenlin, if you are right then all those howls are ..." Laurallin cannot finish her sentence.

Wordlessly, they turn and follow Sensie down the trail. Sensie stops and they catch up. They have to get back to the open plateau where the horses will be able to run.

Together, horse and Hebelcaan plunge down the path moving faster than safety would allow. The wolf that attacked them trails along behind continually howling out their progress to its brothers. Laurallin and Kenlin run on, occasionally stumbling, but never stopping.

In their haste, Kenlin trips and tears a large gash in his left leg. The wound is mostly to his flesh and does not impair the muscle or bone. His string of curses none-the-less causes Laurallin to stop and go back to check on him.

"That damn creature is driving me mad!" Kenlin curses while Laurallin wraps his leg with a makeshift bandage. He lifts the death mask revealing his face. "It tracks us without fear and we cannot escape it."

Less than twenty feet away they hear the creature howling again. "You take the horses and go on ahead."

"No Kenlin!" Laurallin starts to protest.

"Believe me, Laurallin; I don't intend to be a martyr. With a few shafts sticking in it, the wolf might not be so brave. Maybe it will stop following us."

Kenlin starts to lift the cloth to wrap his face in the death mask. Laurallin lifts her hand and stops him for just a moment. In freezing wind, surrounded by howling death, Laurallin leans forward and kisses him, sending a fire raging through his body. She starts to speak, hesitates, and then releases his wrappings and turns away.

Kenlin grabs her arm and spins her back around. His eyes pierce straight through her. His eyes see through all her doubts. He loves her despite it all.

"I will meet you in the open lands below. It's not far away." He lets her go and disappears into the shadows.

Coldly, with a mixed heart, she leads the horses away. She loves Affensash, but is it possible to love two men for different reasons?

On she plunges into the night, the howls growing frighteningly close around her. Both horses grow skittish, but she calms them with words known only by Hebelcaan tribesmen. Down they go faster and faster, the rough terrain starting to break-up. The whole way she whispers stories to the horses about the great Hebelcaan, calming their nerves as well as hers.

Kenlin doubles back, not knowing where the wolf is hiding. He crouches low in the shadows and moves only when the beast howls. He listens for the night sounds that will tell him when and where the beast is moving. The strong winds and answering howls make it nearly impossible.

He suddenly becomes alarmed. What if the beast escapes around him? He could be hiding here while Laurallin walks the horses to her death. He will be too far away to help her.

There is little he can do now. He must practice the patience of a hunter and wait, moving only when it is necessary.

Another howl and he moves again, always trying to stay in the descending path of the beast. Barely breathing, he waits with bow in hand. Then the howling stops! The confused yaps and barking of the surrounding wolves drown out all other sounds in the night until it is too late.

Catching his scent, the wolf finds Kenlin first. The wolf attacks from above, knocking him to the ground before he knows what is happening. His bow falls useless into a snowdrift.

He throws the wolf off of him and tries to run. The creature is on him before he can take the next step. The wolf's deadly claws easily rip through his woolen clothes and tear viciously into his arms. Kenlin grabs the creature by the neck and attempts to hold its jaws away from his exposed neck. The wolf-thing is incredibly strong and easily overpowers Kenlin, knocking him to the ground. Slowly the wolf's jaws descend. Kenlin strains every muscle of his body, but knows that he is losing. His clothes are shredded from the slashing claws. He feels blood dripping down his chest. With a dead man's inspiration he realizes that it is not his blood.

The beast is bleeding from the wound Laurallin gave it earlier. With the last of his strength he heaves up on the beast's jaws to free one hand. Blocking the jaws with one elbow, he moves his free hand down and plunges his fingers into the wound. The beast screams, not howls, and rolls off of Kenlin. Kenlin leaps for his bow and in one continuous motion fires arrows at the thrashing creature.

One thud, two thuds, three, four and five arrows strike the beast before it staggers to its hind legs and runs off screaming into the night. Kenlin stands on wobbly legs and shudders. Those were human ribs he felt when he plunged his hand into the wound.

He has no time to catch his breath before he hears Laurallin's first scream at the base of the mountain.

Struggling down the mountainside, Laurallin stops abruptly when she hears a howl in front of her. There must be another wolf directly ahead on the path she is descending. She changes her direction still trying to calm the horses.

The falling snow is becoming so thick, mostly due to the drifting, that she can barely see twenty feet in front of her. Down she goes whispering a Hebelcaan song to the horses. She turns her head each time she hears a new howl.

Suddenly a howl is cut short and the wolf starts yapping. She's been spotted. She begins a dangerous descent down the side at a dead run. Laurallin knows the plateau must be ahead. If she can reach it before they catch her she can mount-up and possibly out run them.

She stumbles and rolls ten feet before she can stop. Dizzily she tries to stand but slips again and is forced to take two deep breaths before she can reorient herself and rise. When she gets up she sees the plateau. Her elation passes as soon as she hears the snarl. A wolf is waiting for her, yapping at the bottom. Jumping on the back of Sensie, she pulls her bow. Kenlin's stallion is still trailing behind.

Sensie wants to bolt, trusting to her legs to save them, but Laurallin wants to wait for Kenlin. She charges forward at the wolf. Sensie's sudden burst of speed catches the wolf off-guard and they nearly knock it over as it tries to scamper out of the way. Laurallin releases two arrows. Both find their mark and the beast runs off howling in pain.

She whips Sensie around and looks up the mountain. Kenlin's stallion has reached the plateau, but Kenlin is nowhere to be found. Sensie suddenly whinnies and jumps straight to the side. Another wolf comes from nowhere and rakes its claws across Sensie's flanks. Laurallin cries out as her arms are yanked viciously in their sockets, but somehow manages to hang on. The horse starts to rear on its hind legs in an effort to escape the tearing claws on its chest.

Laurallin instead commands her to run forward and the great horse obeys. The wolf is drug under and trampled by the horse's hooves. Laurallin applies pressure with her right knee and Sensie knows to wheel. Once around, Laurallin can see the trampled wolf and puts two more arrows in it as it limps away into the shadows.

The howls are all around her and still there is no sign of Kenlin.

Sensie spins around to warn Laurallin. Dozens of coal black eyes stare from the swirling snow. The howling stops! Sensie makes to charge, but three wolves move to block the path. Sensie stops and wheels around. Laurallin turns her quickly around to guard their back. Laurallin then commands Sensie to step backward towards the mountain rather than turning and running.

The wolves move in, slowly forming a tightening ring around them. They hesitate, afraid to charge, fearing the sting of Laurallin's bow. Laurallin sits pointing the arrow at one wolf and then another, intimidating the wolves, all the while knowing that it is almost over.

Thump. Thump, thump. Arrows fly from above, raining down on the beasts with deadly accuracy. Laurallin chances a glance over her shoulder and sees Kenlin. He is standing on a small ledge with his death mask lowered. His clothes are torn and bloody. He stands there looking very much like the frozen shade of Death.

The wolves attack!

Laurallin reacts shooting arrow after arrow into any wolf that Kenlin has not already targeted. The wolves howl and yap, blood trickling through their thick splotchy fur. They fall and thrash on the ground but refuse to die. After the first volley of arrows, the wolves are stunned and retreat. Kenlin races down and jumps on the back of his stallion. Just off, hidden in the shadows, the wolves howl and begin to regroup, quickly overcoming the shock of Kenlin's and Laurallin's initial attack.

With a quick look between them Kenlin turns his stallion to the right. Laurallin knows it's now or never, and together they charge to the right shooting in front of them to clear the way.

The horses stop with a jolt!

Laurallin gasps as Sensie starts backing up. Wolves! The dozens have grown to scores. Kenlin, realizing the alternatives, goads his mount forward firing all the way. Laurallin follows. Claws rip and tear at horseflesh. The poor animals cry with terror, but continue to lunge forward at the riders command.

Kenlin's bow is ripped from his hand as deadly fangs tear at the exposed muscles in his legs. At one point he is nearly pulled from the horse, but Laurallin is there to right him.

Sensie leaps forward passing over a tangle of snarling wolves, and the way in front of them is free. The horses take off at a dead run, but each stride is tortured by their ripped and torn flesh.

Kenlin is behind Laurallin now, badly swaying from loss of blood. As the first to encounter the wolves, he took the brunt of the damage.

Weakened and tired, the horses are not able to pull far enough away from the pack. The wolf-beasts are fast and strong, nearly pacing the horses stride for stride. Laurallin is forced to shoot the faster ones to keep from being overtaken. Their only hope is that the wolves don't have the same endurance as the horses.

Kenlin is slumping over the neck of his horse. The great stallion's flanks are streaming with blood. Laurallin slows Sensie and pulls to his side. "We have to split up," she shouts over the howls and blowing snow. "One of us might get away."

Kenlin looks up and nods, understanding, but in too much pain to answer. Laurallin's heart nearly breaks. His bronze sturdy body is leaving pools of blood on the freshly falling snow. Worst of all, he did this for her.

"Try to find the Hebelcaan hunters. We are close to the tracks we saw earlier. Bring them back with arrows blessed by the Shaman," Laurallin shouts sobbing.

Kenlin makes no response that he has heard her. A wolf leaps from the snow and Laurallin stops it with an arrow. It falls to the ground in convulsions. The rest of the pack tramples over it continuing their mad chase. When Laurallin looks back to Kenlin, he is holding up his quiver of arrows. She reaches out and takes it.

She commands and Sensie stops. The great horse wheels around. The pack is on her instantly. Laurallin shouts for Sensie to run forward. The horse tries to obey, but the wolves are hanging on. She starts to stumble, but Laurallin kicks them away. Sensie suddenly bolts and breaks free, running for the road. The pack is right after her. The brief stop allowed the slower wolves to catch up.

She looks over her right shoulder, but Kenlin has disappeared into the snowy night shadows. She ties her bow to the horse and leans far over Sensie's neck to maximize speed.

Across the plateau she catches the sound of a distant voice. A man's voice!

"Help," she shouts, guiding Sensie to run toward the sound. The voice becomes louder and she begins to make out a few words. The man is shouting commands.

Too late she hears the words, "Stop her you whelps," and recognizes the voice.

She tries to change direction, but a blue light leaps from the swirling snow and binds her. She falls backwards off of Sensie hitting the ground hard, knocking the wind from her. Sensie stops, but Laurallin manages a whistle for her to go on. She bolts off into the night and disappears.

The pack is all around Laurallin. Her head is spinning as she tries to catch her breath. All she sees are snarling faces and vicious yellow fangs. A voice is yelling and the pack suddenly parts. A man in a rich dark robe pushes and beats the beasts back. Then he turns to inspect his newly snared prize.

Looking down at her is the smiling face of Glenwall. Through tearful eyes Laurallin thinks his face has somehow changed. His beard seems thicker and nearly covers his face. His eyes are wild and lit with a demonic glow. Laurallin faints and tumbles into tender blackness.

CHAPTER FOURTEEN

The Visitation

A person must be born with the talent to become a wizard. As they grow older the local witch maids and magic users nurture this ability along.

- of Wizards, from the treatise of High Fantasy

The little lamps hiss and sputter casting shadows of dancing sprites in the secret corners of the room. The windows rattle with cold, but the sturdy fire keeps the room warm. They take Diane to the second story where she rests under piles of blankets, her golden hair spread evenly around her pale face. Affensash sits beside her, dabbing her forehead with a cloth, wiping the sweat away. He has stacked furniture in front of the door and locked all the windows except one. From there he watches the town while he hears shouting in the streets below. Several times, patrols of militia have passed carrying torches and gleaming blades.

Diane has taken a chill and has not spoken since they arrived at High Tower. The woman who sent them to the inn, a healer by trade, said she would recover soon only if she rests. Her real problem was not illness but utter fatigue.

It is still the first night they arrived and Affensash hasn't had an opportunity to explore the town. He doesn't harbor any hopes of finding Laurallin here. Somehow they must have passed her on the road. Maybe Glenwall was somehow wrong and she was never with the caravan.

Six times, a snowy owl swoops around the open window. Spreading its great white wings, it rises and disappears into the stars. Affensash closes the shutters too weary even to sleep.

Diane's breathing is shallow. He expects it to stop at any time.

The patrols continue unceasingly as Affensash watches through a tiny crack in the shutters.

His reason for being here is remote and distant, shoved to the side by his more tender concerns for those he loves and those he has grown to love. He is a lone man surrounded by the endless black pageantry of the night. People cry in the street below and men shout angrily. The moon shines through the cracks in the window revealing Affensash's vigilant watch over Diane. He appears unimportant and quite lost.

Diane coughs and stirs under the blanket. He wipes her forehead again, stands and walks to the window. Laurallin is out there somewhere. He can feel it in the air. Opening the shutters, he looks over the struggling town. High Tower seems to be made up of three levels. The bottom level, where he is now, is the largest and looks to be semicircular in shape. On this level he can see shops, a tavern, and other odd buildings. Around the perimeter of the town are stone walls giving it the appearance of a large fortress rather than a mining town.

On the second smaller level, there seems to be houses where the miners live. The pitch is too steep on the third smallest level and it is impossible to tell what's up there.

Affensash's mind wanders hazily over the town. Everywhere he hears shouting and screaming. Away on the second level a house is burning, ruining the graceful black sky with flickers of red. He wonders if he just told Elder Enchantraen that everything was all right if the wizard would let him go home.

Tired and aching, he would gladly trade the excitement of the adventure and the beauty of Diane for the quiet dusty comfort of his lab. 'Leave the heroics to heroes' is what his father always told him.

Turning around, he sees Ruefin on the bed licking Diane's face. He runs and shoos the little fox away calling him a hairy pest. Insulted, Ruefin sulks under the bed. Diane begins to stir and her eyes flutter open. She looks up and smiles at Affensash through dreamy blue eyes.

"I was dreaming you were kissing me Affensash," Diane mumbles.

"Well no, not exactly," Affensash replies, giving Ruefin a dirty look when he sticks his head out from under the bed.

"Are we at High Tower?" she asks weakly.

Affensash fills a cup with water and lifts her head to take a few sips.

"Yes we are at High Tower. It is nearly the morning of our first night." He sighs as he eases her back down. "I have heard nothing from Laurallin or Johona. Someone at the gate said no one has entered the town for weeks."

She smiles again and says, "Wizards have ways of entering towns besides the front gate."

"That's true," Affensash says, "but wives of alchemist's don't."

"Of course, I'm sorry," Diane quickly answers realizing what she said. "I am too tired to think straight. I just need a little rest. Tomorrow when my magic returns we will search the town. We will find them." Diane closes her eyes and drifts back to sleep.

A high-pitched scream causes her to struggle, trying to sit upright. A woman runs out in the street below holding a crying child in her arms. Someone is trying to take it from her. The mother's screams batter about the walls of their room.

Affensash pushes Diane back down. "You are too weak to get up yet," he explains to her.

More screams bring terror to Diane's eyes. "Help her, Affensash! For God's sake, help her."

"Who would protect you? There has been screaming like that all night. Don't you think it bothers me?" he asks, fatigued.

Another series of screams is all Diane can stand. "Forget about me. I can take care of myself. Help her! Please go help her or I will go mad!"

Affensash stands; looking at her for a brief moment, then pushes the furniture aside and runs out the door. Out into a hallway he hurries down a flight of stairs. He runs into the street panting. The mother is still there, knocked to her knees struggling with another woman.

"Get away from her! Leave her alone," Affensash yells running up to the woman and shoving her to the ground.

The mother stays crumbled on the ground guarding the child in her arms. The child's arms are bleeding from where the second woman was pulling on them. Affensash steps between the mother and the woman. Like a cat, the woman springs up off the ground. When the woman turns toward Affensash, he can see her clearly in the light shining from the tavern's window. Her eyes are glowing red! She starts to speak, lifting her arms beseechingly to the stars.

"Oh great Baal, hear me now."

That's all Affensash needs to hear. Picking the mother up, he tries to hurry them off to safety. The poor mother and her child are so confused that they start to scream and try to pull away from him. A town patrol comes around the corner.

"Get them," a man shouts.

The woman stops her chant and runs. Affensash does the worst thing possible. He runs too.

He races off directly down the street then dodges into an alley. The militiamen are close behind. Affensash is defenseless. Who knows what they will do to a stranger if they catch him. Already tiring, having no rest, he takes a desperate chance. He turns another corner and doubles back towards the inn. He sees a stack of barrels along a dark wall and ducks behind them.

The patrol charges down the alley. Affensash forces his heaving lungs to stop.

Torches light up his hiding place, but the men are too intent on the chase ahead of them. They run on past him yelling and screaming. When the darkness returns, he gulps in the free air and sighs. He stands up and walks around the barrels. On the other side he looks up and stops dead still. A woman is standing at the end of the alley staring at him. Torchlight passes behind her revealing her shapely silhouette.

"Oh, it's you, Diane. You nearly scared me to death," he says breathing another sigh of relief. He walks toward her.

"The mother is fine. The patrol showed up in the nick of time. They nearly put a sword through my ribs though," he says standing less than two feet from her.

He reaches out to touch her hand when something causes him to stop. The alley is too dark to see clearly.

"You aren't Diane!" he says taking a step back.

"No, but you may take my hand if you want," says a low sensuous voice.

"Get away from me," Affensash says, sensing something terribly wrong in the dark shadow.

"Come here. We need men like you," the voice says, and Affensash can feel her hand brush his cheek.

Panic flushes through his body. His inner voice tells him to run, but he is mesmerized by the sensuous voice. Instead, he stands frozen in the alleyway. He can feel her lips coming closer to his.

A torch suddenly bobs around the corner lighting the alley. Affensash catches his breath when he sees the woman's face clearly for the first time. It is a beautiful ash-white face with full red lips and auburn hair.

She jumps back when the torches appear and runs off into the night. Affensash, abruptly released from the spell, falls to his knees, partially hidden in the shadows. The men run past him chasing the woman.

He stands when they leave, shaking a groggy head, and returns to the inn having saved enough people for one night.

Up the stairs, he gently pushes the door back. Diane's face is struck by the light from the hall. She stirs and rolls over. She is lucky no one came. She is in no condition to defend herself.

Affensash slips in, closes the door, and slides the furniture against it. He starts to tell Diane what happened, but she is sleeping too peacefully to be awakened.

The noise in the street begins to die down as dawn approaches. Affensash checks the room and Diane one last time. Fatigue rocks his bones and he falls against the wall and slides to the floor. He spreads out blankets across the hardwood for a make-shift bed. Ruefin scoots out from under the bed, forgetting about being called a pest, and heads for the comfort of his master's arm.

Sleep edges its way into the corners of his mind. He remembers a peculiar thing Diane said earlier. She said she will feel better when, 'her magic returns.'

That's a curious thing for her to say. In his fading thoughts Affensash, for the life of him, can't figure where her magic could go. One thing is for certain, he thinks, as his eyelids grow heavy, she won't be strong enough to go anywhere tomorrow. It will take her at least another couple of days to be able to get up and around.

Affensash wakes the next morning to the sound of Ruefin wolfing down a plate of sausage. Squinting through one eye, he lifts his head from his roll of blankets and looks around the room. Diane is sitting at a table scratching out words with a long quill pen. She is wearing the same rose pink gown she wore at dinner in Mince. Her hair is washed and pinned up on the top of her head. Every time he sees her like this Affensash is struck dumb and catches his breath.

Diane glances up and sees Affensash, who must have been staring. She stands, running her hands down the edges of her full figure and says, "If you don't like it I can change back to my traveling clothes."

"Ah, no don't think of it," Affensash compliments clumsily. "It's just... I just a ... don't understand how you recovered so quickly. Last night you couldn't lift your head and today ... well," he says getting up, pushing back his rumpled hair.

"I told you my magic would start coming back this morning. I used a little of it to cast a spell to give me more strength. You remember! It's the same spell I cast to help us hold on to the crate when we were tossing around at sea. If you're tired I could ..."

"No, no that's alright," Affensash interrupts, waving her away. "I prefer to be as natural as possible. Not that you're unnatural mind you, but ... ah, you know what I mean." He limps over to the table and begins eating the breakfast Diane placed there for him.

She sits across from him and continues her writing. Between gulps of biscuits and gravy, he tries to tell her about last night.

"We will have to talk to someone first thing this morning. We must know what is happening here," she says going to the window and looking over the now restful little town. "Somehow we need to find the right person to ask. We must be delicate about this, Affensash. Playing into the hands of the wrong people in a town like this could get us killed." She turns and sits back down.

Affensash swallows hard on a mouthful of roll and asks what she is doing.

"I'm writing a note for Laurallin or Johona. We can't exactly hang our heads out the windows and shout for them can we? That wouldn't be discreet. I'll leave this message at a few of the places they are likely to stop by and eventually they should pick it up."

After washing down more roll with a large gulp of milk, Affensash stops and stares at his plate. "Diane, I don't think she is here. I keep thinking that if we really passed her on the road then ... then maybe the pack of wolves was chasing ..."

"Don't think that!" Diane demands. She stands up and walks around the table to place her hand on his shoulder. "You told me she was a Hebelcaan tribesman. I've never met a Hebelcaan that couldn't avoid a pack of wolves. She is fine, Affensash," Diane says, trying to reassure him. "If Johona is here he can help us find her. That's the least I can do to repay all that you did for me last night."

Someone raps on the door with a heavy gauntlet. The door swings open and a fair haired man enters. He stands at the door staring wide-eyed and dumbfounded when he sees Diane.

Affensash bangs his palm on the table and points at the youth. "You see! It's not just me. He does the same thing," he announces, still pointing at the youth staring at Diane.

The man is young; very young. He is tall and slender, wearing a bright chainmail shirt and leather wrappings around his legs. To his side is strapped a full-sized broadsword.

Embarrassed, the youth apologizes, saying, "I'm sorry. They told me at the healer's quarters that I had a new recruit staying in this room." Blushing and apologizing again the young man turns to leave. Ruefin sends a little indignant bark after him.

Diane looks down at Affensash, puzzled.

"Just a minute," Affensash calls after him before the door closes. Getting up and going toward the door, he looks back over his shoulder and pulls out the empty lining of his pocket, as if the action would explain to Diane what he is doing.

"You must be Steven," Affensash says, shaking the young man's hand and pulling him back into the room.

"Yes. Then I am in the right place," Steven says greatly relieved.

"Well, yes and no," Affensash corrects him, going to a chair by the fire to warm his feet from the morning chill. "You see, last night we arrived penniless having just been robbed. Then we needed care for the lady, but as you can see she has made a quick recovery."

"Well I'm happy to hear that," the young man says, obviously disappointed.

"I suppose you have enough to pay for last night's boarding?"

"Oh, I'm sure with her recovery we can scrounge up the necessary coinage," Affensash says feeling quite proud of the way he was handling this.

"Then I guess I really am in the wrong place," Steven says turning to leave.

"Gentlemen," Diane says purposefully, beaming her beauty at the young man. "I'm afraid you have me at a loss. Who is this handsome fellow who has so kindly come to check on my well-being?" She walks up to Steven and extends her hand.

"I am the local constable," Steven says bowing. "The healers told me that I had a volunteer to become my deputy. We have had a lot of trouble lately and I am rather short of men."

Diane turns and looks at Affensash, finally understanding the alchemist's game. Steven was the right person to glean the information they needed.

"This sounds awful!" Diane says. "Please come and sit with us. We were about to come and see you to report our own robbery and tell you about the disturbances last night."

"Thank you anyway," Steven says seriously," but I can't stay. I have more pressing matters to attend to. I am really sorry about the robbery, but it will have to wait until I can take care of other problems."

Steven looks very serious and concerned. Despite his youthful age his words bear great gravity. "I would suggest staying within the walls of the town for a few weeks. Do not venture out of your room at night." Steven turns to leave.

Affensash sees his perfect opportunity to discreetly discover what's going on in town, walking out the door. If he can just find out a little more, maybe he will know enough to satisfy his contract and leave after only one day.

"Wait Steven! If what you say is true and we have to stay that long, then I can assure you we don't have that many gold tams."

Steven's face lights up. "I really could use the help. If you are interested in working for me I could pay your room and board and possibly throw in a few extras."

"I don't know," Affensash says scratching his head. "What do you say, Diane? Should we walk with the Constable and see what services he needs performed?"

Of course Diane agrees. The whole thing seems too perfect. They should be able to get information about Johona or Laurallin and take care of business at the same time.

Affensash grabs Ruefin by the scruff of the neck and drops him in his pocket. Then he straps his case to his back. Steven advises Diane courteously to change if she is going to work for him, and provides her with a less presumptuous dress. He and Affensash wait in the hallway until she is finished preparing.

When she finally reappears, the three walk down and out of the inn. At the inn's front door, Steven bends over and picks up two pails of whitewash and hands them, with brushes, to Diane and Affensash, smiling.

"You need help painting?" Diane asks in total disbelief.

"Now just a minute," Steven interrupts before she can complete her train of thought. "Come with me and I think you will understand."

Affensash rolls his eyes, fearing that his whole plan is collapsing, but Diane signals to play the game a little longer.

As they follow Steven down the streets, Affensash notices for the first time the unusual architecture of the town. The buildings are clean and well kept, especially when you consider that this is a mining town. Lining the roofs, windows, and doors of all the buildings are wonderfully intricate wood trimming in a gingerbread sort of style. The buildings themselves are painted bright yellows and blues, all trimmed in white.

"Why are there no people in the streets?" Diane asks.

Looking around, Affensash suddenly notices that she is right.

"They are waiting for me to signal from the bell tower," Steven says smiling.

They turn a corner and Affensash notices that some of the buildings have big white splotches marring their otherwise spotless exteriors.

Diane stops. Affensash and Steven continue walking a few paces before they notice her.

"If we are in danger, Constable, don't you think we ought to know about it?" Diane says very determined.

Affensash slowly catches on to what she is saying.

"What are the people hiding from?"

"There is some danger, but there is no need to be overly worried," Steven shrugs in answer. "It seems to happen to dogs and small children mostly. Now Mrs. Teasty, the barber's wife, claims she lost her husband to them, but I think she did the poor fellow in by herself."

He turns and starts walking again, but Diane won't budge. After a few paces he turns back around.

"Don't play games with me, Constable," Diane says through piercing eyes. "What is going on in this town?"

The frenzy of Affensash's newly-learned fears sneaks up on him. In the broad bright sun he suddenly feels afraid.

"There's one," Steven says looking over Diane's shoulder. There, on the side of a general store, is a mud-streaked symbol.

"Smudges!" Affensash stammers. "Everyone is afraid of smudges on the wall." He starts to walk over to the wall when Diane stops him.

"I think we had better listen to what the Constable has to say."

"Every night female wizards come out and write these on the walls. It's worse than the plague. Sometimes they write them with coal or mud like this one. They used to write them with the blood of some poor animal, like a dog, or a neighbor's livestock, until there weren't any animals left. Whatever they write them in, they won't wash off."

"It isn't a wizard who plagues your town Steven. Those symbols were put there by witches," Diane corrects him.

"I don't understand," Affensash says, a little worried, hardly believing there is any real danger. "Steven said they are made by females who use magic. You say witches."

"Affensash, I'm surprised," Diane says. "I am a female -wizard."

Steven's eyebrows arch in surprise.

"Can you imagine me scrawling something that crude on the side of a building?"

Both men stand silent.

"You better say no," she smiles. "Remember, Affensash, I also told you that to be a magic-user you must be born with the ability to shape and change the aether. You know I belong to the 'True Ones' Guild and they teach me to discipline my natural abilities. Witches are born with the ability, like me, but have never received any education or training for their talents. Their magic remains weak and limited. Witches are usually more of a menace to themselves than to anyone else because of their ignorance. If one gets out of line it's common to enlist the services of a True Wizard to show them the errors of their ways."

"Wizards or witches, it doesn't matter what you call them. The creatures who write these symbols are powerful and dangerous," Steven interrupts. "These symbols cause fatal illnesses to men, and cause children to disappear. We used to encourage witches to live in this town. We had so few women anyway due to the harsh life. It was mostly witches who helped our carpenters with the architecture. It was they who insisted on the cleanliness. Many of them actually worked as healers."

"Somehow, some way, they became powerful. It seemed to happen overnight. As they became more powerful they also changed the way they behaved. Bad things started happening," Steven starts to choke.

"We drove them off to the mountains." Steven pauses again, "Many of their husbands left with them."

"Is that about the same time the wolves showed up?" Diane asks, trying to connect the two.

"It's hard to say," Steven replies, scratching his head. "I think the wolves were there before, but we didn't really start having trouble with them until the witches were driven out."

Steven pauses and thinks again. "Let's get this symbol down and talk later."

Affensash slips his case from his back. "Hold on just a moment. I want to try something." Affensash fumbles in his case and takes out a long hollow reed.

"Be careful Affensash," Diane says a little worried. "That symbol is a crude copy of a rune of power. The father of my Guild, Elder Edla, spent most of his life interpreting the ancient runes. I learned on the Isles that if properly duplicated, they can be a very real danger. This one is very crude, but parts of it are correct."

Affensash nods his appreciation for the warning, then dips the reed into a vial and sucks up a yellowish liquid. Placing a finger over one end, the suction holds the liquid inside the reed. Cautiously he walks to the symbol.

"That's close enough!" Diane warns.

Affensash starts wobbling as if he were standing on the edge of a cliff. When he regains his balance, he places one end of the reed in his mouth and his finger on the other end. Slipping his finger down, he leaves a little crack and blows a fine mist towards the symbol.

A gentle cloud floats towards the symbol. The edge of the cloud touches it. The little droplets start to sparkle, white and amber. Suddenly they hiss and the whole cloud burns white hot and vanishes. A docile swirl of smoke climbs upward.

Everyone stands motionless. In time Diane asks, "What's next?"

Affensash stands in front of them and says nothing.

"Affensash! What's next?" Diane repeats.

"It wasn't supposed to do that," Affensash says in timid tones.

"Just back slowly away from it," Diane coaxes, realizing that Affensash may be in trouble.

Affensash takes his first step stiffly backward. The next two follow rapidly. He pulls out his book and starts copying the symbol.

"Let me try now, Affensash," Diane says smiling.

Walking to the wall, she passes her hand slowly near the symbol but never touches it.

"You're right Steven," she says still looking at the muddy splotches. "I can feel power pulsing from it."

"Can you make it vanish?" Affensash asks.

Diane studies the symbol, quietly contemplating the possibilities, "I might be able to, but my powers have not fully returned. Let's not tip them off that I am here."

She steps back and examines it again. "It really looks like any other witches scrawl," she says very puzzled. "I don't understand why it is so powerful. You two had better stand back. This particular symbol is copied after a rune that does harm to men."

After magic and alchemy have proved inadequate for the moment, she turns to a more tried and true method. She grabs a brush and paints.

Diane turns to Steven and says, "Maybe there is something we can do for you after all, Constable."

Diane and Affensash decide to return to the inn. Steven says he will go to the bell tower and after he has signaled the town he will join them. On their way back to the inn, Diane seems to be concentrating deeply, and Affensash doesn't bother her.

The bell sounds just as they make it back to their room. The people begin their daily routines.

Diane goes and sits down on a chair by the table, still struggling with the riddle of the powerful scrawls.

"My spell must be wearing off," she says rubbing her forehead. "I'm beginning to tire."

"Tell me more about witches," Affensash says sitting across from her while pouring warm wine from a decanter.

"I've told you about everything you need to know. They are women just like me but they are untrained. They haven't any books. Most of them can't read. They usually know one or two special spells that aren't very powerful. Without anyone to teach them they just stumble along, learning by chance what little they know about magic. They choose to do good things or bad things just like any other human. Regardless of what spells the witches know, they are still no threat to a True Wizard," she says mechanically, trying to convince herself that the laws of magic still hold.

"A wizard worth his salt would probably know the same spell and would be better able to cast it because of our training. We manipulate the aether more efficiently. If this is the weird disturbances Elder Enchantraen wanted investigated, Johona will be mightily disappointed. He probably got bored and left." Diane rubs her head again. Through eyes half closed she asks Affensash to help her into bed. "I think I will rest a little before I cast my next spell."

"You are going to be all right aren't you?" Affensash asks holding her hand.

"Well of course, dear Alchemist. I'm just tired from the other night. I'll just close my eyes. You may talk to me if you wish."

Concerned for her health, Affensash pulls a chair from the table and sits beside her. Diane smiles, as she recognizes his concerns.

"What were those wolf men that cornered me at the gate?"

"I don't really know," she says a little confused. "Normally I would say they are werewolves, but we heard them howling all day long. Werewolves don't come out in the day."

There is a long silence as they both consider the events of the last several days, trying to find a common link. Diane starts to slip off, and Affensash still concerned, thinks of another question.

"That reminds me. Why did you refuse to make a pact with those fire creatures at the charred line?"

"Goodness you have a lot of questions," she says, getting a little perturbed. "That's altogether different than witches. Those were demons!" she states, as if that should settle that.

"I don't understand."

"Demons are the inhabitants of other worlds. Wizards have learned how to summon demons from other nearby worlds. One world in particular, called the mirror plane, is a favorite. When these demons cross over they are not bound by the physical properties of our world. This allows them to do things that we cannot. To one such as you, demons appear to be very magical, but they are not. At least not in the True Ones sense of the word. Demons do not rely on aether or spell casting. Some of their abilities, however, are unique and powerful."

"Then why not make a pact to find out who summoned them the first time? It might have been nice to have such powerful allies."

Diane opens her eyes and laughs, "And so goes the age old trap. It seems so convenient doesn't it? Make a pact for a little information and then just forget about it. Sorry Affensash, but it doesn't work that way.

Demons are very persuasive. Usually much more persuasive than the ones you saw. Once a pact is made it cannot be broken. When they do something for you, you must do something for them. While you still owe them you are the one under their power. They usually wait and hover unseen around you to ask for the favor when you least want to give it to them. To get rid of a pesky demon you need a more powerful demon to control it. Even a cooperative demon is sometimes replaced by a more powerful one. After all, if you are going to have allies why not make them the most powerful ones you can find? And so the cycle goes, continually spiraling downward. Constant contact with a creature from another world affects both creatures' minds. No, Affensash. I will make no easy pacts with demons. There are plenty of good reasons why the True Ones Guild bans such practices."

"What kind of powers do these demons have?" Affensash shudders, remembering the night he saw her conjure them up one by one. Taking out his book once more he begins to write.

"It really varies. Apparently, the mirror plane has many types of inhabitants. Each one is affected differently when it is brought over to our world. No two kinds of demons are alike."

"Demons, werewolves, and witches," Affensash says shaking his head. "That's it! " Affensash announces in a sudden revelation. "The witches have learned a summoning spell and have called a demon over to help them."

Diane thinks a moment and then smiles. "No Affensash, I don't think so. That spell is particularly complex and requires a skilled manipulation of the aether. I'm fairly certain that even the luckiest and talented witch could not do it. That also doesn't explain the wolves. I could understand a witch being duped by a demon already here, but... "

"Don't be so quick to criticize the Alchemist, Diane," says a light and airy voice.

Jumping up, Affensash spins around looking for the intruder. Sitting in the chair by the fire is a man in a crimson robe. He has a handsome face with a well-trimmed beard and moustache. His hair is wrapped in a yellow turban.

"Johona!" Diane says excitedly, jumping from the bed and running to him. She leaps to throw her arms around him. She is shocked when her hands pass through his translucent body. She steps back bewildered.

"Please give me a chance to explain," he says chuckling. "I cannot be there with you so I chose to visit you the only way I know how. What you see is a vision being transported by telekinesis. I am not too far away. I thought you would like it better than a letter."

"Oh, I do, I really do Johona," Diane says, overcoming her initial shock. "When may I be with you beloved?"

Johona's face becomes very serious and he turns away. "Soon, very soon. I am staying with the Yeti up in the mountains."

Diane can see the buttoned tufts on the chair through Johona's lucent body. "I think your friend may be closer to the truth than you realize. I have been studying the problem for some time now and I think I have a reasonable way to solve it."

"Wonderful," says Diane turning to Affensash. "You see, Affensash, I told you he was a dear. Maybe you can leave here soon after all?"

"Johona, have you seen my wife? Her name is Laurallin and she was traveling with a caravan when it was attacked."

"No, I am sorry I have not. But I will spread word to the Yeti to look for her in the mountains."

"What are the 'Yeti'?" Diane asks, her eyes shining more brightly than Affensash has ever seen them before.

"The Yeti are the kind mountain folk of the Pentacles. It is through their powers that I am communicating to you. They hide from the townsfolk, but they tell me that a man there by the name of Steven can start you in the right direction. Once you get up here I will send them out to escort you the rest of the way."

"We will come immediately," Diane says exuberantly! "Is there anything you need?"

"Get your hands on as much silver as you can find. They are having trouble with wolves up here," he replies.

"Oh Johona, I can't wait to be with you. Why haven't you written or gotten in touch with me before now?"

Johona's spirited shape turns its face from Diane, the flames of the fire flickering through his image.

"Don't be afraid of the Yeti. They look like large hairy creatures, but they are really quite kind and gentle. They don't know my name. Instead they call me 'Imparshe'. Diane there is something you must know." Johona's image turns to face her. His mouth moves but he can't find the words to say. "There has been an accident..."

Diane walks to him and moves her hand as if to comfort him. She wants to touch him. Her heart is breaking.

A black shadow passes through the image of Johona. He looks at her with endearing eyes and starts to speak, and then his image fades and is lost.

Someone knocks on the door. There is a long pause then a second knock. "That's probably Steven. Come in," Affensash calls.

"Sorry I'm late. I was stopped by the butcher who wanted to report some stolen meat," Steven says, entering the room rubbing his hands for warmth.

Diane is standing by the fire with her back to Steven when he enters. When she turns around, he can see for the first time that she has been crying.

"I'm sorry," he says, honestly disturbed by her tears. "It looks as though my timing is still bad."

"Sit down, Steven," she mutters. "I'm all right. Actually I'm just happy." Sniffling a little, she motions for him to sit in the chair Johona first appeared in.

Affensash is silent, not knowing what he should or should not say, remembering the warning to keep a low profile.

"It doesn't look like we will be able to help you just yet. I just received word and I must leave shortly. Affensash could stay and help if he wants," she says realizing that he doesn't have to accompany her.

"No! I think it better that we go together. I'm sure Steven will tell me if anyone else shows up from our caravan," Affensash says, mistaking Diane as trying to get rid of him.

"Yes I can do that, but I really don't advise leaving these walls. Between the wolves and witches I don't think you can survive a trip back to Mince," Steven says very concerned.

"We aren't going to Mince. We are headed for the mountains," Diane states flatly leaving no room for argument.

"I am very sorry to hear that. What could possibly attract you to the mountains other than your own deaths?" Steven asks, grimly fidgeting with his boots.

"We are going to visit the Yeti. You are going to give us directions," Affensash jumps in, afraid the conversation will go sour before they can get the information they need from Steven.

"That is quite a visit indeed," Steven says, obviously taken aback by Affensash's statement. "The Yeti don't accept visitors. They like to keep to themselves."

"Well we have someone special waiting for us there. His name is 'Imparshe'," Diane says. Taking a pen she spreads paper out over the table. "Please, if you would kindly show us the way."

Steven stands, rubbing his chin. "I can show you the directions, but I can't tell you the exact location."

"That will be fine."

"The road you traveled here runs north and south. The same road leaves the town on the north and travels up to the top of this mountain. That section of the road is in ill-repair. We don't go up there anymore. It leads to an old mining site that has been closed for decades after many of its tunnels caved in. We call it 'Death Watch' in reference to all the widows who saw their husbands and sons die up there. Avoid the road and the old mine. Travel instead to the west of it about a mile. Follow the side of the mountain and keep as straight a line as possible. The Yeti tribe is somewhere out there," he points to a section of the paper to try and give Diane a general idea about the distance she must travel.

Diane picks up the paper, folds it neatly, and puts it away.

"Please stay just a little longer," Steven pleads. "I have sent for Eastern soldiers. Maybe they will escort you. At least stay and let them rid the area of the wolves."

"Thank you for your concern, but that just isn't possible. I have to see someone right away," Diane says turning to Affensash with a twinkle in her eye.

Affensash remembers that Diane was asleep through most of the night and doesn't seem to understand the danger Steven is warning them about. Affensash knows enough about her personality, however, not to try and interfere once she has made up her mind.

Ruefin sits gnawing on the edge of Affensash's robe. He bends down and picks him up.

"Steven, could you watch Ruefin while we are away?"

Diane looks quizzically at Affensash. Affensash and Steven exchange a knowing glance, both realizing the potential danger. Steven shakes his head yes.

Scribbling something on a new piece of paper, she hands it to Steven.

"Please be so kind as to fill this list for me. We especially need the silver. You can have the third horse we used as a pack horse for payment." Diane smiles broadly.

Leaning over, she gives Steven a peck on the cheek. "It is kind of you to be so concerned, but we have to leave as soon as possible."

Red-faced and flustered, Steven can't seem to refuse her and turns to run her errands.

"Imparshe," he says mumbling as he leaves and walks down the hall. "That's odd. I believe that's Yeti for 'crippled one'."

CHAPTER FIFTEEN

The Order of Beasts

These creatures can or have been teleported from other planes. This fact means that demons are not bound by the natural laws that exist on this world. This is why most demons appear highly magical and have large amounts of magical defense.

- Creature Descriptions from the treatise of High Fantasy

When Laurallin comes to she finds that her nightmare is far from over. Her hands are bound and she is being half-dragged, half-carried over rough and snowy terrain. In leaps and bounds, the wolf-beasts scale the cliffs that Kenlin and she had found so difficult to cross. The night hides most of the pack from her sight. Laurallin guesses that an elite subgroup of the original pack is taking her to her destination. They howl and bark around her, darting in and out of sight.

They take turns carrying her. She often sinks through their grasp. Each time her feet touch the ground she tries to run to avoid the scrapes and bruises on her legs. Each time they lift her off the ground her feet are a little bloodier. Listening to their yapping and howling, she discovers that it isn't all senseless barking. They are communicating to one another over long distances. The members of her pack howl and are soon answered by their brothers far ahead. She isn't certain, but she thinks the pack is changing its direction according to how their brethren answer.

Sleek and gray, the wolves run tirelessly, panting and howling in never-ceasing rhythm. They are immune to Laurallin's outbursts of pain and crying. They don't care how they get her to whatever place they are taking her, as long as they get there soon.

At one point Laurallin tries to twist free and run. The wolves holding her snarl viciously and nip with their fangs, cutting her neck, leaving her bleeding even more. She soon stops any resistance and uses her strength to try and survive the mad rush through the night.

Hours pass, and onward they scramble over cliffs and barren rock. Laurallin's natural strength is working against her for the first time. It is keeping her conscious when all she wants to do is faint to escape the agony. Her body becomes so tormented that she starts to hallucinate. She remembers seeing a man dragged by a horse one time. When the horse stopped, she remembers sympathizing with his pain, but she never really thought about the fear he must have gone through while being dragged.

Faces spin around her, coming out of the cold night: Kenlin, Affensash, and baby Dannia. How in god's name can she miss baby Dannia when she is in so much pain? She does miss her and she wishes she were home feeding her right now.

A sudden revelation comes to her. She is going to die.

Pain!

A wolf drops her and her legs slide across sharp rock. She kicks, but can't get her footing. The pace is too fast. She stumbles and the front wolf drops her. Her body slides across the snow and down into a gully. She lies there feeling numb from the waist down. For a moment it feels like she is in her warm bed with Affensash snuggled beside her and Ruefin curled up at the bottom, warming her feet.

Thick calloused claws grab her and pick her up. They are running again. At last, thank god, at last she is fainting.

Why she comes to again she doesn't know. The sun is shining and still, the pack is running. Running and panting. She was right. There are only ten or less wolves in the pack. They are on level ground, possibly the road. The pack stops and drops her. Her head twists to the side. It is Glenwall staring at her. She doesn't even know why she asks. To someone who is dying it seems like a foolish question.

"Where are you taking me?" she pants, barely able to form the words.

"Good," he smiles. "I thought we were losing you. Drink this, you will feel better."

He shoves a wineskin in her mouth and Laurallin drinks involuntarily before she discovers that it isn't wine.

"That should keep you going for a little while. We are taking you to a safe place to hide you. You are going to be the bait for your husband and his foolish helpers."

Laurallin looks up dazed.

"Yes, I know your husband. Just as I have told you before. I have even tried to kill him three times," he laughs through white, fang-like teeth. "Your husband is quite a resilient fellow. Twice I sent demons after him on the Mystic Isles. Can you imagine that? I nearly killed him under the very nose of Enchantraen," Glenwall says with a mad light gleaming in his satanic eyes.

Laurallin doesn't understand any of this, but she stares, unable to look away.

"Your husband travels in dangerous circles. My master is not as worried about him as he is about the wizards that accompany him. I told him it would be no problem. If we get the alchemist, the others will follow, and we can stop them all."

Glenwall grabs his head and shakes it as if in sudden pain. He rises and walks away.

Laurallin vaguely sees him mount up. She laughs, coughing blood with it. Great father, she thinks. The bastard's riding a Hebelcaan mare. It is not a full-blood mare, but it has Hebelcaan blood just the same. She wonders if the tribe's profit from selling the horse to an Easterner was worth the price she is paying now.

"Pick her up and be more careful. Keep her alive a little longer." Glenwall shouts then turns and rides off.

Oh god, she thinks. We are running again.

The wolves heed Glenwall's orders and are more careful about dropping and dragging her. Either that or Laurallin has become too numb to feel it. The drink Glenwall gave her was bitter tasting, but it is doing its job. Her head is clearer and she is stronger than the night before, despite the fact that she has traveled so much farther.

Finally the wolves stop, easing her down on a grassless knoll. They leave her there for... she can't guess how long. Two crouch in hiding near her, and the others leave to hunt. They return with a downed deer, dragging its carcass less than fifteen feet from her.

The wolves growl and snap at each other, tearing large chunks of meat from the bones with their teeth and claws. Laurallin tries to roll away, not to escape, but so she won't have to witness their gruesome feast. She rolls a small way down the knoll until something in the snow stops her. She looks over to find that she has rolled into the half eaten carcass of a human. With her hands bound, lying in the snow, she can't roll away.

That is all Laurallin can take. She starts screaming uncontrollably until claws lift her and place her back on top of the knoll. She doesn't know how long she laid there screaming. She only remembers that Glenwall suddenly showed up and forced the wineskin in her mouth again.

Gladly, she drinks deeply, pleading for more just before passing out.

When next she opens her eyes, she realizes her hands are free. She is leaning up against something. Behind her she hears Glenwall fumbling with leather straps. He jerks her arms back and tries to tie them. He curses again. Looking over her shoulder, she sees him growling and chewing on his fingers. They look thick and hairy. Obviously, they have lost some of their dexterity because Glenwall can hardly force them to tie the knots.

When he is finished, Laurallin has the presence of mind to know she could jerk free if she can summon the strength. Looking around at the snarling pack, she realizes that she has no place to run, and trying to escape would only cause her more pain.

Glenwall sits slumped behind her still chewing and examining his fingers.

"More please," she says through dry parched lips.

Glenwall comes around in front of her, his lips curled up in a smile. He looks more human now than demonic as he did during the night. He places the wineskin in her mouth and Laurallin drinks, sucking at the opening to take it in quickly.

"Easy," Glenwall smiles, "this is very addictive. Soon you won't be able to live without it." He grabs her chin and lifts it. "Maybe that doesn't matter so much anymore," he says with a laugh. "Just stay healthy long enough for us to get word to your husband. He may want proof that we have you before he will come."

Laurallin isn't sure whether it's the false strength of the drink or the fact that he is so openly using her to kill someone she loves. Whatever it is, she is glad for it, because she suddenly wants to live again. She doesn't want to become a feast for these beasts.

Through a raspy dry voice Laurallin says, "Don't worry, I will live just long enough to see you die. My husband is coming."

The wolves are lying around at the base of the knoll. Their stomachs are full and they doze, sunning themselves in the spring sun. They are curled into balls with flies buzzing around their ears. Occasionally, they twitch and yawn, or lick their lips, while stretching a hind leg. Laurallin can see them clearly now. They are not wolves. They are twisted mimics of men. They are a hairy mockery of the natural order of beasts.

The snow is melting around the base of the knoll, uncovering more carcasses and bones of animals and humans alike. Glenwall sits beside her staring at his hands and blinking at the bright sun.

After hours of rest, Laurallin finally speaks again. "Why would you want to kill them? Is it because of my husband?" she asks staring boldly at Glenwall.

Glenwall turns and looks at her, his face calm and looking very human. "It's not because of your husband; it's because of what he was sent here to do," Glenwall says, pulling up a walking stick and fiddling with the bark.

"It seems you know more about this than I do," Laurallin says, lifting her face to the sun, soaking in what little comfort it can offer.

"He was sent here to take notes about my master. I probably could have sent him sailing back to the Isles with a head full of the wrong information except, you see, your husband takes very good notes. We will take his life and the lives of Diane and her fiancé. We will also take his book."

"Who is Diane?"

"Diane is a True Wizard like me, except that she is a fool. She is traveling with your husband because she fears for his life," Glenwall laughs. "She doesn't realize it yet, but by accompanying him, she has all but signed his death notice. I can't fool her or Johona. I will have to kill them all."

Laurallin shudders at Glenwall's cold, callous way of referring to death. He said it emotionlessly, talking about it as you would talk about fixing lunch. "You aren't a True One, Glenwall!" she says with venom in her throat.

"You are right," Glenwall says, standing and wheeling in front of her. "I used to be just a True Wizard but now I am more."

He paces in front of her lifting his arms. "I am physically stronger than ever. Youthful blood is flowing through these veins. My spells are much more powerful." He bends down and looks Laurallin in the face. "Did you know I'm a fourth plane wizard by True Ones standards? Hell, I can cast spells now more powerful than the Elders themselves," he says nearly shouting.

"You are a dog boy," Laurallin says quietly under her breath.

"What did you say?" Glenwall asks, not believing what he heard.

"You sweep kennels and play trainer to a pack of dogs, Glenwall," Laurallin says shouting now. "Look around you. These things are neither wolves nor men. They are beasts, sick and depraved beasts like you!"

Glenwall slaps her across the face. Laurallin thinks about breaking free of her loose bonds and attacking him, but the wolves start stirring at their shouts.

"What would a herder know about the subjects of gods," Glenwall touts. "I have been given the greatest gift of all! Immortality!"

"Freak! Who did you lose your soul to, Glenwall?" Laurallin shouts back, undaunted. "How many lives did you give away and how many more will you have to trade?"

"I made a pact with Baal, the greatest being to walk this world, and I made it openly and freely."

"So you are in league with a demon," Laurallin hisses.

"Do not call him that," Glenwall says, threatening her with the back of his hand. "I have worked with demons before. I know the difference. Those creatures I called at the fire were demons. The creatures I sent against your husband were demons. I was their master and they did what I bid them to do. When I called Baal over from the other side he didn't want to come. I actually had to persuade him! You would be lucky if he allowed you to join us, but I'm afraid you won't ever be given the chance."

"Are these the men who joined you, Glenwall? Are these pathetic beasts part of your malevolent schemes of immortality? Look around you Wizard. You have dogs serving you and like a dog, you are serving Baal."

Glenwall hits her with a closed fist. Even though it bloodies her lip, she stays seated, resisting the urge to leap at his throat.

"You don't know the half of it. How can you make those judgments?" Glenwall says holding his head as if it is in pain. "He knows the True Ones magic and is better at it than the Elders. He has given me more power. He can take untrained witches and feed enough aether through them to make them equals to the strongest wizards. He is the new Edla. He is the founder of a new magic. We will replace the True Ones. We will do things with magic that have never been dreamed of before," he goes on almost getting frantic in his preaching.

"What new things? Tie women to posts and call demons to drink good men's souls? You are a beast no better than this pack of beasts who serve you," Laurallin shouts refusing to listen anymore.

Glenwall lifts his hand to strike her once more.

"Look at your hand. Go on, look at it!" Laurallin demands.

Glenwall pulls it away shaking.

"Look at the hair and how your fingers grow thick and useless."

Glenwall stares, tears welling up in his eyes. "It is hard to trace the patterns," he mutters softly. "Wizards must trace patterns. What will happen to me if my magic goes away?"

The sun is temporarily blotted out as a large shadow passes over it. Some of the wolf-men lift their heads and sniff the air. Others whimper in their sleep.

Glenwall stands and spins around. A black shadow crawls across the land and stops before him. The wolves leap to their feet yelping, running, and then scattering in all directions. Glenwall falls to his knees. The shadow speaks.

A clear male voice, young and sweet, touched with a tone of importance, "I have found him. Johona is with the Yeti. He gave himself away when he formed his image for Diane. We can take them all in one stroke as soon as they join him. When they are gone we will have enough time to finish our task before the next spies arrive."

"Wonderful," Glenwall says. "When my work is done may we sit together and talk? I am worried about my hands."

"Don't be concerned. I see nothing wrong with you. I look forward to sitting and talking once more," the shadow replies. "We have missed you since we sent you away."

"What shall I do with her? We no longer need her as bait now that you have found Johona."

"If she can serve us no longer, do with her what you will. When you are done, kill her. Remember, the soul is mine." The voice stops, and the shadow fades.

Glenwall turns, pulling his dagger from his belt. Just then Laurallin hears a whinny from a small clump of trees in the distance. A running wolf must have flushed a horse out by accident.

"I could do anything with you that I want," Glenwall grins. "Believe me, I could do things to you that you have never dreamed of." He stops, staring down at her to see if she understands. "Instead, I will prove you wrong. I am no beast! I will kill you cleanly with no suffering."

The dagger lowers slowly for her throat.

Laurallin kicks, doubling Glenwall's knee back. He cries out in pain as he stumbles and falls. With two quick jerks she pulls her hands free and stands. Grabbing Glenwall's stick, she beats him over the back as he clutches his knee, until he collapses.

Frantically spinning around, she goes to steal Glenwall's horse. The wolves are scurrying back now that the shadow has left the knoll. Holding the horse's reins, she starts to mount up.

She can't believe her eyes. Sensie is running up the knoll towards her. She is being chased by two wolves. Her poor friend looks as badly beaten as she does. Sensie must have followed her, the silly creature. Foam is coming from her mouth as she gallops to Laurallin's rescue. Laurallin looks at the fresh horse and then back to Sensie. The wolves are already closing in on her even though she is riderless.

"Silly friend," Laurallin whispers choking back the tears. Why didn't she run off when she had the chance?

Glenwall stirs and starts to rise. Laurallin beats Glenwall's horse on the rump and runs it off.

"No need making it easy on you," she says thinking out loud.

Laurallin whistles and Sensie's ears stand up as she runs. Just as the horse reaches her, Glenwall lets out a low animal growl and springs. Sensie spins around as Laurallin knots her hand in Sensie's main and pulls herself up. The poor horse is soaking and heaving badly. Laurallin kicks at Glenwall and Sensie bolts off, the wolves nipping at her hooves. Sensie is still carrying most of her things, including her bow.

Glenwall is howling his deep demonic song, calling for the pack to chase her. She fires a few arrows at the closest wolves, who then slacken their pace, waiting for the others to catch up. With Sensie's heaving chest, Laurallin knows they won't make it. But this time, she thinks, it is going to be different. This time she will die like a Hebelcaan astride a four-footed friend, instead of dying like some wizard's plaything.

Sensie is running towards a line of trees. Laurallin twists around to fire directly over the horse's rump at the trailing wolves. Sensie suddenly balks.

Just to the other side of the trees is a shear drop off. It is too late to stop and Sensie and Laurallin leap together, plummeting down. Laurallin is caught completely off-guard. She is still turned the wrong way when it happens. She is too surprised to even cry out.

Splash!

Ice cold water flows over them. Laurallin gulps, her lungs full, but rises to the surface coughing it back out. Sensie rises next to her and starts swimming.

All Laurallin can do is to grab onto Sensie's tail as the horse passes her and is helplessly pulled along.

CHAPTER SIXTEEN

A Hero's Reward

There are five planes of spells that are categorized according to increasing difficulty and the amount of aether that must be used to cast them. As a wizard increases in experience, he advances in skill levels and thus progresses from one plane to the next. As he progresses, even his first plane spells he learned as a child become more powerful.

- of Wizards, from the treatise of High Fantasy

The snow has left the boughs of cedars and one by one the limbs rise back into place. The sun turns the harsh frosty ice into cool water that seeps through the grass leaving the ground soft and spongy. Spring is dancing with the sun this day. The warbler sits singing in the tree. Each song makes it spread its wings and puff up shaking its head, as if remembering the sweet grass and the tasty butterfly.

Spring!

The warbler knew it and so did Diane. Despite Diane's sensuous pleas and aggravated badgering, Steven took his time about filling her list. It was harder for Affensash to feel irritated with Steven. Steven thought he was doing it for their own good. The Constable just didn't want them to go, and he especially didn't want them to go at night. He stalls just long enough for daybreak. After the bells have been sounded, things start to move along and the final preparations are completed.

Everything on the list is there except the silver. Steven explains that the town has a great need for the metal and after he gives Diane all the silver coins from his own pocket, she forgives him.

Steven leaves them with a parting remark that will haunt Affensash for some time.

"We really loved the witches," he says, "before we had to drive them out. My wife is up there." Then he kicks the ground and turns and walks away.

The day is clear and sunny, displaying a vivid panorama of the cool mountain view. Affensash is personally glad Steven delayed them. He still has occasional flashes in his mind of the woman in the alley. Last night seemed unusually cold and Diane needed the extra rest.

In an effort to stay off the main road, they travel for hours crossing along the steep side of the mountain. High above them mountain goats are carefully perched on the sides of the lofty cliffs. The pitch is steep and dangerous. At some places they are forced to dismount and walk the horses.

Today, nothing daunts Diane. She sings happy songs, real songs, on her way to see her lover. Diane is in tune with the mountain and its pageantry of spring. It only hurts Affensash. Each verse and smell of new life in the pines reminds him that Laurallin is lost. She is lost and he has no idea where to begin looking.

The wolves howl and carry on, but nothing changes Diane's mood. No matter how Affensash expresses his fears of the wolves and the witches, Diane shrugs them off. She really hasn't experienced either the way Affensash has. To her his explanations sound like an exaggerated tale of an alchemist. She continues to feel safe because, after all, she is a third plane wizard.

Diane continues singing all morning and her tune carries the power of a stream washing over the mossy mountain rocks. By noon the sun pours down, but the pine trees hold up the rays and splay them in cathedral patterns across the ground. They travel on through the crisp scented pines for most of the day. As evening approaches, an irritated Affensash begins to wonder if the Yetl are going to find them tonight or tomorrow. It really doesn't matter because they brought provisions to camp, but the thought of hairy beasts coming for them in the middle of the night makes him feel uneasy.

As the sun rolls along the horizon, the wolves' baying and Diane's unusually good spirits begin to fray more deeply at his nerves.

Diane does most of the work in setting up camp while Affensash looks for firewood; the night will still be cold. He finds a fallen tree and with the help of the horses, he carries large chunks of it into the camp. Tonight he wants a big fire. The wolves are too close.

Diane prepares a wonderful meal from the provisions Steven gathered and Affensash sits watching her across the fire. Even in her heavy woolen coat that she slips on as the sun fades, she is beautiful.

"I'm glad you liked the meal," she smiles cleaning up. "It's one of Johona's favorites. I thought I would practice on you to see if I still had the touch. I'm afraid you might have to eat the same thing again tomorrow night. I plan to fix it as our first meal," she giggles.

It is hard for Affensash to imagine what kind of man could so enamor one as Diane. Affensash could never think of loving someone like her. When this is all over and he looks back on it she will be the one bright spot to remember.

It is a clear night and there is no sign of the Yeti. They sit and chat in small conversation. They are so distant from each other's feelings that it is impossible to speak meaningfully. Diane is still beaming as though experiencing first love and Affensash searches the shadows anxiously.

"The Yeti aren't coming tonight," Diane finally concludes.

"Well if we have to sleep here in the open can we at least sleep in shifts while the other stands guard?" Affensash pleads.

Diane concedes happily, knowing she probably won't sleep anyway. Affensash takes the first watch as Diane lies down with that same irritating smile she wore all day.

Sitting near the fire, Affensash listens to the howling. At times the wolves seem to be coming closer, but they always veer away just before he decides to wake up Diane. His real worry is for Laurallin. What if she is out there and the wolves pick up her scent? Affensash shivers at the thought.

With Diane asleep, he experiences the mountain loneliness. A mass of clouds cross the moon and Affensash sits listening to his heart beat in the darkness.

Alone.

In the morning Diane is cooking again, looking none-the-worse for being awake half the night.

"When do you expect the Yeti?" Affensash asks, stretching and reaching for a plate of food.

"You heard as much as I did. Really, Affensash, sometimes you act just like a child," she chides.

Affensash's ego sinks to his cold feet and he doesn't feel like making conversation for the rest of the morning.

Diane is very good at plotting a straight path through the wilderness. The terrain is very open, but badly slanting, making Affensash feel like one leg is shorter than the other. The trees are the big furry pines. The snow is nearly gone, which makes it easier to spot the Yeti when they finally come.

Affensash sees them first. After his glimpse of them he is glad they didn't sneak up during the night. He stops the horses and dismounts, watching the Yeti appear and disappear through the foliage as they approach.

The Yeti stand over seven feet tall. Their bodies are covered in thick white fur that they shed during the warm months. Already, they are looking shaggy. Their hands are twice the size of any other man that big. Affensash almost laughs when they come near enough to see their faces. The Yeti's most endearing feature is the expression on their faces. Their mouths are always set in what humans consider a smile. The two greet Diane and Affensash with waves mimicking what humans would do.

One of them walks up to Diane and tries to speak her name. The Yeti don't talk. It sounds more like a monkey squeak, but Diane recognizes it. It is Johona's way of telling her that these are the right beasts. Friends. Silently, the two motion for Affensash and Diane to follow.

When the Yeti walk they make no sound. Their feet are covered with such soft fur that the twigs don't break beneath the heavy weight. Or maybe they do break and the sound is too muffled to hear.   Affensash is never really sure.

The horses are able to keep up with the Yeti when the land is level. The wonderful creatures show great patience when Affensash and Diane are forced to dismount and walk. Several times in the beginning the Yeti are forced to retrace their steps when the path proves too difficult for the horses to travel.

After a time they learn to judge the horses limitations and they plan the trail ahead accordingly. The journey is enjoyable and steady. The trip teaches them a lot about the silent furry creatures. The Yeti are able to project their feelings onto others. The whole way they emit a feeling of warmth and calm that affects Affensash and Diane so deeply that they actually feel better-rested the farther they travel. By late evening, Affensash is feeling so good that he starts to sing a little song of his own. He quickly stops though when he notices that the sound is upsetting to the Yeti.   A Yeti loves the quiet. Diane coaxes him into humming and the Yeti seem to prefer that.

As night closes in, they are still walking and have hummed every song the two of them know. They laugh at each other from time to time knowing how ridiculous they must look to an outsider. The feeling of being with the Yeti is too good to resist. It seems like they haven't been this happy for a long, long time.

The wolves are closer than ever, but the Yeti continue onward, totally unafraid. Of course their feelings give Diane and Affensash courage. Affensash is certain he will find Laurallin soon.

The trees begin to thicken and the ground becomes softer and more level. Affensash is sure he would have missed the entrance to their home if the Yeti hadn't taken him right up to it. In a gathering of tall pine trees, there is the opening to a cave.

When everyone has entered the cave, one of the Yeti signals for them to stop. The other goes back to cover up the tracks to the entrance. The fluffy feet of the Yeti are perfect for such practices.

The first room of the cave is quite ordinary. When the Yeti returns, the other rolls a large rock to the side and Affensash, Diane, and the horses enter. When the rock is rolled back the second room becomes totally dark. One of the Yeti tugs on the reins of the horses and neither Diane nor Affensash feel any distrust as the horses are led away.

The remaining Yeti takes Affensash and Diane into a well-lit third room by having them follow him down a twisting, winding trail. Affensash guesses that the trail was made this way to slow intruders and to block any light from entering the second room.

The third room is lit by some type of phosphorescent rocks that glow when the Yeti approach them. From here, they pass into a fourth and then fifth room. Each room is larger and better lit.

At last they enter what must be considered a master hall. The room is bright with several colors of glowing lights. Everything about the Yeti has been so very plain and simple until now. Here the walls are lined with ice and snow chairs, some of them being so elaborately carved that Affensash believed them to be ivory at first. Then he sees reflections off the puddles of water on the floor.

There are several other Yeti waiting here who stand up when they enter. All the Yeti present, five to be exact, circle around Affensash and Diane quietly looking down at them. They seem to be particularly fascinated by Diane's golden hair. One of them tentatively touches it, but then withdraws his hand as if afraid he would harm or mar its sheen in some way. After several minutes of standing and saying nothing, Diane speaks the first word to them.

'Imparshe'

The mood and good feelings of the Yeti change almost immediately. At once, it is replaced by a feeling that frightens Diane, almost causing her to scream.

Sympathy!

"What? Why are you doing this? What is wrong?" she asks, her heart beating erratically.

Unable to speak directly to her, one Yeti leads her into another room where she finds him. He is sitting in the corner of a room lit with yellow phosphorescent lights.

"Johona," she whispers and starts to run towards him.

He raises his hand and she stops. She starts to question but her eyes find the answer first. Johona is strapped to a small wagon. Vines are wrapped around his legs holding him into his seat. The one Yeti in the room starts to emit feelings of gentle understanding.

"Stop that," Diane turns, tears already in her eyes. "I have my own feelings."

Understanding her, the Yeti leaves the two alone.

"I'm sorry, Diane. I tried to tell you that there was a terrible accident. I was all but dead when the Yeti found me and nursed me back to life."

Diane goes over and touches his legs. The bones are shattered. His legs feel lumpy like they have healed together in the wrong places.

"It is unfortunate, but the Yeti are better healers of the mind than they are of the body," he says with a small fragile smile. "You know, until now I didn't even think much about it. The Yeti have a way of making you forget about your shortcomings," Johona chokes turning his head away from Diane.

Diane cannot restrain her tears any longer, but she is not sure why, "I would have been there with you if you had only waited. I didn't get your message." She kneels, cradling his head in her arms.

"It wouldn't have done any good. All eight wizards I came here with are dead. Most of them were a higher plane than you. You would have just been another body."

"What happened? Why didn't you protect yourself?" Diane asks, still sobbing and stroking his hair.

"There is a great beast that hides among the mountains. We threw up our protective spells, but when it couldn't break through, it just swatted us off the ledge," Johona's voice becomes firm but resentful, as if he has told this story a hundred times. "The beast lured us to him, played with our magic, and then tossed us over the cliff. The creature's only mistake was not staying around to see if any of us lived. I did, and I intend to make the beast pay for that mistake."

"Let's go home, Johona. I know healers that can fix this," Diane pleads, not totally convinced what she says is true.

"Diane," he says taking her head between his hands, "There is something up there that intends to destroy everything around it. We can't go back just now. We have a duty, a responsibility to others."

"No Johona!" Diane says jerking her head free. "You always talk about responsibility. Why is everything you do always earth-shatteringly important? Let's be selfish just once. Let me take care of you. You're broken. Eight of our best wizards are dead and you sit in a beggar's cart preaching duty. What about us? What about the small and simple things like us?" Diane stops, determined not to let a cry ruin her meaning.

"That's my Diane," Johona beams. "So gentle, always holding back, afraid to hurt my feelings," he says with a smile. "I know you better than that!" he says suddenly very serious. "You are always the first to give help when those around you need it."

"It is you who needs help now. Let's leave here together. We can tell Enchantraen what we found. When you are better we can come back," Diana says pleading.

"Did you hear that Snow Walker?" Johona bellows. "She still loves me!"

An extra-large Yeti sticks his head through the door.

Infuriated, Diane turns and glares at Snow Walker. The Yeti knows enough about humans to leave.

"This isn't just a childish prank of yours, Johona," Diane says, still not believing what has happened to him. "We have a lot to talk about and a lot to consider."

"I know," Johona says, becoming very solemn. "I wish I could get up and tell you that everything is going to be all right. But I just can't. These damn things won't move," he says, beating on his legs, "and I really can't be sure they ever will. Maybe I really have done it this time."

He stops as though struggling against his own self-pity. "Just listen to me, Diane. There is something up there that must be stopped. You decide, but only after you hear just how important this is. I have nothing to report except that everyone is dead. We must know more before we go back."

Diane holds her head in her hands, confused. This is all too much, too quick. She can't pinpoint her feelings. Is she this concerned over Johona, or is she just being selfish and sorry for herself? She feels as though she has been hurt as much as Johona. She doesn't know why. It will take some time to sort it out.

"Oh, Johona," she cries again, walking over to him and giving him a kiss, "what have you done? You have broken my heart and my world all at once!" Diane grabs him and squeezes with all her strength. She doesn't know whether she should hit him or love him. They sit in each other's embrace not knowing what to say or even what to feel.

Hours pass in a continuous embrace and they learn, if just for the moment, how to accept their situation.   It takes more than hours for such an adjustment, but it is only hours that the lovers have left.

Affensash remains outside with the Yeti. He tries to sit, but without the extra fur it is just too cold. Many Yeti pass through the great hall and soon Affensash is able to distinguish one from another. He begins to understand that there aren't many of them in this particular colony.

Without a formal language to communicate in, Affensash finds it very difficult to befriend the lovable creatures. While he examines the rooms, they stand and watch Affensash as if they expect him to give his approval of their work. Not really knowing what to do, he simply smiles and goes on looking intently around.

After some time in the same room, shrouded in complete silence, Affensash becomes bored and falls asleep.

He is awakened shortly by the sound of two Yeti wrestling in the great hall. At first he is concerned that the two large creatures might hurt each other. Later, Affensash decides to call it 'rumbling'.

Affensash doesn't begrudge them for the loss of sleep. He fell asleep in a great puddle of melting snow anyway. Fortunately, he was awakened before it soaked him to the skin.

When the first match is over, Affensash notices that the victor challenges a new Yeti. Snow Walker, the biggest of the Yeti that Affensash has seen, has won many times in a row. They are playing by some kind of rules that Affensash does not clearly understand.

Soon, Affensash begins to enjoy the 'rumbling'. It is strange to see them wrap around each other until you can't tell a head from a tail. He laughs at the big rolling balls of fur, and that draws the big Yeti's attention. Snow Walker becomes irritated by it and actually challenges Affensash.

Affensash slaps his chest, grabs a big handful of hair and jumps on Snow Walkers back. Darting from one side to the other, Affensash is able to avoid the Yeti's strong grasp. Affensash formulates a plan about how to win the contest and lets Snow Walker catch him. Before the big Yeti can start squeezing him in the traditional Yeti manner, Affensash grabs two handfuls of the Yeti's facial hair, places his feet against the creature's chin and pulls. Shortly, Snow Walker is forced to let him go. Affensash looks around the room like a Yeti victor looking for the next challenge.

Just then Diane reappears looking very tired. Her soft blue eyes are lined in red from crying. Her face still carries the look of shock. Affensash stands in the glowing light unmoving. The last thing he expected was to see Diane like this. He is too stunned to react.

Snow Walker walks past her on his way to the room where Johona is staying. His long white fur brushes her face, waking her from her state of shock.

"Oh Affensash," she says crying and running to him with open arms. She buries her head in his shoulder. Affensash's vision is suddenly blocked by a blonde blur of hair and he does the only thing he can. He folds his arms around her and holds her close, comforting her from some unknown ailment. He gently strokes her hair saying nothing until the sobs subside.

"I was holding him and we were talking. He just suddenly fell asleep in midsentence," she says choking back the tears.

"The Yeti say that all of his internal wounds haven't healed," comes a voice from a shadowy doorway.

Affensash releases Diane and prepares for the worse. He knows that voice. Glenwall walks out of the shadows and stands in the full light. His rich robes are clean and his hair is freshly washed. He smells of heavy perfumes. Diane and Affensash stand riveted to the rock floor.

"I am very sorry for Johona," Glenwall says, "I told him we should leave this place for the Isles immediately, but he won't listen."

Diane walks forward, her mouth still open, "How, how did you get here?"

"What? No hugs for an old friend?" he asks lifting his arms.

Diane goes to him giving him an uneasy embrace.

"The ship weathered the storm. I made for shore as soon as I could to see who survived. I know it was wrong and I should have gone back to the Isles and reported what happened, but I was worried sick about you. I found poor Terrell's body, and naturally feared the worse for you and Affensash. After my men couldn't locate you, I headed for Mince. To my surprise, I found Laurallin waiting for you also," he half-lies, pointing, then walking toward Affensash.

"Is she with you?" Affensash asks, forgetting all else.

"No, I am sorry she is not," Glenwall says lowering his head in mock sympathy. "On our way to High Tower we were attacked by wolves. The wolves were accompanied by a demon. As I battled with it, the others ran and we were separated," he lies again in a deeply touching tone. "I have been wandering the mountains looking for you."

"What do you mean... *they* ran?'" Affensash asks, not knowing what to make of his story.

"She is with a handsome young man named Kenlin," Glenwall goes on.

The name is one that Affensash recognizes and therefore adds believability to the liar's tale.

"They escaped with the wolves hot in pursuit. I can't tell you if they survived."

Affensash sits down on a cold wet chair looking down at the floor. He has been hit doubly hard. The wolves were chasing his wife while he rode right by her. She is now with Kenlin. He can only hope her old boyfriend can keep her safe.

"How did you get here?" Diane asks, still suspicious.

"When I was running and hiding through the mountains, I came across a pack of those wolf-men attacking a Yeti. They had the poor creature down and half torn apart before I could chase them off. The creature led me here only yesterday and died before the others could save him. You can't imagine the shock of finding Johona here. If it wasn't for him, they probably would have left me wandering the mountains alone. Johona said he knew and trusted me so they brought me inside."

Glenwall walks over to Affensash and places his hand on his shoulder. "I'm sure she is all right," he continues in his masterful lie. "Once we finish this thing of Johona's, Diane can take him back, and you and I can go looking for her."

"Thank you, Glenwall," Affensash says, feeling very sick.

"This whole thing has really taken a turn for the worse. Maybe Elder Enchantraen will let you go home? Has the Elder contacted you yet?" Glenwall asks, slyly interjecting his real concern about Affensash. Glenwall knows he has to avoid alerting Enchantraen too early.

"No one has contacted us, Glenwall," Diane interrupts. "We haven't been in one place long enough."

Diane squares away in front of him and crosses her arms. "You realize that most of our troubles happened because you failed to complete your spell on the ship. We have nearly been drowned at sea, frozen to death on a mountainside, challenged by demons, and chased by a pack of wolves several times since then!" Diane says sternly, expecting a detailed explanation.

"Is that why you are treating me so badly?" Glenwall asks with an innocent expression. "Is that why you are questioning me? I feel bad enough. I lost a good friend too you know," he says, raising his voice in reference to Terrell. "I have also nearly been killed several times looking for you and praying for your safety. I didn't have to risk my life pitting myself against those wolf-things every day. Can you throw away my friendship because I failed in casting one spell in the middle of a raging storm? If you can be so heartless then we should all be without friends in this cold harsh place," Glenwall says, turning his back to them with a fake choke in his voice.

Diane goes over and puts her hand on his shoulder, "I am sorry old friend," she says ashamed of herself. "We have all been through a lot and have lost so much. We have to pull the pieces together and go on from here."

She motions Affensash to come over as Glenwall turns back around. She puts one arm around each of them and hugs them together. "We can do it. We must be strong," she says.

Affensash is still uncertain, but is moved by the moment.

Glenwall gives Diane a kiss, sealing her fate.

Snow Walker enters the room. Glenwall sees him first.

"He wants us to go in and see Johona now," he says to the others.

"How do you know?" Affensash asks, turning around to look at the Yeti.

"After you have been with the Yeti, they let you know everything they want you to know. By tomorrow you will be able to understand them too."

They walk together back to the room where Diane first saw Johona. He isn't there, but Snow Walker points to a hidden doorway towards the rear. They pass through it and Johona is sitting behind a large ice block table. There are large stones covered in sticks positioned around the table.

"I told Snow Walker that humans prefer to sit on something other than chunks of ice. He was kind enough to help me with these," Johona says smiling the whole while. He keeps his eyes locked with Diane's, trying to read her real thoughts.

They file in and sit down. "I'm glad we have all finally met. I trust we are still friends?" Johona asks in a weak voice, looking directly at Affensash.

Affensash ignores him and instead concentrates on the table top. It is a carving of a map. It looks to him like a map of the Pentacles, or at least a part of the Pentacles. It is an ice map in detail.

"It is a shame that the Yeti spend so much time on these ice sculptures," Johona says observing Affensash's reaction. "The spring heat will penetrate these walls soon. I guess it mirrors their feeling of life.

Nothing is permanent. It is all temporary. Beauty is for the moment, and the moment is worth spending all your efforts on to make it wonderful. Each year they carve the ice, working in the intricate detail, knowing full well that in the spring it will be gone. They don't seem to mind. They seem to have a feeling that collecting and hoarding such items would somehow enslave them to this world. You can look around and see that the Yeti have no real possessions," Johona muses.

"Can you imagine if these were done in precious metal," Glenwall breaks in. "They would be worth a king's ransom."

To Affensash, it seemed that Glenwall completely missed the point. "A King's ransom maybe, but it would be the King's men coming to steal them," Affensash challenges, trying to shed a little insight on the Yeti ideals.

"Unfortunately, the Yeti are not why we are here," Diane says. "I think Johona has some news for us."

A sick look comes over Johona's face. Everyone around the table becomes silent and Diane's sarcasm hangs heavily in the air.

Johona takes a deep breath and looks around at everyone's face.

"When I first arrived at High Tower the local people flocked to me pleading for help. Husbands, wives, and children were missing, and more were disappearing every day. I led a group of eight wizards up into the mountains accompanied by a larger group of townsfolk. We captured a wolf and tied the beast down. As all of you have seen, these wolves are not common. Some of my companions worked their craft on it and were able to temporarily dispel the enchantment."

"The wolf turned back into a man. The townsfolk recognized him as one of their missing people. The strangest part of all was that we could not cure the poor man. Imagine that. Nine skilled wizards could not remove the mark of the beast. He turned back into a wolf within moments. We eventually had to destroy the poor creature when all of our attempts failed."

"I sent the townsfolk home, realizing for the first time the real potential danger. Then I led the wizards on up the mountain. Several nights after we had captured the wolf, we found a large desecrated area on the side of a cliff. It looked like a bonfire had been lit. We sifted through the ashes and found bones, a lot of bones." Johona stops and looks around the room, catching the eyes of each listener to make sure they caught his point.

"The bones all belonged to children. We buried what we could; the ground was still frozen then, and looked for clues as to what happened. We found markings and scrawls on the ground and rocks that made us think of witches, but there was also evidence that something else had been present."

"We found a trail leading off in this direction." Johona points to an area of the map.

"That leads to the old mining area that Steven called 'Death Watch'," Affensash breaks in.

"Yes it does," Johona confirms. "Along the trail, we found a woman lying in the snow. She was an ordinary woman; looking very much like the townsfolk we sent away. She was half dead and nearly frozen. We managed to revive her. When she came to, she looked at us as though we were going to harm her. Apparently, she was involved in the debauchery that went on at the bonfire. We started to question her when she uttered one simple, seemingly harmless phrase. She said 'Forgive me Baal.' Each of us could feel the change immediately."

"The air became supercharged with aether. The woman threw off the wizard holding her and stood up. She seemed immediately healed. Her simple looks had been heightened. She was no longer plain, but vibrant, beautiful, and as we quickly learned, a witch. She raised her hands to cast a spell. Her words were clumsy and her patterns sloppy, but when she released her binding spell it flew at us with such force that five of us immediately fell, wrapped neatly in her light-blue web."

"The four of us remaining attacked. Against her, our spells were weakened. No binding spell of ours would hold her. Neither sleep nor paralysis nor control could stop her. She laughed at our efforts. Suddenly, she was called away and vanished right before us. Nine wizards stood on the side of a mountain staring at each other in disbelief. We had just been eluded by, of all things, a witch. Dumbfounded, we released our friends and continued on up the mountain."

"The next day we detected a great force somewhere in the mountain. We attempted to probe it with our magic. That was our undoing. Whatever it was became aware of our presence and attacked. We threw up our defenses, but it broke them down one by one. Then, when it was done playing with us, it knocked us from the cliff like you would a fly from the wall. The rest I have already told you," Johona concludes, staring at his legs.

No one speaks.

"I have thought about it a lot since then. From what I recall, and from what I have been able to gather, there is a beast hiding in those mountains. The beast is a demon named Baal. It has the ability to use and manipulate the aether in a way no wizard has ever known. It can feed unbelievable power to witches and cut short the spells of True Wizards. It can charge men with power, giving them strength and cunning, causing them to walk night and day with the mark of the beast on them."

Johona's eyes blaze. "It uses the wolves to clear the mountainsides of any intruders. The packs have killed most of the wildlife and are hungry enough now to start attacking the town. The beast plays with the witches, learning all it can about our magic. It has learned a great deal. It is learning more. When I use my magic, it is able to find me and strike at me from a distance. It was the beast that cut off my visitation to you, Diane."

"It has stopped me every time I try to call magically to the Elders for help. I have been among the Yeti long enough to be able to sense it. Every day I smell the air and it is stronger; deadly and malevolent: evil."

"Then I think it is clear," Diane suddenly stands, "We should leave this place now. We should go and warn the Elders and let them decide what to do."

"Exactly," Johona says, expecting her to say that, "except for one thing. It won't let us! I have tried to leave this place several times and it tracks me down. The Yeti have lost three of their kind to the wolves protecting me. We must leave, but Glenwall and I have devised a plan that we must attempt first."

Diane shoots a knifing glance at Glenwall.

"Now wait," says Glenwall defensively, "I only suggested this after I tried to get him to leave this place."

"Hear me out Diane," Johona says, "I think the beast is a demon, even though I have never seen it. I also think that this 'Death Watch', as the townsfolk call it, is the demon's gate. We want to go here," Johona points again to the map. "With the three of us, we could create a magical wall to trap the demon in its lair. The beast might not be expecting that, and it should at least buy us enough time to escape and warn the others."

"That would mean getting closer to this – Baal!" Affensash thinks out loud.

"Not a pleasant thought, but our only alternative is to run headlong down the mountain without a plan," Glenwall says, defending Johona's idea.

Diane sits back in her chair smoothing her robe. "Nice Johona. Very nice. What we have is wolves, witches, and demons preying on the poor simple folk of a town. We can rush in like heroes and save the day," she says sarcastically.

"Stop it, Diane," Johona retorts with a trembling voice. "I am sorry about what has happened to me, but don't let that muddy your thinking. It isn't as simple as 'saving the day'. It is also our best chance of getting out of here alive. You do want out of here?"

Diane stands, her eyes starting to tear. "Excuse me," she says quietly and walks out.

Affensash follows after her. He catches up to her in the main hall. She is standing in a shadow, weeping softly. "I am so sorry, Diane," Affensash says.

"It's hardly your fault, gentle alchemist," she half-laughs. "I am so mixed up right now. I thought I was stronger than this."

"His plan sounds reasonable ..." Affensash starts to say.

"Oh his plans always sound reasonable. Look at him. He's the crippled one. I'm sure that was a reasonable plan too."

"Don't be so harsh on him," Affensash says firmly. "The injuries are to *his* body after all."

This only makes Diane feel worse and Affensash is sorry he said it just as soon as he is done.

"Can you think of anything else to do at this point?" Affensash asks, putting his arm around her.

"I can't think at all right now," she mumbles through more crying.

"Talk to him some more," Affensash says persuasively. "Listen to him with your head and let your heart rest. He needs you; we need you."

"You're right, Affensash," she says calming down. "This is too important to let self-pity get in the way."

"I will go along with anything you decide. I really can't make a judgment on these magical matters. There is one thing though that I don't agree with you about."

Diane looks at him very puzzled.

"I don't trust Glenwall."

"Why? It was I who told you he should have completed that spell. I trust him. Johona trusts him."

"I don't have a clear reason. I just sense something. Maybe it's because his robe is so bright and clean. If he really has been suffering as much as he says, why isn't it soiled and dirty?" Affensash questions.

"Because I changed it when I got here," says Glenwall stepping from the doorway where he was obviously eavesdropping. Glenwall crosses the hall and stands menacingly over Affensash. His eyes are piercing with unspoken threats. "If you doubt me, alchemist, come out into the open with it."

Affensash takes a step back from his intimidating glare. Diane hurriedly steps between them.

"He is only thinking about me, Glenwall. We have been through a lot together. He speaks to me as a friend, and it is between friends that his doubts will remain," she says, turning him towards Johona's room.

Glenwall shakes his head. "It's no good trying to talk with Johona now. He fainted shortly after you left. It would be better if we let him rest."

Glenwall turns back around to make certain Affensash can hear his words. "With Johona so weak you will need my help badly. I haven't told anyone yet because it hasn't been confirmed by the Elders, but I am now a fifth plane wizard."

Diane's eyes widen.

In a calmer voice Glenwall says, "Johona told me he wants to try his plan in the morning. He feels that the beast knows his whereabouts and that it will be coming for him soon. Sleep on it. In the morning we either go with Johona's plan, or make a headlong run back to High Tower. We can't stay here."

He walks over to the wall and picks up his walking stick. "I am going to scout the area and look for any signs of the beast's coming. Let me know what you decide in the morning." Glenwall turns and is gone from the hall. Unknown to Diane and Affensash, he is smiling quietly to himself.

Affensash walks up to Diane who is still looking out the door Glenwall exited. "I still don't trust him."

Diane turns and kisses Affensash. "Thank you for your concern. I'm going to stay with Johona tonight. I will tell you anything else I find out."

Affensash blushes, but says in earnest, "If you want to go, that's fine. I promise you that while you do your work I will guard you from Glenwall."

Diane gives him a weak smile and disappears into Johona's room.

It is impossible to tell what time it is in these caves, but Affensash is bone-tired. He searches the hall for a comfortable place to sleep, but can't find anyplace dry enough. He finally gives up and starts searching through some other rooms. He finds Snow Walker sleeping on the floor of a room near Johona's. The creature looks so comfortable that Affensash walks up and lies down next to it.

When the Yeti doesn't move, Affensash rolls over and loses himself in the creature's soft warm fur. With the Yeti emitting good feelings, Affensash is soon drugged with sweet dreams and has the most pleasant night of his journey.

CHAPTER SEVENTEEN

Falling Angels

The general theory is that aether entwines the world in a fine mesh. This remember is only a theory and is denied by many knowledgeable wizards outside the True Ones Guild.

- of Wizards, from the treatise of High Fantasy

In the morning Affensash is awakened by a gentle tugging on his shoulder. He brushes away the fur and sees Diane smiling down at him. The first thing he notices is the red outline of her tired blue eyes. Affensash and Snow Walker stand up and stretch in unison.

"I have talked it over with Johona and I've decided to go with him to cast the spell," Diane says very seriously.

"Good. I'll get my things and we'll be off," Affensash says with a yawn. The big Yeti shuffles on out of the room bumping against a rock, not quite awake.

"You don't have to go if you don't want to," Diane reminds him.

"What! Do you think I'll have a better chance running back to High Tower alone? The wolves would catch me before I could get an hour from the cave," he says teasing Diane hotly. "Honestly," he says smiling now, "I said I would go with you and I meant it. I knew that it was going to be dangerous even before we left High Tower."

"Thank you, Affensash," she says with an earnest smile wrinkling her forehead. "I thought about running back to High Tower, but after being in that town I know it can't offer us any real protection. We would be as trapped there as we are here."

Snow Walker comes back pulling the wagon he built for Johona.

"Hello, hello friend Affensash," Johona says jubilantly. His hair is wrapped in the turban that Affensash first saw in the vision. "Diane told me a lot about you last night. It seems that she has become quite fond of you. You better watch it though. With my new pair of legs," he says pointing to Snow Walker, "I can still give you a pretty fair run for her heart."

Affensash is too ashamed by the statement to say anything witty in reply.

Diane is not amused either.

"It will be good to have a handpicked man of Elder Enchantraen's along with us; even if you are an alchemist," he chuckles and extends his hand. Affensash shakes it, saying nothing. Snow Walker pulls him away. Just before they exit through the door that leads to the great hall he calls behind him, "Don't be late! We leave promptly in one hour."

Once he is out Diane turns and smiles again at Affensash, "Don't pay any attention to him. He never really had a good sense of humor. He has a good heart despite all his other faults. He is also the best fourth plane wizard I know."

Affensash smiles, discovering for the first time, that he has learned how to relax in her presence. "Will the Yeti come with us? We could use their protection against the wolves."

"Snow Walker is the only one. The rest are moving from this place. The weather has changed and they feel exposed now that humans have discovered their habitation. The Yeti are not fighters, despite their size and strength. It is probably better that they don't go."

Affensash is disappointed, but finds some solace in the fact that the one Yeti will be Snow Walker. He really doesn't want them for the protection. They're just good company for a trip like this.

"Affensash," Diane says, "I'm scared."

The statement was so simple and so unexpected that Affensash once again is at a loss for words. He just walks over and puts his arms around her. After a reassuring hug, Diane leaves to prepare for the trip.

Affensash eats a cold breakfast of early spring berries. When he is finished with his meal he walks through the cave looking for the Yeti.

After some time he becomes afraid of getting lost in the twisting passages and turns back. Alone in the quiet dark passages, he decides that they have already left. He is very saddened by that fact. He somehow feels he has been cheated. He wishes now that he didn't leave Ruefin back with Steven.

Out in the great hall Affensash finds that it is also deserted. He hears voices from the entrance and discovers that the hour is up and everyone is waiting for him. Johona looks bright and cheerful. If you didn't know better you would think they were on their way to some social event. It is only Diane, and naturally Snow Walker, who are silent. Glenwall is the first to see Affensash.

"Very good! We are ready then," says Glenwall.

Picking up his walking stick, Glenwall starts up the mountain. Affensash follows last. Ten feet away from the Yeti home, he looks back at the cave entrance trying to mark the spot in his mind. It is already difficult to see it. The Yeti are masterful in their concealment. It looks as though all the distinguished terrain features have been removed. Twisted trees, uniquely shaped boulders, and odd blooming shrubs are gone, leaving little to fix the location. Affensash knows he will never find his way here again.

Glenwall walks next to Johona's cart theorizing the whole way about the beast's possible moves and rationale. Diane walks gloomily along, looking very forlorn and forgotten. Affensash walks next to her. Listening to the philosophical discussion, he is the only one who seems concerned about the dangers.

The day is bright and the wind is even warmer than it was yesterday. An oak tree stubbornly lets loose last year's dead leaves preparing for spring. The path they take is not particularly difficult. According to Johona's map, they should near the place they want to start the enchantment before the day is over.

Once the spell is cast it will take another day to make it back to High Tower. They plan to travel through the night to make the best time possible. The spell they cast will only contain the beast. They have to make every moment count after that to get as much distance between them and 'Death Watch' as possible. Johona estimates that they have to make it back to Mince, because from there they should be able to get word to the Isles and the Elders.

Affensash tries to break Diane's moody silence. "When this is over, will you be able to help me search for Laurallin?" he asks hopefully.

"I don't know, Affensash," she says as if suddenly awakened. "I suppose I will have an obligation to get Johona back to the Isles where he can be properly cared for." She sees Affensash's obvious disappointment and quickly adds, "But let's wait and see how things turn out. I would like to help you if it is at all possible. We should be able to ask the Elders for help also."

Once talking, Diane finds it difficult to stop. All night and all day she has been thinking about the beast in the mountain. The words spinning around in her head come tumbling out of her mouth. Affensash isn't sure he understands it all, but he listens intently like a good friend.

"This Baal seems to be a demon from another world with the power to manipulate the aether. You remember what the aether is, don't you, Affensash? It's the magical power that surrounds us. It's what the wizards use to shape their spells. This demon, a beast by all accounts, seems to have the ability to direct the aether, cut it off, or channel it in any direction it wants to. It's almost as if it can see the aether. Wizards can't see the aether; we can only feel it and know when it's around. Can you imagine that, Affensash?" Diane asks shaking her head.

"No, ah, I really can't. I'm afraid I don't follow your concern."

"To openly confront a beast like that with magic would be like a blind man attacking a gladiator with a sword. Both opponents have a sword, but the blind man has to grope around before he can strike. The gladiator on the other hand, just waits for the blind man to make a mistake and plunges his sword in the first opening. If it's true, that beast could see our weaknesses and plunge for the opening at its convenience! It could toy and play with us at its leisure!"

"Maybe we should turn back," Affensash says feeling very cold.

A wolf bays not too far away.

"We won't be any better off if Johona is correct in his assumptions. Believe me, all night I tried to refute his logic and find another, more passive way. I couldn't." She suddenly chokes and looks down.

"He will be all right," Affensash says, mistaking her sadness.

"Oh, I'm sure he will. Look at him up there. He's at the height of his glory. It's me I'm ashamed of. I never thought of myself as a cruel person. But when I saw him ..." she chokes again. "I didn't feel the least compassionate. He brought this on himself by his own ambition. I wanted to dash his dreams just as he has shattered mine!"

"Well that just disproves another alchemy theory," Affensash says, taking an exaggerated breath.

"What do you mean?"

"It just proves that wizards are people like anyone else. I was wrong about you, Diane. When I first saw you I thought you an angel. You even had me going a couple of times. You're not. You're just a woman. But you know, I think I like you more because of it."

Diane wipes away a long tear, looking down at the ground. She reaches over, grabs his hand and squeezes. They walk that way for hours saying nothing, listening to little pieces of conversation between Glenwall and Johona, and watching for a chance wild flower and perhaps the fairies dancing beneath them.

By noon the wolves get uncomfortably close. Johona's head suddenly tilts back then falls forward. Diane and Affensash rush forward, but it is Glenwall who checks him first.

"He fainted again," Glenwall says and motions for Snow Walker to keep going.

Diane tries to tilt Johona's head into a more comfortable position, but it is so limp that it just bobbles with each bump of the wheel.

"What's going to happen if he faints like that when you are trying to cast the spell?" Affensash asks with pity in his eyes.

Glenwall laughs, "We will simply have to cast it again. We aren't going up here to call the beast out and challenge it. We are only going to get close enough to cast a spell to cage it up. If we do it right we will be halfway down the mountain before it even knows we were there."

"It won't be that easy," Diane breaks in. "We have to get dangerously close before we can cast the spell. Affensash, your concerns are well-founded if we are spotted by the beast. We will need Johona's help to fight off the beast's minions no matter how mighty Glenwall has become in our absence."

The surrounding hills are suddenly alive with barking and baying wolves. Affensash spins around, but can't see any of the creatures.

Infuriated by Diane's interruption, Glenwall decides to ride ahead, saying he will check the surrounding area for any traps or danger. He tells them he will be back in an hour.

Johona starts to stir in his wagon. Diane props his head up and walks along beside him.

"We will travel this way for most of the day," she explains to Affensash. "We will come up the side of the mountain and step back onto the road just in front of 'Death Watch'. There, in the road, we will cast our spell."

"Will it hold the beast?" Affensash asks.

"I have never known or heard of a creature that could break this spell once it is cast. From what I've heard of this demon, I'm not sure. I'm going through with the plan because I still believe it is our best chance."

Johona stirs again and opens his eyes.

"Johona can be persuasive at times, but I know how to tell him no when he is wrong." Johona smiles and Diane tenderly kisses him and wipes his forehead.

When the terrain becomes too difficult for the wagon, Snow Walker simply picks it up and tucks it under his arm. Several times they are forced to climb up the sides of cliffs on their hands and knees. Snow Walker knows these mountains like no other and is able to pick the easiest trails. Johona is wide awake now and talking nonstop just like before. By noon they come to a large tree where they stop for a last meal to keep up their strength.

Glenwall returns.

"The wolves are all around here," Johona says covering his eyes from the sun and peering across the countryside. "What did you see when you were scouting?" he asks Glenwall, still looking around.

"I thought I was chasing a few of them, but I never really saw any. I don't expect any trouble from them. I'm sure they sense our power and are afraid to attack."

"I'm not so sure," Johona says, suddenly fixing his eyes on one location.

Affensash sees Johona's hand move in a blur of motion. A light-blue flash follows and the tip of his finger lights in a small flickering flame. He flips the flame in the direction he is staring. The flame jumps from his hand and rockets away, growing as it picks up speed. When it hits the top of a boulder, it is a full-sized fireball and explodes, knocking a chunk of the rock away.

A sudden yapping emits from behind the boulder. A wolf leaps to the top of the rock fully aflame and howling in pain. Totally enveloped in fire, it leaps from the mountainside and free falls downward like a blazing comet.

"Maybe they will keep their distance now," Johona chuckles.

Affensash turns to Diane with his mouth open. "I've never seen anyone trace a pattern that quickly."

"I told you he was good. He can almost cast two spells to my one. Even though I'm biased, I would rather have Johona with me to fight this thing than another fifth plane wizard like Glenwall."

Glenwall doesn't seem to hear her remark and continues his meal without a word.

The rest of the day is spent traveling through considerably harder terrain than before. They are mostly going up over sheer rock cliffs. Affensash has to help Snow Walker balance the wagon. The Yeti has the strength, but climbing and holding the cart upright is a little like balancing a teacup on your head. The hand over hand exertion tires everyone quickly. They are wizards after all, not soldiers. Their power is in the mind, not the body.

A large ledge provides a moments sanctuary.

Everyone, including Johona, is silent, trying to save their energy for what is ahead. Affensash can feel the tension mounting in Diane the closer they get. Every now and then he catches her mumbling phrases of the spell they are going to cast; practicing to relieve her nerves.

Glenwall is doing surprisingly well. He seems relaxed and, out of all of them, the least taxed by the climb.

The drop behind Affensash is far and frightening. He thinks instead about the lofty mountains and spring. He tries to recreate Diane's feeling as they traveled to see Johona. With each panting breath he tries to recall the smell of green.

By late evening they are close. Affensash knows they are close by the expressions on Johona's and Diane's faces. They crawl to the last plateau and rest.

"Up there is the road," Glenwall whispers.

Affensash looks up and before them is the steepest cliff yet.

"Affensash, why don't you stay down here until after we cast the spell? You will be much safer if anything goes wrong," Glenwall says trying to sound concerned.

Affensash looks at Glenwall, then at Diane. Locking his eyes with Diane's he says, "No thank you Glenwall. I'll take my chances with the rest of you up there."

Diane smiles and Glenwall shrugs it off.

Everyone sits silently collecting their thoughts. The wolves are howling, but none of them bothered to follow them up the steep cliffs. The wizards are confident they possess the power. The probability of over-kill is what has made this trip so philosophical.

It is Johona that finally breaks the silence. "It is now or never. Let's go and get this over with so we can all relax and have a warm meal tomorrow at High Tower."

Diane kisses him and after a long embrace they begin the last climb.

All goes well as they near the top. Affensash struggles to help Snow Walker balance the wagon. The big-hearted Yeti doesn't seem to tire or begrudge his burden.

Glenwall looks down to Diane and says that he will go on up to scout for trouble. He doubles his speed despite his bulk and soon disappears up the mountain. At last, the rest of them reach the plateau and the road.

Tentatively, Diane steps up first. Glenwall is nowhere to be seen.

Affensash climbs up next, breathless, and Snow Walker follows with Johona. Affensash looks across the road to the other side. It isn't nearly as steep as what they just climbed and might be a good way to escape if things go wrong. All four of them crouch behind a boulder, looking and waiting for Glenwall.

They can see the entrance to the old mine. It is dark and deserted, with evening shadows already covering nearly a third of it. There are wolves up here. Affensash can hear them, but they are not howling as they were below. Their sounds are muffled and subdued.

"Are you sure the beast is in there?" Affensash finally asks, feeling very tense himself.

"Oh, yes it's there all right," Johona replies. "Its' stench is strong to a wizard's nose. I'll wager that this is the place the beast was first summoned to our world."

Suddenly, Glenwall reappears, climbing down from above them. His abrupt appearance causes Diane to catch her breath.

"There are wolves up there, but so far we are unnoticed. This place is asleep. We better not wait or they will catch our scent and be after us before we can complete our work."

Johona looks deeply into Diane's eyes and an unspoken love passes between them. With the help of Snow Walker, Johona is lifted out of hiding onto the road.

The other wizards follow. Johona in his wagon, with Snow Walker standing behind him, are closest to the steep cliffs they just ascended. Diane is standing beside him holding Johona's hand, and Glenwall is standing next to her on the far side with his walking stick at his feet. They are all facing the mine's entrance. Affensash remains a few feet away still in hiding.

Johona lifts his hands and the others follow in unison. He begins the chant purposefully, going slow so that the others may follow him. It is important that they all complete the spell at the same time to make it as potent as possible.

Affensash watches breathlessly, a million thoughts racing through his head. He watches Johona calmly lead the chant until the blue patterns begin to form in the air. Diane's face is locked in a deep expression of concentration, carefully matching her patterns with Johona's.

Only Glenwall seems to be aware of what is going on around him. Although he traces the same patterns, he is continually looking away; first up the cliffs and then over to Diane.

Johona's last words suddenly ring in Affensash's ears as he watches the wizards trace and retrace the patterns. 'I'll wager this was the place the demon was first summoned to our world.' He begins to wonder who would summon a demon like that to menace the world. If the witches could not do it, it would take a very power-hungry wizard to take that kind of chance. Glenwall said he was now at fifth plane and more powerful than ever!

Affensash sees Glenwall's face clearly for the first time. He is staring at Diane, his lips curled in a wolfish grin and his eyes gleaming with lust.

Affensash moves! He is too late.

A dagger appears in Glenwall's hand from nowhere. Diane, concentrating on her spell, doesn't see it until the dagger is buried deep into her chest.

"No!" Affensash screams, already halfway there.

The cliffs spring to life with howling wolves. Two of them jump down on Snow Walker. They leaped from so high that they strike the Yeti with enough force to knock him off balance. Snow Walker and the wolves tumble down the cliff together.

Diane falls to her knees, holding her hand over the hole. The blood runs through her fingers.

Johona comes out of his trance and starts to react, but Affensash reaches Glenwall first.

Glenwall raises the dagger to strike again. Affensash leaps between them and catches the dagger in his arm. The pain burns and Glenwall howls in fury, throwing Affensash to the ground.

Johona stops the charge of four wolves with the wave of his hand. They die as they run. Ten more wolves leap to replace them and he is overwhelmed.

Glenwall's dagger strikes Diane again. More blood gushes. She kneels there stunned, looking up at Glenwall.

"No!" Affensash yells again and stands up, grabbing Glenwall's wrist. With demon-like strength, Glenwall forces the blade down, ripping up and down Affensash's collarbone. Affensash's hand goes numb and Glenwall shoves him away.

Diane has sunk to a sitting position, staring at her own blood running down the road. Glenwall strikes again and again. Tears are streaming down Affensash's face. From the corner of his eye he sees Johona being drug over the cliff by the wolves.

Affensash's good hand lands on Glenwall's walking stick. With a cry of anguish he swings it wildly, striking Glenwall's arm holding the dagger.

Glenwall grunts in pain, and the dagger flies from his hand and clatters across the road. Enraged, Glenwall wrestles the stick from Affensash's hand. He strikes Affensash in the midsection and then swings down across the back of his neck.

Affensash falls, fighting to stay conscious. He is crying openly now in pain.

Glenwall turns back to Diane who is lying flat on the ground, but with her eyes still open, knowledgeable about what is happening.

Helpless.

He strikes her with the stick across the face and starts to bludgeon her around the head.

Affensash mechanically stands, not knowing Diane is dead. Glenwall howls satanically and Affensash stumbles into him.

"Get away maggot!" Glenwall screams in fury. He lifts the stick and strikes Affensash again and again. Each swing is bone crushing, but Affensash refuses to fall.

Quickly and silently, help flies through the air.

Glenwall suddenly stops his blood thirsty beating and staggers back. Through the blood streaming over his eyes Affensash sees an arrow transfixing Glenwall's throat.

Affensash hears a rain of arrows fall around him and the wolves running for cover. Looking down the road, in the darkening shadows of the coming night, Affensash barely makes out the form of the single rider on a horse.

Laurallin!

Sensie races up beside Affensash and Laurallin jumps down. Without a word, Laurallin boosts Affensash on the back of the horse. Affensash weakly protests, but then he sees Diane lying peacefully on the ground.

Laurallin is back up on Sensie sitting in front of Affensash. "Hang on Aff. We are going home," Laurallin yells as Sensie wheels around.

Glenwall stands in the great horse's way, pulling the arrow from his own throat. Sensie rushes ahead knocking him down. Two hooves trample the fallen body.

Laurallin looks back over her shoulder and sees the wizard rise and motion for the wolves to pursue them.

A howling pack jumps from the cliffs and fills the road, no longer stunned by the surprise attack. Sensie runs full out down the road leading to High Tower.

Affensash has his arms around Laurallin's waist, fading in and out of consciousness, barely aware of the wolves' pursuit.

On they run through the closing night with the pack from hell baying after them. Laurallin tries to loose some arrows, but her husband's swaying body ruins her aim. Finally, she ducks low over Sensie's neck letting the brave horse run her heart out.

Affensash looks back under his arm rubbing the blood from his eyes. The wolves are gaining. He realizes through his clouded mind that Sensie cannot carry both of them and escape the pack. He looks again and the wolves are closer. He decides to sacrifice himself to save his wife.

They ride further as Affensash tries to regain control of his muscles. He can nearly feel the wolves' breath hot on his back. He decides that he will fall from Sensie's back. His body will slow the wolves and with less weight to burden her, Sensie may be able to carry Laurallin to safety. Even in his fading mind he knows that the horse will at least die trying.

CHAPTER EIGHTEEN

Death Do Us Part

They can only be hurt by silver or magic.

> *- Creature Description, from the treatise of High Fantasy*

"Hang on Aff! We're going to make it," Laurallin shouts encouragement to Affensash.

In his blood-filled mind Affensash smiles thinking, *I know you will; I know you will.* He squeezes her slim waist remembering how good it has felt to hold her all these years. Then he lets go.

A horn sounds ahead of them. Laurallin feels Affensash slipping away and grabs for him, righting him on the horse.

Affensash hears the horn too. He looks over the top of Laurallin's back and sees why she said they were going to make it. A patrol of Eastern cavalry lines the road ahead of them. Their pennants held high, Affensash sees them regrouping into a charge formation.

The man-wolves see them too. In their beastly brains they quaver, recognizing the danger, and begin to falter.

The wolves lag behind and the soldiers part to let Sensie run past them. The Captain shouts an order and they skillfully reclose the line. Laurallin lets Sensie canter to a halt.

She and Affensash slide to the ground together. They smother each other in kisses, each thankful to be together at last.

When they pull apart they see each other closely for the first time. They look terrible. Both of them are cut and badly bruised. They both start crying, each for the other and begin hugging each other again. Sensie stands frothy white and quivering beside them; her muscles twitching from fatigue.

Affensash's wounds are the most recent, and bleeding badly. Laurallin shreds pieces of her clothes to bind and stop the bleeding.

Affensash tries to speak but his lips are swelling from being struck several times across the face.

Laurallin places her hand over his lips with a look of understanding.

The Eastern horn blows. Laurallin kisses Affensash on the forehead and then stands to watch.

The Captain has ordered a charge and the soldiers' race forward in a precise line. They hit the wolves with the full impact and weight of the horses behind their piercing lances.

The wolf pack scatters. The wolves who are hit growl and fight fiercely. The wretched beasts won't die by normal lance or bow, but they feel the pain. Laurallin sees some of the soldiers dragged from their saddles. One wolf tears at the flesh of a soldier even though the soldier's lance protrudes through both sides of the wolf's body. Still, the wolves are quickly routed and Laurallin is relieved to see that the Captain calls back the soldiers who broke rank to pursue them.

"There is no need chasing something you can't kill," he shouts at the soldiers.

From up the road an abhorrent light begins to glow. It starts as a dim red vestige and continues to spread like a wild cancerous growth. The horn sounds and the patrol reforms into their riding formation. A soldier gallops to Laurallin's side.

"Your horse looks spent," he says looking down at Laurallin and her bleeding husband. "Take a couple of our horses. You will have to keep up or the Captain will leave you behind."

The soldiers are already passing by them retreating to High Tower. He motions and another soldier rides up with two horses. Affensash tries to rise, but can't. Laurallin, with the help of the soldier, lifts him to the saddle and quickly straps his legs around the horse's belly to hold him on.

The last of the patrol passes and Laurallin mounts up, grabbing Affensash's reins. She gallops quickly after them desperately trying not to fall too far behind. Sensie follows Laurallin with no prompting.

Peering back over his shoulder, Affensash sees that the glow has spread to the size of a frightful setting sun.

Laurallin is so exhausted that she can barely ride. The wolves have hounded her unceasingly for days. She only managed to escape them by walking up and down in the mountain streams; that tactic, and of course Sensie's unbelievable ability to run. But every time she left a stream, a new pack would pick up her scent and hound her once again. She looks over her shoulder at Affensash and thinks proudly, *I got him*!

The patrol is going at an excruciating pace; too fast to continue it all the way to High Tower. Laurallin assumes the Captain is trying to escape the deadening glow. She hasn't slept for days and she knows they are not likely to sleep tonight. Just one more day to High Tower and she and her husband will be safe, she thinks to herself. The irony that her life now depends on the training of the conquering Eastern soldiers is not lost on her. These men know how to fight.

Affensash's wounds are bad. The bandages have stopped most of the bleeding, but he is wildly swaying in the saddle. His face is puffy and blotched. There must be internal bleeding, Laurallin frets.

On into the hellish night Laurallin follows the soldiers retreat with Affensash trailing behind her. The wolves are howling madly, obviously influenced by the loathsome red light. The countryside is glowing, reflecting the light, more frightening than any one of Laurallin's nightmares. She will never forget this night. It's as though the land has been struck by a giant viper and blood-red venom oozes over the mountain.

Laurallin's strength is diminishing, but she refuses to release the reins of her husband's horse. Somehow those thin leather lines have become the only link between their souls.

"Aff, can you hear me?" she would call back from time to time.

Affensash would nod his head, too weak to answer. That was all the encouragement Laurallin needed to keep going. She would not live through this night if he didn't. Now that they are joined together she is certain that the link will hold them to either live, or die, as one.

Laurallin doesn't know how long they flee. The horn blasts, and the patrol comes to an immediate halt.

She slides down and runs to Affensash's side. He is still conscious, but in terrible pain. Every hour on the road he is growing weaker. Laurallin lifts a canteen to his mouth and forces him to drink. The Eastern soldiers are attending their horses. The Captain passes up and down the line making certain the men are doing what is right for their horse and not resting. He comes to where Laurallin is administrating to Affensash.

"Can he ride?" the Captain asks coldly, his face hidden in his helmet.

Laurallin looks up not knowing how to take his meaning. "He can ride, but we need to rest longer. Is there anyone with you practiced in the art of healing?"

"Ma'am!" the Captain sneers, still giving orders. "We have healers, but they will not administer aid to him until we reach High Tower."

"But he is hurt. I think he is bleeding on the inside. He may not make it to High Tower!" Laurallin pleads, imploring him for compassion.

"That would be unfortunate ma' am," the Captain says, again with little emotion in his voice. "I have a duty to my men. I must get as many men back to High Tower to join with the main body of troops waiting there. We must ride hard through the night. We have reports of a huge pack forming in these mountains and we will not be caught out in the open with so few soldiers. I cannot sacrifice my responsibilities to my soldiers for just one man."

"I bet you could if he was an Easterner," Laurallin sneers back.

"That is an opinion we will have to address later. My advice to you now is to keep him as close to the patrol as possible. We will not slow if you fall back, and we will certainly not stop if he cannot ride. Prepare to mount up. If he falls, I want my horse back."

The Captain spurs his horse to the front of the column. The horn sounds and the Eastern soldiers mount up.

Laurallin forces more water down Affensash. "Listen," she says leaning and talking directly into his ear to make certain he hears. "We are going to make it. You sit and relax. You can't fall off the way I have you strapped on."

Laurallin starts to walk away, but she gets no response from Affensash. She goes back to Affensash. "You better live!" she says once again in his ear. "I haven't found you just to watch you die before I can get you alone, " she says and she kisses his face. She sees Affensash faintly grin. She knew if he could hear, that would make him respond.

She mounts up, grabs the reins, and falls in line with the patrol. They ride for hour after hour. The red glow has stopped growing and is actually receding behind them as they run further away. The wolves are still howling, to the point of mass hysteria, but they are moving no closer to the patrol.

Laurallin decides it is going to be a matter of surviving the ride. She checks on Affensash as often as she can. She adjusts the straps that hold him on the horse, but he is still growing weak. Finally, Laurallin herself becomes too exhausted to check on him anymore. It takes all her strength to keep the horses following the fleeing patrol. She wishes someone had strapped her to the saddle as she grows weaker still, and finds herself struggling just to hang on.

The last hours of the nightmare are spent with both Laurallin and Affensash doubled over their horses. Laurallin doesn't know if she is leading Affensash to his bed or to his grave. He hasn't moved or made a sound for a long time. She is fighting fatigue, trying to stay awake. She passes in and out of consciousness barely managing to stay with the patrol.

The horn sounds and then is quickly answered by another! Laurallin strains to lift herself up. It is High Tower! She sees the gates open. She sways and feels like she is going to faint. Not yet, not yet, her mind panics. We are not safe yet.

They pass through the gates and Laurallin hears them close behind her. There are many soldiers who come to lead away the horses. She gets down and staggers to Affensash. Her eyes are blurring and she is unable to focus them long enough to check her husband.

Soldiers help to untie him, and they ease him to the side out of the way. They lead the horses to the stalls. The patrol's soldiers are given orders to proceed to their quarters.

The street is emptying and Affensash and Laurallin lay to the side unnoticed. Laurallin bends over to kiss Affensash, both as a sign of affection, and to see if he is still breathing.

They sit, and still no one comes.

"Help," Laurallin says too weakly to be heard. "Help," she says louder believing they have been forgotten.

"Help!"

Desperately she tries to rise to her feet. If she could just get up and reach the Captain, she would force him to help her. Firm hands grab her from behind.

She looks back and sees a fair-haired young man lifting her.

"Allow me to help," the young man says.

Laurallin turns to face him, but loses her balance and falls. He catches her and eases her back down.

"I am a friend of this man," he says pointing to Affensash. "Are you a friend also?"

Laurallin looks up confused. "Kenlin?" she says, feeling an unexplained fire rush through her aching body. "Kenlin, help us!" She grabs the man she thinks is Kenlin around the legs.

Steven is embarrassed, but understands her desperate delusions. He and a deputy pick both of them up and carry them to the inn where both their needs may be attended.

Sensie is taken away mistakenly by an Eastern groomsman who thinks she is the property of the patrol.

The next thing Laurallin feels is a wet tongue slobbering over her.

"Ruefin!" she chokes.

A woman appears and shoos the little fox away. The woman examines her and then says, "Strip her!" Laurallin tries to fight, but she is too disoriented to be effective. The woman's face reappears in her vision looking down at her. "She can stay," the woman announces.

Laurallin feels warm water and sponges scrubbing her wounds. She winces in pain and tries to kick. Once again the woman's face appears.

"For god's sake honey you have done enough. You brought him here. He's safe! Now relax."

The words 'he's safe' is all she hears. It acts as a trigger to turn off Laurallin's natural fighting instincts.

She did it! Her body has done all she has demanded. Muscles relax and tension flows from her like water through a broken cup. Laurallin smiles, finally allowing herself to do what she should have long ago; she collapses into sleep.

The ways of the world go on around them. Eastern troops march in the streets below bringing temporary peace to the town. New troops arrive to reinforce the ones already stationed in High Tower. The days pass while the healers busily work on both of them.

Laurallin is recovering the quickest. Days later, when the healers finally leave the two alone having done all they could, Laurallin crawls from her bed to lie next to Affensash.

Another day passes and the two spend it together in sleep. The problems of wizards and demons are not theirs for the moment. For now they only have to contend with their dreams and personal nightmares; their love, and violent visions.

On the morning of the fifth day, Laurallin is able to rise on stiff but sturdy legs. Affensash's wounds are healing fine, but his head occasionally burns with a fever from his infections. The fever keeps him weak.

Laurallin checks him and is pleased with his slow, steady recovery. She stretches, feeling life pumping through her veins once again. She pours a pitcher of water into a washbowl.

In the corner of the room she finds a mirror. A real mirror! She walks up to it and stares. She's a mess. Her hair is tangled and her face is smudged and streaked. They gave a nightgown to her to rest in. She unties it and lets it drop around her ankles. With a flip it goes off spinning into the corner.

Standing naked in front of the mirror she is pleasantly surprised. She expected to see large gashes and wounds from the wolves on her legs. Instead, there are slim red streaks that seem to be healing, covered with a light muddy solution.

She turns, examining herself. Her waist has thinned even more, making her breasts seem larger. She runs her hands gently over them wondering if they have actually grown. Her legs are firm and the muscles in her stomach are toned and flattened.

She is alive! What she wants more than anything right now is to be a woman; to be a woman and to be treated like a woman. If she could just bolt the door and keep the world away from them she would be happy.

She grabs a cloth, dips it in the water and scrubs vigorously. She searches the room and finds, to her satisfaction, a rose-colored gown hanging in the wardrobe closet. She pulls it out and examines the size. It is a bit too large in the chest and just a little short. Laurallin doesn't mind. She has never worn anything made of this kind of fabric. Her only alternative is the 'frumpy' sleeping gown or her riding clothes.

Affensash lays quietly for the best part of the morning. Laurallin notices that the healers have covered his knife wounds with thick muddy compresses. It must be the same substance they put on her, except hers was a much thinner solution.

Her heart hurts to see him lying there. At least he doesn't appear to be in much pain. After watching Affensash for several hours, reassuring herself that he is really here, she takes a deep breath and walks towards the window.

She passes by the mirror and catches a glimpse of her reflection. To Laurallin, the gown is beautiful, making her feel the same. She curtsies before the mirror and spins around once with a smile, allowing the hem to fly up and dance around her knees.

She pulls back the shutters and light beams into the room. Spring has quietly come upon them at last. The sun is warm and the air has that titillating tingle that makes everything seem new.

Looking out over the town, she contemplates the terrible days that proceeded. She had been dreaming an awful lot about Kenlin. She is glad that Affensash didn't hear her call his name the night they arrived. She looks over her shoulder guiltily as if Affensash might hear her thoughts. She believes Kenlin is all right. He can escape the wolves if anyone can; Kenlin can handle himself.

She remembers the time he grabbed her in the stream; his arms forcing her to him, breaking down her resistance of right and wrong, the sudden fiery kiss, the power in his body, and his furious passion. Laurallin feels her body flush, starting with her head and moving hotly down her thighs.

She turns away from the window embarrassed by her reaction. The flushing hot feeling turns to little tingling goose bumps.

"It's spring. It's just spring. I want to be home," she says taking a deep breath.

Affensash stirs in the bed and his eyes open. Laurallin rushes over to him wetting a new cloth as she goes. Wiping his brow she says softly, "Good morning, sleepy head. I hope you don't plan to lie around all day."

Affensash looks up trying to shake away the frightening feeling of his deep nightmare. "Diane!" he says, mistaking Laurallin who is wearing Diane's dress.

Whomp! He is hit in the face with the wet cloth.

"No. It's Laurallin! Remember, Laurallin, your wife? I'm the one you left sleeping in her bed. I'm the one who had your child. I'm the one who saved your ass!"

Affensash realizes his mistake and hurries to explain. When he tries to rise, his shoulders wrench with pain and he falls back down with a moan. Laurallin picks up the rag and blots his face tenderly.

"I'm sorry," they say together.

"That dress," Affensash begins to explain again.

Laurallin stands, spins around showing it off and says, "I thought you would like it. You've never seen me dressed like a princess."

"You are lovely, but it is Diane's." Saying her name aloud brings back the sudden terrible memories.

Laurallin's mood shifts to embarrassing disappointment and then becomes very serious. "Was she the woman with you at 'Death Watch'?"

Tears immediately spring to Affensash's eyes and she knows the answer.

"I saw it, Aff. I tried to get there sooner; I just couldn't."

"I promised her I would protect her," Affensash says, choking with a sarcastic smile.

"You nearly did, Aff. You took yourself past what would be expected from a friend. You nearly gave your life trying to keep that promise. I don't think anyone can fault you for that."

"I'm not worried what others might think. I'm the one who has to live with this failure. I should have done more."

Laurallin grabs his head and cradles it in her breasts. "Oh, I see," she whispers, suddenly recognizing her husband's deep feelings for the woman.

Someone knocks on the door and the man she first mistook for Kenlin enters, followed by a healing woman.

"Very nice," says Steven. "I must say Madillyn, you do good work," he says admiring Laurallin in her dress.

Laurallin blushes and the healing woman gives him a 'humph' and goes about her business. Madillyn grabs Laurallin's arms and turns them over in her hands. Then she makes Laurallin lean her head back and stares into her eyes.

"Good! Very good," she mutters, "You are a strong one."

Suddenly, she reaches down and pulls Laurallin's dress up to examine her bare legs. Laurallin catches her breath and Steven quickly turns around.

Laurallin is about to take a swing at the healer when the old woman drops the dress and says, "Let me give you an ointment for those red streaks. It will make them go away and no one will ever know you were scarred by the wolves."

Madillyn turns and sees Affensash's destitute expression. "Color's bad on this one. Is he your husband?" she asks Laurallin.

"Yes he is ..."

"Good," she interrupts. "I don't have time today. You can help me redress his wounds."

Without waiting for a response, Madillyn pulls the covers down, and starts undressing Affensash. Laurallin feels uneasy about that and takes over the job herself. While Laurallin prepares Affensash, Madillyn starts mixing another muddy solution in a bowl.

When Laurallin is finished, the healing woman tosses her a wet rag and a clean bowl. Madillyn shows her how to remove the mud packs and clean the wounds. Then Madillyn examines each wound and, once she is satisfied, rubs on sweet smelling oil that deadens the stinging pain.

"He will heal soon. The worst is over for him," she tells Laurallin, pulling the covers up over Affensash's naked body. "I'll leave you the bowl of solution. Put it on each of his wounds just like you saw me do."

Madillyn stands and turns to walk out. "Come along, Steven. She can take care of your friend. We have many more worse off than these two to see this morning."

Steven bows in an overly grand fashion, smiles and follows her out. Laurallin has a thousand questions to ask the young man, but it looks as though they will have to wait.

"Steven is a good man," Affensash says as he leaves.

Laurallin sits on the bed beside Affensash rubbing his chest. "You look so much better without that mud all over you," Laurallin smiles down at him. The sun shines through the open window striking her hair, stirring a warm natural fragrance in the air.

"I missed you," Affensash says, as if he just saw Laurallin for the first time. He tries to rise again and pain shoots through his arm. Laurallin grabs his head and buries it once again in her bosom. She gently massages his back and neck.

"Hey," Affensash says, suddenly remembering what Laurallin had said on the road to High Tower. "Just why did you come all that way to rescue me?"

Laurallin laughs in surprise, remembering what she said to him while he was strapped to the horse. "I knew that would make you respond if anything could."

Her hands rub down his body until she suddenly discovers just how responsive her husband is.

Affensash tries to rise and grab her in his arms. The pain shoots through him once again and once again he falls back.

"Maybe we will have to wait a little longer," Affensash puffs as he falls back on the pillows.

"Maybe and maybe not," Laurallin laughs, swinging her bare legs across him on the bed.

Affensash reaches up and gives her a long tender kiss. The long separation floods through their bodies.

Laurallin throws the covers off the bed and lifts her dress.

Affensash places his fingers to her lips and says, "Not with that dress on."

They stare at each other with compassion, each feeling the other's pain and desires. Laurallin smiles lifting the dress over her head, and tosses it. It lands on top of the nightgown in the corner.

Laurallin is a child of a nomadic tribe; an educated tribe, but still full of time-worn tradition. She lays sixteen candles around the room. The glow chases away the spiritual darkness with dancing ambers. The time of a husband wife reunion is supposed to be special. The glow is to remind them that together they are unique. The feeling is one of being removed and set away from the world. With a deep sigh she holds him in her arms.

After dinner that evening Affensash is tired and in need of much rest. He spends the rest of the day trying to explain to Laurallin what happened to him. The only problem with the explanation is that Affensash still doesn't know everything to tell.

Affensash tries to explain that they took him away from her to become a spy. "Maybe not a spy," Affensash blushes at the word spy; the word doesn't seem to fit with Affensash's image of himself, "a scout to report on any odd occurrences happening in the Pentacles."

They both got a good laugh at that statement.

"Exactly to whom I'm supposed to pass the information onto is still not clear."

He tries to explain the discovery of Baal. The fear is still real and not too far away. It creeps along the shadows' edge and reaches for him in the candlelight. He can't find the words. Nothing in Affensash's vocabulary comes close. Saying that it is a demon that can manipulate the aether is too academic. The demon is more than just a threat to magic. It is a repugnant beast that feeds on the weaknesses of men. It captures spirits and twists them into ugly perversions of humankind. It is the visage of death; a ghoul in a mask of terror.

"There is already death in this world and enough injustice without inviting more. This new power for destruction must be removed, cut away like an unwanted growth, and sent back to haunt its own world."

Laurallin listens, not fully understanding. She feels the fear though. Brave words, but fear none-the-less, that conjures up her own personal nightmares.

Even now Affensash does not care about magics and their uses. But when he tries to talk about the people actually caught up in the struggle it is different. He can tell Laurallin about Elder Enchantraen and Jabir. He can even explain Glenwall's twisted mind and how he struck again and again with the knife long after it was necessary. But when he tries to say the name of Terrell or Johona it becomes difficult. It is impossible to say Diane's name aloud.

"I have failed her," he says over and over again. "When she needed me I wasn't strong enough." A light breeze stirs the candles. "I tried to tell them that I was an alchemist not a hero. I am just an alchemist." The words tumble out and lie quivering on the floor. He is like a dying man confessing his sins.

Laurallin listens astutely with as much caring in her eyes as is in her heart. He is fighting for his sanity and she can see that.

Change is coming.

It tears at his cocoon, threatening to throw him prematurely into the unjust world. Glenwall's dagger hacks at his laboratory door. There will no longer be an easy peace for Affensash within those four walls.

She knows what is best for Affensash. For now it is best to listen to him; to listen and try to understand. Affensash may have a lot of weaknesses, but one of his strengths is what he is telling her now. Not the words so much, but how he says the words. That shows the real meaning of his character. She already knows he doesn't care about politics or magical cult struggles. What concerns Affensash is what always concerns Affensash; it is hurting him now, making him shiver in his sleep. His strength is his compassion for people. When he talks, he talks of people suffering, not of ideals. Even if Affensash doesn't understand it yet, Laurallin does. He has become a part of the struggle. He can no longer sit passively in his lab, regardless of how much they both would really like to.

Several times he threatens to drift into a doom and gloom depression. Luckily, Ruefin comes to the rescue, as the pet always seems to have the knack of doing. Running around the room and chewing on the chairs somehow makes Affensash remember the Yeti. He has nothing but good things to tell Laurallin about the Yeti. Fortunately, that is the last thing he talks about before losing his energy. He has ridden the crest of his fears and his light fever. He falls to sleep on a happy thought.

Laurallin loves her alchemist. Unfortunately, he doesn't leave her any time to tell him about what has happened to her. She very much wants to talk about Kenlin. It weighs heavily on her conscience. It consumes her like a secret burning guilt. Now it will have to wait.

At times, Affensash's intense compassion for others overshadows her needs for companionship. Just like today, she can never cut him off to express her own pains and suffering. Cutting him off in a time of need always makes her feel selfish and unworthy. But, like many times before, she now feels hurt and unsatisfied for having played the good wife and listened. She is a little hurt and now feels even more guilt.

Laurallin walks over and shuts the window. Her mother never explained how complicated a husband and wife relationship could get, she thinks smiling to herself. With or without Affensash's permission, she has to find Kenlin. She feels responsible for him in many ways; but besides her moral obligations there is a deep burning need inside of her to know; to face him and stare bold-face at her own shameful feelings.

She pins a little note on Affensash's pillow in case he awakes before she returns. Putting the rose-colored gown back on she locks the door behind her and she and Ruefin slip out to the streets below.

The streets are teaming with Eastern soldiers. The pubs are full to the rafters. Brawls break out sending soldiers tumbling into the streets. Laurallin is smart enough to avoid the drinking holes, but she realizes that she must get information. She searches the crowds for the kindest looking faces. "Excuse me," she asks over and over again, "On your way to town did you see any Hebelcaan riders?" Time and time again the answer is no.

There are at least four different units of soldiers stationed in town, she estimates. She is mad at herself for not being able to tell which soldiers belong to which unit. She must ask at least one soldier from each unit since the units arrived in town at different times.

No one has seen the Hebelcaan. Maybe she was overconfident about Kenlin and he didn't survive. The thought makes her shiver.

In a crowd of rowdy soldiers, she bumps into Steven. "This is not a good time to be walking unescorted through town!" he says, dragging her into the shadows at the side of a building.

Ruefin growls and his tail stiffens when Steven grabs her shoulder. Laurallin assures Ruefin that it is all right and the little fox returns to his business of sniffing and rummaging through every trash pile he can find.

Laurallin explains that she is asking about her tribesman and Steven concedes to escort her until they have asked at least one soldier from each unit. Unlike Laurallin, Steven can distinguish Eastern soldier's ranks and units. Before he agrees to help, however, he makes her swear to return to her room when they are finished.

The first soldier that Steven points out proves to be the lucky one. "Yes, we did see a group of riders," the soldier says squinting in the darkness to discover who is asking. "There were about fifteen or twenty of them to the north of here between town and 'Death Watch'. We didn't talk to them though. We were busy with wolves and the wolves were busy hunting something."

Laurallin's heart gives an involuntary leap.

"Say!" the soldier challenges, "Isn't that the girl they picked up in the mountains the other day?"

"Yes, I'm the one. They picked me up with my husband," Laurallin answers before Steven can warn her.

"The healer told us they were too weak to talk! Listen Constable," the soldier says sternly. "My Captain wants to see them right away. Bring them to him first thing in the morning and I will forget about seeing her here with you tonight. Understand?" the soldier says thumping his finger on Steven's chest.

"She will be there tomorrow, but I don't know if her husband is well enough to come," Steven says, wishing he had warned Laurallin earlier.

"No more of your Western foolery," the soldier barks. "Just get her there!" He turns and walks away.

"What do they want with us?" Laurallin asks Steven, watching the soldier walk away.

"You are the only people they know who have walked back from the old mine. They want to ask if you know what's going on up there."

"I could have told him that just now. I haven't got the slightest idea!" she says a little relieved, expecting much worse.

"Let's go back to the inn," Steven says, motioning down the street. "It will be safer there."

As they walk, Ruefin runs in and out between their legs, burning off some of his pent up energy. "Steven, you are the one who asked the soldiers to come to town, aren't you?" Laurallin asks curiously.

"Yes I did; that is at least half of them. I didn't bargain on so many showing up. I guess that when I tipped them off to trouble in the Pentacles the word spread to some dignitary. It seems that one of their High Lord Generals is going to visit the 'Apothecary' soon and these troops have been assigned to secure the area. Their Captain feels that we are close enough to the alchemy school that our trouble could endanger their General. He was delighted to come at my invitation. Personally, I think he's overdone it a bit."

"Do you think the Captain would help me search for a lost friend of mine?" Laurallin asks hopefully.

"Not a chance. Some people trapped here for months have asked for an escort out. He has refused them all. It seems that impressing this General is the most important thing on his mind right now." Laurallin looks down at the ground despondently. "Take heart though! The last of the Captain's troops have arrived and as soon as he cleans up the mess at 'Death Watch' we should all be able to come and go as we please."

Laurallin scoops up Ruefin and walks through the front door of the inn. "It may be too late by then," she says quietly.

"Who is this person you are so concerned about?" It is either the question, or the way Steven asks it, that suddenly makes her feel uncomfortable.

"He is a friend of mine. That's all. I've been running in those mountains for a long time and I know how dangerous it is. I'm just worried about a friend."

Before going back to Affensash as she promised, she makes Steven take her to see where Sensie is stabled. To her relief, Sensie is being well-cared for. Her wounds are wrapped with a mixture of Eastern and Western healing techniques and are applied with bandages. Rinsing and washing her down, Laurallin knows that Sensie understands what she is feeling without having to say a word.

At the door of Affensash's room, she fumbles with the key and unlocks the door. They both hear Affensash snoring inside.

"Tomorrow I will have to take you to see the Captain," Steven says apologetically. "I hope you don't mind."

Laurallin shakes her head, but the worry obviously shows on her face.

Steven, mistaking her concerns say, "Oh, don't worry about your husband. I will assure the Captain that he is still too weak. He can rest all day tomorrow."

"Thank you, Constable," Laurallin says, smiling and opening the door. "I will see you then first thing in the morning."

When the door closes, she puts Ruefin down and leans her back against it. She can hear Steven's footsteps receding down the hall. The room is dark, but she still sees the guilty expression on her face in the mirror. She wasn't thinking about Affensash's well-being just now when Steven was trying to reassure her. She was thinking of Kenlin and what else she might try to do to find him.

Affensash snores and rolls uncomfortably in his bed. Laurallin wraps her arms tightly around her waist. She needs someone to hold her.

In the morning, Laurallin goes down to the kitchen and helps the cook make Affensash's favorite breakfast. She carefully carries her tray of treasures up the stairs and waits for her stirring husband to wake. Blueberry pancakes, sausage, and an over-sized glass of orange juice!

Affensash is delighted. He quickly gobbles it down, starting his day off in a much better mood than the previous one. Affensash kisses her in gratitude and laughs at being pampered by one who knows his likes and dislikes so well. "Laurallin, I don't know how you found me," he says with admiration in his eyes.

She places her hand on his lips and says, "Please, Affensash, let's not start the day out talking about it. There are so many other things we have to discuss."

A knock on the door stops her before she can go further. Steven and Madillyn enter on their rounds again, just like yesterday.

"Listen, Aff," Laurallin quickly interjects, not wishing Steven to let it slip before she has a chance to tell Affensash. "While Madillyn takes care of you today, I'm going to talk to the Eastern Captain in town." Affensash sits up surprised, knowing how little she likes Easterners. "He wants to ask a few questions and I have a few of my own to ask him," she quickly tries to reassure him.

"I will go with you!" he says, but when Affensash tries to rise, he discovers that he is still stiff, and Madillyn pushes him back down.

"It will be a few more days before you can get up. If you push it any faster than that you will get worse instead of better, and you might end up lying on your back for weeks!"

Affensash's shoulders ache too much to argue right now.

"I won't be long," Laurallin says, smiling and giving him a kiss.

Steven opens the door and they start to leave.

"Steven," Affensash calls after them. "Does the Alchemy Guild have any labs or equipment in this town? I'll be coming into a little gold soon and I would like to spend my time working rather than just sitting here."

"I will see what I can do. If you're smart you will listen to Madillyn. She's never wrong about matters concerning healing." Steven closes the door and he and Laurallin hear Affensash moan as Madillyn begins removing his bandages.

"I hope your husband will be well soon. Madillyn thinks it will take a little time."

"He will be fine physically. The hardest healing will be inside," Laurallin says, turning a corner and heading down the street.

The air is cold enough that they can see each other's breath.

"I suppose he is lucky to have you here," Steven says, trying to make it sound complimentary.

Laurallin takes a deep breath, "Yes I suppose it is up to me."

Steven is no fool and realizes that Laurallin is very troubled about something. Thinking it a private matter, he lets it pass and walks on.

"I didn't hear any bells this morning," Laurallin says, suddenly noticing the crowded streets.

"We haven't had any trouble since the Easterners arrived. I just stopped doing it. Captain Rollins has taken over my patrols."

"I bet you are very pleased with the Easterners then," Laurallin says smugly.

"Well of course I am, but I don't make any pretenses about why they are here. If it were just to protect us they probably would never have showed. No! Captain Rollins has made it clear that he is here to secure the area for the arrival of one of their High Lord Generals. You know I hate to say it, but the Eastern patrol that found you was on its way to talk about a truce with whatever it is up there. It's lucky that the wolves were excited enough to attack the patrol. If they hadn't, it's hard telling what the good Captain would have done."

"That's easy. He would have sacrificed this town for the good of one of their Dark Lords," Laurallin says coldly.

"I wouldn't let Captain Rollins hear you talk about a High Lord General that way. He is very fond of the word treason. He's nearly accused me of it several times already. "

"I think I like you Steven," Laurallin finally laughs.

They near two soldiers standing outside a doorway. Steven warns her one last time to guard her words and then they both enter, passing by the silent guards. They find the Captain in a smoke-filled room, mostly from his own pipe, looking over a series of maps.

"Good to see you Constable," he says, motioning for Laurallin to be seated. "Can you tell me how accurate these maps are?"

Steven walks over to the table and notices the signatures on the maps' legends. They look like Eastern names. It is probably maps the East used when invading their land years ago. Steven studies them for a moment and finds them to be fairly accurate.

"The area just to this side of the old mine is not that steep," Steven says pointing to the map.

"Could horses cross it?" the Captain asks with great interest.

"Well, once you have passed this point on the road I don't think the horses will have any trouble."

The Captain is pleased, "Excellent! I won't have to keep my men lined up in a row. I can position them in a better formation."

Laurallin sits quietly, watching the Captain, studying the face that was hidden before in the helmet. The Captain is a very typical Easterner. He has dark curly hair and sports an unusually large nose. Laurallin has always wondered if they really found a big nose attractive. The Captain is not physically large nor particularly muscular. Like most Easterners, he is overly conscious of trying to please his superiors. He takes his orders seriously.

When the Captain is through with Steven he seats himself in a plush red chair and stares at Laurallin through cold blue eyes while lighting another tobacco load. "You know you were dammed lucky we found you when we did," the Captain says, pausing to take three quick puffs.

"I was also 'dammed lucky' to have a horse that could keep up with you as you ran away," Laurallin says wincing, already regretting her sharp tongue.

The Captain starts to say something then checks his words, takes a few puffs, and thinks again. "What were you doing up there anyway? Steven tells me that there has been trouble at 'Death Watch' for some time."

"I was up there to find my husband, but I don't suppose that is what you want to hear. My husband was there to magically seal a demon away until they could call on the True Ones Elders for help."

The Captain chokes on his next puff. "I see. Then your husband is a wizard," the Captain says, steadying his puffs.

"No. He was just traveling with two who were. Unfortunately, you didn't arrive in time to save them."

"Can either you or your husband tell me with some understanding what is up there?" the Captain asks disappointingly. He knows that it would be more helpful to get his information from a wizard whose background would lend to better understanding.

"I'm afraid that neither I nor my husband is very astute at magic, but since my husband is ill you will have to listen to my interpretation. There is some type of hideous demon up there. Now a demon by itself is not that bad, but this one has high ambitions and uses its magic to twist peoples' minds. It takes men and turns them into beasts, and witches into powerful sorceresses. I'm afraid you will have to ask the demon what its' intentions are. I don't routinely speak to or pretend to understand those creatures," Laurallin says, knowing exactly how that sounded. She wasn't doing very well.

"I see," says the Captain, flipping a match and trying to light his pipe again. "Would you say this demon was particularly strong?"

"I wouldn't go there with the group you have here in town, if that's what you mean."

Suddenly losing his patience, the Captain stands and leans across the table. "Just answer the questions. Leave your prejudices out of your answers if you don't mind."

"You saw the wolves! They couldn't be killed even when they were impaled on your lances. Those were once men, Captain; good and caring men."

"We have ways to take care of things like that," the Captain says. "We estimate maybe one hundred wolves. Would you?"

"I don't know," Laurallin says uneasily. "To me it seemed like there were thousands." This time she speaks earnestly, but the Captain takes it to be another glib remark.

"You Westerners are all alike. You are scared little farm boys and girls who don't know how to fight. I have two hundred of our best troops outside this door; the same men who destroyed your pretty little kingdoms. They know how to fight. All I'm trying to do is get some straight answers out of you so that we can attack with the best possible plan."

Laurallin turns red with rage. "I am Hebelcaan. You never defeated the Hebelcaan!"

"Is that a challenge? You know I could order a few thousand soldiers right now to High Tower. I think I have a pretty good idea where the tribe might be grazing this time of year."

Laurallin becomes very quiet. She has heard tales about cities and villages being burnt to the ground because of an Eastern officer's temper. She doesn't think a Captain has that kind of authority, but she doesn't want to press the matter.

"I have seen your troops," Laurallin says trying to relax. "You have no bowmen, and I didn't see any great magical or alchemy equipment. You asked, and I say that you shouldn't go."

The Captain's patience is exhausted. "The General is due in the Pentacles in a few days. I have assured him that I would secure the area so that his vanguard could cross the mountains undisturbed. I am going to do that young lady. In fact, I'm going to do that tomorrow." He stops, contemplating a moment, and takes two more puffs. "Yes, I think you should come along. It would do you good to carry the news back to your tribe of how well the Eastern soldiers fight. The Hebelcaan may be brave, but we are brave *and* disciplined!"

"But her husband is ill and needs someone to look after him!" Steven objects.

"I will send a few men to do that very thing," the Captain says with a smirk.

Laurallin stands, but the room quickly fills with soldiers, having been given some unseen signal by their commander. All she can do is stand and stare grimly at the Captain. This isn't the first time being too proud has gotten her in trouble.

"Don't worry. He won't be harmed; that is, he won't be harmed if we return. We will take this girl and a few others from town with us. You see, Steven, when we got your message we didn't know whether to expect a trap. Since we can't seem to get satisfactory explanations, we will take along a few prisoners just to make sure this isn't some Western scheme at petty revenge. If you are indeed innocent and are simply being plagued by wolves then all will turn out well. But if this is some trick, I assure you more than just the prisoners will be killed." He walks over to Steven with two other soldiers at either arm. "I think you understand, don't you, Constable?"

Steven turns and gives Laurallin a look of apology. "I will make sure that your husband is cared for." Rough hands grab him and he is escorted out to the street.

Laurallin's hands are tied and she is led downstairs to a room with no windows. There, seven other people are already being detained. They throw her roughly into the room and close and lock the door behind her. In the darkness she backs up against a wall.

"What are you here for?" asks a strange voice of another prisoner.

"For having a big mouth! For having a very, very, big mouth," Laurallin huffs despondently, disappointed in herself. She does her best to get comfortable. It will be a long wait until the morning.

Madillyn persuades the two Eastern soldiers, at knife point, to leave her patient alone. Finally, they decide they could just as easily guard Affensash outside the room where he lies. He isn't exactly supposed to be a prisoner.

Steven doesn't tell Affensash that Laurallin was taken forcibly away. He is afraid the alchemist would try to follow, and if the soldiers didn't kill him, his wounds certainly would. Instead, Steven brings him alchemy equipment and props it up around his bed. He tells Affensash that Laurallin left for a day under the protection of soldiers to try and track down the Hebelcaan and warn them of the danger.

When Steven and Madillyn finally leave him, Affensash struggles to get out of bed. He doesn't trust their explanation at all. Laurallin would have told him if she were leaving. After all, they just had this discussion about leaving without saying goodbye. Steven's explanation that she had to leave immediately or be left behind seems like a convenient lie.

He cracks the door open, already in pain just from standing. He sees the two guards and quietly closes it again.

Walking across the room causes him so much pain that he has to sit down in a chair to rest before he can go further to the window. He opens the shutters with a creak and looks down. He'll never make it.

Tink.

Gathering bed sheets and blankets, he ties them into a makeshift rope. He'll never make it, but that doesn't mean that he won't try.

Tying one end to the hinges, he tries to ease up onto the windowsill. Even this causes him pain. That's when he sees it; a small silver hook and thin thread of a rope.

"We are not falling out the window again are we?"

Affensash looks down and is shocked to see the small Tuatha girl from the Mystic Isles.

"If we are falling again just give me a few moments to get up there and out of the way," she says, steadily rising on her rope.

Affensash falls back in the room and sits, still not believing what he sees. The Tuatha lightly climbs through the window and Affensash puts his finger to his lips motioning at the guards by the door.

"I have come for the report," she says smiling.

"You're a little late aren't you? I've nearly been killed several times. My wife too! Right now I can't find her. I don't suppose you could help me down?" He rubs his sore shoulders and notices that his wrappings are already starting to bleed.

"I have not seen your wife, and you don't look like you are ready to travel. Can you tell me what you have discovered?"

Angrily, Affensash looks up. "I wouldn't tell you this except that the message has been too costly to my family to keep it a secret. Tell Elder Enchantraen that Diana, Johona, Terrell, and I don't know how many others, have been butchered. Killed by Glenwall."

Affensash can see the shocked reaction on the Tuatha's face. "Tell the great wizard if he had chosen a better spy, then Diane might have been saved," Affensash rasps with as much bitterness as he could inflict in his voice.

"There is a demon at 'Death Watch' that can manipulate aether like no other beast on earth. It is loathsome. It turns men to beasts. It rewards witches for doing its evil business. It brings to our world a new shame for mankind by playing on their greed. It manipulates our basest nature as well as your magic! "Affensash stops for a moment, blinking furiously.

Looking up with a single tear in his eye he says, "Tell the Elder that my wife and I are tired of magics, but wish this beast to be gone and that is why I am giving him this information. Explain to the wizard that alchemists don't care about feats of power. We want none of this. Do you think you can explain all that to your Elder?" Affensash asks venomously.

"Yes, I think so," the Tuatha replies, looking very downcast.

"Good. Then maybe you could explain to me why my wife would leave without telling me to go look for a Hebelcaan ... "Affensash stops himself in midsentence. He doesn't even see the Tuatha slip back out the window and disappear.

Maybe Steven was telling the truth!

Affensash suddenly remembers a Hebelcaan tribesman that might explain Laurallin's behavior. He sits there with his mouth open, not wanting to hear the answer to his own question.

Maybe, just maybe, she left him to find Kenlin.

CHAPTER NINETEEN

When Witches Wail

Undead are creatures that were dead and magically brought back to life. The fact that they have returned to life by magic means they have a high resistance to normal physical assaults.

- Creature Description, from the treatise of High Fantasy

Laurallin is briskly lifted from her cell by the rough hands of a soldier and pushed into the line of the departing prisoners. It is the next day and the Easterners are preparing to move out. The day is warm and sunny, but this is spring in the mountains and anything is possible as far as the weather before the day's end. Her eyes have a hard time adjusting to the harsh bright light. When she can finally see again, she finds the soldiers pushing the prisoners onto horses. The horses have been tied together in a line, and each prisoner has been bound at the wrists like Laurallin.

Down the line Laurallin hears one horse neighing and starting to buck when a soldier tries to push a prisoner into the saddle. Laurallin squints and sees that it's Sensie. "Hey, that's my horse," she yells and starts to break from the waiting line and go to her friend.

The hilt of a sword pummels her on the side of the head. She staggers back and her vision blinks to black, but comes back again.

"Stay in line," comes the soldier's voice thick with an Eastern accent.

"That's my horse," she groans rubbing the side of her head. "She will kill the poor bastard if they try to force him to ride her!"

The soldier grunts and goes to the others who are forcing the prisoners onto the horses. They motion for her to come forward. "Go ahead Miss. If you're so fond of this nag you can have her." Laurallin doesn't say a word. With her hands bound together she reaches under Sensie, loosens the strap and lets the saddle fall to the ground. She runs her hands down the horse's flanks saying soothing words. Walking to face Sensie, she gives her old friend a gentle hug.

"It looks like they have taken good care of you." Sensie's sides are still badly scarred but the wounds are healing. She looks a mess, but as Laurallin carefully examines the wrappings and scars, she sees they will all heal. "What do you say? Are you ready to run again?"

She is still wearing the rose-colored gown and she is embarrassed when she can't find a lady like way to mount the horse. Finally, she jumps up and straddles Sensie, listening to the jeers of the soldiers. She tries to pull the gown down around her bare legs. She refuses to ride side saddle like the rest of the female prisoners. She, after all, was a Hebelcaan, not one of those little pink town girls.

The rest of the prisoners are placed on horses and the line is led out into the main street where the full unit of Eastern soldiers are mounted and waiting. The prisoners are taken to the rear of the main unit. On each side of the prisoners are two soldiers, who will ride to keep them in line. Behind the prisoners four more soldiers ride, guarding the rear.

The Captain and two of his lieutenants ride up and down scrutinizing the unit. When the Captain reaches the prisoners, he stops to look them over. Standing high in his stirrups he shouts, "We are expecting a lot of trouble out there, but we are prepared for it. If we win this day and discover that your town officials have been honest with us, you will all return to your families tomorrow. I warn you to stay within the protection of the soldiers. Any of you attempting to run or escape will forfeit your life immediately. We are going to battle. We cannot waste time with prisoners. Do not talk to each other or cause us any distractions. It is to your benefit that my men stay as alert and ready for danger as possible. On this day, our fate will be yours."

Laurallin had a thousand things to say about that speech, but decides to remain silent. It was her comments that got her in this trouble to begin with. The Captain and his lieutenants turn and start to ride back to the front of the line. The Captain spots Laurallin from the corner of his eye and smiles at her and tips his plumed helmet. Laurallin glares!

The unit starts to move out down the streets. Most of the townsfolk are locked inside their homes. Those in the street scurry to get out of the way, afraid they might be made the next prisoner. The procession travels down toward the main gates of the town. The soldiers hold their lances high, each with a tiny banner tied to the end. The officers' plumed helmets blow and bob giving the whole procession the kind of grandeur befitting a conquering army.

"You go to meet death face-to-face," an old woman's voice cackles.

Laurallin looks through the town and spots an old woman sitting on the steps of some fallen religious relic.

"You and Enchantraen both will be defeated!" she shouts. "Old Harrlow knows. Old Harrlow can see these things! You and Enchantraen will be defeated!"

The Captain starts to send two soldiers to silence the old hag, but decides not to. Butchering an old woman would only make the soldiers uneasy. Ignoring her taunts will show them that he doesn't put any credence to her words.

The unit rides on past her. Laurallin thinks a moment and remembers where she has heard that name. Affensash told her that Enchantraen was one of the Elders.

What does the old woman mean? There are no Elders riding with them, certainly no Western wizards! The old hag must be mad and shouting the most powerful names she can think of. Isn't there enough magic flying around this town without fakes adding to the chaos?

The unit and the prisoners pass quietly through the gates, starting their uneasy trek to 'Death Watch'. Once away from the town, the Captain orders a small vanguard of ten men to ride ahead and scout for an ambush. Laurallin looks down the lines of soldiers. She was right. None of them are archers. The Easterners aren't very good with the bow, but their cavalry units are well-known for being the best in all the lands. However, the high mountain ranges are certainly not the place for horses and lances.

Laurallin keeps looking over their faces hoping to discover wizards hidden among them. Although she is not very good at spotting such things, she doesn't see any who even remotely remind her of magic-users. The entire procession is taking on the semblance of a pompous funeral march. The soldiers ride on up the road making excellent time.

Noon comes and passes, but the soldiers don't stop. Surely the Captain isn't going to make his men fight on empty stomachs, Laurallin begins to wonder. Then Laurallin notices for the first time how quiet the mountains are. Too quiet. Where are the howling wolves? She hasn't heard the first baying or growling howls since they left High Tower. She tries to formulate several reasons for this in her mind, but none of them make sense. Helplessly captured, she realizes that she is going to be a part of the Captain's dance with death regardless of whether she can make any sense of it. To try and ease the tension, she turns her attention to Sensie; stroking and thanking the horse for all her brave friend has done.

Sensie's flanks are scarred and badly marked by the wolves. Laurallin realizes how lucky she was to receive treatment from one as skilled as Madillyn. She feels confident that Affensash will recover also. She wonders about Kenlin. He was so badly hurt the last time she saw him.

Her eyes drift to the mountainsides. There! She suddenly spots a group of horsemen way off in the distance. She catches her breath, squints and looks again. She can't tell for sure. They are too far away, but they could be Hebelcaan. Maybe Kenlin found the tribesmen and is searching for her?

She decides on a calculated risk. She places her hands to her mouth and shouts, "Kenlin! Kenlin, I'm here!" hoping that the mountains will carry the echo to his ears.

A soldier rides up next to her and swings his fist to silence her. She ducks and he misses. "Are you warning someone we are coming?" the soldier barks, but backs away when he sees the Captain riding towards them.

"There is my friend," Laurallin shouts pointing toward the small specks perched on the mountainside. "Those are Hebelcaan," she says, trying to diffuse the tense situation. The Captain gives a quick glance back over his shoulder.

"I don't see how you can know that! Listen, young lady," the Captain commands, remembering that she was asking about her tribesmen before, and then changes his mind. Turning to the soldier he says, "If she is wrong about them being friendly, kill her first. If she shouts again, kill her immediately."

Laurallin turns to the Captain. "I thought you might want to send someone after them. You could use their strong bow arms in this fight."

"I decide whether we need help from Westerners or not. You sit on that damned horse and keep quiet. Pull that skirt down," is his last command as he turns and rides back to the front.

Laurallin tugs on the hem of the gown a little embarrassed, but hopeful that her voice carried along the mountains. At least it might cause her tribesmen to look around. If Kenlin is with them he will come to ask the soldiers if they have seen her. She wants to see him again, more than she wants to admit consciously to herself.

They ride on for several hours. Then the horn blows. In one great motion the soldiers stop what they are doing and immediately change formation. Laurallin isn't sure what is going on, but then she sees the soldiers dismount and start to unpack their saddles. "They're making camp," Laurallin says to the prisoner in front of her. The prisoner, a distinguished looking older man, starts to answer, but a soldier walks by and he remains silent.

The prisoners are helped from their saddles and are led away. They are seated in a circle and two soldiers work ropes around their legs, binding each to the other. "Hey, we are not prisoners of war. Don't you think this is a bit much?" asks one of the prisoners, speaking for the first time.

"Prisoners are prisoners," replies a soldier quietly. "This is the way I was trained to do it. Now shut up before the Captain hears you." The rest of the prisoners remain silent as the soldiers do their duty.

Other soldiers are erecting tents and finding logs and sharp sticks to make barricades. The soldiers are fast and efficient and their tasks are soon complete. Only one soldier remains to watch over the prisoners. They are bound so tightly that escape seems impossible; not that any of them want to. They have all lived in the area long enough to know that they are safer with the soldiers than alone and unarmed in the mountains.

Laurallin can hear the Captain and his lieutenants barking orders, and she sees riders disappearing to scout and guard the area. Other guards are stationed on foot closer to camp. Even Laurallin can tell that it would nearly be impossible to catch the camp unaware. These kinds of military disciplines are foreign to the Western armies. It is easy to see how better trained the Easterners really are. Most Western soldiers are militia called to battle at a moment's notice. They fight with their hearts, while the Easterners fight with organization and training.

After a little time, the camp begins to settle and the prisoners begin to mumble amongst themselves. The guard allows them to talk to the person sitting next to them, but if a prisoner tries to talk with a friend he recognizes that is sitting too far away, the soldier raps them on the back of the head with the butt of his spear and tells them to whisper. The distinguished looking man is sitting next to Laurallin.

"I am Talbort," the man politely introduces himself. "I am a retired army officer from Nautpolis. I have been living in HighTower for the past eight years . That's why I'm here. How about you?"

Laurallin recognizes the name of the Western city-state and smiles politely back. "I'm Laurallin, a Hebelcaan, despite the way I'm dressed. I'm here because I have too much to say." Talbort laughs, but quickly changes it to a cough when he sees the soldier coming.

"I used to fight against these same soldiers," Talbort says looking around the camp. "I know the Captain. I hate to admit it, but he is a good soldier. We will make it back all right," Talbort says, trying to sound confident.

"Why is he stopping so early in the day?" Laurallin whispers back.

"He's trying to time his march to arrive at 'Death Watch' during the best part of the day. He doesn't want to fight in the night any more than you do."

"There aren't any wolves around," Laurallin says after a little pause. "When I was here last time they were chasing me in hellish packs!"

"I don't know," Talbort says shaking his head. "We can only hope that the Captain knows what he is doing."

Laurallin sits back, taking little comfort in that thought. The soldiers go about their business, breaking into small groups, laughing and joking to themselves. Time passes slowly and Laurallin spends most of it searching the mountainsides for any sign of Kenlin or the Hebelcaan.

Laurallin finds the plumes and some of the soldier uniforms to be a bit odd-looking out here in the wilderness. "I hope these soldiers fight as well as they are pretty to look at," Laurallin sighs after a while.

"When the fighting begins the plumes come off," Talbort offers. "These are veterans of the wars. I'll wager most of them have been soldiers for all of their adult life."

"You sound as if you admire them."

"I don't admire them; I just respect them. You would too after years of fighting and losing against them. I believe the Captain was right when he said, on this day our fate will be their fate," Talbort says defensively.

Laurallin realizes that this conversation could easily end up in an argument and quickly changes it. "Say, who was that old woman yelling at the troops back in town?"

"That was old Harrlow. That crazy old witch nearly got her head sliced off," Talbort chuckles.

"A witch! You mean Steven allows a witch to live in town? No wonder you have so many problems at night," Laurallin says grimly.

"Not from old Harrlow," Talbort laughs with eyebrows arching in disbelief. "There used to be a lot of witches at High Tower. When they all started going a little crazy, being called to serve this Baal-thing up in these mountains, they were driven out. Poor old Harrlow was left behind. I guess she's too crazy for even a demon to fool with. Harrlow has sat on those steps and cackled prophecies for ages. She needn't be feared."

"Is she ever right?" Laurallin asks the obvious.

"Usually she is half-right. Most of the time her thoughts are so jumbled that you can't make heads-or-tails of what she says. Like today for instance. She might have got everyone scared cursing the soldiers, but then she called out the name Enchantraen. Elder Enchantraen is a war-wizard from Nautpolis. That wizard spent most of his life fighting men like the Captain. He's a legend where I come from. I'd sure the hell know if he were traveling with us."

Laurallin stops and pulls her knees up to her chin, wrapping her dress around her feet. She sits there curled up contemplating Talbort's words in moody silence. The rest of the day, and on past the evening meal, she sits listening to the conversation of others. She decides once again before nodding off to sleep that she hates magic. It really does seem to complicate more than help matters.

The camp is up and stirring in the eerie hours before sunrise. The prisoners are unceremoniously wakened and escorted to their horses. In less than an hour they are saddled up and moving out once more. The morning is quiet. No wolves are howling and there is no red glow coming from 'Death Watch' as there was when Laurallin last saw it. The soldiers ride for several hours while Laurallin dozes off on Sensie.

A horn blast startles her and she looks up to see the soldiers moving into a new formation. They are near 'Death Watch' and the Captain is preparing. Talbort was right, the plumes do come off, and so do a lot of the other glittering decorations as the soldiers shift restlessly in their saddles.

Finally, the horn signals again and the formation starts to move forward. The vanguard has pulled back closer to the main unit. The Captain canters to the front. The road is too constrictive for good fighting so the Captain maneuvers for the open terrain that Steven had pointed out on the map.

The opening to the mine looms around the corner as the troops advance. Above the opening are steep cliffs that rise for hundreds of feet. To the left is the steep drop-off that Affensash first climbed up, and to the right is the open rocky plain.

The prisoners are ordered to dismount to the left side near the drop-off so that one soldier can easily guard them. The horses are led away and staked to the ground. Still, there was no sign of trouble.

The Captain barks orders to his troops and once again the formation changes to take advantage of the terrain. The Captain then orders the trumpeter forward to the vanguard and moves in closer to the mine's entrance. The soldier blows a long challenging blast on the horn. They sit there before the gaping maw of the mine's entrance, shifting uneasily, listening to the creaking leather, waiting for a reply.

It comes.

A single figure emerges from the entrance and approaches the vanguard. It is a woman, scantily dressed in thin flowing robes. Her full figure is immediately obvious to the troops as she confidently walks straight towards the Captain. The manner of her strut tells them she knows how to handle her body in a base sort of beastly way.

"Greetings, Captain. Have you brought your troops all this way to be entertained by my master's gracious hospitality?" she asks in very slow syrupy tones.

"That is very close to the truth," the Captain bellows, undistracted by her looks. "A few days ago your master saw fit to attack one of his High Lord General's patrols. I have come, as the rightful conqueror and owner of this land, to correct that wrong, and to take a just payment for that mistake."

The woman throws back her head and laughs, her deep auburn hair flying and cascading down her bare back. "Come Captain, there is no need to be so rigid and stiff. I'm sure we could work out some personal satisfaction to atone for our mistake." The woman gently places her hand on the Captain's leg.

"Tell your master that all he has to do is bring his weapons forth and place them on the ground before me. When he has surrendered thus I promise I will be as lenient as my code will permit."

The woman pulls away from him laughing. She saunters ten feet away, turns and looks back at the Captain. "Are you sure, Captain, that we can't work it out another way?" she asks compellingly.

"Enough!" Captain Rollins replies loud enough for the rest of the troops to hear.

"Then see if these hands are more tender than mine!" The witch lifts her arm and the earth trembles. The ground begins to break and crack, vomiting clods of dirt into the air. The soldiers fight to calm the horses. The ground splits and ghastly white arms rise up grabbing at the horses' legs. The prisoners scream in terror.

"We found them buried in the mines. We thought you might like meeting some of your old friends," the witch screams, pointing to the crowd of cowering townsfolk and laughing.

Small mounds erupt and men stand up from their graves. Emaciated, ashen-faced and rotting, they stand tearing at the legs of the soldiers in the vanguard, trying to pull them from their horses. The Captain orders the trumpeter to signal and the poor soldier manages a blast before he is drug from his saddle. The smell of rotting flesh now blows past the rest of the soldiers.

Bravely the men stand their ground, their horses nervously stamping beneath them. At their Captain's signal they remove the pendants from their lances revealing bright silver tips.

"I told you the Captain was no fool," Talbort wails hysterically, pointing to the lances. The soldier guarding the prisoners gives him a tense glare and warns him to stay quiet.

The first line of the unit advances in good order then breaks into a full charge. The impact of the charge knocks the undead men down, freeing the surviving vanguard soldiers. The momentum of the charge carries the soldiers past the vanguard towards the entrance. Rotting flesh hangs from their lances. The Captain shouts for them to return as the witch disappears into the mine.

Screams of laughter erupt from the cliffs above the mine's entrance. Witches by the score appear naked-breasted and taunting the soldiers. Even to Laurallin the women are physically beautiful. Their mannerisms and jeers are so disgusting, that no thought could be given to any type of physical attraction by the soldiers. They begin casting their crude but powerful spells. Lights and fireballs plummet down on the soldiers. Some of the witches begin tossing baskets full of huge snakes from the cliffs causing the horses to panic. More of the dead miners erupt from the ground and lumber towards the soldiers. The scene turns bloody, like a vivid painting by an insane artist.

The Captain orders the unit to retreat just out of the witches' spell range.

Then they come!

From the steep side of the road, just behind the troops, rabid howling wolf-men scamper up the cliffs. The soldiers remain calm. The unbelievable howling nightmare does not shatter their discipline. They wheel, lower their blood-soaked lances, and charge in a straight line, killing all who stand before their silver spears.

Still, the wolves come leaping over the wretched bodies of their fallen brethren. The soldiers are at the disadvantage once the wolves leap past their lances. Their swords can't kill the snarling beasts no matter how many times they beat and hack them away.

Soldiers are dragged from their saddles. Laurallin sees many of them desperately trying to pull their lances from the impaled body of a wolf so they can use it against another. One soldier near her is unsuccessful and is thrown from his horse. The wolves have his arms ripped off before his twitching body hits the ground.

The witches shriek and hoot from the safety of the cliffs, casting spells when a soldier is unfortunate enough to come within range. Those who aren't casting spells are disrobing and rotating on the rocks in lewd motions, displaying their beautiful bodies. Laurallin shies away, ashamed to be a woman. It is a fathomless scene of malign terror. Laurallin thrashes in her ropes trying to break free.

The prisoners plead to be released, but the soldiers are too busy fighting for their own lives. A wolf breaks through and charges the one soldier guarding the prisoners. The soldier swings and hits the wolf, but the impact of the wolf's attack knocks the soldier on his back next to Laurallin. The wolf howls in unthinkable pain, nearly disemboweled by the soldier's swing.

Horrified, the soldier watches. The wolf regains control, stands and comes after him once more in pain-driven fury. The soldier bravely stands and raises his sword. The wolf leaps, breaking through the soldier's defensive swing and carries the soldier back down; rabid jaws going for his throat. It is Laurallin who saves the soldier by kicking the wolf away.

When the wolf rolls off the soldier it stands to attack her. Helplessly bound, she kicks again before the wolf can completely regain its balance, sending the beast spinning over the cliff. The wolf lands thirty feet below, groans, quivers for a second, then rises and simply turns and joins the others re-scaling the cliff.

"Release us!" Laurallin implores desperately. "We can help."

Convinced, the soldier slashes with his sword and she is free. He hands her his dagger and turns to meet the next charging wolf. Laurallin lashes frantically at the prisoners' bindings. Most of them run off as soon as they are free and are chased down and torn apart by the much faster wolves. Some, however, form into little groups, working together to throw the wolves down the cliffs as they had seen Laurallin do.

The soldiers fight on in a desperate struggle, but not one of them routes. The silver is taking its toll and some wolves stop moving.

Laurallin realizes from the outset of the battle that brave men die just as easily as cowards, and that the soldiers are outnumbered. She runs for Sensie. The wolves see her break from the protection of the group and are after her. She is running as fast as she can, and through the blood pounding in her head she hears them howling. If she could only make it to Sensie she might break through. At least with her horse under her she would have a chance.

A wolf's jaws clip her on the back of the heel, sending her spinning to the ground. She tries to rise, but realizes that the wolves will be on her before she can stand.

The air whistles around her. Arrows! The wolves howl in pain and fall away.

She stands and sees the small band of Hebelcaan riding up the road. She recognizes Kenlin's firm, confident outline even though his death-mask is lowered. Her heart nearly leaps from her chest. Kenlin has come for her!

This time Kenlin has come better prepared. The Hebelcaan shoot another volley with deadly accuracy and the silver-tipped arrows take the wolves down, clearing a path. Laurallin unties Sensie and cuts the reins of the other horses. The tribesmen ride through the pack shooting down any wolf that stands in their way. Laurallin leads the horses to the townspeople. There are very few left alive, but those who are able mount up. Laurallin looks to where the majority of the Eastern soldiers are bravely making their stand. The soldiers look trapped. The road between them and the Hebelcaan is clogged with wolves. More wolves than even Laurallin knew existed.

Kenlin is beside her. He removes his death-mask and kisses her roughly.

"If those are your friends, then it is time to die," he says lowering his mask once again and preparing to lead the Hebelcaan into their last charge.

"Stop!" Laurallin shouts. "They are not our friends. They forced us up here! "Laurallin explains, pointing to the few remaining townsfolk. "We owe these people more than we owe the soldiers. If we die, let's die fighting to get home."

With light pressure from his knees, Kenlin turns his stallion around. The initial path they shot through to get to Laurallin has closed behind them. The wolves are coming at them in packs. Kenlin realizes they may not make it and squeezes Laurallin's hand, possibly for the last time.

At his signal, the tribesmen release a volley and charge. They shoot with deadly aim, but many of the riders are drug from their horses and die by a wolf's sharp teeth.

Laurallin hears the Captain shouting behind them. "Come back you cowards! Come and die like men!" Even over the witches cackling she can hear the Captain's determination. To Laurallin, the Hebelcaan do not seem like cowards. Her kinsmen are falling all around her, some of them sacrificing their last arrow to protect another.

Since the prisoners started from the rear of the Eastern unit, it takes only a short time to break away. The few who survive are free from the wolf packs and Kenlin and Laurallin are among them.

Down the road they ride at a full gallop. Laurallin allows herself one last glance back at the nightmare of the naked, taunting witches, the vicious tearing wolves, and the bravely dying soldiers. But over it a large dreadful shadow seems to hang.

Strange that she didn't notice it before. Then a harsh sickening odor comes to her nose. It is the same beastly odor Kenlin described when they caught Glenwall with the rabbit in the woods. Could this be the same shadow she saw then? Is it the same shadow that came to Glenwall on the knoll?

She turns back around, unable to watch any longer. The few wolves who try to follow are taken down by silver-tipped arrows; the rest turn back to feast on easier game.

The Hebelcaan ride on silently with their masks lowered, watching for any sign of pursuit. When Kenlin thinks it is safe, he signals for a stop. The tribesmen dismount and inspect the horses and townsfolk for wounds.

Laurallin rushes to Kenlin's arms. "I was so worried! I was beginning to think you didn't make it."

Kenlin answers her again in a long savage kiss that sends exaltation up Laurallin's spine and leaves her breathless. "Where have you been? I've seen every part of these mountains more than I ever want to see again."

Laurallin pulls away from his encompassing arms suddenly ashamed of her actions. "I have been in High Tower with .... with my husband."

Kenlin is undaunted and pulls her back to him with an understanding embrace. Laurallin doesn't fight; she relaxes and enjoys the feeling it sends rippling through her body. Her mind becomes unmoored and she drifts helplessly through steamy clouds of passion.

Danger is not that far behind them. To make it to High Tower they will have to ride into the night. They mount up and ride like sparrows from the hawk. The horses do not seem to mind running their hearts out; with their burning, tired muscles they leave the nightmare behind them.

On they ride, wishing only to escape. Laurallin is dazed and lost in a world of confusion. There was Kenlin next to her; close enough to touch. Yet she still wants to see Affensash; to find quiet and comfort away from this madness. None of it makes sense. None of it was right. At times along the way she feels no better than the witches on the cliffs, taunting and teasing herself, and those around her.

Hours after sunset the riders reach High Tower. Laurallin seems to be the only one who is not relieved when the gates open. Steven is there with others to take the horses and offer aid to the wounded. Separated from the others, he sees Kenlin embracing Laurallin. He guesses that Laurallin's problem has finally come home. Steven, once again, comes to her rescue and offers her temporary asylum.

"Laurallin," he shouts, walking to her to warn the two of his approach. They break off their conversation. Steven sees Laurallin's tear-streaked face. "I am so happy that you made it back. I need you to come with me. It's urgent."

Laurallin starts to move away from Kenlin who quickly objects.

"Now don't argue with the Constable," Steven laughs, but manages to let Kenlin know he is serious. "The other men will show you to your quarters."

Taking Laurallin by the arm, he escorts her quickly away down the street. They walk together silently. Steven is aware of what is going on and Laurallin is too ashamed to say anything. They come to the inn and Laurallin decides she better take this moment to explain.

"I don't want to know a thing," Steven says, stopping her with a smile. "All I know is that Affensash has been going crazy since you left. I had to lie to him to keep him from killing himself riding after you. Tell him whatever it is you wanted to tell me." He smiles thoughtfully as he watches her walk up the stairs. "I want to see both of you in the morning. A stranger arrived in town. I need to know if you two know anything about him."

Laurallin looks back and nods absently. When she reaches the hallway she freezes, unable to continue to the door. One leg is shackled with guilt, the other with fatigue.

Suddenly there is a big explosion from inside of the room. The door is jolted open and black smoke bellows from the room. Ruefin comes running out smoldering.

Laurallin grabs him as he tries to run by her.

"Ya-hoo!" screams Affensash from the room. "Steven," he shouts at the top of his lungs, "They are going to give me my pistols this time for sure." Affensash rounds the corner into the hall grinning. Behind him the room is filled with smoke. He sees Laurallin and the smile drains from his face. They stare at each other for one brief, apprehensive moment, neither one saying a word.

"He's here in town isn't he?" Affensash finally asks.

Laurallin simply nods yes.

CHAPTER TWENTY

Small Affairs

Only alchemists should use gunpowder weapons since only they know how to make the powder, load and activate the guns.

- of Alchemists, from the treatise of High Fantasy

Affensash looks in the mirror trying to clean the black smudges from his face. Laurallin has gotten a broom and is trying to sweep up the shattered glass and bubbling chemicals. Ruefin is keeping his distance.

"What is it this time? An ointment to cure foot sores!" Laurallin says, complaining and talking just to fill the nervous silence.

"No, it started out as an elixir to cure wolf bites, but I dribbled a little. One drop hit the floor; well, you see the results!"

"Great. What are you going to sell it as; Affensash's Extraordinary Room Demolisher! One drop will paint your walls black! Two drops will take down the house!" Laurallin says, scrubbing vigorously at a large black spot that prefers to smear rather than wipe away.

"I think you missed the point, dear," Affensash says disgustingly. He stares at her with a large black smudge still on the end of his nose. "That was one drop. A whole vile of the stuff will cause a lot more than a house to disappear. The Guild has never been able to make a potion that gives off more than a little bang. I'm telling you. This time it's important. I'm going to earn my pistols for sure!"

"I'm proud of you, but I don't think I like you inventing things that are going to harm people."

"Well this could be used for a lot of good things. They could use it to clear roads, and for mining, and lots of worthwhile causes," Affensash defends himself, wiping off the last of the black powder.

"Nice thought, but you know it won't be used just for that. Your Guild has a very violent side. This Jabir will sell it to the East for a handsome profit. Maybe you ought to think about it for a while. That's all I'm trying to say."

"You know you scared me when you left without a word," Affensash finally gets the courage to inject his real thoughts into the conversation.

"It didn't happen exactly the way Steven told you," Laurallin quickly puts in.

Affensash sits down in a chair massaging his stiff shoulder. "Then you didn't leave to find Kenlin?" Affensash asks with a trace of hope in his voice.

"No. I was forced to leave with Captain Rollins as a prisoner. It was Kenlin who found me and saved my life," Laurallin says very hesitantly. Glass scrapes across the floor as she pushes it along with the broom.

Affensash scratches the back of his head. "Great! It didn't happen the way I thought it did, but it still happened. I am sleeping in bed while an old lover gallantly sweeps in to rescue you."

"He is not an old lover," Laurallin says throwing the broom down. "He is an old friend! And I did not leave here intending to find him!"

"Well then an old friend who wants to be a lover, if that makes you feel any better!" Affensash snaps back. Laurallin turns to walk out the door.

"Don't go," Affensash says remorsefully. Laurallin stops, facing the door. "I'm sorry. I just don't understand."

"That's usually the problem," Laurallin says spinning on her heels. "You are so caught up in your little projects that you don't have time to try and understand. You don't want to take the time. Tell me, Affensash. Why is every project you are currently working on always so important that you don't have time for me or your family?"

"Have I really been that bad?" he asks, ignoring the question but listening instead to her feelings.

"Yes! No! Sometimes!" Laurallin shouts exasperatingly. "Oh, why is everything so complicated with you? Why do I have to love you and hate what you do at the same time? Why do I have to be bored with you and then feel like I can never live without you?"

Affensash starts to say something then stops. "You just said you loved me. Did you mean it?"

"I did not say that! Yes, of course I love you," Laurallin retorts, but it lacks the feeling Affensash yearns to hear. Affensash starts to rise and walk over to embrace her. She raises her hand to stop him. "That doesn't make everything all right. You realize that you never even asked me how I got here or what kind of danger I went through. I came a long way before I finally caught up with you."

Affensash stumbles on his own thoughts realizing she is right. "That's because I took it for granted that it didn't bother you," Affensash says very perplexed. "You have always told me stories about how rough it was when you were growing up with the tribe. You always made it sound like life and death matters occurred every day on the plains."

He stops and scratches his head, feeling stupid. "This was the first time anything like this has ever happened to me."

"Being chased by wolf-beasts and demons is not an everyday occurrence. I'm your wife. I'm flesh and blood with feelings. I was scared! I almost died!"

Affensash sits in his chair stunned. He never really thought about Laurallin being afraid and needing to talk about it. All their life together she has been the one calming him down. She always took things in stride.

She is right.

"Hmm," he says wistfully after a pause, "It used to be enough."

"What?" Laurallin asks, barely hearing him.

Shaking his head clear of his deep concentration, he explains. "You just said you loved me, but that wasn't enough. I used to think that was all we needed."

"I'm tired Aff. I don't understand what you are saying," she says, rubbing her forehead and pushing her hair back. "I was nearly eaten by wolves and devoured by demons today. I guess you're right," she laughs bitterly; "It is getting to be an everyday occurrence."

The little jab hurt more than Glenwall's knife wounds. He has never known what to say when he realizes he is dead wrong.

"I'm going to bed now," Laurallin says, wishing very much to avoid any more fighting. All she wants is to forget about men and hide under the warm covers. She isn't sure how much more of this she can take. She lies down in the bed; rose-colored dress and all. Laurallin picks up the second pillow and tosses it at Affensash. "You do understand that, don't you?" she asks and rolls over completely exhausted and for the moment uncaring.

Affensash sits by the open window as the moonlight feathers in around him. He tries to get comfortable in the chair. He studies Laurallin's sleeping form and wonders about himself. He has heard women complain about their husbands not being understanding, but his case was a little extreme. He had really ignored her. He can't even recall one conversation they had that concerned her, and only her, since she arrived at High Tower. How could she love him? That was the kind of question he always asked, because he never really understood why she loved him in the first place. It was pointless to try and figure out now if she still cared. One thing stood out clearly inside Affensash's worried world. He loved her. He loved her more than he ever has. With the death of Diane, mortality had come all too close to his awareness. Life in this world was short, really short, and Affensash was on fire with a want to spend it with Laurallin.

He stands from his chair and starts to walk to the bed. Laurallin is wrapped in the soft night shadows; the moon caressing her feet and partially outlining her bare legs. He wants so much to wake her and ask for forgiveness, to somehow take her from this place and give her everything he has neglected and stupidly overlooked through the years.

"I love you," he whispers into the night at the recumbent personification of his love. 'I love you,' is all he manages to produce from the turbulent struggle of love and rage that threatens to shatter his heart and leave him no better than the living dead. He sits back down with shaking hands.

This time the decision wasn't his. Laurallin had to choose. He could not force her, no matter how hard his soul pleaded to intervene. "I love you," he says with a yearning heart held powerless to be heard, or to express its trembling desires. He fluffs the pillow and succumbs to the ruthless sleep of the black night.

Something flies through the window and strikes Affensash on the side of the head!

He stifles a cry of pain and stands looking out the window. He can see two figures walking peacefully down the street, but he can't make out what they are saying. He starts to yell an obscenity at the men who must be playing a practical joke, but decides not to when he hears Laurallin roll over uneasily in her sleep. He suppresses another desire to crawl into the bed next to her and sits back down and dozes off.

A knock in the late hours of the morning wakes them both. They stumble to the door together and bump into one another before realizing they are both trying to answer it. They stare at each other for a moment, both through red-rimmed eyes, each waiting for the other to speak.

A second knock breaks the standoff and Affensash opens the door.

Steven enters, shaking his arms briskly at his side, and marches over to the fireplace hoping for a fire. Disappointed, he turns around, "It's a little chilly for my liking. It's good cold-catching weather; freezing in the morning and hot by noon, causing you to sweat just before it gets cold again."

Neither Laurallin nor Affensash bother to reply. Each turns to fidget with their own morning preparations.

"Wonderful," Steven mumbles under his breath, made aware of the tension between them. "Happy, happy, happy," he mumbles again, a little too loud, and Affensash shoots him an aggravated glare. "Well," he goes, on determined to say his piece regardless of whether they want to hear it. "No soldiers returned last night. I guess that means the Captain and all were lost to that thing and its demented followers."

Steven's comment was meant to be as light-hearted as possible under the circumstances, but it still sends shivers scrambling down Laurallin's spine.

"There are a few soldiers left in town and they are still patrolling the streets. Two of them left this morning to try and report what has happened, and to warn off the High Lord General. I told them they wouldn't make it, but you know how Eastern soldiers are about duty. If they do make it they will return with a full army next time."

An inner fear creeps through Laurallin and spills out along her tongue. "An army won't do! Baal was just playing with the Captain. The witches sat on balconies and threw more taunts than spells. Baal himself never even bothered to crawl from his hole. He was too busy to be bothered by a few hundred of their best soldiers. No Constable, an army won't do. I have crept along the edge of damnation twice now. I know how close that big gaping hole is to being Hell's own gate."

Laurallin's words shock Affensash. He has never heard his wife talk this way. There was fear in her voice and a sick sort of understanding of death.

"Happy, happy, happy," Steven repeats, rubbing his hands together, and turns to look out the open window. "A visitor strolled into town yesterday," Steven continues, still determined to speak his mind.

"What do you mean, Steven?" Affensash finally speaks up irritated. "Get to the point."

"I mean a small caravan arrived. There were six of them in all, I think. They carried a canvased litter and simply walked up to the gates and knocked. When the soldiers opened it they explained that they were merchants with a load of salt and spices. The soldiers asked how they managed to fight their way through the wolves. Personally, I thought that was a good question. The merchants replied that they hadn't seen any wolves." Steven stops and spins around to look at Affensash, hesitating a brief moment to let the absurdity of the statement sink in.

"I watched the soldiers from a nearby alley," Steven expounds, now that he is sure he has their attention. "Naturally, the soldiers were as skeptical as you or I would be. They demanded to look inside the litter. They started to examine the litter, but then each of the merchants tapped a soldier on the back of the head and the soldiers smiled, and let them pass."

"What? Are you insane? Why didn't you warn the soldiers? Why didn't you tell me last night? I would have helped you," Affensash blurts a string of indignant questions.

"Now wait! Neither one of you was in a very receptive mood. Besides, I'm still the Constable around here. I followed the little procession until they rented a vacant house on the second level of town. I watched them through most of the day. I have my only deputy watching the place right now. Nothing has happened. All of the merchants just entered town, went to the first available house, and have been closed up inside ever since."

"That is strange Steven. What if they are creatures sent from Baal?" Laurallin asks, more than a little concerned.

"I thought of that, but all of the men I have seen associated with that demon have turned beastly in nature. These men seemed quite civilized. I can't be sure, however. Whoever they are, they wanted to get into town unbothered and unnoticed by the Easterners. Now that in itself is not bad. I was hoping you knew who they were and could shed a little light on the subject."

Laurallin and Affensash look at each other for the first time since Steven entered the room. Neither of them seems to know.

"Well, I thought it was worth waiting to talk to you first. The town could use all the help it can get right now. I hoped they were friends. I will go tell the soldiers and flush whoever it is out." Steven shrugs and starts for the door.

"Just a moment, Steven," Laurallin reflects, smoothing at the wrinkles in her dress. "Since you have waited this long and there hasn't been any trouble, maybe we should go together without the soldiers, just in case the merchants are unexpected help?"

Steven turns with a smile, "I was hoping you would say that. With just one deputy it is a little too chancy to go it alone."

Laurallin looks directly at Affensash. "I think we should ask Kenlin along with us. If there is trouble his bow arm could help."

Affensash starts to protest, but Steven intercedes. "Was that the Hebelcaan you rode in with last night? Sorry, but I had to lock him up. It seems he wouldn't obey the curfew laws and kept sneaking out of his quarters."

"Steven!" Laurallin explodes unamused. "How could you? That man saved my life!"

"I told him twice to stay in his room and then I caught him tossing rocks through open windows. I am the law in this town," Steven says jingling the keys on his belt.

Before he can stop her, Laurallin jerks the keys away from him and stamps towards the door. Steven looks at Affensash for advice. Affensash is rubbing the side of his head just realizing what struck him in the night. Gritting his teeth, Affensash grabs little Ruefin and falls into line right behind her. Steven closes the door and does the same.

Out and into the street the three of them go; Laurallin taking long huffy strides, and the other two scurrying to keep up. A group of Eastern soldiers sees her coming and parts to let her pass. They read the expression on her face as being too dangerous to interfere with.

Affensash is in no great spirits himself. He is tense and angry that Kenlin would dare to try and contact his wife while he slept in the very same room. The audacity of the tribesman! She was his wife! His wife! And he was going to make that barbarian understand that!

Laurallin shoves open the door to the jail, rattling it on its hinges. Kenlin bolts upright from his cot when he sees Laurallin. Her hair streams behind her and she tosses a chair aside on her way to free him. She fumbles with the keys until the door finally clicks and swings open.

Kenlin pushes the door to the side and grabs her, pulling her next to his bare chest.

Just then Affensash and Steven round the corner into the jail. Affensash stops dead in his tracks. There was his wife in the arms of another man for the entire world to see.

His definition of Laurallin as his wife suddenly seems all wrong. She looks, now that she is in another's arms, like a ... like a woman; an independent person free to choose and go as she will. The embrace was for only a brief moment when Laurallin pushes away, but the sight was forever burned into Affensash's memory. The sudden shock, the sudden rearrangement of his world that so very much revolved around the definition of Laurallin as his wife was stricken instantly, and erased. She was suddenly different, and he was somehow changed.

Laurallin, free of Kenlin's arms, is somewhat embarrassed herself. Her upbringing did not allow her to engage in such practices in public. She was married and had just been caught breaking her vows. Kenlin had just shamed her! She feels dirty, but more than that she feels confused.

Affensash stares at Kenlin. The brave Hebelcaan stands tall and strong, looking at Laurallin with imploring eyes. His muscular frame and confident stance offers her promises of hope and protection. To Affensash, Kenlin looks like everything he could never be to her. Kenlin seems like a direct opposite of himself. He could easily understand why Laurallin would prefer Kenlin over himself. Kenlin somehow looked better, even to Affensash; his bitterness and fiery determination to make the tribesman pay for his desires drains away, washing with a gush from his body to the floor, and lies there alongside his shattered world and broken heart.

Steven breaks in, trying to divert an obvious conflict. "Sorry, Kenlin. Laurallin has explained how I have done you a grave injustice detaining you here against your will. I hope you don't bear a grudge."

"No, of course not," Kenlin says, taking his eyes away from Laurallin. He turns and sees Affensash for the first time. Affensash's face is so destitute-looking that Kenlin actually feels a pang of regret in his heart.

Lauralllin watches the two of them, her eyes darting back and forth, not knowing what to expect. Will they fight? Will they call each other names or just flip a coin for her affection? She wishes that she wasn't here. She wishes that she were gone from this place, alone with baby Dannia.

Steven walks to his desk, seeing his morning breakfast covered on a large plate. He grabs a piece of unleavened bread, breaks it in half, and tosses the pieces at Kenlin and Affensash. The two break their stare in order to catch the bread. A third piece is flipped to Laurallin and all three eat greedily, none of them willing to look at one another for a while.

"Well, Kenlin!" Steven begins in an enthusiastic tone of voice, trying to dispel the tension. "We came here to see if you would come along with us while we investigate a newcomer in town. We have some concerns that this visitor may be dangerous and Laurallin advises that we may be in need of your bow arm. What do you say? Would you be willing to follow us to the second level of town and take a look?"

"Of course I will come," Kenlin says, trying to catch a glimpse of Laurallin from the corner of his eye. He wants her approval before deciding what to do. She won't look up.

"Good! I thought we could count on you. Eat quickly. It's time I relieved my deputy. We can check it out this morning and then all of you can be free to roam the town for the rest of the day."

Laurallin stands and walks out the door, wishing the most to be free of the situation. Kenlin stuffs the last of the bread in his mouth, grabs his bow, and follows.

Affensash leans against a chair, stroking the fur of Ruefin, sulking in deep contemplation.

Steven crosses the room and slaps Affensash hard on the shoulder. Searing pain shoots through his arm, lifting him from his stupor. "Fight," Steven says brutally. "She's worth fighting for, so fight!" His own wife was lost to him, Steven thinks. This fool of an alchemist can still touch his and wants to let her walk away.

He spins Affensash off the chair and out the door where Laurallin and Kenlin stand waiting in the street. Steven sees them and smiles. "This way," he points and leads them all down the street to the road that heads to the second level of town. They all walk silently onward, but the nearer they get to the danger the more important it becomes, outweighing even their own gloomy, self-scrutinizing thoughts.

Kenlin takes a few quick strides and catches up to Steven. "Just what do you plan? Do you want to storm the place and take them by surprise?"

"No, I don't think that would be appropriate if they were either friend or foe. I had something a little more stealthful in mind." Steven suddenly stops and motions for them to move quietly down an alley. "The house the merchants occupy is across the street," he whispers as they transverse the back alley. "We can enter the back of a house here that sits directly across the street from theirs and then decide what to do once you have seen their place."

Down past several more houses, Steven finally pulls up behind one of the houses and raps out a code on the door. A click is followed by an opening latch and the four of them file in.

The house they enter is boarded, closed on the front, making it dark and musty smelling even in the early part of the day. Steven asks his deputy if anything has happened, but the deputy, really a fat lazy miner pressed into duty, stretches and scratches his bulging belly and shakes his head no. Steven gives him a copper piece and sends him on his way out the back door.

Affensash and Laurallin are already peering out the cracks in the front of the house looking at the merchants' house across the street. Kenlin is testing the tension in his bowstring and looking down the shafts of his arrows to choose the straightest ones.

"I don't like the looks of that place," Laurallin says to Steven. "There aren't any easy ways to approach it without being seen." The merchant's house is a long and narrow home sitting in between two others, with narrow alleys to either side.

"Is there anyone living in the houses next to theirs?" Laurallin asks.

Steven and Kenlin walk to the front next to Affensash and Laurallin and peer out through the cracks. "Yes, there is always someone at home in those houses. I thought about that, but I don't know either of the neighbors well enough to ask questions. I'm afraid one of them may have invited the merchants to town and I might prematurely tip my hand."

"It looks like we're left with the simple, direct approach," Kenlin concludes. "We will just have to walk down the street, slip into the alley, and listen at a window. We'll have to risk being seen."

"Can't we wait until it gets dark?" Laurallin interjects, worrying about creating any unnecessary trouble.

"No," Steven says absolutely. "I have waited too long already. We have given them too much time to create any mischief they desire. I need to know if there is going to be trouble now! Listen, everyone. Laurallin's concerns are just. At the first sign of trouble we run for it. The soldiers can handle any of the rough fighting. Does everyone understand that? No trouble!"

Everyone, including Affensash, shakes their head yes.

Kenlin sweeps up an old cover that the deputy used to sleep on and wraps his bow and quiver into a neat little bundle. He is the first to slip out the back and down the alley. The others are quick to follow, with Ruefin and Affensash lagging behind.

They head down the back of the houses before entering the street, trying to cause as little suspicion as possible in case someone should happen to see them. Laurallin and Steven wait until Kenlin is about twenty feet down the street before they step out of hiding, and Affensash follows twenty feet behind them. They proceed down the street towards the merchants' house as though they were simply going about their daily activities.

Kenlin gets just to the other side of the house and ducks quickly into the alley, stopping below a window. There he shakes loose his bow and nocks an arrow while listening intently at the window. Laurallin and Steven slip in immediately behind him.

They hear voices coming from the house; many voices in serious debate over some matter of importance. Kenlin can tell by the tone that it is urgent, but he can only catch small phrases of their conversation. He starts to rise and go nearer the window when they all hear a heavy thump on the roof above them. They freeze, afraid to move. The conversation in the house stops. Then suddenly, from above, comes a low, deep growl.

"Wolves!" Laurallin hisses, placing her hand on Steven, who seems to be in shock.

Kenlin rolls and falls against the wall of the house on the other side of the alley. This way he can get a clear shot at the thing on the roof and still cover the others' retreat out of the alley. With his back pressed hard against the wall, he pulls the arrow back to his ear.

There! Just over the edge is a large black...a large black...

"Shoot my panther tribesman and I will drop you where you stand," comes a deep bass voice from the back of the house.

Kenlin keeps his arrow pointed at the large black panther on the roof, but allows himself a glance down the alley. There he sees a burly man with a glistening tipped arrow aimed directly at his head. Kenlin sweeps his arrow around and points it at the stranger down the alley.

"Shoot at me and that panther will rip your throat out before you can scream for help," the man says very seriously, and the panther hunches to the edge of the roof and growls as if to confirm his master's threat. "Now that gives you two options," the burly man surmises in quiet forceful tones. "I'll give you a third. Lay that bow down and we might all walk out of here alive!"

Kenlin fights to control his breathing. If he lays his bow down, they will all be at the mercy of this stranger and his beast. No, he can't chance that for Laurallin's sake. Better to die and be sure that the others escape. His eyes narrow, finding just the right spot to kill the man with his first shot. His fingers tremble as he starts to let go of the string.

"Benolic!" comes the voice of Affensash, at last ducking down the alley.

Kenlin's fingers hold the string taut at the very last fraction of a second. "What is the bodyguard of Elder Enchantraen doing here?" Affensash asks, casually and altogether too loudly. Kenlin and the burly man both lower their bows. "I thought wherever the bodyguard of Elder Enchantraen was seen that...."

"Enchantraen was sure to follow!" comes yet another voice from around the back of the house. The great wizard himself walks around to stand behind Benolic, dressed in a dull red robe, but still looking ominous. "Listen, spy," the Elder challenges. "It has taken a lot of work to get into this town unnoticed. Instead of shouting my arrival in the street, why don't you and your curious colleagues come inside and sit down?"

The great wizard turns in a whirl and disappears back behind the house. Benolic smiles and bows deeply, motioning for them to follow his master. All of them stand still, wary, except for Affensash.

"It's all right, really. That is the Elder who started this whole thing." Affensash walks past them towards the back door. "Come now, Steven," Affensash says wryly, "surely you have heard of Enchantraen the great war wizard?"

When Steven nods yes, the rest fall into line and follow Affensash inside the house.

The door leads to a large dusty room. Enchantraen stands at the head of several large boards propped on barrels that form a table. Around the table are six plainly clothed men that appear to be merchants, but it is obvious now that they are wizards in disguise. Across the table are several intricate, well drawn maps.

"This is the spy I told you about," Enchantraen says, motioning towards Affensash in an overly grand fashion. "The Tuatha delivered your message to us, and I must say we certainly got more than we bargained for with our contract between our guilds."

"No one mentioned you were coming. What are you doing here?" Affensash asks, still a little shocked to see the great wizard himself in High Tower.

"Believe me, Affensash, I had no idea of the danger I was putting you in when I sent you here. You have more than completed your contract. I have doubled my payment to Jabir and it will be waiting for you and your wife when you return home."

The reference to Laurallin makes him involuntarily wince. He manages to ask again why Enchantraen is here.

"You of all people should understand why I am here. What you have uncovered in these mountains is the seething personification of despair. It was summoned to this world by a True One and has used its great power to infect my Guild. Our own wizards are in league with this beast and are using their raw new power to torture, butcher, and enslave the good people who resist them. Friends can no longer trust friends, and husbands their wives. It has taken its trickery and deceit as far as the Mystic Isles, and even I must be wary to whom I speak."

There is a long silent pause as Enchantraen gathers his thoughts. "Would you believe me if I told you that Glenwall was once a kindly, benevolent wizard in our Guild, who used to take the Tuatha sailing and fishing with him on the ocean? These wizards can attest to that if you don't believe me," Enchantraen says looking around the table. "Tell them,

Affensash! Tell them what you told the Tuatha. How many times did Glenwall strike Diane after she was dead? How many times did his dagger blindly seek to torture someone who had already passed beyond his brutal passions?" the great wizard asks contemptuously.

Affensash tries to push the vision of Diane's death from his mind. His heart swells and pumps despair and failure through his body.

"I have come to stop it before it can do any more harm. I will send it back to its own world where its own kind can deal with it."

Everyone stands in quiet reflection. They hear the great wizard's determination, but they also realize the appalling danger. Enchantraen draws his power, no matter how magnificently, from the aether around him. They fear Baal can see the aether. Baal may be the master of the craft. Baal can see what Enchantraen can only feel. "I suggest Affensash that you leave in the morning. My plan is to start an attack tonight. By the morning Baal and his cast of ghouls will be too busy to worry about you fleeing along the road to Mince."

"You can't go up that road to 'Death Watch'," Laurallin suddenly breaks in. "I have been there twice. You might as well send the demon a letter first telling him when to expect your arrival!"

Enchantraen smiles, making Laurallin feel very foolish for her sudden doubting outburst. "That is what we were just discussing. Steven, maybe you can help us?" Enchantraen smooths out the wrinkled parchment of the maps so that all may see.

"Wait,'" Steven blurts. "That is a map of the mines at the third level of the town. Those are supposed to be secret, known only to the master miners."

"Please don't worry about that just now. The information will not be abused. With Baal in your mountains you have no hope of ever resuming mining again. Now listen! We believe that this shaft extends the furthest into the mountain."

Steven nods that it might be so.

"Good. Then we could take this shaft and at its end we should be close to an old mining shaft from 'Death Watch'."

"You will be close, but the shafts of the two mines are still separated by a hundred feet of rock. The vein of ore just didn't run that way through the mountain," Steven concludes, "so the miners never connected the new mine with the old mine at 'Death Watch'."

"Steven, I have powers to create such passages in shafts that are that close together. I could temporarily create a passage to the old shafts and come upon the demon from his backside!" Enchantraen says, closing his fist as though he were capturing and crushing Baal that very moment in his hand.

"But even if that were true the old shafts of 'Death Watch' are unstable. That's why the old mine was closed in the first place. Many of these old shafts shown on this map may have collapsed. There is no guarantee that they will stand, even if you manage to reach them," Steven retorts, as if the plan were mad.

"That is why I have been trying to convince my good friends not to go. The demon has chosen his lair well. That is the risk I must take. I know the dangers as well as the rest of you, but can you name another better suited for the challenge!" Enchantraen glares around the table and no one, even among his friends, are willing to return his stare.

"My friends," he says pointing to the six wizards, "will remain in the new mine to keep the passage open until I am through. Chances are I will be too exhausted to try and reopen it myself."

The room is silent except for Benolic's big panther who is cleaning himself in the corner. "Benolic, you and your panther must return to the Isles. Too many people know we travel together. Go back, and anyone following us will think I have gone back also."

Enchantraen's words are so final that Affensash guesses that all objections have already been heard and dismissed. Affensash looks around the room at the downcast faces. His eyes finally come to rest on Laurallin. She is standing, unknowingly, next to Kenlin.

"I am not going back just yet," Affensash suddenly announces.

"What," is the unspoken word that forms on Laurallin's lips?

"I want to go with you," Affensash states boldly to Enchantraen.

"No, Aff!" Laurallin shouts bewildered. "The old witch said Enchantraen would be defeated!" Her sudden revelation sends a ripple of outrage across the table.

Enchantraen lifts his hands. "That changes nothing," the Elder protests. "Old Harrlow could not have known of the surprise we have planned for Baal when I meet him."

"Listen, Elder," Affensash bravely challenges Enchantraen. "You brought me here and I, more than anyone else, have witnessed the atrocities of this beast. I know better than you what doom you are headed for if you fail. I demand to go. I demand the right to redeem myself and the wrongs done to me and those around me!"

"Please don't, Aff," Laurallin pleads.

"All my life I have been a victim of what goes on around me. All my life I have watched others take charge and shape the events of my life. For once I want to be in charge of what happens to me."

Laurallin turns to Enchantraen, her eyes imploring him to tell her husband no, believing Affensash has other reasons for wanting to go to his doom. Enchantraen ignores her gaze and studies the eyes of Affensash, using them as a window to his heart.

"I shall be honored to have you come with me Affensash," the great wizard says after an intense pause. "You know, Affensash, great events sometimes turn on small affairs. You may well be the unexpected force that Baal finds incapable of handling. I am honored. I am honored indeed!"

Laurallin lets her breath out with a long sigh. "Then I will follow my husband and make it three times that I have walked into this Demon's Lair."

"And now I must go also," says Kenlin gritting his teeth. "We all leave tonight as Elder Enchantraen planned!"

All three have decided to go for different reasons. All three have decided to go because of love.

Kenlin turns and kicks the front door open, walking out into the street.

CHAPTER TWENTY-ONE

Vows Respoken

A wizard casting a spell acts as a conduit for aether energy. The amount of aether a wizard can conduct is a direct function of the wizard's skill level and is expressed as manna.

- of Wizards, from the treatise of High Fantasy

What Affensash had thought was going to be a beautiful day has turned sour and dismal. After leaving Enchantraen, he and Laurallin had gone their separate ways. Sitting on a barrel at the side of the inn, he watches Ruefin dart in and out of the rain. Each time the little fox returns to a dry place beside Affensash, he shakes his fur furiously. Then, Affensash pretends he is angry and is going to chase him. Ruefin runs around him and always escapes by going back into the rain.

The rain is good for Affensash. He has always felt most comfortable when the weather reflects his mood. This was perfect weather for the few hours that remained before he starts the walk to 'Death Watch'. He had meant everything he said to Laurallin and Enchantraen. Right now his whole life was reshaping around him. The old habits and familiar ways of thinking no longer comforted him.

He is at an important crossroad in his life and knows it. But as long as he has to undergo such enormous change, he might as well force some of those changes to his liking. In the past he has always been motivated to accomplish things for himself, and only for himself. Looking back on that doesn't make him feel proud. This will be one of the changes to his liking.

When the trip to 'Death Watch' is over he will feel better about his new self. If Laurallin were going to leave him this would give him enough pride and confidence in himself to continue on, alone. Another thing he would like to change is his physical self. That, he well knows, isn't possible. The new Affensash is still going to be small-framed and of slight build, but at least he could have a bigger heart.

Baby Dannia is his only real worry now. He can't stop Laurallin from going. It is pointless to argue with her. Every argument he used she would just use the same one to explain why he should not go. She has been through as much as Affensash, and therefore, has every bit as much right to go. What about Dannia? If something were to happen she would be without both parents.

With Diane's murder still fresh on his mind, Affensash is certain something is going to happen. The frail mortality of life has become very obvious. Many on this trek to 'Death Watch' are not likely to come back. Who would it be? Which life is Death going to snatch from them, leaving the rest with the empty hollow corpse? One, two, or maybe all of them? It just doesn't seem fair that Dannia might have to pay the price for his sacrifice. Death is coming. He could smell it in the air. It has been summoned to 'Death Watch' to clean up whatever Baal discards.

The red glow has been growing from the old mine through most of the day. With the rain clouds blocking out most of the natural light, the mountains are illuminated by the red abhorrent light. Even the bottoms of the black rain clouds are lined with the faint red glare, giving the world an eerie taint of death. As the day wears on, the glow becomes more intense, until the puddles that Ruefin and Affensash are playing in begin to reflect the red light, making them look more like pools of blood instead of water. Did Baal know they were coming? Why did he choose now of all times to exert his mastery over our land?

Finally, Affensash gives up and he and Ruefin go inside to have a warm meal in the dining room on the Inn's first floor. After eating his fill, he goes to his room and isn't surprised when he doesn't find Laurallin there. He crawls into bed, listening to the rain splatter in great gusts against the roof. Eventually it slows down into a rhythmic pattern, and he and Ruefin manage to sleep the last few hours of the day.

When he awakens, he packs his alchemy case, including a vial of his new potion, picks up Ruefin, and leaves. His stomach churns as he nears Enchantraen's house and thoughts about backing out at the last minute cross his mind. Maybe he was doing this to prove something to Laurallin? He remembers having the same last minute fears on his wedding day. A last-second opportunity arose to duck out, but he didn't.

Decisions that have far-reaching consequences always make him squeamish. He isn't going to change his mind. He knows that. He just wishes that the new Affensash will stop the doubting and start out on a more positive note.

When he arrives, Kenlin and Laurallin are already waiting. The wizards are dressed in miner's clothes and have picks and shovels to complete their disguises. Laurallin and Kenlin are still dressed in their Hebelcaan clothing. Laurallin looks thin and brown. Her hair is neatly combed and lying loose around her shoulders. Her legs are bare and smooth showing no signs of the red streaks from the wolves. She smells of the sweet healing ointment that Madillyn has been giving her. Her eyes however, are red and swollen, as if she has spent the whole night crying.

Affensash sees her and wants her! He wants her physically and emotionally. Another thought crosses his mind about sweeping her up in his arms and running from this place. But again he stops himself, cooling his passions with a reminder that the choice is not his. It seems as though the new Affensash is going to be in love with Laurallin, just like the old. It also seems that the new Affensash is overthinking things, just like the old. If they both live through this he will have to deal with it later.

Enchantraen forces them all to cover up in woolen cloaks before leaving. Walking slowly up the streets they all look very much like a party of miners off to work. The need for surprise is of the utmost importance, but the weather makes Affensash feel like they have already been discovered.

The rain continues, and increases, as they reach the third level. This area of the town, which Affensash hasn't seen before, is strictly for mining. There are mills and dirty brown buildings lining the outside of the mine's entrance, very much in contrast to the cleanliness of the rest of the town. Steven had said the witches that used to live here were responsible for the designs in the cleaner levels.

There hasn't been any mining for months. Most of the miners are gone, and those surviving are needed for the town's protection, rather than worrying about its income. Steven managed to send away the few left that stood guard at the mine's entrance.

Enchantraen and the whole procession hurry under a wooden roof that arches over the entrance of the mine. There, they gladly take off their woolen cloaks. The wizards waste no time in striking flint to light the torches. One by one they sputter and flare around the party. As they wait for the last one to be lit, Affensash looks despondently around him.

They are surrounded by splashing pools of water, blood-red from the glow. The torchlight glitters in the closer pools, reflecting like flecks of a broken mirror. Baal must know, Affensash concludes. He has never seen a day so frighteningly dismal. He stares at the reflecting torchlight imagining them twisting into corpses' candles. He doesn't notice when the last torch is lit and the group begins to move into the mine.

Laurallin waits for him to go, but when he doesn't move she touches him lightly on the shoulder. He looks up with a jerk. Their eyes meet and lock together. Neither one moves, but neither one understands the other's feelings. Laurallin kisses him on the cheek and walks after the wizards.

Affensash follows; the last of his thoughts for escaping coming to an end as he realizes he is finally and fatally committed.

Enchantraen leads the way inside. Directly behind him are three of the wizards, then Laurallin, Kenlin, and Affensash. Behind them follow the last three wizards. Kenlin walks closer to the front group of wizards, while Affensash is nearer the back. Laurallin walks an uncomfortable distance between them both.

The middle of the mine is heavily rutted with wagon tracks. For many years miners and mules have pulled the precious rocks from the deep black hole. The air is damp and Affensash believes it is because of the rain outside. As they move further and further into the blackness it becomes apparent that the mine has always been damp. The moisture originates from within. The torchlight rolls across the high walls of the main tunnel. The rock is flecked with worthless sparkling crystal, and together with the dampness creates a glistening, magical feeling as if they were entering a fairy world.

The walls are high and not at all as cramped as Affensash expected. He dislikes close, constricted places. They proceed along quietly and cautiously until the walls of the main tunnel begin to widen and spread even further.

"I have always marveled at what man is capable of doing with long persistence," Affensash finally says to the wizards that follow.

"It wasn't just man who made these passages," replies Gondollan, a stout, red-faced wizard. "This mine is honeycombed with natural passages and rooms of its own. This tunnel, according to the map, should lead into a huge natural room the size of a coliseum."

Affensash looks at him incredulously, but soon the walls veer and shoot up sharply again to heights unnatural for man to create.

They travel methodically along, too solemn to engage in conversation. The wizards stop several times along the way to light new torches when they find them at even intervals along the tunnel. Laurallin makes several attempts to drop back and walk beside Affensash, but he doesn't want to have anything to do with her. He couldn't bear to hear her excuses, or to listen to her while she prepared him for the worst. In his own mind, it was over and he had lost.

It was easy for him to make that conclusion while watching the two Hebelcaan walk in front of him; a perfect physical match for each other. Kenlin was making strong, even strides to the left of him with his bow strapped across his back. Laurallin was on the other side in her Hebelcaan clothing, with her bow also strapped across her back. Trailing behind them is Enchantraen, the only person who seems to outshine them.

Affensash never felt so out of place in his life. He doesn't belong among these kinds of people. He feels like a monkey scampering after his human masters. They have two arms and two legs, and they all put their pants on the same way; yet it isn't the same. A monkey just doesn't wear the same kind of pants!

It was odd to feel this way about Laurallin, his own wife. Somehow she has become more than just his wife. He never saw her so trim and so confident. She has become, in many ways, like Diane; aloof, knowledgeable, and untouchable.

The thought of Diane sends sudden panic through his blood. Oh god, what if Laurallin dies the same way? What if she falls right before him while he stands helpless and watches? His legs suddenly burn with energy and he thinks about running to her, grabbing her, and protecting her – this time. The thought of Laurallin actually being hurt sends racing nightmares up his spine. There they stop short and crawl along the base of his skull.

The party pulls up, Enchantraen lifts his hand and everyone stops, quietly standing in the flickering torchlight.

Water?

The sound of rushing water clearly echoes down the tunnel. Enchantraen pulls out a map and a wizard rushes to his side with a torch. Kenlin joins them and they stand together, pointing in different directions, too far away from Affensash for him to clearly make out their words.

Finally, Kenlin leads Enchantraen off to the side and reveals a large, second passage that cuts away from the main tunnel. They motion for the rest to follow. They all start to move forward again with Enchantraen now sharing the lead with Kenlin. Laurallin looks back over her shoulder, and Affensash catches a glimpse of one long tear streaking down her cheek.

The sight startles Affensash and weakens his pig-headed resolve. The next hour he spends trying to reassess his conclusions. Was that tear for him, or for their past life and ruined marriage?

The side walls and ceiling gradually rise, and the sounds of rushing, splashing water become louder. They stop at the edge of the room that Gondollan, the red-faced wizard had told Affensash about.

Indeed the room is enormous. Just how big is impossible to tell, for the torchlight will not reach to the ceiling. The walls of the room are stratified in various colored rock. Some layers are red and brown, but the higher layers are tinted in blues and greens, adding more intrigue to the solitary magical kingdom.

From high above and out of the darkness, a waterfall cascades. It plummets down splashing against the rocks, ripples over, and continues downward in sheets of misty rain. At its base is a large pond that must connect to an underground stream that carries the freshwater the rest of the way down the mountainside.

Over the roar of the waterfall, Enchantraen, Kenlin, and the wizards consult their map. Enchantraen spots a large wooden elevator just to the other side of the falls and determines that to be their next destination. They start off once again, skirting the edge of the sparkling pond.

Laurallin is not the type to overreact. She hisses through her teeth pointing out over the pond. The sound unnerves them all as it echoes throughout the cavernous room.

Kenlin reaches for an arrow and the wizards drop everything to prepare a spell. Affensash counts four heartbeats before a set of three werelights appears over the wizards' heads and dart away from them across the pond. The three little spheres of light race around the pond in a frantic search. Suddenly they stop, circle, and hover over a bobbing object in the water.

The enchantment of the mine is suddenly lost, illuminated by the three harbingers of truth. A dead body floats in the pond. As if reaching out with his hand, a wizard casts a spell and the body moves towards the bank.

Enchantraen walks to the side of the pond to examine it as it draws near. He motions for the wizard pulling the body to stop. It is too late. Everyone sees why Enchantraen doesn't want the body brought on land. The corpse is only half there! The other half appears to be gnawed away. With a wave of his hand the corpse goes under, out of sight, to a watery grave.

Turning around, Enchantraen announces grimly, "It must have been a miner. It is impossible to tell from how far up the river the body was washed. I had hoped to travel the new mine without any incident, but it seems that the demon's claw extends even here."

While the wizards exchange a few mumbled thoughts, Laurallin walks into Affensash's arms for a tender comforting moment.

Kenlin turns and points to the man-made wooden elevator acting as if he doesn't notice. "This is the way up to the next level of the mine. We must take this elevator, and then another, before we are to reach the farthest tunnels."

Silently, the party continues around the pond, Laurallin staying back with Affensash. The high black ceiling takes on the feeling of a weighty doom; a doom that you know is there, but you can't quite see. No matter which way you may run, or where you may choose to hide, it is always there waiting.

They reach the elevator and the wizards begin to file in.

"I can't shake the feeling that we are being watched, Aff," Laurallin says, hanging back afraid to let the others hear.

"I doubt that Baal itself has come here. From the looks of Enchantraen's maps, he has plenty of room to haunt the old mine," Affensash says, trying to be reassuring.

"Still, I feel something! I wish I could see the roof of this place. It feels like a hundred eyes are peering down at us."

"It won't last long," Kenlin breaks in, overhearing their conversation as they enter the elevator. "This will take us to a man-made tunnel that is much smaller. We won't feel so vulnerable there." Kenlin manages a smile, but Laurallin can only return a small, appreciative glance.

The elevator begins a long creaking ascent up the shaft as the wizards take turns pulling on the thick ropes. The actual tension on the ropes is light. The elevator was made to carry much larger loads of rock and men. The wizards not pulling on the ropes keep a careful vigilance for trouble. Both Laurallin and Kenlin nock an arrow and stare over the sides. No Hebelcaan feels comfortable in a cage.

When they reach the top and the big wooden doors slide open, Ruefin rises out of Affensash's pocket and shakes a lazy head. "How you can sleep through all of this is beyond me, Ruefin," Affensash muses, "but I think if my pocket were big enough I would crawl into it and do the same thing."

Laurallin's little laugh surprises Affensash. It has been so long! She always liked his little quips, no matter how unfunny they seemed to others.

The top of the shaft is littered with carts and mining equipment. The edge of the tunnel near the elevator has been cut away and is much broader than the rest of it. The tunnel slopes slowly upward into the mountain.

It is getting late in the day by the recollections of Affensash's and Ruefin's stomach. The group decides to continue, knowing that the quicker they arrive, the less chance they have of being discovered.

True to Kenlin's words, this tunnel is not nearly as large as the one they left below. There are still deep ruts down the middle indicating that it is a heavily used area of the mine. As they walk along, the wizards find more torches, usually at the intersections of new tunnels. At each of these intersections Kenlin and Enchantraen refer to the map and confirm which direction to travel.

Finally, at one such intersection Ruefin bites and pulls at the pant leg of Affensash. "I think we had better stop and eat. If we don't, Ruefin will eat my pants off, and the rest of this journey could prove quite embarrassing."

Laurallin suddenly drops to her knees and lets an arrow loose down a black mine tunnel. The other wizards immediately spring into action. Flames dance on the fingertips of two of them. A third recreates the werelights and sends them racing down the tunnel. The tunnel makes a sharp turn and dead ends. There they see the shaft of Laurallin's arrow, quivering in an oak brace.

"What is it?" Enchantraen demands of Laurallin.

"I don't know! I felt something staring at us from the darkness," she says white-faced and staring at the werelights.

"You felt? You mean you didn't see?"

"No, I didn't see anything."

"Listen," Enchantraen says consolingly while he motions for his wizards to dispel their incantations. "You need to control your nerves. Each time one of these overprotective wizards casts a spell they use up a little more of their power. We have to be careful not to cause them to waste it."

She overreacts.

If there was one thing Laurallin couldn't stand, it was being spoken to in a condescending tone of voice. She rises to her feet and squares away facing the Elder. "Look. I don't like wasting arrows either. I felt something very real. I have felt it following us since we left the waterfall." She pauses taking a deep breath. Then she marches forward, grabs the map from Kenlin's hand, stares at it a moment, and heads off taking the lead.

"Ruefin, I think we will have to wait for our supper," Affensash mumbles in a low voice. Dropping the growling fox back into his pocket, he hurries after the group. Laurallin is a Hebelcaan and is most comfortable in the great expanse of the outdoors. Slowly, she is adjusting to the mine and that same courage is returning.

The trip through the mines is exhausting due to the long hours of continuous, upward climbing. Affensash never gets the same feeling of being watched as Laurallin. To keep up his strength, and to quiet Ruefin, he grabs small pieces of cake and cheese and nibbles them along the way. Everyone else seems to be impervious to growling stomachs, too caught up in the urgency of the quest to give much thought to personal matters.

Affensash was feeling better about Laurallin, and this made him even more hungry. Maybe Steven was right, Laurallin was a woman worth fighting for. Why would he ever give up?

This stretch of the climb takes them far past dinnertime. Finally, Enchantraen calls for a stop and they prepare a cold meal during a short rest. The torches' hiss is the only sound that they can hear in the dead, quiet mines.

Several wizards stand guard just out of torchlight while the rest prepare the food. Laurallin sits devouring a half a loaf of bread, but continues looking around uneasily. Maybe the black shades had finally gotten to her? Maybe the whole trip has been too much. It makes Affensash feel uneasy. This isn't like his wife. She always has good instincts, but then she is always able to pinpoint her doubts. This time she isn't able to say what is wrong. She is dealing in the world of magic and the supernatural. Those things traditionally make her feel uneasy.

A small rock clicks down the side of a wall. This time a wizard is the first to notice. His hands flare and he throws a flaming fireball. The ball hits, chars the rock, and bounces along a small ledge, rolling until it bursts apart against a boulder.

As little shards of rock and flame tumble down the side of the wall, Enchantraen bellows, "What is it? What do you see?"

There is a pause as all the others sit poised, ready to strike at anything that retaliates. Nothing happens.

"I don't know," says the wizard that threw the fireball. "I saw something move along the ledge."

"How do you know it wasn't a friend?" Enchantraen asks exasperated. "What has gotten into you people?"

"I don't know," says the wizard who cast the spell. "I just knew that whatever it was, it wasn't friendly. I could feel its evil closing around us."

"That's it! No one is to shoot or cast a spell without my permission. If you disobey me it had better be a life or death situation, or I vow to make it one! I can't stand a bunch of nervous book-learned wizards enchanting and trying to kill every cave creature in this mountain. With this much noise we might as well go up and knock on the demon's front door," Enchantraen shoves the rest of his meal back into his sack.

He stands, picks up a torch and starts off again. Everyone else scrambles nervously to follow.

The other wizards seem to take offense at being called book-learned wizards. It is true that they have not lived the life of a war-wizard, but they were hardly a bunch of cloistered neophytes. They are high level wizards who earned their skills after years of painstaking research and practice. They are True Ones. Still, they all understood their Elder's hot temper, and each of them learned to accept it long before they volunteered for this trip.

Many hours later they reach the second elevator. It is located in a much smaller room than the first, and it seems to be the focal point of several major tunnels. This elevator goes up and disappears through the rock ceiling. It is impossible to tell how far it runs, but it gives the impression of going much higher than the first.

After a quick examination of the elevator, they proceed in and close the door. Just like before, the wizards methodically work the thick ropes, trading off when they are tired. They switch more often than before. Everyone except for Enchantraen and Kenlin seems to be tiring quickly.

On and on they rise, occasionally passing a level, but refusing to stop, determined to make it to the top level in one trip; past one level and then into rock, out and past another.

Kenlin and Affensash take their turn at the rope as they ascend the cold, dank shaft for hundreds of feet. The labored breathing of the men mixes with the creaking rhythmic sounds of the pulleys.

The elevator jerks once, rumbles, and then falls!

The sudden change in direction sends everyone spinning inside the small cage. Ruefin is nearly dashed against the shaft's wall. Affensash's quick reflexes save him. Enchantraen alone manages to stay on his feet.

The elevator has already gained incredible speed plummeting downward, accelerating as it goes. Enchantraen remains calm. Lying on his back Affensash can see Enchantraen forming blue patterns that float around his head. From Affensash's vantage point everything seems to stop and drift into a dream state.

The elevator begins to slow, or at least it seems to slow. Either that or the wizard begins to move in a fast, blurred motion. Enchantraen races around the elevator lifting the wizards to their feet.

No matter how hard Affensash tries to recover, he simply can't match their incredible speed. Just like he had seen them do before, the wizards form a circle and begin to chant a spell. This time their chant is fast and comical sounding. It's as though their voices have been raised an octave.

By the time Affensash, Laurallin, and Kenlin rise to their feet, the spell is completed. A blue force strikes the roof with such power that some of the timbers crack and threaten to splinter.

The elevator changes direction and shoots upward.

Again, the sudden change in direction sends Affensash, Kenlin, and Laurallin spinning to the floor. All of the wizards find no trouble in keeping their balance. The three try to rise again, but this time it proves impossible. An odd force like gravity is holding them down. Affensash can almost feel the skin on his face pull tight by the great speed of the elevator's ascent.

Crash! The top of the elevator splinters away.

They have reached the top, smashing into the ceiling. The wizards secure the elevator and leap out. Affensash tries to rise and follow, but his muscles feel out of control as though he had been drinking. Laurallin and Kenlin are struggling around him, no better off. He manages to rise to his knees and look out the door. Through the crowd of wizards he sees a strange creature pinned against a rock by wizardly threads of light-blue binding.

The creature's hide shimmers with scales of gold. Its long thin body thrashes and twists unceasingly beneath the blue bindings like a tortured snake. The creature's form is partially blocked by the back of Enchantraen, but Affensash can hear it growling curses at the Elder.

Baal! The thought suddenly sounds in Affensash's slow-moving brain. The great wizard has already got him cornered and is about to destroy him.

With a great thrust, the demon snaps the blue bindings like pieces of rotten twine. The air is shattered by the roar of a hundred lions as the demon lunges for Enchantraen's throat. Still moving in slow motion, Affensash attempts to cover his ears from the deafening blast, but it is over before his hands can reach his head.

The great war-wizard merely slaps the creature back with a blue glowing hand. The demon spits green flecks of blood, says something, and then tries to attack once again. With the back of his hand, Enchantraen knocks the demon's head back and snaps its spine. In great venomous clouds of green mist the demon's body dissolves, returning to its netherworld.

Affensash's body tingles as the magic around him is released, and he finds himself moving again at normal speed.

"What is going on?" shouts Kenlin, as though he were betrayed. "How dare you cast a spell to slow us down? We have a right to protect ourselves also!"

Enchantraen turns on Kenlin as though he were going to strike him. "Watch your accusations tribesman! I'm not used to hearing such threats, even from friends."

Kenlin does not flinch and his eyes still demand an answer.

"I did not cast a spell on you! Instead I cast a spell on the others to speed them up. It was the only way I could give the wizards enough time to complete their own spells to lift the elevator before we were smashed at the bottom."

Laurallin moves forward and places her hand gently on Kenlin's arm. He turns and she smiles, sympathizing with his pent-up frustration at not being able to defend himself. A man like Kenlin wants to live or die by his own abilities. The thought of a wizard interfering and keeping him helpless would naturally set his temper on fire. Once he realizes the truth, he just shakes his head and laughs, slowly letting the adrenalin leave his body.

"Is that it?" Affensash asks in disbelief. "Is that all there was to the demon Baal?"

Enchantraen jerks his head back in surprise. "That wasn't Baal! Really, Affensash, I don't think you understand the true danger of our mission. That thing was simply a creature of Baal called to help him. It was a lesser demon called over to our world to *serve* Baal. Lucky for us, it wasn't an obedient servant. It was meant to guard the innermost tunnels of this mine. It seems Baal was clever enough to anticipate this possible move against him. That demon you saw was a little too greedy. It smelled the blood and sweat that the miners left in the rocks. Its hunger got the better of it and it moved inward in hopes of stalking some human meat for itself. It was too ignorant to realize who we were before it sabotaged our elevator. When the elevator rose instead of falling, we surprised it."

Affensash smiles recalling the power that emanates and flows through the Elder's veins; then he notices the other wizards' sullen expressions. "What is it? What did I miss?" Affensash asks confused.

Gondallon, the red-faced wizard that spoke to him before, enlightens them all on the gloomy discovery. "That demon Elder Enchantraen just slew was called here by Baal, who is as you know, a demon himself. That means that 'Death Watch' has been transformed into a 'Demon's Gate! Where one demon has been summoned by another you can be certain others have followed. Walking into 'Death Watch' will be like walking into a basket of cobras!"

Together, Affensash and Laurallin turn to stare at Enchantraen, their eyes asking if the statement is true.

"Really, Gondollan! You needn't be so blunt. What he says is true," Enchantraen says, answering the unspoken question. "I would understand if you decide not to go any farther. As for me, all it means is that I must make every effort to avoid confronting any more of his minions. We must avoid them at all cost for two reasons. One, they will drain us of our energies, and two, they may escape to warn Baal of our coming. This time we were lucky. The next time we can't trust to luck. Our next confrontation must be with Baal himself!"

The wizards and Kenlin surge forward around Enchantraen at once, demanding to be heard, each with their own suggestions and questions. Affensash chases after Ruefin who is getting dangerously close to the edge of the torchlight.

Laurallin follows after him. They catch up to Ruefin and sit together on a rock, while the others continue in heated debate.

"Aff," Laurallin says, looking up with moist brown eyes. "I've decided something very important that we must talk about."

Affensash feels his heart lurch and thrash around in his chest like the demon in the bindings. He can't bear to hear what she might say. If she were to say she was leaving him now he knows he won't have the strength to live through this quest. He raises his hand and places his fingers on her lips.

"Please don't say it now. Wait until this is over. The time is not right. I have to do this for me. Do you understand? For me!"

"No, I don't understand. I thought you might change your mind now that the danger has become so much worse. A demon's gate is no place for us. Please tell me you're not doing this. You have nothing to prove," she says visibly upset.

"I don't think I'm doing it to prove anything to anyone. It is to prove something to myself. You are right about one thing, however. A demon's gate is no place for us. Don't go with me because you feel you have an obligation. You don't! I'm telling you, Laurallin. Don't do it out of feelings of guilt and obligation! You owe Dannia more than you owe me."

Laurallin looks down, stroking the soft fur of Ruefin. "That's what I meant to tell you. I will follow you because I want to, not because I have to! Do you understand? I want to!"

Affensash listens, but is half afraid to hope for the total implications of her statement. Lucky for his churning emotions, the group starts off once more. For the moment he can concentrate on his aching feet and leave his heart for later.

The last part of the trek through the mine is by far the most difficult. The wide spacious tunnels give way to small cramped offshoots. The whole group finds themselves walking for hours in a bent-over position, which causes terrible cramping in the legs and lower back. The wizards begin casting strength spells, like the spell Diane used on Affensash, just to keep the group moving. It takes several castings and many hours to reach the farthest end of the mine.

Finally, the group is crawling on their hands and knees. When the passage narrows to a belly crawl, the worst fears begin to set in on Affensash. The whole mine feels like a crypt and he is crawling head first into his casket. He finds that he has to fight back his fears, as they threaten to overwhelm him. Fear surges in waves. He aches to push up and break free, but he knows if he tries it will fail and he will go mad.

At last Enchantraen halts in a wide section of the tunnel where everyone can crawl to face each other. Only one torch remains burning as the wizards try to reserve the others for the long wait ahead.

"This is where the new mine ends," Enchantraen says breathing heavily. "No one is obligated to go with me. When we are on the other side, if those who go prove unable to keep up, I must warn you now that I will be forced to leave you behind."

Affensash only half hears the Elder's words; his blood his pumping through his head with a great swooshing sound. The maddening feeling of a coffin closing its lid washes in on the next wave of fear. Through a panting sigh he gasps, "Hurry!"

Mistaking Affensash's panic to be a sign of bravery Enchantraen laughs, "I wish I had such courage. "His hand moves and light blue patterns spring into the cramped tunnel. Heat surges past Affensash and the confining rocks give way around him.

CHAPTER TWENTY-TWO

Demon's Gate

Passage: *It is used by wizards to pass through walls or blocked passageways. A succession of these spells would create a corridor even through mountains.*

- The Spell Book, from the treatise of High Fantasy

The six wizards walk behind Enchantraen. Affensash picks up a torch and he, along with Kenlin, Laurallin, and Ruefin follow. Leading the way, the great wizard traces light-blue patterns in the air as he walks. The rock melts and fades around them. The result of the spell produces heat that steams the water from the rocks and makes the mystical tunnel one large sweatbox. The passage it makes is cylindrical and slick on the edges. The torchlight reveals each new section that the wizard creates. They all move slowly forward listening to Enchantraen's rhythmic chanting.

The Elder's spells are consistent and flawless, but the strain is beginning to show after each careful repetition of the spell. The tunnel is perfect and unchanging. The heat and steam drain the strength of even Kenlin and Laurallin. At last the final spell is cast and they all stumble into a cold damp natural tunnel in 'Death Watch'.

Enchantraen walks down the natural tunnel to investigate. It appears that they are lucky and have opened onto a main passage that should allow them all to continue standing upright and unhindered. Everyone remains silent expecting to hear howls or demon laughter.

All is quiet.

When Enchantraen returns to the group, he walks to the passage he made so cleanly through the rock. "If Baal has been tracking us by our use of aether he certainly will know we are here now."

The words of the crazy prophet sound in Laurallin's ears, 'Enchantraen will be defeated.'

The dampness of the passage has soaked the cloths of Affensash's torch and it begins to sputter. "We had best light another," Enchantraen says, "That one is about done." The torch sputters one last time and fades. In chilly darkness, Affensash asks for another. There is silence. Someone chuckles.

"We forgot the torches," Laurallin concludes. They all sit in the eerie darkness. Enchantraen finally laughs, breaking the tension.

"Don't panic," Affensash whispers. "I can help." He opens his case and rustles blindly through the cloths that wrap and protect his precious chemicals. Recognizing one vial, he takes it out and tucks it under his belt. Removing a second vial, he shakes it and a faint light appears. His light potions are faulty. In daylight the glow would be unnoticeable. Here in the pitch blackness it gives off enough light to see the outline of the tunnel around Affensash's feet.

"Well, this will have to do," Enchantraen says, suddenly looking very old and tired in the faint light. "If there comes a need for better light I will summon up my werelights, but I wouldn't want to do that for a time. The passage spells have left me rather weak. It will be necessary to conserve as much of my power as possible for Baal. Well now," he says standing trying to wipe off his soaking robes.

He turns to the six wizards who accompanied them. "You six must stay. Two of you must use your power to keep the passage open. It will take much less manna to maintain it than it did for me to create it. If Baal is tracking us by our use of magic he will send the wolves. Four of you are to watch for the wolves at all times. Fight! If things do not go as I planned I will summon help. That help must come through your tunnel. You must be ready at all times."

The six already knew this having discussed the plan back at High Tower. There was no need to argue it now. They know that they are most likely the decoy and the wolves will come for them. In this way they can best serve and protect their Elder.

"Which way do you think we should go?" Enchantraen asks the rest of the party.

Looking down the tunnel, both ways seem to be equally as large, and neither way gives any indication of tapering off. Ruefin is scurrying down one way, sniffing and darting around in his usual manner. The little fox stops, turns around and heads back the other way.

"Well, we might as well follow Ruefin," Kenlin says in his deep bass voice.

"No, we should go the way he was originally sniffing. Ruefin always tries to avoid trouble. He probably picked up the scent of a wolf and high-tailed in the other direction."

Enchantraen shrugs and says, "You've got the light Alchemist. I'm following you."

The tunnels of 'Death Watch' are stifling dark and the air is almost suffocating. It is hard to understand. Affensash feels the walls should scream in agony, but they can't. The caves and manmade tunnels are quiet except for the occasional sound of water dripping down a cold wall. At each intersection he expects to come across the great lurking form of Baal, waiting for them in the shadows to pounce and render their limbs from their body.

Enchantraen begins to recognize markings on the walls that are also on the map. Soon he gets a general idea of their whereabouts. Finally, he is able to guide their steps in a more purposeful direction. To the surprise of everyone else, he is heading towards the main entrance of the mine.

Eventually, Ruefin becomes tired of scurrying around in front of the group and drops back tugging on Affensash's robe to be placed back into his familiar pocket. Everyone is very quiet, each feeling the heavy, foreboding atmosphere of the mine, and each struggling to deal with it in their own way.

For Affensash, the way is easy. He shakes his vial furiously from time to time causing it to glow brighter. It's as if he expects the aura of the tiny light to fight back the darkness and shield him from the malignant despair that hangs so heavily in the air. It was, after all, natural for an alchemist to rely on his craft during his most desperate moments.

The feeling that death is lurking in each shadow becomes so strong that Laurallin and Kenlin nock an arrow and begin scouting ahead of the others. They run along just at the edge of the party's sight, ducking in an out of the shadows, always seeking concealment behind the large stone outcroppings that line the tunnels. At each turn in the path, one of them takes the lead. Crouching low, they run to the very edge and listen around the bend. When they hear nothing, they swing around and aim their arrow down the tunnel, watching and listening for any movement. While one watches, the other stands behind to protect from any sudden attacks. Their precision as a team is perfect. They move with stealth through the mine as one.

Even though the procedure is sound in providing reasonable protection to the group, Affensash finds it unnerving. Each time, he expects a giant clawed hand to reach out of the darkness and snatch the one in the lead. Each time, his heart stops and a sick feeling passes through his stomach.

Enchantraen follows behind them all reading the map. The Elder seems to have turned inward, relying on the others to guide and look out for dangers. During the brief pauses before going around corners or large bends, he recites or meditates on his craft. The repetitious casting of the passage spell really seems to have left him tired and vacant. As the smell and brutal existence of the demon becomes stronger to everyone's awareness, Enchantraen seems to slip further and further away.

Deep within the tunnel a series of growls erupts. The sounds are distant, but just how far away they are is impossible to tell in the echoing confines. Affensash is almost relieved when he hears it. He is prepared mentally for the physical offensive. Each moment waiting in the purgatory of the silent mine threatens his sanity.

Both Laurallin and Kenlin stop and look around a large sweeping corner. They motion for the others to come up. Peering around the corner, they can see a faint light at the far end of the tunnel. It appears as though the tunnel feeds out into another one well-lit by torchlight.

Just as the light filters down to them, so does an even stronger feeling of dread. No one, not even Enchantraen, can understand it. The feeling of despair becomes so strong that no one can believe it might be caused by their own personal anxieties. Something is there, almost as thick as a physical presence; it hangs black and blotted in the air like a corpse that died days ago.

The sounds of growling are coming from the light. Enchantraen motions for Affensash to put away his vial. Again no one speaks, each afraid to inhale too much of the repugnant air, jittery about what it might do to their souls.

Enchantraen's full attention is back on the party now. His firm confident leadership restores their courage. He takes the lead, moving slowly through the darkness, and then faster as the light becomes more prevalent. Laurallin and Kenlin follow, trusting to their bows, and Affensash taps the vial tucked in his belt for reassurance. Ruefin sleeps.

Step by careful step, they approach the light. New noises arise, more distant than the growling, and are therefore drowned out during most of their approach. It sounds like human voices laughing and singing! There is music! Who or what could play music in this small corner of hell?

They make it to the end of their tunnel undetected. With his eyes barely over the top of a large stone, Affensash peers into the ghastly tunnel. The new tunnel is very wide and tall. It stretches in a straight line for as far as he can see. Torches sputter and burn on the walls every thirty or so feet, apparently having trouble staying lit in the thick grim air. Smoke bellows and curls from them, making a dark heavy cloud along the ceiling. The rotten wooden beams braced against the walls and ceiling are sagging, leaving little piles of crumbled dirt where the rocks gave in. Dampness runs down the walls, leaving dismal little puddles in the deep wagon tracks. Sixty to seventy feet down the tunnel sits a wolf-beast hunching over the half-eaten carcass of a man.

Kenlin's jaw locks into place and he starts to rise to get a better aim at the wolf. Enchantraen sees him and swiftly pulls him down.

The wolf lifts and turns its head from side to side scenting the air, then bends back down ripping more muscle from the bones. A slow uneven creaking of wood on wood echoes down the tunnels. A swaying lantern appears and its light becomes brighter as it makes its methodical way towards them. The wolf jolts, sniffs the air, and scampers off down another tunnel in the weird half-walk, half-run of the misshapen creatures.

No one moves, listening to the hooves pounding on the tunnel's floor. The cart looms out of the thick black shadows; a wooden cart that at first appears to be pulled by a large draft horse. As the torches fight back the blackness it becomes plain that it is no draft horse. It is a strange, four-legged beast with a shaggy coat of black fur that clings in bunches to its body. Its head sways from side to side, and as each of its hooves strike the ground little puffs of steam rise and swirl around its legs.

Atop the cart, outlined by the lantern, is a man with a large black-brimmed hat. At least, he closely resembles a man, as much as his beast resembles a horse. His eyes glow bright amber. His face is drawn and pale, ghostly white and pitiless.

The cart pulls to a stop in front of the body. The man stands with a grunt and searches with his eyes through the darkness for the wolf that ruined the carcass. Realizing that the wolf is gone, he goes on about his obscene chore.

A small light, the flicker of a flame, darts from the cart behind him. It hovers over the body then crawls into the mouth. The carcass jerks as if the dead could feel pain. Through its pores a red light quivers and the veins and bones become illuminated from the inside out. Then the body flares! Quickly, and all at once, it disappears in a fast phantasmal flame. Leaving no ash, it is gone.

A sudden glow emits from the back of the cart and the man-thing is outlined clearly for one brief moment. The new light details a pair of slow beating wings protruding from his back that were hidden by the shadows before. The flame rides in the back of the wagon where it teleports the hollow corpses. The phantasmal flame only burns away the soul and leaves the body as it was.

"Baal?" is the word that Laurallin mouths as she looks at Enchantraen. The Elder simply shakes his head no and motions for the others to be still.

The cart slowly turns around and heads back up the tunnel. The cart's bed is piled with corpses and the hollow bodies of men and women, including the one it just picked up. Down the tunnel it travels, following the snatches of weird gaily playing music.

As the cart pulls away from those in hiding Enchantraen finally whispers, "Baal has no need to retrieve the carcasses of his victims. No, that is just two of the demons Baal has summoned here to do his bidding. Unless I miss my guess, the demon that pulled the cart was the most powerful and intelligent of the two. Several times I felt it probe the shadows for us. I thought we were going to have to fight right then and there."

The creaking fades away as the wheels of the cart slide in and out of the well-formed ruts.

"Let's go," Enchantraen says, stepping into the lit tunnel and easing into the closest shadow. Kenlin remains in the dark tunnel dumbfounded. "Come on I say," Enchantraen whispers louder this time. "We have to follow those demons! The wolves are afraid of them. If we can keep pace and stay unnoticed we should be able to travel the whole length of this mine without fear of being sniffed and tracked down by the pack." Everyone hangs back, still uncertain. "Come on! Eventually that cart will become full and they will probably take it to their master. I can't think of a better way to find Baal than to be led to him by his minions."

Laurallin is the first to accept his frightening plan and walks out into the tunnel to follow the cart of death. Down the long tunnel the companions go, moving in and out of the shadows. Each step into the torchlight brings new threats of discovery and with it the awful fear of what could follow.

Enchantraen has taken on a double duty. Along with remaining as physically hidden as possible, he must constantly test the air and remain prepared to fight against any magical intrusions that the shaggy demon may set upon them.

The music becomes louder, and with it drifts sounds of laughter made horrid by the repugnance of the mine's atmosphere. Laughter in this place could only be an insane response to torture and pain. Yet the laughter becomes louder and sounds more like the revelries at a grand ball.

As the cart creaks along the sound of violins begin to mix with it! Kenlin and Laurallin exchange glances of disbelief. The whole thing is insane! It was like listening to a full orchestra with a dense, splitting headache. It leaves them all sick and suspicious, but they follow the death cart down the tunnel anyway, and are forced to tolerate it.

The torch mountings are closer together the further down the tunnel they travel. The light from the dancing flames becomes brighter and the safety of the shadows becomes less and less. Finally, Enchantraen stops, stooping in one of the last shadows.

When the others catch up he says, "We cannot go any further like this. All the demons need do is turn around and we will be discovered. I can shield us from normal sight with a spell, but do not get comfortable with its protection. Demons have many ways of sensing a mortals' presence that don't all rely on sight. Even with the protection of my spell, take every opportunity to hide and do not expose yourself in the open!"

Everyone nods dumbly, not fully comprehending what he is trying to say. As Enchantraen begins forming the light-blue patterns, Ruefin pops his sleepy head from Affensash's pocket. Enchantraen touches the fox on the tip of his nose. As quickly as a flicker of a torch flame, the little creature disappears! Affensash's pocket wiggles and goes slack. Kenlin pulls the pocket out roughly and looks inside to see if Ruefin slid back down. The fox was gone!

With the second touch Affensash disappears, then Lauralin, Kenlin, and last of all Enchantraen. They all sit very still having seen their companions vanish, uncertain and alone.

"No one move yet!" comes the reassuring voice of Enchantraen. Little blue patterns appear from nowhere as the Elder chants yet another series of spells.

In a blink they reappear to one another's sight. "We needn't travel alone. This way we are visible only to each other. No other human can see us."

Dread passes through Affensash and then falls away as he resumes following Enchantraen and the cart. Things are changing. The empty malign feeling is replaced. It feels as though a dusty cup is filling with a honey-sweet wine.

As they walk further into the brighter light the music picks up its gaiety. The earthen floor has cracks showing sections of smooth polished marble below it. The demons and the cart change also. The shaggy hooves begin sounding like the pounding of horse's hooves on clean, round cobblestones. The demon-man shifts in appearance. His wings disappear and he takes on the visage of a peddler riding through any one of a number of Western towns.

As they follow, hugging the walls, the cracks in the ground become larger, revealing more and more marble tiles. The walls become lined with pillars that are at first crude, but later refined, as they travel further into the light.

It is too much too quickly; a complete change in mood like the bizarre blending of fine architecture with the rough workings of the mine. It is too much. It is something everyone has seen before, but it is all disjointed and unbelievable.

The music and laughter closes in around them. Everyone stops, uncertainly testing the air for any new signs of danger. The cart continues on steadily, away from them. All hopes of hiding among the rocks are gone. The rough jagged walls have turned into glass smooth marble. They are forced to decide whether to trust Enchantraen's spell and go on, or to come up with a better alternative.

The cart suddenly veers to the left and disappears into a large opening unnoticed before. As the cart passes through the opening, a red glow flashes brilliantly into the corridor. A feeling of elation ripples down the tunnel like a giant wave. It washes over the group and passes by them leaving goose bumps over their bodies. Affensash takes an involuntary step forward towards the opening.

Enchantraen's hand goes out and stops him, "Even though it felt good you should ask yourself, did it feel right?"

Affensash stops and looks at the Elder with blinking eyes. "No, I guess it wasn't right. I don't really understand what I felt."

"I think we have come to the nexus of the 'Demon's Gate '. There was a reason we had such ill feelings as we came this way. It is as though the life has been drawn from the air; like it has been drained away. Perhaps this is where it has gone?" Enchantraen contemplates his theory for a moment, "I must know!"

Kenlin steps in front of Enchantraen as he tries to move forward, "Without you we will have to fight our own way through the hundreds of witches and wolves that roam this place. We are not likely to make it without you. Jeopardizing your life jeopardizes us all. I'm afraid I can't let you do that. I will go instead and tell you everything I see."

Enchantraen starts to push him aside when Affensash speaks, "He's right Elder Enchantraen. I will go with Kenlin, and Laurallin can remain here with you."

"I don't know what to tell you to look for. I don't know what you'll see. Allow me to at least watch through your eyes."

Affensash acts confused, but does not refuse the Elder. Enchantraen begins a small eloquent chant. Briefly, patterns appear then vanish. Affensash suddenly finds it impossible to focus his eyes. When they do adjust he finds himself staring at himself! Affensash gasps, and then his vision blurs once again. It snaps back into focus and he is looking at Enchantraen.

"Don't pass through the opening for any reason. The sensation rippled over us after the cart passed through it. My guess is that the magic is not activated until someone passes through," Enchantraen says slowly and methodically, making certain both Affensash and Kenlin understand.

Both of them start down the corridor completely in the open, trusting to Enchantraen's invisibility spell. Speed, more than secrecy, is important now. Affensash trembles at the Elder's warning. What if he is pushed or drawn through the opening? He can hear the sounds of laughter and music becoming more distinct as he approaches. The eerie misplaced sounds send chills through his body.

Suddenly padded footsteps resound in the corridor behind him! He whirls around, his hand reaching for the vial tucked in his belt. He exhales one long breath when he sees that it is only Laurallin taking Ruefin back to their place of hiding. The loyal little fox must have started after him and Laurallin stopped him and picked him up. Laurallin gives Affensash a concerned look, then turns and hurries back to Enchantraen.

The opening turns out to be a large marble archway supported by two pillars.

The marble is a dark-rose color, flecked with veins of gold so vivid that they seem to pulse with energy. Above the archway is a chiseled inscription, beautiful to behold, but written in a language foreign to them both. Affensash glances hesitantly around the corner of the archway, ready to jerk his head back at a moment's notice.

Through the arch he sees an enormous ballroom. The walls of the room are lined with seamless panels of marble, the same deep red color as the arch. Large potted plants and ferns, some the size of trees, are thick throughout and mainly clustered around streaming fountains. Large pastel colored fish teem in the fountain's waters and float from tier to tier, glowing with their own inner light.

Against the far wall an orchestra of forty instruments plays freely and unceasingly. Indeed, they are wondrous instruments, for they play joyous sounds with no fingers to pluck their strings, and no breath to blow their pipes.

A dense saucy incense drifts in the air, spewing from balls of delicately worked silver that float unattached.

The ceiling is vaulted so high that a series of swings hang frailly from it, held aloof by living vines woven with tiny blossoms of pinks and purples. The swings are set to glide into gaily-lit alcoves and then back out over the cascading fountains.

Carved in the great sheets of marble walls are half-urns crowded with dainty flowers that bloom and close, as if the days and nights spin secretly around them. Within the center of the flowers are shining stamens, the room's greatest source of light.

Dancing wildly through the forest of plants are groups of brightly clad men and women. A few couples are isolated from the others, hidden in thick clusters of ferns or deep within the alcoves. Affensash can see them embracing each other in the act of love.

The crowning glory of the huge festive hall is the thorny wreath of death. Littered around the room are the fallen twisted bodies of the gaily-clad revelers. With arms and legs stiff from rigor mortis, many still bear the strange tight smile across their lips that they had when they fell.

Affensash feels nauseated. Why can't those still living see?

Just inside the archway rests the cart piled with bodies. The flickering incandescent demon is busily at work. Floating from corpse to corpse, it crawls into the mouths. Like an insatiable pest-maiden the flaming demon magically burns the souls, stacking the cart with hollow corpses five high.

Affensash and Kenlin have seen all they can bear. They turn back, dreadfully astonished and questioning the believability of their own senses.

"I have seen," Enchantraen says stiffly before anyone can speak. "Save yourselves the painful explanation. We are at the nexus of the demon's power. There is another opening on the other side of the arch. Quickly! We can hide there."

Glad to release pent-up fears, they sprint down the corridor after Enchantraen. Affensash allows himself one glance as he passes by the arch and sees the demons still busily working at their harvest.

The next opening is twenty feet down the corridor. Enchantraen hesitates at its entrance, and then goes inside. The others nearly run him over when he stops.

This room is equally as large as the ballroom. Down its center runs a well-polished walnut table that can seat over a hundred people. Presently, the room is dark and vacant.

"This is where the demon will come to feast. We will wait here. When our magics meet it will be on the battleground of the demon, but the time will be of our choosing."

Enchantraen motions to piles of thick furs, dimly visible, that cover couches lining the walls. Here, even though they are still protected by Enchantraen's invisibility spell, they hide themselves. As Affensash sinks down into the piles of furs, his head suddenly becomes light. His vision spins like he is heavily drunk on wine. He finds it impossible to focus his eyes on the black twirling room. In the warm quiet comfort of the furs he tumbles off to sleep, forgetting for now that he is deep within the demon's lair. They all are forced to sleep while waiting for the incubus of dark-death to saunter in to feast at his well-planned banquet.

CHAPTER TWENTY-THREE

Confessions and Courage

Within lies the ancient tomes and writing of our most worshipped predecessors. Between the leather covers of this most ancient reading is the sum total of all the old scrolls and the power of our kind.

- opening to The Spell Book, from the treatise of High Fantasy

No one had guessed that Baal had laid so subtle a trap, but that is what the fur-covered couches were meant to be. All who hid in them were now fast asleep. Fortunately, the trapper is not diligent in checking his traps and the prey is set free. Dazzling light flares inside the dining hall. The companions stir from their easy slumber.

Affensash starts to rise confused, as if in an early morning state of grogginess. He tosses one fur off and reaches for another when it growls and he realizes he is about to toss Ruefin. Cheerful talkative voices filter into the room. Affensash quickly remembers where he is and sinks back down into hiding.

Through two sets of massive double doors, several lines of ladies file in chatting and giggling in a bright colorful procession of lace and gentle fabrics. Dressed even more flamboyantly than the revelers in the ballroom, they prance in and seat themselves around the great table. One hundred of them enter, all stunningly beautiful. Scattered oddly on the shoulders of some are snowy-white owls and jet-black ravens. Each woman is full-figured, in her prime and unblemished. Each is a personification of beauty by herself and breathtaking. Affensash immediately recognizes them for who they really are. Witches!

Affensash is reminded of Diane. Diane's beauty was equal to theirs, but yet somehow markedly different. He struggles to determine that difference as he looks over the table. Was he simply being biased and too full of self-guilt to admit that anyone could be as beautiful as Diane? Studying them carefully as they carry on in trite conversation, he decides not. True, these women have the same curving eyebrows and the round full figures. Many of them are crowned with the same golden hair, but still they lack something! None of them shines with the inner beauty that Diane possessed. It wasn't that Diane had been perfect. Affensash had seen the rude, self-centered side of her that we all possess and struggle daily to control. These witches look more like Diane did when she tried to flippantly impress Steven. They don't shine with the truer inner beauty that was natural to Diane.   There is no sparkle in the eye. It isn't real.

Affensash can't believe it! Here he is sitting in the demon's lair judging women like the local farmer would his livestock. That is the magic of Baal's palace. It is rich in treasures that cloud the thinking; treasures that were stolen or sucked away from areas that did not seem important to the demon. Affensash realizes he should feel scared. He can't! He would rather trot up to the table and greedily join in the coming feast.

The women become suddenly quiet. A small door opens on the wall near the head of the table. Radiant light bursts into the room and Affensash must temporarily shield his eyes. He fights to see the silhouette etched in the middle of the light.

The witches clap and the figure enters. It is a boy about the age of sixteen. He walks with the sure grace of an athlete and sits himself on a throne at the head of the table. His features are sharp and finely chiseled. His hair is thick and blonde dropping to his shoulders in fine perfect ringlets. He is wearing a wine-colored tunic, bare on one shoulder, over a taut bronze frame. His body shines so brightly with the power of youth that he casts a distinct well-formed shadow. His eyes glitter like tiny dancing torches as he looks around at the witches, resting for a brief moment to embrace each one with his vision.

Despite all his virile charm, his demeanor is cold. His lips are pallid and his face shows only the mechanical parody of a smile. Unable to remove his eyes from the boy, Affensash discovers his most amazing feature. The boy's chest does not rise and fall! The breath of life is not within him. This time Affensash is certain. The boy is Baal.

As if summoned by an unseen gesture, the doors that Affensash and the others had originally entered open. A single servant enters pushing a cart of golden plates to serve the one hundred. One shining bright candle is placed in the center of the table. An odd unrecognizable odor wafts around the room.

Plates are placed before the witches and each one hurries to gobble it up, not waiting for the others to be served. The witches stuff huge portions into their bulging cheeks with their bare hands. When they are done they shout for more and pound their plates on the table. The plush refined dining hall turns into a trough for pretty, squealing pigs.

Affensash turns away and catches a brief side view of Enchantraen hidden among the furs. The great Elder's head is buried in his hands looking nauseous and sick. In amazement, Affensash's eyes dart back to the feast. He believes he sees the faint outline of beating wings protruding from the servant's back. The brilliant candle seems to preside over the ghastly meal with a new demonic splendor.

Just then Ruefin sneezes and growls angrily, shaking his ears. Affensash barely manages to restrain the little fox from jumping out among the witches.

Over the clink of the golden dishes and the squeals of the witches, Ruefin's tiny sneeze is heard. The entire hall becomes deadly quiet. Affensash believes his heart is going to shatter through the bones in his chest.

"Well, what an unexpected surprise," says the boy after forcing air into his lungs so that his mouth could form the words. Despite his harsh gasping for air his voice is rich and melodious. "Ladies please! Will someone make room for our guests?" he says sliding his chair back.

Twenty witches jump to please their master, but only four reach his chair in time. The others despondently sit back down. One witch, with hair as blue-black as the raven resting on her shoulder, goes to stand just behind Baal's chair, playing with the curls in his hair. Her dress is deep blue, trimmed in silver; low cut and showing half her bosom.

Another witch, with a large snowy white owl, rests on her knees at his left and leans against the arm of the chair stroking his hand. The last two, blonde haired witches, sit curled around his feet purring like well-fed cats.

A flash of blue lights hurts Affensash's eyes and Enchantraen walks from concealment, umbrellaed in a half-sphere of promenading patterns. Confidently, the Elder strides to the center of the room. Kenlin and Laurallin rise, arrows flashing to their bows. The servant of Baal's calmly places new plates on the table.

"You seem to have overlooked the fact that we on this world are not cannibals as those on yours!" Enchantraen taunts, but the witches are not riled. Indeed even Affensash finds it difficult to become agitated. It's as if great waves of serenity flow from Baal making it impossible to become angry with the fair-haired youth.

Enchantraen, however, is a man of strict morals. It was those morals, not his magic that stripped away the demon's guise and allowed him to see Baal as his true self. A demon prince!

"How dare you," Enchantraen continues threateningly, "come invited to our world by one of my pupils to commit such atrocities? Not the atrocities of bastardizing our craft and teachings," the great Elder sneers, pointing to the witches around the room, "but the atrocity of destroying virtue and dignity; of enslaving these souls with cold harsh murder!"

Baal laughs and claps his hands. The witches mimic him, but some shift uneasily in their seats. "Pretty! Pretty! I love the fervent burning speeches you True Ones like to give. Glenwall used to rant for hours like that when I first met him."

Enchantraen's fingertips glow. He touches his throat and his voice suddenly rises in commanding tones. "Women of High Tower I have come to take you back to your town and husbands. There, all will be forgiven. They miss you. The community you helped build has been broken since you left your homes."

"There is no more need for this debauchery of pride and shameful degradation. Look at how far you have declined in so short a time. You feast on your own flesh for god's sake! Will that plate next be filled with the flesh of the woman sitting next to you, or will it be filled with your own? Where are your husbands? Or better yet, what have you done to your children? Do their bones lie among the ashes on the mountainside where they are blown and twisted about by the foul wind?" Enchantraen stops, glaring around the table.

His words reinforced by his magic are beginning to bring back deeply forgotten memories in the witches. "Continual self-indulgence is fruitless and devastating. I have come here not to hurt you, but to walk with you from this den where meaningful life has been lacerated and left bleeding in your hearts."

Baal, having heard enough, rises and snips at the air around Enchantraen with his eyes. It's as if he is cutting at the threads of aether that power the True One's spells. First, Enchantraen's voice spell is cancelled. The Elder's sphere of warding begins to falter and Enchantraen stumbles like a puppet cut from his strings. Fortunately, the Elder stumbles into a new web of aether and the half-sphere holds.

"It is as I told Glenwall," the demon bellows and gasps in fresh air to continue. "We are no longer amused by pretty speeches!"

Baal's voice suddenly takes on the same echo of power that Enchantraen's had. "All these women need do is look as you suggested. If they look, their eyes will tell them that they are no longer strapped with the responsibilities of a dirty miner's wife. Because of that they have grown beautiful; more beautiful than they ever imagined possible. Look for yourself Elder! They are young! Each one of them is a queen! And really, can you ever have too much?"

Without his spell, the Elder's words still have validity. "I don't mean to look with your eyes! Your vision is the plaything of demons. It lies. I mean look with your souls. Look with the sanctity of your morals and know the truth."

Baal is up and like a giant scythe, he swings his eyes across the top of Enchantraen's head. Again the threads of aether are broken and the warding sphere sputters. Groping like a blind man, Enchantraen finds a new cluster and the spell holds firm a little longer.

With blazing eyes Baal points to Enchantraen. "You are an Elder, are you not? You represent years of study and training in your guild's craft. You are simply jealous of the gift I have given my friends. I have given them your power *overnight*! Where you would wish to hold them down and keep them ignorant, I have given them knowledge equal to your long years of study. They are now queens because of me; queens of magic!"

"Show this nonbeliever," Baal says glancing around at the witches with his strange resplendent eyes. "Teach those who would oppress you and forever hold you down. Demonstrate to this man the first lesson of the new order of magic!"

Chairs rumble as they scoot back and the witches rise. A bevy of voices speak at once, jumbled and disorderly, very different from the precise chanting of the True Ones. For a brief moment the whole thing is chaotic and insane.

Then Baal, like a grand maestro, directs the threads of aether around and through the witches. Caught in his web, their spells suddenly flare and take hold. Scores of incandescent balls of fire leap into the witches hands. They toss them at Enchantraen causing ruin and destruction as they bounce off his sphere and roll about the room.

Deafening thunder rips the air as another score of witches discharge bolts of lightning cutting like white knives toward the Elder. Baal directs even more aether into the shrieking witches and circles of clear acid begin to rain down around the wizard.

This is not all!

Simple attacks of flame, lightning, and searing death are not enough. The ground at the True One's feet erupts, rocketing huge chunks of marble to the ceiling where they burst apart and shower back down in a maelstrom of hard death. Thick bubbling lava seeps up through the open wounds in the earth clouding the room with rolling, searing steam.

Affensash drops to his knees during the first wave of attacks. He covers his ears; unable to stand up to the ear-shattering booms and vociferate chanting of the witches.

Enchantraen's sphere hisses and bright blue flames lick the edges as the True One steadily powers it to ward off the witches' death chants. Instantly, the whole cacophony of terror is stopped by one soft thud.

Silence!

Affensash looks up to see that Enchantraen still stands with his sphere blazing around him. The room is so quiet Affensash believes that he has gone completely deaf. Then he sees Baal. The young boy is standing, looking down through wide eyes at an arrow shaft protruding from his chest.

With flashing hands Laurallin nocks and looses two more arrows that strike where the demon's heart should be. The arrows are shot so accurately that the second nearly splits the shaft of the first.

Baal looks up confused. Either this was the first time he had been hurt on this world, or he was stunned that it was a woman who had delivered the blow. Whatever the reason, the shock does not last for long. A lurid smile passes over the demon's pallid lips as he stares at Laurallin.

Baal inhales sharply and the shafts quiver in his chest. Inhaling again, the shafts are drawn inward, sucked into his body and disappear! The demon's laughter reverberates through the mine. Baal's shadow begins to enlarge and creep across the room towards Laurallin.

Affensash scrambles to rise, but it is Kenlin who steps in the way to halt the shadow's slithering advance.

Large black claws tighten around the bronze warrior's ankles. Bones snap and Kenlin cries out in pain. The shadow tries to force him to his knees, but Kenlin knows that if he succumbs to the pain and falls, his body will be crushed as easily as the bones in his feet.

From the glistening blue shell, Enchantraen finishes his spell. Baal's body sizzles red as though his blood were boiling and oozing from his pores. "It was a wizard who brought you here and it will be a wizard who sends you back. You are not fit to live in our world. We have devils of our own, and evil enough!"

Baal arches his back and lifts his arms in pain. Agony crowds his lungs and desperation fills his beastly brain. He is leaving! He is being banished back to a world, sterile and void compared to the riches of this one.

The witches!

No, they can't help him in time. Without knowing how to work in unison, their spells are not powerful enough to overcome the Elder quickly.

He is losing!

His body is beginning to dissolve. Through his boiling brain he knows that it is all but over. In a last desperate attempt he lowers his eyes and slices across the room.

Again and again he chops at the aether like a mad woodsman. The aether shreds and falls away. All the mystical power drains from the room and Elder Enchantraen's warding sphere sizzles and stops.

Powerless!

That is not the only spell that stops! The beauty of the witches fades. Their gowns hang loose on their once voluptuous bodies. Without the mark of the beast upon them they can see themselves for what they have become.

They are really starved and wretched-looking creatures. Many of them have infected unattended wounds that immediately cause them to wail in great pain. Their features are twisted and uglier due to long months of abuse and neglect. With the fading aether, they realize that they have not only lost the unreal beauty of the demon's magic, but most of them have become so disfigured and scarred that they will never be able to reclaim any of the beauty that was naturally theirs.

One by one they turn with beseeching eyes towards Baal.

Baal is gone! At least the illusion that pretended to be Baal is gone. The great beastly shadow that crawled and slithered along the ground was always the real demon. That unearthly shadow was now inches away from Enchantraen who has slumped exhausted on the floor.

The witches scream and run in terror from the hall. They run, trying to escape from themselves more than from Baal.

Enchantraen himself looks very old, worn out completely by the magical combat. When his warding spell collapsed so did the spells of strength. He lies on the floor waving his hands blindly, trying to find the aether to rekindle his spells.

Baal doesn't need magic to kill him now. He can crush his bones with his claws and there is nothing the Elder can do. Like a dry twig the bone in the Elder's forearm snaps. Enchantraen refuses to cry out, instead repeating over and over the spells that will not ignite.

Laurallin hears the prophet's words again, 'Enchantraen will be defeated.' Then another bone snaps. She leaps with steel hard nerves and struggles with the demon to lift Enchantraen to the table and away from the shadow.

Hideous laughter cries from the deepest vaults of the mine as the demon slithers its way up the legs of the table and bounces over the chairs.

Laurallin fires arrow after arrow at the advancing shade. The shadow has enough form that the arrows hit and the demon squirms, feeling some affect, but not enough to stop him.

"Aff! Help me please!" Laurallin cries when the demon is almost upon her.

Affensash struggles through calculating thoughts. His mind churns through variables and formulas that might stop the demon, but nothing seems probable.

A loud buzzing sound suddenly shakes the roof. Enchantraen laughs and coughs at Laurallin's side. "The Wind Drakes have arrived! The Tuatha are here. They are later than I planned, but now we know the passage is still open, and the six True Ones fight on," Enchantraen laughs again.

The shade of Baal draws back, realizing the danger in the Elder's words. Through the arched doors stream young children chanting and holding brands of hissing blue flames high above their heads. The aether floods back into the room like water through a broken dam. The children line the walls of the room singing their magical requiem loud and clear.

Enchantraen's strength spells return and he rises. Baal too is affected by the sudden return of aether and the image of the young boy reappears.

"You see, demon," Enchantraen says, regaining his strength and some vigor. "I listened to the Soothsayer and believed her."

Enchantraen's face breaks into a broad smile sensing that victory is near, despite his shattered arm. Flexing his fingers he looks down at Baal and says, "In the battle of the masters of magic, I'm afraid I have won!"

The Tuatha sing their chant in unison, rivaling a choir of angels. The room glows in the pale blue light of their brands. Enchantraen adds his voice to the choir and begins his last spell that will exorcise the demon from this world.

Baal crosses his arms and smiles as though he were content to listen to the music of their magic. Enchantraen is barely able to move his fingers through the pain in his broken arm. Spell casting requires two hands so he tries to block the pain from his mind.

Halfway through the enchantment Baal attacks, revealing the reason for his smiling face. The battle of the master of magic is not over.

Baal first sought to defeat Enchantraen by overpowering him through the witches. When that failed he canceled all the aether, hoping to win the physical struggle of demon against the frail strength of a man.

The Tuatha are ushering new aether into the room. They can replenish the magical energy faster than Baal could ever hope to exhaust it.

Baal is the master of aether and aether is the root of the True Ones magic. He can see it! Baal doesn't have to grope for a way to defeat the Elder. He knows exactly how to do it.

Stretching out his mind, he finds the edges of the magical threads that he originally severed and pulls them back into the room. He guides the floating aether strands toward the brands of the Tuatha.

The sudden reoccurrence of the magical energy feeds directly into the aether-producing brands causing them to burn and hiss furiously, over-fueling them like lantern oil on a fire. Baal feels the heat from the supercharged brands and pours even more aether into them.

The result is a large, loud explosion that rips thunderously through the mine!

The Tuatha are thrown to the ground by the score. Bodies slam into other bodies. Flesh burns and the children cry.

Finally when the explosions subside, only Baal, of all the magic users, remains standing among the wreckage. The rest lie burnt, dead, or unconscious in tiny heaps around him. The Wind Drakes are dead before they can manage their first attack.

A brutal laugh of triumph erupts from the demon's lips. He knows he has beaten the best of the old magic users.

Baal laughs and turns on those remaining. Kenlin is propped in a chair fighting to stay conscious. His ankles are bleeding and already swollen. Laurallin was flattened by an exploding brand and is struggling to lift herself to her elbows. Affensash stands facing the demon with a small vial in his hand.

The battle has left Baal tired, but not too tired to recognize the threat Affensash holds. His burning amber eyes pierce into the souls of the three. Then he inhales sharply, filling his lungs for his final assault.

Persuasion!

"You know I have been studying a little about your craft. There is already a lot I could do for you Alchemist."

"I don't think so," Affensash says with a touch of trembling in his voice. He raises the vial.

"If you throw that, Kenlin will have your wife for his own!" Baal says smiling.

"What? How could you know that?" Affensash says lowering the vial.

"It doesn't take magic to see what is happening between them. Look! Have you ever seen a better match? How can you blame her? Just look at yourself and now look at Kenlin. You know, Affensash, if you allowed me I could make you greater than he," Baal says with his last bit of breath and then strains to gulp the next lung-full of air.

"Oh Aff," Laurallin pleads, pulling up to a sitting position. "That isn't true. Don't let him twist your mind!"

Affensash turns his head and looks at her with eyes pleading to see the truth. "It isn't true? Laurallin, he isn't saying anything that I haven't already thought."

"Aff that is how he works. He is preying on your feelings!" Laurallin says beseechingly, "Throw it quickly while you still can!"

"Do I lie, Affensash? You are standing closest to me. When the blast goes off can you be sure you won't die also? If she loves you why isn't she concerned about that? If she loves you why isn't she concerned about that?" Baal asks, his eyes sparkling brighter. "Laurallin! Tell me to stand by Kenlin instead of your husband if you love Affensash the most."

Laurallin looks at Baal then back to Affensash, "Aff, I can't do that!"

There is a long pause and tears well up in Affensash's eyes. Laurallin looks back up.

"How can I purposefully ask you to kill a friend? Aff, do you really believe I would want you harmed? He is confusing you. He is twisting things from a question of love to a question of murder!"

In a strong melodious tone Baal steps up his attack. "If I sound accusing, Laurallin, I don't mean to be. It is natural for you to grow restless after a few years of marriage."

Turning to Affensash, his eyes blaze and his mouth turns up mechanically at the edges into a smile. "We could begin by granting you your pistols. Cartloads of alchemy material were brought to me for my studies. Look in that chest against the wall." Baal points to a chest on a table a few feet from Affensash.

Without turning around, Affensash steps carefully backwards and lifts the lid. Two marvelous pistols gleam inside! They have pearl handles and their muzzles are coated in gold. Without hesitating, Affensash takes them out and tucks them into his belt.

Baal takes Affensash's actions as a sign of cooperation and sighs in relief. "Very good! You know it is only human to grow tired of another human after a while. I think we should work on that next."

"Stop it," shouts Laurallin. "Stop it, you morbid beast. Don't pretend to understand what I think."

Turning tearfully, she looks deeply into her husband's eyes. "Aff, I never stopped loving you. I just grew tired of the daily inescapable drudgery. It isn't our life together that I grew tired of. Kenlin reminded me of all of the good things I loved about my family and tribe. He was a chance for escape back into worry free days. It was what he represented that led me astray, not Kenlin.

"It is silly, Aff. I know I cannot go back, but for a small time I just remembered how simple it used to be. Aff, I know this is confusing. It isn't even very clear to me."

Laurallin looks over at Kenlin struggling with the pain in his legs, but listening. He still has his bow across his lap, ever-ready to come to Laurallin's aid.

"I'm sorry, Kenlin. No one has done more for me and has expected so little in return. I know in my heart that if I went with you I would bring my own troubles with me; new ones would just be added. I am not a child anymore. I am a woman with a woman's responsibilities."

Turning and wiping the tears from her eyes, she glares at Baal, "Damn you demon! You have friends everywhere. You are in league with the demon in my heart. Well damn you! I'm not perfect, but I can accept that, and having accepted that I can beat you. I will not let you break my heart by destroying those I love!"

Laurallin jumps down from the table, staggers, but regains her balance determined to fight the demon hand to hand if she must.

Baal is unconcerned about Laurallin. Instead he looks into Affensash's soul to see if he has lost his power over him. In answer Affensash tosses the vial.

The vial seems to float slowly through the air. Affensash sees Elder Enchantraen lying unconscious on the table. Many of the Tuatha are already dead and others are coughing, trying to hang on to what little life they have left. Laurallin falls flat on the floor covering her head, tensing for the explosion. The vial takes its last turn in the air and stops inches from the floor, caught in the claw of the demon shade.

Baal laughs a strange jubilant laugh that seems to come up from the ground shaking the marble walls. A slow scraping fear cuts at Affensash's already braided nerves. The demon laughs again and Laurallin covers her ears with her knees as if to restrain her pounding terror. A third laugh follows with a single boast.

"Fool!"

Laurallin knows all is lost. Then she sees Kenlin straining through his pain and lifting his bow.

Hope returns.

Kenlin pushes past what is physically possible and pulls the bow back and fires!

The arrow sparks as it skitters across the floor shooting wide past its mark. Kenlin drops his head back, blind with pain and lost in his failure, with no strength left to try again.

Demonic laughter!

In the room of despair, no one sees Affensash's steady hand aiming the wheel-lock pistol. No one notices when the trigger is pulled, the hammer falls, and the powder hisses and ignites.

A bang is followed by a tiny tinkle of glass as Affensash nicks the top of the vial held in the demon's claw. The shattered glass is followed by a killing explosion. The room turns blood-red and Affensash's body is blown back, spinning across the room.

It has been hours since the explosion. Tiny fires smolder among the wreckage. Flames are burning, reluctantly shedding light on the unjust suffering around them.

The witches fled down the mountainside when they first learned the truth about Baal. They ran bare-breasted, and screaming for mercy, many of them insane with terror and forever lost within the secret horrors of their own minds. Those who kept their minds pleaded endlessly for the rest of their shortened lives to be forgiven.

Laurallin's father arrives with the Hebelcaan. The tribe had been stopped down the mountain by the wolves and could not make it in time to rescue his daughter. When Baal was destroyed, so was his hold over the beasts. The wolves changed back and fled with the witches.

The Hebelcaan remove bodies and neatly make a long line, children and witches side by side. It doesn't seem to matter now. Those alive are rushed down the mountainside to be cared for by the healers in High Tower. Many are too weak to survive the desperate flight down the mountain.

Baal has been exorcised. The evil light of his existence has been snuffed out and removed from the world. The Hebelcaan, in their haste to gather and save the living, ride swiftly down the mountainside; missing a small light of another kind.

A torch sputters deep within the mine; the last of its light filters through the cracks of a locked cell door. Two eyes stare widely. A mouth makes gurgling sounds that could be calls for help.

A wizard who cannot speak is no wizard. You must chant to cast the spells. A servant who cannot serve Baal is no servant.

Glenwall batters his bloody hands against the rock walls, but there is no one in the mines left alive to hear.

The torch sputters and goes black.

CHAPTER TWENTY-FOUR

Reunited

At second plane the alchemist may purchase the wheel-lock pistol, but at third he may use the musket!

- of Alchemists, from the treatise of High Fantasy

The world rocks left then rights itself abruptly. Laurallin's eyes flutter open from the harsh jolt. The sky is aqua blue. It is late in the day. Hay is stuffed comfortably around her. The wagon hits another rut and jolts again.

Alive! She is alive! Blood tingles through her veins. She is surprised. Laurallin looks down her body and finds careful bandages around her wounds. Sensie prances behind the wagon and flips her mane when Laurallin moves. Her hair is nestled in a lap. "Aff," she cries and rises from the hay. She is startled when she sees that it isn't Affensash.

"You have been unconscious for a long time," Kenlin says. The big tribesman is propped in the corner of the wagon bed sitting up. His healthy bronze color is back in his face, but his legs are wrapped and blood oozes through the bandages on his feet. Laurallin places one hand to cover her mouth when she starts to cry. Tentatively, she reaches out with the other and places it trembling on Kenlin's shoulder.

Kenlin looks deeply into her tearing eyes. He sees gratitude, concern, forgiveness, and everything else except what he wants to find there.

Love.

Kenlin looks sadly at her face trying to memorize each line.

The Hebelcaan tribe stretches in a long line down the road on their way back to the grasslands. A tribesman signals that Laurallin is awake. The wagon stops.

Laurallin's father gallops down the long line and pulls to a halt behind the wagon. Tsester, his proud tall stallion, bows its' head.

"I see you are a good Hebelcaan, daughter. I told them it would take more than a few wolves to drag you down."

Laurallin stands uneasily on the back of the wagon and hugs her father around the neck. A little squeal comes from his back. He turns in the saddle and Laurallin sees Dannia flaying her arms and gurgling. He eases the straps off his back and Laurallin smothers her baby in sweet kisses. Cuddling the child in her arms and never taking her eyes off her she asks, "Where is Aff?"

Her father is silent.

"Your husband has been rushed to High Tower. He is alive, but he is not well. He may not recover," Kenlin answers instead.

Laurallin slides the straps of the papoose over her shoulders fastening Dannia to her back. She whistles and Sensie canters to her. She jumps from the wagon to the horse's back. Sensie spins in a circle and stops. Laurallin looks down into the wagon at Kenlin.

He smiles a sad soft smile and no words are spoken.

Laurallin clicks her tongue and Sensie bolts for the open road in front of the tribesmen. Both Sensie and Laurallin are still streaked in red and wrapped in bandages. The two are a matched pair, and with Dannia on her back, she charges from 'Death Watch' rushing once again to her husband's side.

At High Tower Laurallin finds Affensash resting in the care of Madillyn. He is unconscious, but in little pain. Laurallin combs back his thick matted hair. She washes the areas of his body that can be washed. Large areas are deep black and purple where the explosion tossed him against the marble.

She tries to set up little routines for her and the baby as the hours stretch into days. She hovers around the room doing wifely chores like mending clothes and cooking. She tries everything to re-establish a feeling of care and trust, but he does not move. For hours she sings children's rhymes that her mother used to sing about the Devil and the Dew Walker. She cuddles Dannia, praying that they won't lose him.

Elder Enchantraen remains in High Tower and visits Affensash regularly. Dignitaries and important wizards come to see the Great Wizard, but he refuses to leave Affensash to return to the Isles.

Once, in the latest part of the night, Affensash's breathing became irregular. She sent for Madillyn. As soon as the healer arrived Affensash stopped breathing altogether. Elder Enchantraen had come along that time and together they managed to revive him. Laurallin still shudders thinking what might have been if the Elder had let duty outweigh friendship.

Days of fatigue and worry sap Laurallin of her strength. Her vigilance over Affensash costs her. After many days she spends the time dazed and dull-witted. It is for the better. She doesn't have to think through the consequences of Affensash's possible death.

She lights the sixteen candles in the room and keeps them burning day and night. She wants their husband-wife reunion to be special when he wakes.

It is.

Early one sunrise Affensash comes back to her. His eyes open and they see each other. He is too weak to speak and only stays awake for a brief moment. But there is kindness in his eyes and understanding. That is enough for Laurallin.

From then on Affensash gains strength steadily like the spring sun. Soon he is up and walking. Together they take short walks through the town, rehabilitating his muscles.

On one trip they witness the arrival of a full-fledged Eastern army. It parades through the streets taking credit for banishing Baal. The townspeople cheered, but it made no difference to Laurallin. She knows that her fate, the Hebelcaan, and these people, has been decided not by a great pompous army but by one single alchemist.

With the arrival of the troops, Elder Enchantraen is forced to make a quick departure. Before he leaves, Affensash knows he has made a powerful friend.

Jabir never shows. Instead, a sack of gold tams appears with a message of a job well-done. That doesn't bother the two of them either. They need the time to become reacquainted with each other and to rediscover their love.

Rumors spread through the town that a High Lord General is on his way from the Apothecary to congratulate the troops. That's when Affensash knows it is time for them to leave also.

Buying a fresh horse for himself, they say their good-byes to Steven and depart High Tower with a glad feeling in their hearts. The day is a warm and peaceful one. It would be better spent sprawling in the sun, but getting away from the town's turmoil is an even better feeling.

"You know," Affensash says. "I think we should plan a trip every now and then."

Laurallin laughs and pats Sensie on the flank as they ride. Dannia is strapped to her back. Ruefin sticks his head out of Affensash's pocket, panting.

"No, I'm serious. I think Dannia should get to know her grandparents and stay in touch with her tribe."

"I think I'd like that, Aff, but what about your work?"

"I do have a lot to do with the invention of my new explosive, but I still think I would like to learn to hunt. The Guild has a musket I would like to earn that shoots straight over long distances. What do you think? Wouldn't that be nice?"

Affensash takes out his new pistols. "Did you see that shot I made? I think I'm going to be pretty good with these things." He twirls his new pistols around his fingers and Laurallin laughs again.

Baby Dannia's head bounces with the gentle sway of Sensie and she gives one last, "plehhhhh..." before falling to sleep on their way home.

ANCIENT TOMES
by this author include:

    When Magics Meet is a novel based on the writings found within the *High Fantasy* series of books. The rules for magic, combat and discovery are all derived from these ancient tomes. Alas these books are no longer in print and can only be found in the dusty moldy corners of libraries or buried deep within the backrooms of faraway places known, to a few of us, as "bookstores".

Written in the 70's and published in the 80's and 90's, when role-playing games were emerging in literature, the High Fantasy series of books were made available by the second largest role-playing publisher in the world. It has been thirty years, but the author has agreed to bring his world back in the form of three new lines of books. These publications include a new line of traditional novels, interactive novels, and a series for young adults.

www.ingramcontent.com/pod-product-compliance
Lightning Source LLC
Chambersburg PA
CBHW070200260626
47160CB00002B/397